The Lovers
Echoes from the Past
Book 1

by Irina Shapiro

Copyright

© 2017 by Irina Shapiro

All rights reserved. No part of this book may be reproduced in any form, except for quotations in printed reviews, without permission in writing from the author.

All characters are fictional. Any resemblances to actual people (except those who are actual historical figures) are purely coincidental.

Contents

Prologue 6
Chapter 1 7
Chapter 2 10
Chapter 3 24
Chapter 4 33
Chapter 5 41
Chapter 6 51
Chapter 7 62
Chapter 8 71
Chapter 9 78
Chapter 10 84
Chapter 11 91
Chapter 12 99
Chapter 13 110
Chapter 14 121
Chapter 15 128
Chapter 16 136
Chapter 17 139
Chapter 18 141
Chapter 19 150
Chapter 20 156
Chapter 21 162
Chapter 22 171
Chapter 23 177

Chapter 24 181

Chapter 25 188

Chapter 26 193

Chapter 27 199

Chapter 28 210

Chapter 29 217

Chapter 30 221

Chapter 31 226

Chapter 32 229

Chapter 33 239

Chapter 34 245

Chapter 35 248

Chapter 36 258

Chapter 37 266

Chapter 38 271

Chapter 39 280

Chapter 40 282

Chapter 41 287

Chapter 42 291

Chapter 43 297

Chapter 44 301

Chapter 45 304

Chapter 46 315

Chapter 47 323

Chapter 48 329

Chapter 49 333

Chapter 50 339

Chapter 51 344

Chapter 52 347

Chapter 53 353

Chapter 54 356

Chapter 55 362

Chapter 56 366

Chapter 57 374

Chapter 58 377

Chapter 59 384

Chapter 60 390

Chapter 61 392

Chapter 62 398

Chapter 63 401

Chapter 64 413

Chapter 65 419

Chapter 66 425

Chapter 67 430

Chapter 68 434

Chapter 69 439

Chapter 70 443

Chapter 71 444

Notes..450

Prologue

The darkness was absolute, the interior of the chest smelling rank and damp. Their bodies were pressed together, crammed in an unnatural position, limbs stiff after hours of immobility. At first, there was still hope, but it had run out, as had the air, as the tight-fitting lid prevented even the smallest amount from seeping in. His arms felt like lead, but he gathered what was left of his waning strength and lifted his hand to her face. He didn't need to see it; her features were burned into his brain, as were those of their child. *Please, God, keep the babe safe.*

Her skin was still warm, but she was already gone, as surely as he would be in the next few minutes. His lungs were already burning, a sheen of sweat covering his face. He pressed his lips against her unresponsive mouth in a final kiss as a last thought flashed through his dying brain:

It was all worth it.

Chapter 1

October 2013

London, England

Sean Adams leaped from the cab of his digger and pushed his way through the crowd of men gathered around a large opening. For a moment, he thought it was a sinkhole, here in the middle of London, but what he was looking at was some kind of subterranean chamber that had been uncovered as a result of his efforts. The ceiling of the chamber—nothing more than a thin layer of rotted wooden beams—had caved in, revealing a narrow space beneath, the walls of which were solid stone. The men peered into the hole, curious to see what it held.

"Step aside, step aside," Foreman Milne bellowed. He stood at the edge of the opening and shone a torch into the dark recess of the chamber. "What have we here?" he asked no one in particular as he removed his hard hat and scratched his egg-shaped head. Foreman Milne was a good-natured man most of the time, not averse to joining his crew for a pint and singing loudly and off-key once he'd had a few, but at this moment he was vibrating with irritation. He had no time for delays; he was on a schedule, and the management was breathing down his neck.

"What is it, boss?" someone called out. "A buried treasure?" The men chuckled. They found all kinds of rubbish at every new site: bits of furniture, rusted prams, sometimes even old cellars that had been used as air raid shelters during the last war, complete with tin cups, wooden benches, and old newspapers. But this looked different. The chamber was completely empty, except for one large rectangular object.

"Bring me a ladder, lads. A long one," the foreman called. "Adams, you're with me since we have you to thank for this 'fortuitous' find."

Sean reluctantly followed his boss into the dank hole. The roof was mostly gone, but the walls were still intact, built of rough-hewn stone nearly a foot thick. They were cold to the touch, even on a pleasant day like today. The opening looked like it might have been a large well in its day, but there was no indication that it ever contained any water. The walls were not covered with mildew, and the packed earth at the bottom was dry as bone.

"Toss me down a pair of cutters," the foreman called out to the men gathered at the top. "This thing appears to have a lock on it."

The two men stood awkwardly next to what appeared to be an oversize sea chest. It took up most of the space, leaving barely any room for Milne and Adams to stand. The chest looked sturdy and was secured with a chain and an old-fashioned padlock, which was rusted with age and neglect. Foreman Milne gently kicked the chest with his foot, and the two men heard something rattle within. He then ran a finger along the lid. It came away dusty, but the wood beneath appeared to be in good condition. The chest was elaborately carved and painted, the colors still vibrant despite the layers of grime.

Sean was bursting with curiosity and wished Milne would just get on with it. His brother, Joe, worked on a site where they'd found a leather pouch full of antique coins. The story had been in all the major newspapers and even on the telly. Joe had been interviewed, and the segment appeared on the news. The coins were now part of an exhibition at the British Museum, and Joe still told the story of his historic find every time he had a captive audience.

"Shall I do it, boss?" Sean asked the foreman, his voice quivering with excitement. The older man shrugged and moved aside as much as the small space would allow, his face creased with displeasure. He handed Sean the cutters and leaned against the wall, his arms crossed, his posture indicative of the impatience that he was trying to keep in check. Foreman Milne wasn't the type of man who suffered from acute curiosity or an overactive imagination. He assumed they'd found some rubbish that would need to be cleared away, resulting in wasting several hours of their time. To him, it made no difference who opened the chest.

Sean cut the rusty chain and kicked away the lock when it clattered to the stone floor. He took a shaky breath before lifting the lid and peering inside.

"Jesus, Mary, and Joseph," he breathed out as he quickly crossed himself. Sean stepped back, nearly colliding with Foreman Milne, who'd taken a step forward to shine a light into the chest. It was full of bones, the skulls grinning eerily out of the gloom.

The men above were craning their necks for a better look, blocking nearly all the light in the process. Someone already had his mobile out and was snapping pictures of the chest, the flash blinding in the dark space.

"No photos," Milne bellowed as he stood in front of the open chest. "Get away with you."

"Sean, call the police. Now!"

Chapter 2

October 2013

Surrey, England

Quinn threw another log on the fire and went to pour herself a cup of tea. A steady rain had been falling since the night before, bringing with it a howling wind and a bone-chilling damp, which seemed to seep into the stones. The room was lost in shadow, the lowering sky and pouring rain having leached all light out of the October afternoon. But the fire glowed in the hearth, casting shifting shadows onto the stone walls and filling the room with a welcome warmth, the crackling of the logs momentarily blocking out the moaning of the wind.

Quinn sat down on the sofa and wrapped her hands around the hot mug. The heat felt good, so she held the mug for a few minutes without drinking, absorbing the pleasant warmth, which brought her a welcome sense of comfort. Despite the cold and the rain, it felt good to be home, even if that home wasn't quite as she had left it. She'd returned to England only a few days ago, landing in Heathrow on a golden autumn morning. She'd collected her cases from the carousel and made her way out the door toward the queue of taxis waiting at the curb.

She filled her lungs with crisp air and smiled at the brilliant foliage, which stood out in jarring contrast to the cobalt blue of the cloudless sky. After months of relentless heat and merciless sun of the Middle East, it was lovely to feel a cool breeze on her face and the nip of the coming winter already in the air. Quinn looked as if she'd just come back from a tropical holiday, her face and arms tanned to a golden glow. Still, the six months she'd spent on a dig in Jerusalem had left their mark, both physical and emotional, and she was relieved to be home at last. No one paid her any attention as she waited patiently in line for her turn at a taxi. To anyone who bothered to notice her, she was just an average young woman, casually dressed in jeans, T-shirt, and a worn leather jacket. Her dark hair was pulled into a messy bun atop her head, and her face was devoid of any makeup, except for some lip balm she'd put on before disembarking the plane. She looked like any other tourist, but in archeological circles she was a star, at least until the next big find.

Unearthing the Roman sword dating back to the Great Revolt of 66 CE was a tremendous coup. The sword had been discovered lodged in the drainage system running between the City of David and the Archeological Garden, and it was found only a few feet away from an ancient stone depicting a menorah. The menorah had been etched into the stone with something crude and sharp, like an old nail or a chisel, but it was close enough to Temple Mount to be of tremendous interest and confirmed what the original menorah might have looked like. Researchers from the Israel Antiquities Authority put forth various theories on the significance of the find.

Quinn had to admit that she had been more interested in the sword. It was still in its leather scabbard, which was miraculously well preserved. The scabbard kept some of the decorations from being obliterated by time and the elements, allowing a glimpse into Roman craftsmanship of the period. The sword likely belonged to a simple infantryman, but it was so much more than a sharp hunk of metal. It was not only a tool but also a work of art, a lovingly crafted weapon that would have been treasured and well maintained by its bearer. The sword would remain in Jerusalem, but Quinn had published her findings and had agreed to interviews with CNN, the *British Archeology Magazine*, and the

Archeological Journal, scheduled back-to-back for the day after her arrival. The sword might be thousands of years old, but the news of its discovery would fade fast, and the interviews had to be published while public interest was still at its peak.

And now she was finally at home, having fulfilled her obligations and free until the spring semester began just after the new year. She'd intended to pick up a few classes at the institute, devote time to research, apply for new grants that would fund the next dig when they came through, and spend time with Luke. At least that had been the plan while she was still in Jerusalem—but things had changed.

It felt strange to walk into the house and face all the empty spaces. They glared at her like hollow eye sockets, eerie and blank. Luke had cleared out before she returned, partially to avoid awkwardness and partially because he'd been in a rush to leave. He hadn't even given her the courtesy of breaking up with her in person. He'd dumped her via text, telling her that he had accepted a teaching position in Boston and would be gone by the time she returned. This was no longer their house, their little love nest, but it was still her home, and despite the sadness that filled the quiet rooms, she loved it.

Quinn snuggled deeper into the sofa and gazed with affection at the familiar room. The house had once been a private chapel, built by some devoted husband for his devout Catholic wife, but it had been confiscated by the Crown during the Dissolution of the Monasteries and allowed to fall into disrepair once everything of value had been stripped, sold off, or melted down. It stood empty for centuries, forgotten and desolate, before being offered to Captain Lewis Granger, a distant cousin of the family that still owned the estate at the beginning of the nineteenth century.

The young captain had been embroiled in a scandal involving the young wife of a well-respected general, dishonorably discharged from the army just before Waterloo, and sent home to England. He had disgraced himself to the point where he could no longer show his face in London, at least for a time, and so he appealed to his cousin, begging for sanctuary, which Squire Granger reluctantly offered. Lewis Granger might have been a libertine and a gambler, but he had a penchant for architecture and history. He turned the ruin into a home, rebuilding the crumbling structure with his own two hands and the help of a few lads from the village, who were more than happy to earn a few quid during a time when well-paying jobs were scarce and returning soldiers tried to pick up the pieces of their lives and find any employment going.

Squire Granger had been so impressed with Lewis's efforts that he bequeathed the chapel to Lewis in his will, and it had remained in the family until the last descendant sold the house to Quinn three years ago. Niles Granger was a young man who was thoroughly at odds with Lewis's legacy. His spiky hair was dyed platinum blond; he wore unbearably narrow trousers and horn-rimmed spectacles, proclaiming himself to be a hipster and an artist. Niles had no interest in history or architecture, and he wanted nothing more than to get away from all that "old shite," as he so eloquently described it. He unloaded it gleefully and never looked back, using the profits to buy a dilapidated loft with space for a studio, where he created works of unfathomable modernity using splashes of bright colors, bits of trash, and phallic symbols strategically displayed for maximum shock value.

The rest of the estate had been bought years earlier by an eccentric millionaire who converted the huge manor house into Lingfield Park Resort. Despite its proximity to the resort, Quinn's house felt completely private. The chapel was nestled in the woods at the edge of the property; none of the guests ever ventured in that direction, warned off by the "Private Property" sign nailed to a tree and a lack of a walkable path. There was a narrow lane, just wide enough for one car to pass on the other side of the house, which led into the village, but the lane saw so little traffic that Quinn felt as if she were living alone in the woods.

Now, three years later, Quinn was still charmed by the stained-glass windows set high in the stone walls and vaulted ceilings painted with an image of the heavens. Not much had remained of the original chapel, but there was something about it that always made Quinn feel welcome and at home. She supposed it was all the hopes, dreams, and prayers that had been absorbed by the stones over the years. Prayers didn't just dissipate into thin air—they soaked into the walls, buttressing the structure with their strength and healing energy. As an archeologist, she found it immensely appealing to live in a place that was imbued with so much character and steeped in history.

When originally built, the chapel had been one large open space, but Lewis Granger had divided it into two rooms, the back room serving as a bedroom and furnished with an antique four-poster bed and carved dresser, which Niles had been only too happy to throw in as part of the deal. The dark wood was polished to a shine, the bed hangings made of embroidered damask in mauve and gold. Once that bed had been the center of Quinn's universe, the place where she spent lazy afternoons with Luke as they made love, shared their dreams, and made plans for the future. Now, the bed was used only for sleeping and reading when sleep wouldn't come.

Quinn still felt fragile and bruised by Luke's sudden desertion, but now being on her own didn't seem as frightening as it had two months ago when she suddenly found herself single. She'd felt adrift for a while, remembering several times a day that she no longer had anyone to return to. But like all shocks to the system, the knowledge eventually became part of her new reality, and Quinn threw herself into her work, eager to feel like her old self again. There had been a few offers and casual flirtations at the dig but nothing that blossomed into anything real; she supposed she hadn't allowed it to. She hadn't been ready to move on.

At first, Quinn managed to forget about Luke for a few hours at a time, then for whole days, but now she was back home, and her loneliness was suddenly sharper and so much more oppressive than it had been in Jerusalem, where she was surrounded by people. The silence of the chapel, which she normally found soothing, weighed heavily on her, its density disturbed only by the sound of the falling rain and the ticking of the clock.

Quinn took a sip of tea and closed her eyes. She hated rainy days; they forced her to stay indoors. On fine days, she went for long country walks, walking until she exhausted herself enough to enjoy a few hours of dreamless sleep. But on a day like today, there was nothing to do but brood. She didn't even have a dog. Her job demanded frequent absences, and it wouldn't be fair to leave a puppy behind to be looked after by someone else for months on end. She did wish for a companion, though. Perhaps she could get a little dog and leave it with her parents when she went overseas. The thought cheered her up as she imagined a furry little ball of affection snuggled in her lap, making her feel less alone.

Quinn nearly spilled her tea when there was a loud knock at the door. She wasn't expecting any visitors, not so soon after arriving at home, and there was no one she could think of who'd just drop by unannounced. Quinn set her mug down and went to answer the door. Perhaps it was one of the guests from the resort who'd ventured too far off the path and got lost. Quinn opened the door, surprised to find an actual visitor.

"May I come in, or do I have to stand here in the rain?" Gabriel Russell asked as he smiled down at her.

"Of course. Sorry, Gabe. Come on in. May I offer you some tea?"

"You sure can. And add a dollop of whiskey, for medicinal purposes," he joked as he took off his wet coat and hung it on a coatrack before taking a seat on the sofa in front of the roaring fire.

Quinn held out the mug to Gabe and reclaimed her spot on the sofa. The melancholy that crept up on her earlier was gone, and she was suddenly grateful for the unexpected visit. Gabriel Russell wasn't just her boss but also one of her closest friends. They'd met years ago on a dig in Ireland when she was just a student and he was the dig supervisor and had remained close ever since, always staying in touch even during the most tumultuous moments of their lives. Gabe invited her to join the faculty at UCL Institute of Archeology when he accepted the position as head of the Archeology Department, and they shared a nice, comfortable relationship unmarred by stodgy professionalism or academic rivalry. They wanted different things, and Gabe, who preferred a desk job to digging in the dirt, supported Quinn and rejoiced in her success. Luke had taught several classes at the institute as well, using Quinn's friendship with Gabe as a way in.

Gabe was in his late thirties, with shaggy dark hair worn just a little too long and dark blue eyes fringed with ridiculously long lashes. His nose was a trifle long, and his eyebrows curved like wings above his hooded eyes, making him look stern and unapproachable at times, but that was only until he smiled. Gabe had a radiant smile that made him look sheepish and endearing at the same time. He could probably charm the knickers off Her Majesty, if they ever had occasion to be in the same room, which was why he was as popular with the faculty as he was with the students.

Few people knew this, but Gabe could trace his roots back to the Norman invasion, having descended from Hugh de Rosel, who'd accompanied William the Conqueror to the shores of England and had been rewarded for his loyalty with estates in Dorset. Gabe's family still lived in Berwick, although Gabe was the only male left of the noble line. It was Gabe's grandfather's obsession with history that influenced young Gabe and led to a degree in history and archeology.

Quinn folded her slim legs beneath her and turned her gaze to Gabe as she took a sip of her own tea, eager to hear what brought Gabe to her door on such a filthy night. He'd never been one for unannounced visits, so whatever it was had to be important.

"It's really coming down out there. I nearly missed the turn; I didn't see the sign for the village. Are you over the worst of the jet lag?" Gabe asked as he studied her features. Gabe had always detested small talk, but after several years of interdepartmental politics, he learned not to blurt out what was on his mind, as he had done when he was younger. Quinn smiled into her mug. She found this newfound political correctness somewhat amusing but went along with it nonetheless. Gabe would get to the point eventually, and she was in no rush for him to leave.

"It took about two days to adjust, but I'm back to my usual routine. It's nice to be home."

"Oh? Looking forward to a nice long winter, are you?" he joked.

"After roasting in the desert for six months, a cold winter sounds like a dream come true. I won't even complain about snow."

"We'll see about that. I wouldn't say no to a couple of weeks in a warm sunny place. Haven't had a holiday in longer than I can remember. Ibiza would do me very well right about now."

"Maybe you can take Eve after Christmas," Quinn suggested. Gabe always spent Christmas with his parents, but liked to take off for a week after the holiday, having had enough family togetherness, particularly since his mother had a long list of chores for him to complete before returning to London. Being an only child, it fell to him to see to the never-ending repairs needed to maintain the family home. His father was getting on in years and could no longer manage the upkeep on his own, but was too stubborn to hire a handyman.

"Actually, Eve and I are no longer, but that's not why I'm here," Gabe said but didn't elaborate. Eve had been the latest in a string of women in Gabe's life, an editor at a fashion magazine who was glamorous, vivacious, and dangerously independent. She was the type of woman who had lovers, not partners, and Quinn strongly suspected that she'd moved on to someone else while Gabe wasn't looking. Quinn never could understand why a man as intelligent and warm as Gabe always went for women who could never quite give him their full attention and bailed at the first sign of trouble. She had never known Gabe to be truly in love with any of his amours and wondered what kept him from finding someone who could really touch his heart.

Perhaps he feared commitment, or was wary of getting hurt. After her experience with Luke, Quinn could commiserate. She'd always craved a relationship that could sustain her, but her choice of partners hadn't been any wiser than Gabe's. There had been a few men who professed to love her, but sadly, she'd never become their number one priority and was discarded as soon as something better came along, as it had with Luke. The future she offered him couldn't compete with a professorship at Harvard University.

Quinn was actually surprised that Gabe made no mention of Luke's departure. Luke would have informed him since he'd been on the faculty and would have had to give notice. *Perhaps*

Gabe even warranted a phone call or an e-mail, and not just a text, Quinn thought bitterly.

"So, why *are* you here on a rainy Friday night?" Quinn asked, her expression coy. The last thing she wanted to do was discuss Luke or Eve, but she was too curious to remain silent any longer.

"Have you seen the news?" Gabe asked as he took a sip of his whiskey-laced tea and sighed with pleasure as the alcohol hit his bloodstream.

"No, why?"

"Human remains were discovered yesterday at a construction site in Mayfair. They'd just broken ground a few days ago for another building of luxury flats few of us can afford. It seems there was a hidden chamber below ground that never appeared in the blueprints."

"And they called you?" Quinn asked, unsure of why exactly Gabe was involved. "Hardly your area of expertise."

"The foreman called in the Met and the coroner, but they quickly ruled it out as a recent crime."

"So, why's it on the news? Don't skeletal remains normally get reburied or left where they were found?" Quinn asked.

This wasn't the first case of human remains being found during excavation. The ground beneath London was full of surprises. Workers routinely came across remains of plague victims who'd been carelessly thrown into pits and buried en masse. At times, they even dug up what used to be whole cemeteries and reburied the dead in another part of town. Unless the remains belonged to someone of historical interest—like Richard III, whose remains had been resting under a parking lot for centuries—they didn't get much press. These were nameless, faceless relics of another time, a time when people were buried in paupers' graves and plague pits and forgotten about. There wasn't much to be learned from these remains, historically speaking, so they were usually just left in their final resting place as a sign of respect or moved somewhere safe.

"This find was special," Gabe replied with a sigh. "The remains were in a large chest of some kind, padlocked and chained. The two skeletons inside were lying face-to-face, as if sharing a final kiss as they lay dying. Clearly, they didn't die of natural causes, especially since there are scratch marks on the inside of the lid. Those two were murdered, their bodies hidden and denied proper burial."

"Do you think they were someone of historical significance?" Quinn asked, her interest piqued.

"I have no idea, but some tosser took pictures with his mobile and sent them to the media. *The Globe* picked up the story, and it went from there. The skeletons are now being referred to as 'the Lovers,' and they've become a real human-interest story. The public want to know who they were and what happened to them," Gabe said with a faint lift of his eyebrows. "If the media runs with this, we'll have another Romeo and Juliet on our hands."

"They'll lose interest in a few days," Quinn replied. She was very familiar with the fickle nature of the public. Unless the find was significant, people's attention very quickly strayed to something more current.

"I don't think so. I've actually had a call from someone at the BBC just this morning. They're thinking of doing a program based on various finds of historic interest that have cropped up all over the country these past few years. Think of them as historical scavenger hunts, if you will, like *Time Team*. Interest is high since Richard's remains were found earlier this year. People are intrigued by the notion that they are going about their daily lives and not suspecting for a second that they might be walking over the mortal remains of a royal."

"In all probability, those poor people in the chest were as far from royalty as one can get," Quinn said. Modern people didn't invent crime; murder had been around as long as humans themselves, and many a murder had gone unsolved, especially in times before the creation of a police force or forensic science.

"It's still good publicity for the institute and might result in some generous grants from the powers that be."

"Why do I have the feeling there's more to this?" Quinn asked with a smile. She could see the sheepish look on Gabe's face as he met her gaze. He was getting to the good part.

"I want you to take on this project, Quinn. You are the best forensic archeologist I've ever worked with, and you can use your gift to learn about the victims," he added softly.

Quinn's eyes flew to Gabe's face in alarm. They never discussed her "gift." She'd told him about it a long time ago, in a bout of alcohol-infused self-pity in a pub in Ireland, and now she couldn't take the revelation back. Gabe had respected her confidence and never brought it up again, allowing her to forget that there was one other person out there in the world who knew of her uncanny ability to see into the past. She'd never told anyone else, not even Luke, frightened of the implications the knowledge might have on her life and her work. It was her ability to see into the past that had influenced Quinn's choice of career—that, and a desperate need to tell the stories of people who could no longer speak for themselves. But she could hardly use the information she'd gleaned as scientific research. Every bit of information had to be documented and supported by fact, so Quinn kept a lot of what she saw to herself, using her secret knowledge as a road map to finding out more about the people whose possessions she came across and dressing the information up as scientific discovery.

Quinn had been able to learn quite a lot about a twenty-two-year-old man called Atticus, a dark-eyed, handsome youth who came to Judea from a province of Rome in search of glory. He died far from home and left behind a child born to a Jewess who'd been married off in haste to hide the disgrace of having lain with a Roman soldier. The sword that belonged to Atticus had been rescued from the clutches of history, but not his story; it would die with Quinn since there was no one she could share it with without betraying her ability—no one except Gabe.

Gabe came to her because he was fully aware of the limitations of this particular assignment. In all probability, historians might never be able to put a name or a face to the two skeletons in the chest, and his only hope of making this project appealing to the BBC was to truly dig deep and find out who the victims were. He was using her most treasured secret against her, knowing that she was likely the only one who could find out the truth about the two people locked in an eternal embrace in that dark chest.

"Why are you doing this to me, Gabe?" she asked warily, her voice devoid of any hint of accusation. She knew why. Gabe would give anything to possess her gift, if only for his own academic ends. He genuinely loved history, and to see into the past as it had really been rather than as it had been imagined was something that, as a historian, would send him into raptures.

"Quinn, your ability is nothing to be ashamed of. You've been given an amazing gift, one that's invaluable in your chosen profession. You can not only use physical evidence to find out more about your subjects but actually see into their lives, hear their thoughts. Why are you so reluctant to use it?"

"Because publicly admitting to it would make me look like a quack and destroy my credibility as a scientist. Can you just imagine me discussing my *visions* on BBC? People would go from calling me a historian to calling me a psychic, a label I don't really care for."

"But you are psychic, and you are the real deal."

Quinn shook her head. She'd fought her ability ever since she was a child, resentful of the responsibility it placed squarely on her skinny shoulders. She didn't want to see people who were long dead going about their business, nor did she want to hear their thoughts or feel their joy and pain. She just wanted to be a normal kid, if such a thing were even possible. Her life could never be normal anyway, given the way it had begun.

"I'll think about it," she replied with a grudging half-smile.

"All right, do. I'll be going now. I'll wait for your call. If I don't hear from you by Sunday night, I'll give the project to someone else—like Monica Fielding, for instance."

"Like hell you will," Quinn retorted, suddenly furious. Gabe knew offering this find to Monica would shake her out of her complacency. Quinn supposed that every person eventually came across someone who got under their skin for reasons they couldn't quite explain. It wasn't just professional rivalry that pitted the two women against each other, it was a personal one as well. Monica genuinely disliked Quinn and made no secret of it, actually going as far as to question Quinn's credibility in television interviews and periodicals. She had some sort of personal score to settle with Quinn and wouldn't be satisfied until Quinn became a laughing stock and a pariah in the scientific community.

"I'll do it," Quinn blurted out without thinking. "I'll take it on."

"I thought you might." Gabe's victorious smile said it all. "I'll give BBC a call and tell them you're on board."

Chapter 3

December 1664

London, England

Elise de Lesseps smoothed down the skirt of her gown and patted her hair into place, suddenly reluctant to enter the room. She'd been in her father's study countless times, to tidy up mostly, but this morning she felt strangely nervous. This summons felt different, more official somehow. She wasn't here to restore order but to be spoken to on a matter of some importance; she was sure of it.

"Oh, stop being such a ninny," she said sternly to herself under her breath. "There's absolutely no reason to be frightened."

But the brave words did nothing to dispel her sense of foreboding. She'd seen the young man come and leave this morning, had heard the thunder of hooves on frozen earth, and knew that something of significance had occurred. She just couldn't imagine what. Elise refused to entertain the notion that it was bad news. They'd had more than enough of that lately. The anxiety of not knowing made her hand shake as she finally raised it and knocked on the solid oak door.

"Come," her father called out. He stood with his back to the room, gazing out the window. The diamond-shaped panes glittered in the morning light, bright winter sunshine filling the room, which was freezing cold, the fire having been laid but not lit per her father's instructions. Hugh de Lesseps conserved firewood whenever possible; his own comfort was of little importance to him these days.

Elise stood just inside the room, waiting for her father to speak. He finally turned around, his expression unreadable. Elise couldn't help noticing the stooped shoulders or the stern set of his lips. Her father had aged drastically during the past year. His once-dark hair and beard were now streaked with gray, and his powerful frame had shrunk, making him appear older than his forty-seven years. Hugh de Lesseps's deep-set eyes studied his daughter, his head cocked to the side, as if he were listening to some inner voice.

"What is it, Father?" Elise asked, now even more worried than before. "Are you ill?"

"Sit down, child," Hugh said. "I would speak with you."

Hugh lowered himself into the carved hardback chair behind the massive desk and clasped his hands, his fingers intertwined. Normally, her father leaned back, but today he was hunched forward, his shoulders stiff with strain. His eyes slid away from Elise toward the cold fireplace, as if he was reluctant to speak, and he remained silent for a few moments before finally facing her again.

"Elise, I've had a messenger this morning," he began.

"Yes, I saw him leave," Elise replied. "What news?"

Her father took a deep breath as his eyes met hers over the breadth of the desk. "I won't beat about the bush. You're old enough to know the truth, and since your mother died, you have been the lady of this house and a mother to your sisters."

Her father sighed, as he did every time he mentioned his late wife, who'd left them only last February. Nothing had been the same since. The house seemed cold and empty, even on the warmest and sunniest of days. The laughter had died, as had the music. Hugh often called his wife frivolous while she was alive, but he always said it with a smile, glad to see his wife laughing and dancing with her daughters. Their two sons were grown men now, one living in Massachusetts Bay Colony and one in Port Royal, Jamaica, where he was most useful to his father.

Caroline de Lesseps had been a child bride, a girl of fifteen when Hugh married her, and she'd retained something of that innocence and joy, a quality he loved above all else in a woman who never aged in his eyes. She'd been only thirty-six when she died, but to him she was still the young, beautiful girl who took his breath away the first time he saw her. It had been a marriage of convenience arranged by the families of the couple, but the relationship had blossomed into one of love and respect and became a true partnership. Many men married again once the period of mourning was over, but Elise was certain that her father wouldn't look at another woman for a long time to come, if ever. No one could replace his beautiful Caroline, and secretly she was glad.

Hugh de Lesseps pinched the bridge of his nose, as if he had a terrible headache, then looked up at his daughter, his expression one of utter misery.

"The messenger was from Lord Asher. I owe him a great deal of money since the cargo he'd paid for is now at the bottom of the sea. I am not in a position to repay him, at least not at this time. Since the sinking of the *Celeste*, our financial situation is dire, Elise."

The *Celeste* went down in a storm just off the coast of Jamaica in September, taking with it all her father's precious cargo and its crew. Hugh de Lesseps owned one more ship, the *Sea Nymph*, but no ships crossed the Atlantic during the winter, and it would be nearly a year before Hugh saw any profit from the sale of the cargo the crew would bring back from the West Indies.

"Is Lord Asher demanding payment?" Elise asked carefully. She had more of an education than most girls of her station and understood only too well the ramifications of losing the cargo and the vessel. Her father would need ready capital to purchase goods, which would be shipped to Jamaica and sold, the profit used to purchase Jamaican goods that would then be transported to the American colonies. A third cargo would then be loaded on the ship for the voyage back to England, the hold loaded with tobacco, furs traded from the savages, and wooden spars, which would be sold to the Navy for the building of masts. Only once the cargo was sold in England would a profit be realized and the debt to Lord Asher repaid.

"Lord Asher has offered to allow me a grace period of two years to pay the debt, but on one condition. He wishes to take you as his bride."

"Me? Why? I hardly know the man," Elise exclaimed. Lord Asher was a wealthy and powerful man who had the ear of the king and could choose any woman for his wife. Elise had neither title nor fortune, and the dowry her father had set aside for her was hardly enough to tempt a man of Asher's wealth and position. Why would he want her?

"Lord Asher has offered to forgo the dowry," her father added, his expression pained. "It seems he has no need for it."

Elise slowly rose to her feet, her legs suddenly too wobbly to hold her up. She grasped the back of the chair for support as she faced her father. "I don't have a choice, do I?"

"I'm sorry, Elise. I promised your mother that I would see you happy, but if Lord Asher calls in the debt, I will be ruined. Your brothers will lose their livelihood, and your sisters will have no dowry once they come of age. I can't afford to refuse."

"I understand," Elise breathed. She felt faint but remained standing upright, her knuckles white on the back of the chair.

"You will be the wife of a great man. Your sons will be of noble birth, and you will be received at court. I know that Edward

Asher is not your heart's desire, but you will benefit from this union, as will your sisters. Our family will weather this crisis."

"Yes, Father," Elise replied woodenly. "May I go now?"

"Go on. You need some time to absorb this news."

"When does Lord Asher wish to marry?"

"In three weeks' time, at the New Year."

"That soon?" Elise willed herself not to cry, but her voice sounded shaky.

"You will be ready." It wasn't a question but a statement. She would be ready; she had no choice. The bargain had been struck and she was the chattel that would be transferred as payment of debt—human cargo replacing material goods.

Elise didn't bother to shut the door behind her as she fled the room. She needed time alone to sort out her tumultuous feelings and prepare a story for her sisters. Amy and Anne were only thirteen and nine, too young to understand the implications of the *Celeste's* sinking. They'd lost their mother less than a year ago, and now they would lose their sister as well. To show them the depth of her despair would only make the inevitable separation more difficult for them, so Elise had to put on a brave face and make them believe that this match was of her own choosing.

Elise climbed the stairs to her room and shut the door, locking it behind her. The girls would be expecting her in the parlor, but she couldn't bear to face them just yet. She couldn't calmly work on her sewing when she was battling rising hysteria. In three weeks, she would be married off to a man she barely knew. Elise had met Lord Asher once when he visited her father on a matter of business. She'd seen him twice more since then, but no words had been exchanged besides a curt greeting. Lord Asher had bowed to her, his eyes never leaving her face as his lips stretched into a half-hearted smile. Elise assumed he was just being polite, although a man of his station had no obligation to be polite to the likes of her.

Elise sat in front of the cold hearth and pulled a warm shawl about her shoulders, but it did little to warm her. She closed her eyes and tried to picture herself standing next to Edward Asher in church as a vicar bound them for eternity, giving her new husband complete control over her life. Edward Asher was an imposing man, to be sure, but old enough to be her father. *He has to be at least five and forty*, Elise thought miserably. She shuddered and opened her eyes. The only way to accept this new reality was to focus on the positive things about her future husband. Elise was hard-pressed to find any, but she had to, so she began with his looks.

Lord Asher was of above-average height, and despite his age, he was still in good physical form. He didn't run to fat, nor had he lost his hair. She supposed he wore a wig when at court, but when he'd come to visit her father, he wore his own hair, which was a rich brown with only a few strands of gray silvering the temples. His gray eyes were not unkind, and he did smile easily, which spoke of a good temperament. As far as Elise knew, he had no children, at least not ones still living.

Elise supposed that any girl of her station would be honored to marry a man like Lord Asher, who would pluck her from complete obscurity and elevate her practically overnight to become one of the ladies of the royal court. To be wealthy and titled and received by His Majesty Charles II was the stuff of dreams for young maidens, but that had never been Elise's aspiration. She'd never been inside the palace, but she had seen courtiers out and about, carousing in the Strand and enjoying pleasure cruises on the river. They were like peacocks, draped in yards of exquisite fabric and lace, painted like whores, and adorned with bows, ribbons, and ridiculous curly wigs, which made even the most masculine of men look like overgrown poodles. Most people gleefully accepted the new fashions when Charles II took the throne, tired as they were of the black and gray of Puritan rule that had been the order of the day for so long. The theaters had reopened, music and color burst into people's lives with a gaiety most had forgotten, and suddenly, life was good again. Everyone, from the wealthiest nobleman to the poorest wretch, was glad to be alive.

But now, after half a decade of excess and frivolity, the unbearable glitter of royal glamour had begun to fade, and the common people were beginning to tire of the careless spending of their new king, their lot in life still not much better than it had been during the reign of his father and the tyranny of Oliver Cromwell.

Elise had no desire to become one of the cheap, painted ladies of the court, who indulged in sinful games, thinly veiled sexual innuendo, and provocative masques, the only purpose of which was to showcase their charms and catch the interest of a new lover. Elise was a good, Christian woman, and she wanted nothing more than to be like her own mother: a faithful wife and loving mother, with a husband who was loyal and devoted even after decades of marriage. And she'd come so close to achieving that dream.

Elise had been nursing a tender affection for Gavin Talbot, her father's clerk, for the past two years. Gavin was kind, thoughtful, and hardworking. He would never be rich, but through hard work and careful planning, he would surely be able to offer his family a comfortable living. And he was handsome. Gavin had sandy hair and wide blue eyes that shone with good humor. He'd always had a kind word and a smile for Elise, even when she was still a young girl and beyond his notice. Now that she was a woman of seventeen, Gavin was in his mid-twenties and ready to start his own family. No betrothal had taken place, but there was an understanding between them that with her father's permission, they would marry once the year of mourning for her mother was over.

Elise had never spoken to her father of her feelings for Gavin, but she was sure he knew. Hugh de Lesseps was an observant man, a man who was a devoted father to his girls, and who, she believed, genuinely wished for their happiness. He would have consented had this catastrophe not struck their family, Elise was sure of it.

And now Gavin was as far removed from her as the moon. Her father had a debt to repay, and she was the currency. There was no one else. Elise bit her lip to keep from crying. She had no choice. If she refused, her father and brothers would be ruined, and her sisters would have no chance of a respectable marriage. It was her duty to honor her father's wishes and make a good marriage that would benefit the whole family. Few girls had the luxury of choosing their own husbands, and even fewer had expectations of a happy marriage. Lord Asher would be good to her, and she would want for nothing. Perhaps she could even help Amy and Anne make an advantageous match when the time came.

Elise sprang to her feet when she heard footsteps outside her door and the excited voices of her sisters. She forced a smile onto her face just as the two girls burst into the room. "Father says there's to be a wedding," Amy exclaimed. "Oh, that's so exciting. I can't wait until I am a bride." She sighed dramatically and did a little pirouette.

"Father says there's to be dancing and a great feast. Do say we can come, Elise," Amy pleaded.

"You'll have to ask Father. You two are too young to attend, but perhaps you can watch from the gallery, if the wedding is to be held here."

Amy continued to perform dance steps as she gazed at herself in the cheval glass, but Anne stood quietly by the door, her eyes shiny with unshed tears. She was the more sensitive of the two and had taken their mother's death very hard. Her grief was still as fresh as it had been when their mother breathed her last, and

Elise worried how she would cope once her big sister was gone. Amy was too young and frivolous to give her sister the support she so sorely needed.

"You're going to leave us," Anne whispered as she ran to Elise and wrapped her arms around her waist. "Oh, what are we going to do without you?" she said and began to sob.

"Come now, Annie. It won't be so bad. I'll be a great lady, and you might be able to visit me in my house across the river. Just think of it."

Anne's eyes grew round with wonder. She'd never been across the river. There was no call for the girls to leave their house in Southwark; everything they needed was right there. But Lord Asher lived in the Strand, where Elise's new home would be. She'd never seen Lord Asher's house, but she'd heard her father speak of it. Grand, it was, he said, and well appointed, with tapestries on the walls, carpets on the floors, and fine furnishings. There were many servants: maids, cooks, grooms, and gardeners. Perhaps Hugh de Lesseps viewed this turn of events as fortuitous. Elise only wished she could bring herself to feel the same.

Chapter 4

Elise woke every morning with an ever-increasing feeling of dread. A week had passed since the discussion with her father, but she had yet to see either Gavin or her betrothed. She strongly suspected that her father had sent Gavin away under some pretense or other. Gavin was frequently away for several weeks at a time, undertaking tasks that were too menial or arduous for her father. Hugh de Lesseps was no fool; he needed to make sure that the wedding went off as planned and that his daughter was still a maid on her wedding night. Giving herself to Gavin only weeks before her wedding would ensure that if she got with child, her husband would be none the wiser should the babe not be his. Elise had to admit that she felt a frisson of anger at the thought. She might have feelings for Gavin, but she was a woman who valued her honor and would never disgrace herself or her father in that way. Elise and Gavin had shared a few tender kisses, but it never went further than that. Their affection for each other was pure and true, and the fact that Gavin never tried anything untoward with her was a mark of his love and respect.

Elise forced herself to throw off the covers and took a resolute breath before stepping onto the chilly floorboards. Her feet burned with cold as she hastily washed, dressed, and brushed her hair. She was shivering by the time she pulled on her woolen stockings and shoved her feet into her shoes, which were no warmer than the floor. She turned to go downstairs, where at least a fire was lit and it was a few degrees above freezing. She'd stop by the kitchen to discuss the day's menu with Cook and warm herself by the hearth. Elise was glad that her sisters, at least, had a fire in their room. Anne had a weak chest, so it was imperative to keep her warm at all times. When their father instituted the new economies, dispensing with fire in the girls' room never entered his thoughts.

Elise gathered her shawl about her shoulders for added warmth and turned toward the door, suddenly catching her reflection in the cheval glass. She looked pale and melancholy, her eyes large in her unsmiling face. What did Lord Asher see in her? She stood before the mirror and stared at her reflection. It wasn't until that moment that she realized how much she resembled her mother. She had the same sky-blue eyes and fair skin dusted with tiny freckles across the bridge of her nose. The same full mouth and high cheekbones. But her mother's hair had been a deep auburn, whereas Elise's was more of a pale red. It looked bright and coppery during the summer months, but right now it was lackluster and made her appear even paler than she already was. She was small and slight, with a high bosom and a tiny waist.

It was a blessing really that she looked so childish since to look her age would remind people that she was seventeen and not yet married. Most girls her age were already wed and had a child or two, but Hugh de Lesseps needed his eldest to care for her mother when she was ill and look after the two girls until they were somewhat recovered from the loss of their mother. It would be a year since Caroline de Lesseps died in February, so Gavin had planned to ask her father for her hand in marriage at Christmastime, but the sinking of the *Celeste* put paid to that. And now she was to wed Lord Asher. Elise sighed. Her mother always said that life had its own plan, and Elise supposed this was it. No one said she had to like it.

Going to the kitchen lifted her spirits somewhat. The cavernous room was blessedly warm, and the aroma of baking bread and beef broth made her mouth water. She'd had a terrible headache last night and had barely eaten any supper, retiring to bed with a hot brick instead, so now she was ravenous.

"Good morrow, mistress," Cook called out as she extracted fresh loaves from the nook on the side of the hearth. "Can I offer you some breakfast? The master has broken his fast already, and the girls are still abed."

"Yes, please."

Elise took a seat on the long bench and gratefully accepted a cup of hot broth and a hunk of bread smeared with bacon drippings. She bit into the food, momentarily content. It was a long time till dinner; the sky outside hadn't even begun to lighten. It'd be another hour at least until sunrise, and Elise would have to make the most out of the few winter daylight hours to work on her trousseau. Her father had called in their mother's seamstress to make her a gown for the wedding that wouldn't shame her intended, but the rest had to be improvised. Elise hated going through her mother's things, but her father pointed out that her mother would have been glad to see her gowns put to good use. Caroline de Lesseps had a good eye for fashion, and her gowns, although elaborate and richly adorned as fashion demanded, were not gaudy or exceedingly low cut.

Elise spent the previous day altering a peacock-blue silk gown, a favorite of her mother's. It had taken her nearly all day since the stitches had to be tiny, even, and cleverly disguised in the embroidered pattern of the rich fabric. Elise was a few inches shorter than her mother had been, and thinner. Caroline had looked much as Elise had in her youth, but six pregnancies had filled out her bosom and expanded her waist. The bodice needed to be taken in, and the waist tightened so that there would be no extra fabric gathered at the back when the laces were tied. At least the sleeves fit well.

After breakfast, Elise selected another gown to alter and settled in a settee by the window. Once the sun was up, the room would be bathed in bright winter light, and she wouldn't need to waste any candles. Natural light was easier to see by, and hopefully she would be finished before the first candles of the evening needed to be lit. She ran her fingers over the claret velvet as she held the gown up and brought it to her nose. It still smelled of her mother, and the familiar scent brought tears to her eyes. "Mama, what would you make of all this?" she whispered into the folds of the sleeve. "What advice would you give me? Did you feel so frightened before you married Father?"

Elise wished she could hear her mother's voice in her mind, even if the answer was one of her own conjuring, but all she heard was a deafening silence. Anne said that Mother spoke to her, but Elise had had no communication, not even a dream. It was as if their mother had forsaken her, deeming her too mature to need such comfort. Or perhaps, Elise didn't really believe that her mother's spirit was still with them, as her father kept telling the younger girls. Caroline was gone, taking her love, support, and warmth with her and leaving Elise in a vacuum of sadness.

Elise had just finished hemming the claret gown when she spotted movement by the carriage house. Her heart leaped as she carefully set aside her sewing and got to her feet, as if to stretch her legs. Cissy had just come into the parlor to deposit an armload of firewood by the hearth, and Elise had no desire to arouse her suspicions. She was a gossip at the best of times, a shrew at the worst, always looking for juicy tidbits to chew over with the other servants. Hugh had her whipped once for speaking ill of the mistress but had been persuaded by his wife to give Cissy another chance. Elise smiled innocently at Cissy and took a turn about the room, waiting for the girl to finish stacking the wood and leave before making her way stealthily outside.

The carriage house was located next to the stables and visible from all the front-facing windows, which included her father's study. Hugh de Lesseps used to spend hours poring over manifests, figures, and maps, but these days he spent much of his time gazing out the window, his mind refusing to settle to business matters. Elise threw a cautious glance at the windows of her father's study but couldn't see the dark silhouette behind the sunlit panes. She quickened her step and slipped into the carriage house before anyone saw her, breathing out a sigh of relief as she closed the door behind her.

The carriage loomed in the dim confines of the building, its black-painted exterior making it look forbidding and grim without light reflecting off the windows and illuminating the padded interior. The carriage house was Gavin and Elise's special place, the only place where they could steal a few moments of privacy, away from the prying eyes of the family and servants. Hugh was a man who enjoyed routine, so Elise always knew when the carriage house would be empty. It was there that Gavin had kissed her for the first time and talked to her of the future. And it was there, inside the carriage, that they hatched their plans, talking and dreaming as young lovers did.

Gavin stepped from behind the carriage, his hat in his hands as he peered at Elise through the gloom. He looked tired and anxious, his eyes searching Elise's face for clues as she rushed toward him. Elise walked into Gavin's arms and rested her head on his chest. She'd never taken such liberties before, but this might be the last time they saw each other, so she threw caution to the wind. Whatever happened, she was glad he'd come. Not seeing him before the wedding or saying good-bye would have made things even more difficult to bear.

"Elise," Gavin murmured as he pushed back the hood of her cloak and stroked her hair. "Oh, Elise."

Elise opened her mouth to say something, but the only thing that came out was a choked sob. She hadn't meant to cry, but suddenly her predicament seemed unbearable. All her hopes and dreams were being torn apart, replaced by a black void in which her future now lived. She'd tried picturing her life with Lord Asher but drew a blank every time. She knew nothing about the man, his life, or even his house. She could picture his face, but nothing more.

"Gavin, I'm so sorry," she finally choked out. "I wasn't given a choice. The *Celeste* . . ."

"I know," he replied gently as he continued to hold her close. "Come inside the carriage. I want to talk to you."

Gavin reluctantly let her go, then opened the door of the carriage and handed her inside. The interior felt like a tomb, but it did offer them more privacy should anyone decide to come in. Once Elise's eyes adjusted to the darkness, she felt cocooned within the vehicle, momentarily safe from the world outside. If only they could stay in the carriage forever, hidden from her father and future husband, who would claim her for his own in less than two weeks.

Gavin set aside his hat and turned to Elise, his eyes intent on her face. "Elise, I hold your father in very high esteem and would never dream of going against his wishes, but this is our once chance to thwart your marriage to Lord Asher."

"Gavin," Elise interjected, but he shook his head, wary of the interruption.

"Elise, come away with me. We can leave London tomorrow, or even today. I have enough put by to sustain us for several months until I find employment. We can go anywhere, even to the American colonies. We can be free," Gavin pleaded. "We'll never be rich, but I will take care of you and our future family; you'll never want for anything."

Elise huddled into the corner of the carriage for support, her heart racing wildly as she considered Gavin's words. She wanted to throw her arms around him and tell him that yes, she would go with him, today, tomorrow, next week, or whenever he was ready. She'd sacrifice anything to be his wife.

Gavin's earnest blue eyes held her gaze, begging her for an answer as he reached for her hands. "Say yes. We'll make a life together, a good life."

Elise lowered her eyes, staring at their intertwined hands. If it were up to her, she'd give anything to be with him. No sacrifice would be too great, but she had to think of her family. Her father would be ruined if she ran off, as would her brothers who already had families to support. Her sisters would be left with no dowry, and their reputation would be tarnished by association. Amy would be fourteen in March. In a few short years, she would be ready to be wed, and her prospects would be nonexistent, thanks to a sister who selfishly ran off with no thought to her duty to her family.

"Gavin, I can't," Elise said miserably. "I can't shame my father that way. He's facing utter financial ruin, and this will be the end of him. Lord Asher will see that he's disgraced and bankrupted if I humiliate him by running away. How can I be happy living with the knowledge that I ruined so many lives?"

"Elise, I know you have a duty to your family, but you have a duty to yourself as well." Gavin looked stricken, as if the possibility of her refusal never figured in his plans.

"Do I? I'm just a woman, Gavin. I've nothing of my own, not even a voice. My father speaks for me until such a time as I'm given away in marriage. My only value is in how well I can marry and what I can bring to my family. I want nothing more than to be your wife, but I have no right to be so selfish. I'm the only one who can keep us from total ruin. Please forgive me," she whispered as she looked up into his shocked face.

"So be it, then," Gavin replied, his tone laced with bitter defeat. He pulled his hands away and looked at her tear-streaked face, his eyes studying her features as he wordlessly said good-bye.

"I cannot continue working for your father, Elise. I will wait until spring, then sail to the colonies. There are opportunities for men like me. It's a chance for a fresh start. If you change your mind, before or even after the wedding, you know where to find me. But, by April, I will be gone. I'll wait for you until then."

"Don't. I won't be coming, Gavin. This is good-bye."

Elise leaned forward and planted a soft kiss on Gavin's lips, but he remained unresponsive.

"Good-bye, Elise. May God keep you," he said as he exited the carriage, pushed his hat onto his head, and strode out of the carriage house, leaving her alone and bereft. Elise knew that she'd done the right thing, but it was a cold comfort when faced with a lifetime of sadness.

Chapter 5

October 2013

London, England

On Monday morning, Quinn dutifully presented herself at the morgue where the skeletal remains found in Mayfair had been taken for tests. Over the weekend, she'd scanned all the information available online about the find but learned little more than she already knew from Gabe. The only thing that offered any clues as to the time period of the murder was the picture of the chest taken by one of the workers on the site, but she needed a closer look to ascertain the period in which it might have been crafted.

Truth be told, Quinn was glad to be in London. Having spent her first weekend on her own, she was more than ready to leave the house and grasp the distraction of this case with both hands. She thought that she'd accepted the idea of Luke's desertion, could forge ahead without him, but the time alone proved her wrong. They'd spoken about the future shortly before she left for the dig in Jerusalem. Luke had even hinted that he was ready for the next step, and she'd dreamed of a Christmastime proposal, but she could never have imagined that the next step for Luke would be a professorship in America.

Quinn was ready for marriage and thought that Luke had been too. And she had been eager to start a family, although she hadn't mentioned that to Luke before she left. One step at a time was the way to go with Luke. She'd never known him to be impulsive. Luke was a planner, a list keeper. He wouldn't have been open to having a child right away, but she would have talked him round sooner rather than later. Luke liked kids and mentioned his desire for a family several times over the past few years. It had been Quinn who'd been apprehensive. She'd spent years focusing on her career and making a name for herself in academic circles, but now, at thirty, she seemed to melt every time she saw a sweet baby gazing at her from a passing pram and longed for the feel of chubby arms around her neck. There was a time when having a child seemed like a burden and an unnecessary hindrance to her success, but at this moment, she would give up all the ancient bones in the world for the comforting weight of a baby in her arms. But the promise of family had suddenly been snatched away from her, and she found herself mourning the loss of something that had been within her grasp only a few months before.

Quinn blanched as the smell of strong disinfectant assailed her senses. It failed to disguise the note of putrefaction hovering in the air. In fact, it only served to bring attention to it. Dr. Scott was in the middle of an autopsy, his apron covered with substances Quinn didn't care to name. He gave her a wave through the Plexiglas window and held up his splayed hand, indicating that he'd be done in five minutes. Quinn took a seat outside, reserved for family members coming in to identify their loved ones, and stared out the window. The on-and-off rain that stuck around all weekend had stopped, giving way to a glorious autumn morning. Everything was painted in shades of orange, crimson, and gold, the colors brilliant against an azure sky, the outside a stark contrast to the atmosphere of the morgue, where death ruled with an iron fist.

Dr. Scott finally came out, thankfully sans apron. He'd removed his latex gloves and shook Quinn's hand, surprising her with the firmness of the handshake. Colin Scott wasn't tall, but he was lithe, with graceful hands that looked as if they should be holding a paintbrush, not a scalpel. His long sandy hair was pulled back into a bun while he worked, and Quinn was fairly certain that he was fully aware that his surgical cap exactly matched the shade of his eyes. Had she met him at a social function, she would never have taken him for a pathologist. An artist, maybe, or a musician—even a writer—but never for a man who dissected cadavers for a living.

Dr. Scott's sensual lips stretched into a warm smile as he released her hand.

"Dr. Allenby, a pleasure to meet you. Gabe told me you'd be stopping by."

"He strong-armed me into taking on this case," Quinn complained good-naturedly as she smiled back at the doctor, who didn't seem the least bit affected by the fact that he'd just autopsied a woman who appeared to be in her early forties.

"Me as well, but I was secretly pleased. Unlike those of us in the trenches, the administrators always have to worry about where their funding is coming from. I'd rather get my hands dirty any day rather than panhandle to endless bureaucrats in exchange for measly handouts. Come, let me introduce you to our 'lovers.'"

"Well, since you put it that way, lead the way," Quinn said and followed Dr. Scott down the corridor.

"Actually, Sarita Dhawan, my assistant, is performing most of the tests, but she's very thorough, I assure you."

They entered a separate room, where a young Asian woman was tapping away at her computer, her huge dark eyes reflecting the screen in front of her. She looked up in greeting, a smile transforming her narrow face from serious to radiant in an instant.

"Good morning, Dr. Allenby," Sarita called out from her perch as she gave Dr. Scott a questioning look.

"Can you finish up for me, Sarita?" he asked as he inclined his head toward the room he'd just come from. "Just close her up. I'll enter the results once I'm finished in here."

"Sure thing, boss," Sarita answered as she slid off her stool and reached for an apron and a pair of latex gloves.

"What was it that killed her?" Sarita asked.

"Intracerebral hemorrhage," Dr. Scott replied, his attention already on the metal slab in the middle of the room. Sarita nodded and left the room with some reluctance, casting a look of pure longing at the remains. Whatever Dr. Scott said would be more interesting than closing up a body after an autopsy, a pathologist's version of grunt work.

"Shall we begin?" Dr. Scott asked as he walked briskly toward the slab, rubbing his hands in childish anticipation.

Two skeletons were laid out side by side, the chest they'd been found in discreetly stored in the corner of the room and wrapped in clear plastic to prevent accelerated decay caused by exposure to oxygen and sunlight. Quinn would examine the chest later, but for now all her attention was focused on the remains. Even if she had not known that the skeletons were those of a male and female, she would have been able to guess just by looking at them. The male skeleton was much longer, raw boned, with large hands and feet. The female was dwarfed by the male, her bones narrow and delicate by comparison. She might have been mistaken for a boy were it not for the wider pelvis.

"So, what have you discovered?" Quinn asked as she accepted a pair of latex gloves from Dr. Scott and approached the slab with some trepidation. She always felt a pang of anxiety when confronted with human remains. These individuals had died years before, but her heart turned over at the sight of them. They'd been living, breathing people once, people who loved and hated and worried about things just as any person did today. They had names and people who cared about them, but now they were just two anonymous skeletons lying on a cold metal slab in a twenty-first-century morgue, their bones almost translucent beneath the merciless florescent light coming from the fixture above.

Dr. Scott didn't seem to share Quinn's bout of sentimentality as he reached for a manila folder containing the test results. Unlike her, who dealt with death in a more academic manner, he faced down death every single day and was immune to the ugliness and decay that immediately followed the passing of a person. Dr. Scott was more interested in the physical aspects, whereas Quinn longed to know about the actual person and the life they'd led.

"We've conducted the usual tests: carbon-14 dating, mineral analysis, degree of bone calcification, and isotope mapping to determine the paleo environment and reconstruct the paleo diet of the subjects. What we have here are the skeletal remains of a male and a female, and they are roughly four hundred years old. The male was in his mid-twenties. Judging by his height and the condition of his teeth, I'd say that he came from a well-to-do background and enjoyed adequate nutrition for most of his life. There are bony ridges on his right wrist, so he likely did some type of work that required prolonged use of his right hand; I can't ascertain what kind, but he might have been a craftsman of some sort or a blacksmith—a workingman, at any rate. He'd sustained broken ribs and several broken fingers on his left hand, but they were well healed by the time of his death."

"How did he die?" Quinn asked, staring at the man's grinning skull as if it might offer up some clue to his fate.

"There is no indication that he was murdered before being placed in the chest. His skull is intact, and there are no nicks from a knife on any of his bones. It's possible, of course, that someone could have slid a knife under the ribs and into the heart, but I doubt that was the case since we found no traces of blood, which would have been there had he suffered a violent death. He most likely died of asphyxiation."

"And the woman?"

"The woman was younger, possibly in her late teens or early twenties. Only two of her wisdom teeth had come in, and clavicle fusion hadn't occurred yet. There are no obvious signs of violence, so she likely died in the same way as her mate. I can say, however, that she'd had at least one child, possibly more."

"Is that all you can tell me?" Quinn asked, slightly disappointed. She hoped for something more to go on before starting her quest for the identity of these two, and Gabe had made it clear that time was of the essence.

"Oh no, my dear. I have lots of surprises for you," Dr. Scott replied, his tone jovial. "We have been able to recover several strands of hair, bits of fabric, and scraps of leather as well as several metallic objects that you can evaluate at your leisure."

Dr. Scott led her to a side counter where the specimens were displayed in labeled plastic bags. He was practically glowing with excitement. Quinn supposed that this was a welcome break from autopsying cadavers, a historical puzzle rather than the final journey of someone who was now nothing more than a slab of meat, dissected and analyzed for the benefit of the family who needed answers or for the police, desperate for clues in an investigation.

"Although we found hair, we were unable to extract any nuclear DNA due to the lack of a root. We did, however, find a few broken nails, which were much more helpful. We did extensive DNA testing, and here's what we found. The man's hair was dark; it appears to have been either a dark brown or black, and he had light eyes. He was Caucasian, of Norman and Saxon descent, and he was not related to the woman. Can't say that last bit surprises me," Dr. Scott joked, implying that the man and woman were romantically involved. They might have been, but Quinn didn't wish to jump to any conclusions that might sway her findings until she knew more.

"As I mentioned before, he enjoyed a plentiful diet for a man of his time. He might have suffered from a mild calcium and vitamin C deficiency, but that was common since people subsided mostly on bread and meat and hardly ate any vegetables, fruit, or dairy. The deficiency wasn't severe enough to make him lose his teeth, at least not yet. We x-rayed his skeleton and saw no evidence of disease, which would have appeared as holes or lesions. Bone density is normal. We found that he had a version of the Klotho gene associated with long life."

Dr. Scott smiled ruefully at Quinn. "So, what we have here is a healthy young man, with a predisposition for a long life, who died at an unnaturally young age. We did discover a type of monoamine oxidase enzyme which accounts for impulsive behavior, so he might have been something of a hothead."

Dr. Scott paused dramatically to give Quinn a moment to draw her own conclusions as to the type of behavior that might have resulted in someone being locked in a chest while still alive and left to die a slow and agonizing death. Quinn shuddered, imagining what it must have felt like to be buried alive, entombed with no avenue of escape and the knowledge of certain death. She hoped that the man and woman had already been dead and the chest used in lieu of a coffin, but Dr. Scott immediately disproved that theory by pointing to a small baggie containing slivers of torn nails.

"There were scratches on the inside of the lid, which was what accounted for us finding the broken nails. They were both alive and conscious when they went into that chest."

Quinn sighed, longing for this interview to be over. She felt claustrophobic in this windowless room and couldn't wait to get outside. "Tell me about the woman."

"The woman had reddish-blonde hair and light eyes. Her ancestry was Saxon with a few Scots thrown in. She tested positive for the BRCA1 gene, which meant that she would have most likely developed breast cancer at some point in her life, and showed PER2, which would have made her an early riser. She had a vitamin D deficiency and, judging from the condition of her teeth, didn't get enough calcium in her diet, but otherwise she was a healthy young woman."

"Is that all we know about her?" Quinn asked, hoping for something more to go on.

Dr. Scott gave Quinn a triumphant look that nearly made her laugh. He'd really missed his calling as a stage actor.

"Sarita and I found traces of a third source of DNA," he announced, his eyes shining as he allowed this bit of information to sink in.

"Do you mean you found the DNA of whoever forced them into the chest? Their murderer?"

"I'm afraid not. What I'm referring to is some additional bones that we found at the bottom of the chest. They were tiny and very fragile."

"A baby?" Quinn breathed, suddenly sickened by the scenario playing in her mind.

"Yes. The woman was pregnant. About fourteen weeks. The child was male, and our man here was his father."

Quinn averted her eyes for a moment, embarrassed of the moisture that suddenly blurred her vision.

"I know. It's heartbreaking, isn't it?" Dr. Scott said, having correctly interpreted her reaction. "I was quite overcome myself. And they wouldn't have died quickly, which made it even worse."

"What kind of monster would do that to a young family?" Quinn asked, still feeling weepy. The young woman would have known she was with child by the second trimester, and she would have had to bear the pain of knowing that her child would die with her, never even having drawn breath.

"A monster that likely wore gloves while he went about his business. We found no traces of anyone else's DNA. No hair, no nails, nothing."

"And what of the material evidence?" Quinn asked, finally tearing her gaze away from the grinning skeletons on the slab. She couldn't begin to imagine the look of agony these two actually wore at the time of death, their suffering now erased from history by the decomposition of flesh.

"We found bits of fabric from what we believe to have been the woman's gown. It was made of heavy damask and might have been a deep blue at one point. The dye was made of indigo, so it was all natural—consistent with the approximate time period, which I would place at mid-seventeenth century, give or take a decade or two. The pieces of leather likely came from the man's attire. Perhaps he wore a leather doublet and boots. There are no chemicals found on the leather, so again, it's consistent with the time period when the leather would have been tanned by hand, using only natural methods and organic dyes."

"And the metal?"

"There is a brass belt buckle from the man and two silver shoe buckles that belonged to the woman. And, there is this!" Dr.

Scott pulled out a Ziploc bag containing a piece of jewelry and passed it to Quinn. "Here, you can examine it more closely."

Quinn opened the bag and reached inside, taking out an ornate brooch. The brooch was made of yellow gold, with a sapphire flower in the center of a filigree background set with small, round sapphires and seed pearls, creating an exquisite and delicate pattern. It must have been pinned to the bodice of the blue gown worn by the young woman.

Quinn felt a tremor as she looked at the brooch. She was grateful for the layer of latex between the brooch and her skin. She would examine the brooch more carefully later, when she was alone, but for now she needed to return it to the bag. The brooch, more than anything else, would serve as a bridge between herself and the unknown woman whose mortal remains now rested on the slab. It had belonged to her and was an item that she touched and valued, more so than shoe buckles or bits of fabric. The brooch was the key, as was the belt buckle. The man would have handled it regularly, so the buckle would be imprinted with his memories.

"Thank you, Dr. Scott. I'd just like to get a copy of the test results and take some photos of the skeletons and the chest. You've been very thorough."

"It's not often that I work with people who died hundreds of years ago. I suppose I felt some strange need to give them something of their identity back," Dr. Scott replied. "Although, it won't make a jot of difference to them now."

Quinn nodded, overcome by a wave of sadness.

Chapter 6

After leaving the morgue, Quinn wasn't ready to return home, so she decided to walk to the institute, which was located in Gordon Square. It was a lovely October day, and the sun caressed her face as she strolled at a leisurely pace. The square was strewn with a quilt of colorful fallen leaves, the old trees providing welcome patches of shade for those who chose not to sit on the lawn. Several students were busy studying, their noses in books, while other visitors to the square just reclined on their rugs in the sunshine. Some were reading, others listening to music, and some enjoying a brief nap during their lunch break.

Quinn found a spot beneath an overgrown maple and sat down, her back against the trunk. The visit to the morgue affected her more that she cared to admit. She supposed that she chose archeology and history as her field of study because she lacked a history of her own, and seeing those two nameless skeletons brought home once again the importance of having a name and a past. She'd spent years trying to come to terms with her own lack of one and thought she'd gotten a handle on her desperate need to know where she came from, but today the layers of acceptance and denial had been stripped away, leaving her as emotionally fragile as she had been the day she learned the truth of her origins.

Quinn had been eight years old the day her world imploded. She'd come home from school, excited to begin her project over the weekend. She'd always liked stories, especially ones that took place in the past, and the idea of working on her family tree deeply intrigued her. Her mother was in the kitchen, preparing their tea, and her father was watching a game on the telly, having come home early from work as he did most Fridays.

The house smelled of roasting meat and vegetables, and there was an apple tart her mother had baked that morning. The aroma of apples and cinnamon wafted from the table, making Quinn's mouth water.

"How was your day, darling?" her mum asked as Quinn settled herself at the table and reached for a piece of carrot.

"Grand. We're doing a school project. I'm going to need your help."

"What type of project?" her mother asked without looking up from the potatoes she was mashing.

"It's a family tree, so I need information about past generations of both Allenbys and Grants. I'd like to see some photos too, if you have any." Quinn bit into her carrot and chewed happily, thrilled to have two days off school in which to work on her project and read *The Secret Garden*, which she'd just started the night before.

Quinn looked up to find her father standing in the doorway, his expression odd. Her mother's eyes flew to her husband's face, her eyes wide with anxiety. "No, Roger," her mother said, her eyes locked with his. "Not yet."

"There's never a good time, Sue, but I think this is the opening we've been waiting for."

Quinn's mother looked dejected, as if she had suddenly shrunk a few inches, her shoulders hunched and her lips pursed. Whatever her parents were talking about distressed her a great deal, and she suddenly pushed away the bowl of mash and sat down heavily on the kitchen chair.

"You do it, then," she said, her tone bleak.

"What are you two talking about?" Quinn demanded, suddenly anxious. They hadn't openly mentioned her name, but it was clear that whatever they were arguing about had to do with her. Why was her mother so upset? And what was it that her father wanted to do? Was this about the puppy she'd been asking for? That was the only thing she truly wanted for her birthday, but if it caused her parents so much distress, she'd just wait a few years until she was able to take care of it all on her own. Quinn grew very still, her eyes shifting from one parent to the other. The tension in the kitchen was thick as her father left the doorway and approached her slowly, his forehead creased.

No, this couldn't be about the puppy. This was something else. Something serious. Something she wished would just go away, whatever it was. Quinn was only eight, but she knew at that moment that whatever her father was going to say would change everything. *Are they getting a divorce?* she suddenly wondered. Her heart fell. No, it couldn't be. They loved each other, and they loved her. She was sure of it. But there were several children in her class whose parents were divorced, and they were shuffled from one parent to the other on weekends and for school holidays. Quinn wanted to cry, but she was a big girl, so she bit her lip instead and forced herself to meet her father's troubled gaze.

"Quinn, I want you to know that we love you very much," her father began as he squatted in front of her. "You must always remember that."

"I love you too," she replied, her voice shaking with suppressed tears.

"The thing is . . . Well, this family tree project . . ." Her father grew silent, his face tense as he searched for the best way to break the news he felt compelled to share with her.

"What is it, Dad?" Quinn cried, now truly alarmed.

"Quinn, we always meant to tell you. We just wanted to wait until you were old enough to understand. Your mother and I adopted you when you were a baby."

Quinn stared from one parent to the other. Adopted? She'd never for a moment suspected that she wasn't their child. She even looked like her father; everyone always said so.

"So, who were my parents, then?" she asked, her voice barely audible. She supposed she was glad that her parents weren't getting a divorce, but this news left her utterly gutted. Her entire existence tilted on its axis, her center of gravity suddenly shifting so alarmingly that she thought she just might slide off and fall into some dark void from which there was no return. If there was one thing she'd been sure of in life, it was that Susan and Roger Allenby were her parents. They were ordinary people, who lived an ordinary life, a life of which she had always been the center. She'd wished for a brother or a sister from time to time, but she loved having her parents all to herself and being the focus of all their love and attention. How was it possible that she wasn't theirs?

"We don't know," her mother chimed in as she reached for Quinn's hand, but Quinn pulled it away. She felt too betrayed to allow her mother to touch her just then.

"Did they not want me?" Quinn persisted, her voice shaking with apprehension.

"We don't know anything about them, sweetheart. We only know that we wanted a child very much and were happy when you came along. You made us a family," her father explained as he searched her face for understanding.

"Did you try to have a baby of your own?" Quinn asked.

"Yes, but we couldn't," her mother said sadly. "We tried for years."

"So, I wasn't your first choice. You settled for me."

"No!" her parents cried in unison.

"Never that," her father continued. "We loved you from the moment we saw you."

"Right," Quinn replied bitterly, unable to look at her father for fear of crying. She slid off the chair and ran to her room.

"Tea is in ten minutes," her mother called out after her, but Quinn just ignored her.

"Let her be, Sue. She needs a little time to think this through," she heard her father's voice say.

Quinn spent most of that weekend in her room, reading her book and trying hard not to let the conversation with her parents upset her, but she was upset and confused. Everything she knew about herself was a lie, a fabrication. The school project no longer held any interest for her. These weren't *her* relatives—they were the relatives of her parents, people who had no biological connection to her. Of course, lots of people were adopted and lived a perfectly normal life, but to do that she'd need more information. She needed to fill in the blanks in order to make peace with this newfound knowledge.

Quinn finally emerged on Sunday afternoon. Her mum was in the kitchen again, baking Quinn's favorite chocolate chip biscuits. She'd been trying to cajole her to come out all weekend, bribing Quinn with her favorite foods and the promise of a new bicycle for her birthday. She didn't want a bicycle. She wanted a puppy, one that would be hers and hers alone. It would belong to her, and she would belong to it; they would be each other's true family. Quinn sat down at the kitchen table and accepted a biscuit. It was hot, straight from the oven, but she ate it nonetheless, enjoying the familiar taste of chocolate. At least that hadn't changed.

"Are you still my mum?" she asked, her voice cracking.

"Of course I am, and I always will be. Quinn, I didn't want to tell you, but your father is right. You need to know the truth. If we withheld it from you, you'd find out later and then accuse us of lying to you. We felt it was best to be honest."

Quinn nodded. She didn't question her parents' logic; she understood their reasons for finally telling her the truth. She supposed that it would have come as a shock at any age, even if she were a grown-up. Finding out that you weren't who you thought you were could never be easy.

"Mum, I'd like to know something about my real parents. I love you and Dad, but I'd like to know where I really came from." Quinn knew it would hurt her mother, but she needed to know. She'd tried all weekend to envision the woman who'd given birth to her, but all she saw was a pale oval where a face should have been. Was she young or older, was she dark haired like Quinn, or had she been fair? Did she have green eyes like her daughter, or did Quinn get those from her father? Had they loved each other, or had she been the result of a mistake that neither person wished to repeat? She'd just recently learned about where babies came from, and it was still a shock to think of two people doing *that* willingly—even more so knowing that the gross act adults indulged in could result in an unwanted child.

"Quinn, I'm afraid we don't know anything about them at all, and neither does the adoption agency. You were found in Leicester Cathedral. Someone left you in the front pew wrapped in a blanket."

"Who found me?" Quinn exclaimed, shocked to learn this new version of the truth. Left. Abandoned. Not even given up for adoption, but discarded like an empty coffee cup or a newspaper.

"The Reverend Alan Seaton. He heard a baby crying but thought nothing of it until he came out of the vestry and spotted you there. He called the police, of course, but they had nothing to go on."

"Nothing?" Quinn whispered.

"There was a note tucked into the blanket. I have it if you'd like to see it. I saved it for you. I knew you'd want answers one day, but I'm sorry to say, that's all we have."

"Yes, I'd like to see it," Quinn replied. She imagined she'd be able to see something in the note everyone else failed to notice, but it was just a scrap of paper, torn out of some notebook. Quinn stared at the writing on the note. It was in pencil and said very little:

Quinn

Born September 27, 1983

"Is that it?" Quinn asked, disappointed.

"Yes, that's it. Social Services had no idea whether Quinn was your last name or first name, but they passed the note on to us, and we decided it must have been your given name, so we kept it."

Quinn. Someone had bothered to name her and provided her date of birth. At least she knew that much, but it was very little to go on. It was a dead end, and she had to learn to live with this new reality.

Over the years, Quinn tried to put a different spin on the story of her birth, but the uncertainty of what really happened tore at her soul, refusing to let her find peace. She tried to pretend that her mother was a young girl, who was frightened and alone and couldn't afford to keep her, so she left her in a church where she knew the baby would be found by someone trustworthy and passed on to the authorities. But the fantasy wasn't enough. She longed to know the truth, no matter how painful it might be, especially once she discovered her ability to see into the past.

Quinn supposed that she had it all along, she just never realized it, not having known anyone who died before. She'd been almost eleven when Grandma Allenby died. Ruth Allenby had been Quinn's favorite grandparent, the one she spent the most time with given that she lived only a few streets over. Her mother's parents were good, loving people, but they lacked the imagination and sense of fun Grandma Allenby seemed to possess. At nearly ninety, she had been spritely and young at heart, not like any other old person Quinn knew. Quinn loved having sleepovers at Grandma Ruth's. They spent hours listening to wartime jazz, looking at old photo albums, and telling ghost stories by the light of the old spirit lamp. Quinn's favorite ghost story was about Grandpa Joe, who died long before she was born. Grandma Ruth said that Grandpa's spirit lived in the house and would look after her until she went to join him in heaven. She looked forward to seeing him again after all this time.

"Do you think he'll look old when you see him, Grandma?" Quinn asked, wondering if Grandpa Joe would appear as he did in his fifties when he died or if he would look like Grandma Ruth, wrinkled and frail.

"I bet he'll look just as handsome as he did when I first met him in 1942. He had been a surgeon, and I was one of the nurses at the Alexandra Hospital in Singapore," her grandmother said, her eyes clouded with memories. She didn't like to talk about the war, or the atrocities she had witnessed, but she liked reminiscing about her Joe. She always said goodnight to his picture, which stood by her bed, the sepia photograph framed by a heavy silver frame. Grandpa Joe was in uniform, his lean face serious as he stared into the camera, but Quinn could still see the laugh lines around his mouth and the twinkle in his eye that Ruth so often alluded to. She said it was that twinkle that led to the existence of her father, Roger. Quinn hadn't been at all sure how a twinkle could produce a little boy, but she took her grandmother's word for it. Her grandfather must have retained the twinkle since there had been four other children after Roger.

And now Grandma Ruth was gone; her little house was the same but utterly different without her in it. Quinn hoped that her grandparents were finally together, as Grandma Ruth always said they would be.

"Quinn, darling," her mother said, interrupting Quinn's reverie as she stared at the photograph of her grandfather after the funeral. "Grandma Ruth wanted you to have this."

Her mother held Quinn's hand and lowered a gold chain with a heart-shaped locket into her palm. Grandma Ruth always wore that locket. Joe had given it to her on her twenty-second birthday in 1943. It contained a tiny picture of the two of them, dressed in civilian clothes. They looked so young and earnest then. Quinn squeezed her fingers shut around the locket. She would treasure it always.

Quinn suddenly had an image of her grandmother, as she appeared in the locket, running down an unfamiliar-looking street, the heels of her shoes clicking on the pavement. She seemed anxious and kept turning to look behind her, as if someone were chasing her. Ruth breathed a sigh of relief when she spotted Joe, who jumped from a military jeep and enfolded her briefly in his arms before helping her into the car and speeding away. Quinn heard the whistle of a bomb and then the deafening roar of an explosion as a silver-bellied plane emptied its cargo onto the burning city. Quinn was so frightened, she dropped the locket, and the image of her grandparents vanished like smoke, leaving her confused and disoriented.

Quinn sat down on the bed, her brow furrowed with concentration. She couldn't remember Grandma Ruth telling her that story. She never spoke of bombs or terrifying raids that turned buildings to rubble and painted the sky black with smoke from countless fires burning all over the city. Instead, she told Quinn about dancing with Joe at a jazz club and even showed her some of the dance moves of the time, making Quinn giggle as they did the twist in the kitchen. Ruth reminisced about strolling beneath the palm trees on a moonlit night and how Joe proposed to her over a patient lying open on the operating table because he simply couldn't concentrate on performing the surgery until he had her answer. But, perhaps Quinn had forgotten and chose to remember only the stories she enjoyed.

 Over the next year, Quinn saw countless images of Grandma Ruth, not only during the war but of Ruth as a child, as wife and mother, and later, as a widow. Quinn no longer believed that she was remembering the stories her grandmother told her. No, the stories came from the locket, and she saw them only when she held the locket in her hands and the gold grew warm from the heat of her skin. Quinn didn't know how to navigate what she saw, and at times she was frightened by the depth of her grandmother's sorrow or fear, but there were also visions of love and joy, and Quinn cherished those, knowing that her grandmother would have wanted to share those moments with her.

 Quinn wore the locket all the time; she wore it still, as a tribute to her beloved Grandma Ruth, the person who unwittingly unlocked her gift. Now that she was a grown woman, Quinn understood how her ability to see into the past worked and could even manage to choose what she saw by mentally focusing on a specific year, but it was a secret she kept to herself. She'd tried telling her parents after experiencing those first unexplained visions, but they didn't believe her. Her father rationalized it as a manifestation of grief and a desire to retain a link to Grandma Ruth, and her mother said that the images were simply a figment of her imagination, an explanation that Quinn readily accepted, despite knowing beyond a shadow of a doubt that what she was experiencing was quite real.

As Quinn got older, she realized that the strange ability she'd been born with had to have come from somewhere or someone. She must have inherited it from one of her parents, but of course, she had no one to ask. Quinn made up stories in her head, imagining that this link to the spirit world was passed from generation to generation down her mother's line, the ability bestowed only on the first daughter of the first daughter and so on. It was a romantic tale that helped her make peace with the strange and often frightening images she saw. Quinn learned not to pick up old objects and made sure that she wore gloves when there was no choice. Her gift came in handy in her profession, but she didn't welcome it into her personal life, wary of where other people's recollections might lead her.

Chapter 7

December 1664

London, England

An icy wind blew off the river and nipped at Elise's cheeks as the ferryboat glided across the Thames, its lantern swinging from side to side. It was still lit despite the hour due to the thick fog swirling all around them and making Elise feel as if they were alone on the river. The fog seemed to mute all sound, the only thing still audible were the twin splashes as the oars dipped into the water. The ferryman looked glum as he navigated the boat toward the Strand, his eyes fixed on the smudge of bank looming in the distance. Elise huddled into her cloak, frozen to the bone despite the warm lining of fox fur. Damp seeped into her bones and made her shiver. Or was it apprehension?

Hugh de Lesseps sat quite still, his face turned toward the shore, his hands resting on his thighs. He hadn't uttered a word since leaving home an hour ago, abandoning Elise to her own thoughts, which were less than tranquil. She'd eaten a light breakfast of bread and broth, but now the food soured her stomach, and the rocking of the boat made her feel as if she might be sick. She breathed deeply, hoping the frigid air would prevent her from giving in to the nausea. Hugh sprang to his feet as soon as the boat docked, paid the ferryman, and helped Elise out of the boat. "Come," was all he said as they set off toward Asher Hall on foot. Elise was grateful to feel solid ground beneath her feet. She was still nervous, but at least her stomach seemed to be settling.

Elise followed her father silently down the street, her thoughts on the upcoming interview with Lord Asher. She found it odd that she'd been summoned to call on her betrothed instead of him coming to her, but then again, nothing about this situation was what she would consider to be normal or proper. The wedding was only a week away, but she'd had no contact with Lord Asher, nor had she been informed or consulted on anything. The summons came the previous evening, inviting Elise and her father to call on Lord Asher at his home at midday. They hadn't even been invited to dine, just to attend, which meant that they would be expected to leave as soon as their business was concluded, whatever that business was.

Elise walked with her head down, paying little heed to the grand houses or traffic in the street. Her father pulled her roughly out of the way as a fine carriage rattled down the street, the coachman huddled into his cloak and the horses blowing steam as they raced past. It was too early for a gentleman to be going out, so the occupant was likely just returning from a night's entertainment, possibly at the palace. Had Lord Asher spent the night at home, or had he gone out for the evening to enjoy the amusements the court had to offer? Elise wondered. Would he take her with him once they were wed?

Elise nearly bumped into her father when Hugh stopped in front of Asher Hall. The imposing facade was shrouded in soupy fog, and most of the shutters were closed, as if the occupants were still asleep. Elise was surprised to note that the house was built of gray stone, boasting large windows and numerous chimney pots, at least half of which were belching smoke. Fires had been lit in several rooms, by the look of things, so at least the place must be warm.

The building itself was surprisingly modern and nothing like the half-timbered Tudor houses that lined the narrow streets, their overhanging second stories blocking nearly all light and leaving the streets in shadow even on the brightest of days. Imposing wrought iron gates set into a stone wall bore an ornate "A" on either side, a small sign of vanity on the part of the owner. Lord Asher spared no expense in building his London residence, and it showed.

"Are we early, Father?" Elise asked as she surveyed her future home.

"No, we are on time."

Hugh pushed open the gates and walked down the drive toward the front door. He used the heavy knocker to announce their presence as Elise hovered behind him, her heart fluttering in her chest, which was constricted with rising panic. She considered herself to be a sensible person, but at this moment, she had an overwhelming urge to run and hide. She supposed all brides felt frightened and unsure a week before their wedding, especially if the union was arranged by the families, and they barely knew the bridegroom. There was no reason to fear, she told herself as a servant opened the door and ushered them inside and into a large parlor furnished with several heavy settles and chairs situated against the walls and decorated with lavish tapestries that gave some much-needed color to the dark-paneled room. The roaring fire warmed the parlor, its orange flames dispelling the gloom seeping through the casement windows and providing enough light to supplement the two candles supplied by the servant.

"Lord Asher bids you to make yourselves comfortable. He'll be down presently," the servant informed them before leaving the room. Elise removed her cloak and hung it over a chair but remained standing, far too agitated to sit down. Her father pulled off his gloves, shrugged off his cloak, and took a seat closest to the fire. His eyes strayed to a portrait hanging above the hearth. It was of a fair-haired young woman posed in a splendid gown of aquamarine damask, a sweet puppy in her lap.

"Who is that?" Elise asked, marveling at how little she knew of her future husband and his family.

"His wife," Hugh replied curtly.

"She is beautiful," Elise said as she moved closer to the fire.

"Was beautiful," her father corrected her. "You will be his wife now."

The servant returned a moment later, bearing a tray, which she set on a low table between the two hardback chairs in front of the fire.

"Would you care for some spiced wine, Master de Lesseps?" she asked deferentially.

"Don't mind if I do," Hugh replied, holding out his hand for a cup of wine. "Have some, Elise. You need it. It will put the roses back in your cheeks."

Perhaps her father hadn't meant to sound critical, but she detected a note of displeasure in his tone. She must look a fright. Elise accepted a cup of wine and took a sip. It was delicious and instantly made her feel warmer. She took another swallow, savoring the delicate flavor of cinnamon and cloves with a hint of honey. The wine warmed its way down her gullet and gave Elise a pleasant sensation in her belly. She'd broken her fast hours ago, before the sun was up, and hunger seemed to be contributing to the effect of the wine, which was making her feel light-headed and languid. She had to admit that she welcomed the alcohol-induced calm. It was better than panic.

Elise had nearly finished her drink by the time Lord Asher finally graced them with his presence. He was elegantly dressed, despite the early hour, in an exquisitely embroidered dark-blue velvet coat with wide cuffs, matching pleated breeches, white hose, and shoes with silver buckles. His wig was in the latest style, long and curly, just like those Charles himself favored.

"Good morrow," Lord Asher greeted them, his smile warm and welcoming. "I do appreciate you making the journey on such a frigid morning. I hope it wasn't too arduous."

"It was no trouble, your lordship," Hugh replied as he rose to his feet to shake Lord Asher's outstretched hand.

Lord Asher shook Hugh's hand, but his eyes never left Elise's face. He approached her slowly, a smile pasted on his face. Now that he was closer, Elise could see that there were dark shadows beneath his eyes, stubble on his pale cheeks, and the smell of liquor on his breath. Perhaps he'd just returned home from a night's entertainment. The thought made Elise uneasy, giving her an unwelcome glimpse into what her life with Lord Asher might be if he continued to carouse after they were wed.

"My dear, what an absolute pleasure to see you again. I do hope you're not angry with me for not coming to see you. I've been rather preoccupied with the business of the king, I'm afraid. I wouldn't dare bore you with the details," he added, waving his hand in a practiced gesture meant to disarm her.

"Now, if your papa will allow it, I'd like a few minutes alone with my bride."

"Of course," Hugh readily agreed. "I'll just step outside."

"My man is outside with the signed marriage contract. Perhaps you can cast an eye over it while you wait," Lord Asher added airily, making it sound as if Hugh was in a position to make changes or demands. They all knew that wasn't the case, but her father bowed stiffly from the neck, acquiescing to the request and doing everything he could to maintain his dignity.

Elise felt a pang of unease as Hugh left them alone. She didn't expect Lord Asher to do anything untoward, but it felt awkward to be alone with him. They were strangers to each other, strangers who would be united in matrimony in a week's time.

"Elise, my dear, I am so pleased that you accepted my proposal," Lord Asher said as he took her hands in his, squeezing them lightly. "I feared you'd refuse."

"It was an honor to be asked," Elise replied. She wanted to smile, but something held her back. There were so many things she wanted to ask this man but instinctively knew that she shouldn't, at least not now.

"So like your dear mother," Asher said as he gazed into her eyes. "She was a beauty, you know. I was very sorry to hear of her passing."

"Thank you, my lord," Elise whispered. There was a lump in her throat that made it difficult to speak. Elise wondered what her mother would have made of this match. And how well had Lord Asher known her mother? As far as Elise knew, the two never came in contact.

"Please, call me Edward. We are to be man and wife, after all. And speaking of that," he smiled broadly as he extracted a heavy cabochon ruby ring from his pocket, "please accept this token of my affection and commitment. I expect you must be feeling a bit anxious, but we will be very happy. I promise you that," Edward said, laying his hand over his heart. "I have every intention of being the model husband, a husband you can grow to love and respect."

Elise stared at her hand as he slid the heavy ring onto her finger. She had to squeeze her fingers to keep the ring from sliding off.

"There now, it's official. I suspect you'd like a tour of your future home, but the servants are going about their chores. Best not to disturb them," he added dismissively. "You'll have all the time in the world to explore once we are wed. Now, I hate to rush you, but I must attend to His Majesty this morning."

Lord Asher slipped the cloak over Elise's shoulders and maneuvered her toward the parlor door, the interview clearly over. "Take good care of my bride, Hugh," he said with forced cheer as he clapped Hugh on the shoulder in a gesture of familiarity.

"I will see you in church, my sweet." Lord Asher bent over Elise's hand and kissed it lingeringly before gesturing to the servant, who sprang to attention and opened the door.

"Good day to you both."

Elise followed her father back toward the riverbank. She wasn't sure what she'd been expecting, but it wasn't this strange, impersonal tête-à-tête. Lord Asher seemed eager to be rid of them, and despite his pretty words, she felt he had absolutely no interest in her. She was young and innocent, to be sure, but she could always tell when a man found her attractive. She'd seen the look of desire in Gavin's eyes, and there had been a few others who expressed their admiration. Lord Asher barely looked at her. Why the sudden decision to ask for her hand in marriage?

"Father, did Lord Asher know mother well?" Elise asked as they approached the river.

Hugh shrugged. "I don't believe they ever met," Hugh replied. "Why do you ask?"

"No reason."

"That's a handsome ring your intended has given you," Hugh said as he took Elise's hand and appraised the ring. It was large and awkward, and it made Elise's hand feel heavy. She pulled on her glove, but it bulged beneath the leather, making her hand look disfigured. It was an expensive piece of jewelry, but Elise didn't care for it one bit.

Elise remained silent throughout the crossing but could hold her dismay back no longer once they climbed into the waiting carriage. "Father, I don't understand," she exclaimed. "Why does Lord Asher want to marry me? Surely he doesn't love me."

That naïve statement brought a hiss of annoyance from her father, who tore his gaze away from the window and stared hard at his daughter. "Really, Elise," he said with derision. "Who said anything about love?"

"Well, why else, then? I know you owe him a great deal of money, but why would he want me to offset the debt? He hardly knows me."

Elise could see her father striving for patience as he considered his answer. His eyes softened as he took in her flushed face and anxious eyes. He loved her, she knew that, but he'd always been a bit gruff when it came to expressing his feelings.

"Elise," he began, "your mother and I had a happy union, and perhaps seeing our affection for each other has—shall we say—distorted your expectations of marriage somewhat. Few men of Lord Asher's class marry for love. They choose suitable women who will provide them with heirs to the estate. If they want love, they take a mistress."

"But, I'm not suitable," Elise countered. "I bring no noble title or wealth to the table. I'm just a simple girl."

"You bring youth and beauty, which is what I think Lord Asher desires at this stage of his life. He not only has a title but the ear of the king. He also has tremendous wealth; he doesn't need your money. Perhaps a simple girl is all he wants, not one of the painted ladies of the court who change lovers like they change gowns," her father suggested with a pained expression on his face.

"You mean he wants an unspoiled, unworldly virgin."

"Don't be vulgar, Elise," Hugh retorted as the carriage pulled up to the house. "Every man desires a virgin, and it's his right as a husband to expect one. You should be pleased that a man of Lord Asher's stature has chosen you for his bride. Now, I'll hear no more about this. You will marry Edward Asher next week, and you will be happy to do so."

With that, Hugh descended from the carriage and walked away, his shoulders straight and his gait purposeful. Elise stared at her father's back, suddenly resentful. She'd never known him to be harsh, but then again, she'd never really questioned his judgment before. If she had hoped to gain sympathy or understanding, she now knew that she wouldn't get either. Her father had already said good-bye to her in his heart. She was no longer his to love.

Chapter 8

Elise gazed around the crowded hall but heard nothing, save a steady buzz of conversation that washed over her without leaving an impression. She felt utterly detached, as if she were underwater or someone peering through a window at a riotous gathering, able only to see, but not hear, the people within. Lord Asher's guests were eating, drinking, and making merry, their faces flushed with the heat from the roaring fire and the spiced wine that had been liberally consumed over the past few hours. Course after course of various delicacies had been brought out and cleared away, the sweetmeats still to come. Hugh de Lesseps sat to the left of Elise's new husband, his countenance one of satisfaction at a job well done. His daughter was married, his livelihood protected, and his family once again solvent. He'd barely even looked at Elise since arriving at the church that afternoon, and he walked her to the altar without so much as a fatherly kiss of blessing.

They'd hardly spoken all week; her father locked himself in his study for hours on end while Elise spent the time she had left with her sisters. Much to their chagrin, they had not been permitted to attend the wedding supper since it was held in Lord Asher's home, and the girls were too young to be presented in adult company. The de Lesseps's servants brought Amy and Anne to the church to witness their sister's wedding ceremony but then took the crying children back to Southwark despite their desperate pleas. Normally, the wedding supper would be hosted by the bride's father, but Edward had made his own plans and made no mention of Hugh inviting any of his own friends or relatives, effectively cutting out every one of his acquaintance. Hugh bristled at this injustice, but when Elise brought it up, he snapped at her as if she were at fault and not her future husband.

"You don't seriously expect all those noble ladies and gentlemen to cross the river to Southwark, do you?" her father demanded, annoyed with Elise for broaching the subject. All he could do was put on a smile and attend with good grace. Elise didn't know anyone present except for her father, and at that moment, she wasn't sure she even knew him.

Elise sat next to Lord Asher, her face frozen into an expression of false happiness, desperate for the supper to be over and equally terrified that it should end. She felt as if she'd accidentally stumbled onto a theater stage during a play and found herself among the company of actors who went on with their performance as if she weren't there. She stood there, rooted to the stage, unable to leave but not part of the scene being played out all around her, the inevitability of what was to come in the final act hanging over her like an executioner's blade. She wasn't the first bride to fear her wedding night, she knew that, but that didn't make what was to come any easier.

Perchance it was best to just get it over with—the dread in the pit of her stomach was probably worse than the act itself. Everyone survived the ordeal, and so would she, and she'd learn to accept it as part of her marriage. Some women even grew to like it, or so she'd been told by Rose, the impudent maid who was likely speaking from experience—and the only person Elise could confide in since her mother died. She would miss Rose. She hadn't been allowed to bring her into the Asher household, but it made Elise feel marginally better to know that Rose would look after her sisters and care for them.

Elise was almost relieved when Lord Asher's mother, who'd barely said two words to her since meeting her that afternoon, motioned for her to say goodnight to her guests and retire upstairs. Elise blushed furiously when she heard the lewd whispers and guffaws of laughter, but she smiled prettily, executed a graceful curtsy, and hastily left the hall. She had no idea how long it would take her husband to actually come to her, but being alone in their bridal chamber was preferable to being displayed like a curiosity.

"Good evening, yer ladyship. Me name is Lucy," a young girl mumbled as she sprang from her seat in the corner. She looked sleepy, probably having dozed off while waiting for her new mistress to arrive. "May I be of service?" The girl had dark hair and clear blue eyes that dominated her round face. A deep blush stained her cheeks, the result of being caught sleeping, no doubt. She was about the same age as Elise, but there was a world of difference between them. Perhaps under different circumstances they might have become friends, as she had with Rose, but social boundaries had to be maintained now that she was the wife of a nobleman.

"Yes, if you'll just help me undress, Lucy."

Lucy helped Elise out of her bodice and sleeves and untied her skirt, stepping aside to let it fall at Elise's feet. Elise stepped out of the heap of fabric, and Lucy scooped it up and set it aside to be folded and put away in the trunk. Her movements were practiced and sure and mildly reassuring.

"Shall I brush out yer hair, me lady?" Lucy asked. Elise nodded, unable to reply. Now that she was in her chemise, she felt even more vulnerable and scared. She sat down heavily as Lucy went to work unpinning the elaborate hairstyle that Rose had conjured up for the wedding. The hair cascaded to Elise's shoulders in heavy waves, making her look younger and plainer.

"Oh, ye do have beautiful hair, me lady," Lucy said as she picked up the brush and began to gently pull it through the tangled strands. "Such a lovely color. Just like amber."

"Have you ever seen amber?" Elise asked. Conversation was a wonderful distraction at times, and at the moment, Elise was desperate to focus on something other than what was to come.

"Aye. Her ladyship has a necklace made of amber and gold, crafted in Russia, of all places. It was a gift from her husband, who'd visited many foreign lands. The necklace is truly a thing of beauty, but her ladyship rarely wears jewelry these days."

For a brief second, Elise thought that Lucy was referring to Lady Asher, whose portrait she'd seen in the parlor, but then realized that Lucy was referring to Edward's mother.

"Why is that?" Elise asked.

"I wouldn't know, me lady. She doesn't share confidences with the likes of me," Lucy answered good-naturedly. "She is very stern and rather frightens me at times," Lucy blurted out before realizing her mistake. She looked momentarily frightened, but Elise rushed to assure her.

"Don't worry, Lucy. Anything you say to me will be held in confidence. I thought Lady Asher looked rather forbidding myself."

Lucy smiled, her relief evident. "Me father says that I need to learn to hold me tongue. I do tend to speak out of turn sometimes, and it always gets me into trouble."

"You're not in trouble, Lucy. Does Lord Asher scare you?" Elise asked carefully.

"No, me lady. He's a good master. He's always mindful of the servants and never takes advantage."

"How do you mean?" Elise asked.

Lucy blushed to the roots of her hair, having again said something she shouldn't have. She opened her mouth to explain, then closed it again, like a landed fish.

"I don't rightly know . . ." she began.

"You mean he doesn't take liberties with the female servants," Elise finished for her.

"Aye, ma'am. That is what I meant."

Elise nodded in understanding. Lucy might have spoken out of turn, but it was good to know that her husband wasn't taking willing or unwilling servants to his bed, as many other men did. Elise had begun to wonder if her own father might be bedding one of the servants, a chit named Grace who seemed to suddenly put on airs over the past few months and was showing off a new pair of shoes that she boasted were a gift from an admirer. Elise had assumed that the admirer was someone from outside the household, but she'd seen Grace blush and giggle when she saw her father in the corridor, and rather than reprimand the girl, he smiled at her in a familiar manner, his expression one of indulgence rather than annoyance.

What a lot she had to learn about relations between men and women. Only this summer, Elise would have burned with shame at having such a thought about her father, who was deep in mourning for his wife, but she'd come to see a different, more practical side of him over the past few weeks, and all her assumptions about his character were now being put to the test. Could a man love his wife but still look for pleasure elsewhere? Was it their nature, or was it a lack of respect for the institution of marriage and their spouse? Elise heard that the court of Charles II was like a game of musical beds, but she assumed that such debauchery was limited to His Majesty's cronies. Her father was a good and decent man who always put his wife and family first. Could it be that he was really no better than the faithless courtiers who thwarted the rules of God and man in pursuit of pleasure?

Elise pushed aside this unwelcome thought. Her father's personal business was his own. He wouldn't be the first or the last man to take a mistress, especially since he was now widowed. She only hoped that the liaison with Grace had begun after and not before her mother's death. She needed to believe that her father had been faithful and decent.

Lucy finished brushing Elise's hair and went to poke up the fire in the grate. "Shall I turn down the bed for you, me lady?"

Elise looked with distaste at the massive bed that dominated the chamber. It was carved of mahogany and decorated with crimson velvet hangings embroidered with flowers and birds. She briefly wondered if Edward used this room as his bedchamber or if it had been specially prepared for the bridal couple. Elise climbed into the bed, pulled up the coverlet to her chin, and surveyed the room. She hadn't noticed it before, but there was a second door between the fireplace and the corner of the room. It blended into the paneling, the only thing giving it away was the seam around the door that was barely visible from a different angle.

"Where does that lead?" she asked Lucy, who was putting away her gown and shoes.

"Oh, that leads to his lordship's bedchamber. He prefers it to this room. 'Tis where his wife died." Lucy looked stricken as she uttered the words, clamping her hand over her mouth. The girl really was a wealth of information, through no intention of her own.

"I see. Is there a key?"

Lucy blushed as she shook her head. "No, me lady. Lord Asher likes to keep that door unlocked at all times. He has the key in his possession."

Elise sighed. So, her husband would have access to her bedchamber whenever he wished. She supposed that was to be expected, but that she couldn't even expect that small bit of privacy still rankled.

"If there's nothing else, I'll say goodnight," Lucy said as she sank into an awkward curtsy.

"Good night, Lucy. Sleep well."

"You too, me lady," Lucy said with an impish smile. "I hope to find ye in fine spirits come morning."

The girl was saucy, Elise had to admit that, but she couldn't help smiling. She liked Lucy, and at the moment, she really needed a friend.

Chapter 9

Elise woke with a start. The candle had burned down, and the fire had been reduced to a heap of smoldering embers. A rosy glow illuminated the room, making everything appear dreamlike. The connecting door between her room and Edward's was open, and a silhouette stood over the bed. Elise sat up, amazed that she'd managed to fall asleep in her state of nervous expectation. It had to be after midnight since the house was silent around her, all traces of earlier merriment gone now that the guests had departed.

Edward pulled a new candle out of a drawer and held it to the embers until the wick caught. A little golden flame sprang to life, casting light onto his face. He had removed his wig and coat, wearing only a shirt, breeches, and hose. Edward looked disheveled, his face puffy from overindulgence in drink. Elise assumed that he was about to undress and get into bed, but instead he sat in a chair, studying her with an air of maudlin reflection, likely brought on by drunkenness. He seemed in no hurry to come to bed and just remained where he was, watching Elise, which made her shiver with apprehension.

The door creaked, and a young man entered the chamber on silent feet. Elise stiffened at the sight of him, unsure of why he was there. He wasn't a servant, she was sure of that. She'd seen him before today, with Edward, and then again at the church, but he hadn't been at the supper. She expected Edward to order him to leave immediately, but her husband said nothing, amused by her reaction. He waved the young man into the room and asked him to close the connecting door. Elise turned to her husband, awaiting an explanation as her heart thumped against her breast and her breath caught in her throat.

"My dear," Edward began, his tone solicitous, "there is something I must share with you."

"My lord?" Elise's voice shook. She had no idea what her husband was about to say, but she knew, in that instinctive way one knew things, that whatever it was, she wasn't going to like it.

"Some years ago, shortly after the death of my wife, I suffered a riding accident. I'd been thrown from my horse during a hunt. I'd lost the use of my legs, and the physician wasn't sure that I would be able to walk again, given the injury to my spine."

"But you have recovered," Elise pointed out, unsure of what any of this had to do with their nuptials and the presence of the man in her chamber.

"I have recovered, yes. It took nearly a year before I was able to walk again, but I can no longer ride," he said with a smirk, as if alluding to something else. "The injury has rendered me impotent, so I am quite unable to perform my husbandly duties."

Elise gaped at him. Why had he married her, then? Her father had given her to understand that Lord Asher desired a son to carry on the family name and inherit the vast estate he possessed.

"I don't understand," Elise mumbled.

Edward beckoned for the other man to come into the light. He was in his mid-twenties, with a mane of dark hair that fell to the collar of his doublet and thickly lashed eyes beneath severe dark brows. Elise couldn't quite make out the color of his eyes, especially since the man was looking away from her, his posture rigid.

"This is James Coleman. He's my natural-born son," Edward confided with a sad smile. "His mother worked here as a laundry maid when she first came to London from the country. She was a very comely lass," he added wistfully.

"My lord, what are you trying to tell me?" Elise asked, her voice now sharp with worry.

"What I am trying to tell you, my dear, is that James will stand in for me in the marriage bed. My blood flows in his veins, so his child will be the closest I can get to a legitimate heir."

"You wish me to give birth to your grandson and pass him off as your son?" Elise gasped, Edward's meaning finally sinking into her muddled brain.

"Now you've got it. I always thought you were a clever girl."

"That goes against the teachings of the Church," Elise protested. "If you cannot consummate the marriage, it can still be annulled," she cried. What Edward was proposing was scandalous.

"And your family can still be ruined, my sweet, so think carefully of what you wish to do next. In the eyes of God and man, you're my wife, and I can do with you as I please. You are my property. I'm only asking you to do that which you would have been expected to do anyway. The only reason you are here is because I require a legitimate male heir. Does it truly matter who plants that heir in your belly? Are you so in love with me that you can't bear to lie with another man?" Edward asked, chuckling sarcastically. "Come now, he's a well-made lad."

Elise's eyes slid to the young man who stood silently with his back to the fireplace. He looked angry and humiliated but didn't utter a word of protest.

"Get on with it, James," Edward said, tired of discussing the matter.

"Will you not leave us alone?" James asked, speaking for the first time. He had a deep voice that Elise would have found pleasing on any other occasion.

"It is my wedding night, after all. I intend to enjoy it to the best of my ability, and I need to make sure that you do what's asked of you."

"As you wish," James replied woodenly. He pulled something out of his pocket and set it on the small table by the bed before pulling off his boots and removing his doublet and breeches. Thankfully, he kept on his shirt. Elise felt an overwhelming sense of panic as the mattress sank beneath his weight, and tears stung her eyes as she stared imploringly at Edward, but he seemed unmoved by her plight. He leaned back in his chair and crossed his legs, as if he were preparing to watch a play.

"Lie down," James instructed as he took the vial from the bedside table and poured something into his hand. The smell of rose oil filled Elise's nostrils and nearly made her gag.

"It will make it easier," James explained as he slid his hand beneath her nightdress. Elise gasped as his fingers made contact with her flesh. No one had touched her down there since she was a little girl and required help bathing. The sensation was strange and alarming. James touched her lightly as he applied the oil, not only to the outside but also to the very core of her.

"Try to relax," he said not unkindly. "I have no wish to hurt you."

Elise squeezed her eyes shut as James pushed her legs apart with his knee. She felt his hand move against her pelvis as he took hold of himself and guided his shaft inside her, stretching and pushing until she cried out, shocked by unexpected pain as her maidenhead gave way. James began to move, slowly and deliberately. The pain had passed, replaced by a feeling of intrusion and violation. Her defiler refused to meet her gaze as she looked up at him, her eyes full of accusation. What kind of man was he to perpetuate such sin at his father's bidding?

"Close your eyes," James ordered her, clearly annoyed by her staring.

She did. If she didn't see his face, she could pretend that it was Gavin, consummating their marriage. *Would it feel different than this?* she wondered. Would she welcome Gavin into her body, or would it still feel this wrong?

Elise's eyes flew open as she let out a low moan. She hadn't expected to, but the sensation had gone from being intrusive to something quite different. It was almost pleasurable. Her moan seemed to undo James, who let out a gasp of his own before collapsing on top of her, having completed his task.

Edward chuckled mirthlessly from his place against the wall. "Liked it, did you, lady wife?" he asked nastily. "Too bad I can't bed you myself. You're a tasty little morsel, I'll grant you that. I would have enjoyed you had I been able to do my duty by you. Did you enjoy her, *son*?" His tone was one of derision. He was clearly bitter and angry at his predicament and would have liked to punish them both.

"Get out," he hissed to James. The young man got out of bed, grabbed his clothes, and disappeared into the adjoining room.

"You will lie with James until you get with child," Edward informed Elise, now standing over the bed. "And then, you will do it again, even if the child is a boy. Is that understood?" he asked, his tone menacing now.

"Yes."

"You are to have no dealings with James outside this bed. If I so much as see you talking to each other, I will have you both whipped. You are my wife, and I am your husband. James is nothing but my cock. Remember that."

Elise nodded her understanding. She felt sick to her stomach and wished only to be left in peace.

"Oh, how I wish your mother was alive to see this," Edward suddenly added with a twisted smile. "She rejected me, you know. Once, a long time ago. She chose your feckless father over me. She proved a good breeder. Three sons in as many years, and only one of them dead," he added, his tone musing. "They could have been my sons. Well, I might not have had her, but I now hold the power of life and death over her daughter. Ironic, is it not? I suppose life has a way of righting certain wrongs," he added with a laugh.

With that, he turned on his heel and strode from the room, leaving Elise to gaze after him with a mutinous expression. She adjusted her nightdress, blew out the candle, and pulled up the blanket, but she was unable to sleep. She was seething with humiliation and resentment. Lord Asher had deceived her father about his intentions and acted out of spite because of something her mother had done decades before. Elise was now his to command and pimp. Hot tears rolled down her face as she sobbed into the pillow. What was she to do now? How was she to go on? Edward Asher had no intention of being a real husband to her. She was a broodmare, her presence in his house having only one purpose.

Chapter 10

Elise awoke to find Lucy pushing aside the bed hangings. Cold winter light poured through the diamond-paned windows, its brightness suggesting that she'd slept rather late. A fire already crackled in the grate, making the room pleasantly warm. Lucy poured hot water into the basin and placed a towel next to it in readiness. This was certainly a lot more pleasant than waking up at home and braving the frigid floorboards and a crust of ice in the pitcher.

"What time is it?" Elise asked as she got out of bed and pushed her arms through the sleeves of a heavy brocade dressing gown held out by Lucy.

"Why, it's past ten, me lady. His lordship said not to disturb you, but her ladyship is demanding to see you in her parlor. She's been up for hours. Early riser, she is," Lucy added bitterly. She likely had to get up very early to wait on the old lady.

"Why does she want to see me?" Elise asked, suddenly fretful. Memories of last night forced their way to the surface, their sharp edges no longer blunted by slumber, and made Elise cringe with shame. She imagined feeling many things on her first morning as a wife, but shame and disbelief hadn't been on the list. She hadn't expected to feel happiness, but she had hoped for contentment and relief at having survived that first test of matrimonial togetherness. But the test wasn't over—it had just begun.

Lucy shrugged. "She's got reasons of her own, to be sure. Always does. I've laid out this nice woolen gown, on account of it being so cold," Lucy added, her tone questioning. She didn't know the ways of the new mistress and was feeling her way around, looking for approval of her initiative. Elise smiled. No one had fussed over her like this before. The de Lesseps women all shared Rose, who was the only upstairs maid, and had to wait their turn in the mornings. Rose always saw to Caroline first, then went to help the younger girls. Elise fended for herself, preferring not to wait an hour to get dressed and come downstairs. She was usually the first one up anyway, and she'd go look in on her sisters and offer any assistance in getting them dressed and ready for the day. Her heart squeezed at the thought of Amy and Anne. This was the first time they'd spent a night apart, the first night of a lifetime. Elise forced her attention back to Lucy, refusing to give in to melancholy.

"Yes, the gown will do very well for today. Thank you, Lucy."

"Dolly will bring up yer breakfast presently. Can't see the old dragon on an empty stomach." Lucy giggled, her expression conspiratorial.

"Is she that fierce?"

"That and more," Lucy confirmed as she did up the laces of the bodice. "I heard his lordship say that she was quite a terror in her day."

"That's encouraging to hear," Elise mumbled. She wanted to learn as much as possible before facing her mother-in-law, but Lucy's insolence didn't sit well with her. The girl was too free with her tongue and treated her new mistress as if she were her friend. Elise knew that she should nip the unseemly familiarity in the bud, but Lucy's prattling could arm Elise with useful information, information she wouldn't otherwise be privy to, so perhaps it was wiser to wait and see.

"Rules the roost, she does," Lucy continued. "I hear it were her as wished his lordship to marry again. Said he needed an heir."

"Who would inherit if he didn't beget one?" Elise asked, her curiosity piqued.

"Oh, I wouldn't rightly know, me lady."

Elise suddenly wondered if it was common knowledge within the household that James was her husband's natural son. She couldn't very well ask Lucy, nor could she say anything to the girl that she didn't wish making the rounds of the servants' quarters within the hour. Lucy could be a useful ally, but she could also be Elise's undoing if she weren't careful. She had to tread carefully.

"Ye'd best get on, my lady. Her ladyship don't like to be kept waiting," Lucy informed Elise.

Elise hastily finished her breakfast and headed downstairs to her mother-in-law's private parlor on the ground floor. She'd finally met Lady Asher yesterday upon arriving from the church, the old lady being too frail and susceptible to cold to attend the wedding service held in the church porch. Lady Asher had offered her congratulations after looking Elise up and down, as if she were a prize heifer. *Is she privy to what her son has planned?* Elise wondered as she knocked on the door and was bid to enter.

The old woman sat in front of a roaring fire, her back ramrod straight despite the cushion placed behind it to make her more comfortable. She was tall and thin, her nearly white hair piled so high above her forehead as to make her appear even taller. Her gown was well made but outdated in style. It was dark gray, not a color flattering to most women, and completely unadorned with any lace or jewelry. In an era of excess and overindulgence, it seemed even more out of place, especially against the rich backdrop of the parlor, which was done up in scarlet and gold, clearly her son's choice. Elise subconsciously fingered the brooch pinned to her bodice. It had belonged to her mother, and she wore it every day since her mother passed, almost like a talisman.

A young woman sat in the corner, crewelwork forgotten on her lap as she gazed out the window, a slight smile playing about her lips. She was fair-haired and had the look of Edward Asher about her. She might have been his sister, had the age gap between them not been too great for that to be possible.

"Sit down," Dowager Lady Asher instructed and pointed to the chair opposite her.

"Thank you, Lady Asher," Elise replied. Elise did as she was bid but inwardly bristled at the tone. It was a tone normally used to bring a dog to heel, not to address one's daughter-in-law, but the Dowager Lady Asher clearly wasn't interested in Elise's feelings or comfort.

"You may call me Lady Matilda. You are Lady Asher now. Has the marriage been consummated?" Lady Asher asked without any preamble. Elise blushed furiously and nodded.

"Good. Do you bleed regularly?"

"Yes."

"I have instructed Lucy to keep track of your menses. That way, we'll know right away if you are with child."

"We?" Elise asked, heat rising in her cheeks. She hadn't realized this was to be a group endeavor.

"My son and I. Edward must have an heir. That one over there is no use to him."

The old woman jutted her chin out toward the girl, who seemed not to hear or notice anything other than the branches moving in the wind outside the window. Elise stole a peek at the girl, confused. She was told that Edward Asher had no children by his first marriage, but her mother-in-law was clearly implying that the girl was her husband's daughter.

"Oh, yes. She's Edward's daughter. Two stillborn sons and then a dimwit. Should have been her that died. I'd have had her locked up, you know, but Edward insisted that we treat her with kindness," the dowager said with disgust. Elise gasped, but the girl seemed to pay her grandmother no heed. She either didn't hear or didn't understand. Or perhaps she was used to such abuse and chose to ignore it.

"I must admit that I never expected the bastard to be of any use. I told Edward to wash his hands of the both of them, but he wouldn't listen to me. Inherited his father's misguided sense of honor. His father was a foolish man," she added bitterly. "Felt he had to care for his bastards and instructed Edward to do the same. It's unheard of, but Edward felt some sense of duty. I'm glad to see that the money didn't go to waste. His sister, of course, is a different matter altogether. I was glad to see the back of her, I'll gladly tell you that. Still, I suppose we ought to be thankful. The Good Lord always has a plan."

Elise doubted the Good Lord had hatched this particular scheme, but she bit her tongue and remained silent. Rallying against her situation or the people who created it would do little good, especially until she'd had a chance to study the lay of the land. Her head sprang up as the dowager addressed her again.

"Are you listening to me, you silly goose, or are you as dimwitted as Barbara?"

"Yes, your ladyship, I'm listening."

"Here, take these." The old woman handed Elise a brass ring hung with numerous keys. "You will take over the running of the household, as is right and proper. It'll keep you busy and away from useless pursuits. You will, however, consult me on any changes you wish to make. Is that understood?"

"Yes, madam."

"Good. Now go."

Thus dismissed, Elise left the room. She had no idea what the keys were for, but she would find out everything she needed to know from the servants. They usually knew more about the running of the household than the mistress herself. At least she'd have something to do with her days. Elise wondered if there might be a library. Her father hadn't approved of reading for pleasure, preferring to read scripture every night, but Elise had a fondness for poetry and plays. Perhaps her husband wouldn't notice if she borrowed a volume or two. She'd decided not to ask his permission. Her mother always said that it was easier to apologize for something after the fact rather than openly defy a husband's decree, and Elise was beginning to see the wisdom of that advice.

Elise walked along the ground floor corridor, opening one door after another until she found what she'd been looking for. The library wasn't a large one—downright meager, one might say—but there were some well-thumbed books and several plays displayed on the polished shelves. She was just reaching for a calf-bound folio when James stepped out from behind a shelf, a scowl on his face.

Elise opened her mouth to say something, but the wave of heat that washed over her left her speechless and stained her cheeks beet red. Her gaze slid away from his face in embarrassment, recalling only too well the liberties James had taken with her person last night. She felt a stab of resentment, glad that James seemed equally uncomfortable. He gave her a quick bow, muttered something that sounded like *good morrow*, and left the library. Elise sank into a leather chair and leaned her head back. She felt humiliated and used, but most of all, she felt lonely and scared. There was no one she could turn to for comfort, no one who could be told of her predicament. Lonely tears slid down her cheeks as she recalled Gavin's offer. If only she could turn back the clock, she'd go away with him without a moment's hesitation.

She believed she was doing her duty to her family, but her family had failed her. She'd been sold into what could only be described as sexual slavery. She had no voice, no options, and she wasn't likely to get any sympathy from her new kin. She had to find a way to make peace with her situation and pluck some measure of contentment from this farce of a marriage.

Chapter 11

October 2013

London, England

"Dr. Allenby." The voice came from far away, like a whisper on the wind, as someone gently shook Quinn by the shoulder. "Are you all right?"

Quinn reluctantly returned to the present, blinking in surprise as the brilliant hues of autumn foliage replaced the stark bleakness of the winter morning. A man was squatting in front of her, his eyes searching her face for signs of illness. *Madness, more like*, Quinn thought as she allowed her gaze to finally focus on him. He looked vaguely familiar, but she couldn't quite place him, especially at this moment, when she was still straddling two different worlds and felt disoriented and confused.

"Dr. Allenby?" the man prompted.

"Yes, thank you. I'm quite all right. Just daydreaming," Quinn replied, suddenly self-conscious. How long had he been trying to get her attention? She never allowed herself to experience a flashback in public, only handling objects that belonged to the deceased in a controlled environment and on her own, but her spot under the tree felt deceptively private, and she'd felt an overwhelming urge to get a glimpse of the girl found in the chest. Something about her slight form tugged at Quinn's heart, and she felt a desperate need to at least put a name to the anonymous remains. Quinn hastily stuffed the brooch back into the plastic bag and shoved it into her bag before turning her attention to the stranger, who was still hovering over her.

"Have we met?" she asked, rather more haughtily than she intended. She'd just realized that he called her by her name, but she couldn't recall being introduced to him.

"Not officially, no, but I've read several of your articles and have seen you on television," he replied. His smile seemed friendly, but his gaze was still watchful, as if he wasn't convinced that she was telling the truth and would suddenly have some sort of a fit. "Rhys Morgan," he finally offered as he held out his hand. "From the BBC. I've actually just had a meeting with Gabriel Russell. I spotted you as I was walking past and thought I'd say hello. Are you sure you're all right?" he asked again.

"Yes, Mr. Morgan. I'm all right, as I've just explained," Quinn retorted angrily. She instantly regretted her cutting tone when she saw his expression go from genuine concern to surprise at being spoken to so rudely. She hadn't meant to sound hostile, but she felt foolish in the extreme and just wanted to put her momentary lapse in judgment behind her.

"I'm sorry if I disturbed you, Dr. Allenby. I'll call your office and make an appointment for a meeting in a more formal setting." The man got to his feet and began to walk away.

"Mr. Morgan. Wait," Quinn called out as she scrambled to her feet. "I didn't mean to be rude. You just caught me by surprise, that's all. Shall we start again?" she asked, giving him her most disarming smile.

Rhys Morgan turned back and studied her for a moment, his expression thoughtful. It took him a moment too long to respond but having made up his mind, he walked back to her and held out his hand. "Rhys Morgan," he said again as a small smile played about his lips.

"Quinn Allenby," Quinn responded.

"Can I interest you in a cup of coffee?" he asked carefully. "Or do you already have plans?"

"No, actually I was going to stop by my office to pick up a few papers, but that can wait. A cup of coffee would be lovely."

"Come on, then, there's a little Italian bakery not far from here. They make excellent cappuccino, and their cheesecake is a particular weakness of mine."

"Lead the way," Quinn said as she picked up her bag and slung it over her shoulder. Some residue of Elise's anguish still swirled in Quinn's mind, but she would have to return to Elise later, when she was on her own and could begin to make sense of what she'd seen. At this moment, Quinn was more interested in the meeting between Gabe and Rhys Morgan, especially since whatever they'd discussed seemed to involve her.

The bakery was a five-minute walk from the institute and was surprisingly crowded. Quinn and Rhys settled at a small table by the window that had just been vacated by an elderly couple. Gentle autumn sunshine illuminated the Formica tabletop, where a laminated menu stood propped up by the sugar bowl. Mouthwatering smells of baking and freshly ground coffee filled the small space, and Quinn was suddenly glad she'd come. A cup of strong coffee was just what she needed, and given her recent foray into the seventeenth century, a bit of modern-day company couldn't hurt either.

"A double espresso and an almond biscotti, please," Quinn said to the young waitress who approached their table. The woman wrote down Quinn's order, but her lively dark eyes never left Rhys's face.

"No cheesecake?" Rhys asked with mock disappointment.

"Too rich for my blood."

"Well, maybe you can try mine. It's not to be missed. I'll have a slice of strawberry cheesecake and a cappuccino, Giovanna," Rhys said to the girl, who beamed at him, pleased that he remembered her name.

"Gabriel Russell tells me you've just returned from the Middle East," Rhys said as he silenced his phone and put it in his pocket, a gesture Quinn appreciated. She hated it when people constantly looked at their phones and felt the need to read every e-mail and reply to every text in the middle of a conversation, as if they were so urgent that they couldn't wait until later. Luke always placed his phone next to his plate when they went out to dinner and left it on the nightstand during the night despite Quinn's objections. She gritted her teeth every time it pinged, alerting Luke to a new text or notification. Sometimes he even reached for the phone while they were making love, leaving her boiling with outrage. Quinn found his behavior to be rude, but Luke laughed it off, telling her that she needed to march boldly into the twenty-first century and accept that technology was an integral part of everyday life. So was having manners, in Quinn's opinion.

"Yes, I've been back for just over a week. I hate to admit it, but I think I'm still a bit jet-lagged. It seems to get worse every time I travel." Quinn was giving Rhys a roundabout explanation for her earlier lapse, to which he nodded, understanding and moving on.

"I'd seen the documentary about your incredible find. You spoke about that Roman soldier as if you'd personally known him. It made some obscure foot soldier who died thousands of years ago really come alive for the viewers. How were you able to learn so much about him?" Rhys asked.

"It wasn't that I knew so much about him, per se. I suppose I imbued him with certain qualities and characteristics that I based on previous research into the standards of the Roman army and the type of young man he might have been. Some of it is fact, some just educated speculation."

"Which is exactly what I intend this new program to be, and I would like for you to research and narrate it. We want to make these people seem real and relevant, and creating a dramatization based as much on fact as supposition turns them from forgotten skeletons into living, breathing people once again. Who's to say that it didn't happen just as we envision it, eh? What do you say, Dr. Allenby? Are you onboard?" Rhys asked, taking Quinn by surprise. Gabriel had mentioned the BBC's interest, but she hadn't expected to get an offer so soon, and in such an informal setting. She was interested, of course, but she wasn't ready to commit, not until she'd had a chance to review the proposed compensation and conditions of the contract.

"Forward me your offer, and I will get back to you as soon as I've had a chance to look it over," Quinn replied, hoping that he wouldn't start talking shop right there and then. He seemed to notice her reluctance and nodded in agreement, instantly returning to the previous topic to put her at ease.

"That sword was magnificent," Rhys said as he swallowed a forkful of his cheesecake and rolled his eyes in ecstasy.

"Try it," he insisted. Quinn felt a little awkward eating off a plate of a man she'd just met, but she obediently tried a piece of cake. It really was extraordinary.

"Amazing, isn't it?" Rhys asked enthusiastically, glad to see her reaction. "Baking is a hobby of mine. I started out with bread after my sister-in-law got me a bread machine for Christmas one year. She said it would help me relax."

"And did it?"

"Surprisingly, yes. There's a certain sense of satisfaction in producing something from scratch, especially when it brings people pleasure. I graduated to more complicated recipes only recently."

"Cheesecake?" Quinn asked with a smile.

"Yes, but I just can't get the consistency right. It's always too thick, not light like this one."

Quinn suddenly wondered if he was having her on. She'd never met Rhys Morgan in person before, but she'd heard stories. He was one of the toughest producers in the business, a sadistic perfectionist who routinely made his assistants cry. She'd expected him to be older and stodgier, but the man sitting across from her couldn't be more than forty-five. He was casually dressed in jeans and a dark-blue V-neck jumper that set off his amazing eyes. They were by far his best feature, wide and thick lashed. His chestnut hair fell into his eyes and brushed the collar of the jumper, and his morning stubble gave him a slightly disheveled appearance. He hardly looked like the hard-boiled exec coming from a business meeting.

"So, how are you going to do it?" Rhys suddenly asked, cheesecake forgotten.

"Do what?"

"Find out who 'the Lovers' were. Gabriel said that if anyone could unravel this mystery, it would be you."

"I appreciate his vote of confidence," Quinn replied, mentally sending Gabe a heartfelt thanks.

"I've actually already come up with a tentative title for the series: *Echoes from the Past*. What do you think?" he asked, watching her over the rim of his cup. It seemed that he wasn't quite finished discussing the project.

"It's a fitting title for an archeological program," Quinn agreed.

"I thought that 'the Lovers' might be the subject of the first episode. So, have you anything to go on? Even conjecture must be based on something," Rhys asked, his tone now speculative and brusque.

Quinn shrugged. "I have a few ideas."

"Like what?"

It was a perfectly legitimate question, but Quinn felt herself bristling. She thought they were just having a coffee, but suddenly it was a business meeting, one she wasn't prepared for. She could hardly tell him that she hoped to obtain the information directly from the source and then try to manipulate it in such a way as to fit with scientific research supported by facts.

"I've only just come from the morgue," she replied defensively.

"Sorry, I didn't mean to rush you. I'm sure you have your own process, but surely you must have a starting point."

Quinn was annoyed by the twinkle in his eyes. He was having fun at her expense, enjoying her discomfort. He clearly liked to be in charge, and he'd totally hijacked the situation and turned it to his advantage, making her feel as if she were interviewing for a job and listing her qualifications like some recent grad resigned to take the lowliest position just to get their foot in the door. She didn't have to answer his questions, not before he made her any kind of offer or discussed the project with her in a professional environment. This impromptu interview was at an end.

"I'm sorry, Mr. Morgan, but I really must be going," Quinn said as she gathered her things. She pulled two ten-pound notes and threw them on the table. "Cheesecake is on me."

She saw the amusement on Rhys's face as she left the bakery and headed toward Paddington Station. She suddenly wanted to go home. Not only did his questions unsettle her but she also felt a burning desire to find out more about Elise. Her situation had been unique, even for the seventeenth century, and Quinn was curious to see how the young woman went from being a young, disillusioned bride to a forgotten skeleton slumbering for centuries below the streets of London.

Chapter 12

January 1665

London, England

A thick, soupy fog swirled off the river, enfolding everything in its path and reducing visibility to just a few inches. Buildings materialized out of the fog as one got closer, but their upper stories were lost, invisible. All sound seemed to get swallowed up by the thick blanket spread over the city, and it was eerily quiet for a weekday. The morning was cold, the damp seeping through the layers of clothing and right into the very bones. James kept close to the walls of the houses despite the imminent danger of having a chamber pot upended on his head. It was better than being run over by a draft horse, the driver unable to see a solitary man through the mist.

James heard the splash of water as oars sliced through the murky waters of the Thames. He felt pity for the men who depended on the river for their livelihood; it was no place to be on a day like today. He finally found the corner he'd been searching for and turned into a narrow lane, which was ominously silent. Glowing orbs of light floated out of the fog, reminding James that people were inside their homes, the candles still lit at this time of the morning. James peered at the houses on the left side, searching for the right one. A little girl opened the door when he knocked, her face breaking into a smile as she invited him in and hastily closed the door behind him, afraid that the fog would float right into the house.

"For you, my sweet Mercy," James said as he conjured up an orange from the pocket of his cloak.

"Is there one for Elizabeth?" the child asked as she caressed the orange with her small fingers. Mercy didn't like to share.

"Of course, there is. Is she here?"

"Nay. She's helping Father in the workshop," Mercy replied as she pocketed the orange. "She sweeps the wood shavings and such."

"Where's your mother, then?"

Mercy glanced upward. "She's feeding 'Arry. You can go up; she won't mind."

"And what are you doing?" James asked, smiling at the girl. She had such an air of practicality about her, like a grown woman trapped in a child's body.

"I'm doing the washing up from breakfast," Mercy answered with a frown. "I'm almost finished. Then I must start on preparing dinner."

"I'm sure your mother is glad of the help."

Mercy shrugged. Unlike her sister Elizabeth, who liked to help her parents and glowed with pleasure at being thanked or praised, Mercy didn't do anything voluntarily. She was a spirited child who didn't like being told what to do, especially when it involved housework. James petted Mercy on the head and turned to go upstairs.

Molly sat in a low nursing chair by the hearth, her eyes closed and her head thrown back in sleep as the babe at her breast sucked lazily. She looked tired and pale, her normally smiling mouth downcast. Molly woke with a start, surprised to find someone watching her.

"Oh, it's ye," she said as she glanced down at the child who held the nipple in his mouth but didn't seem to be actually nursing. Molly adjusted her bodice and pulled the blanket tighter around the sleeping child.

"How is he, Moll?" James asked as he leaned against the wall, arms crossed. There was nowhere for him to sit other than the bed, which didn't seem appropriate, and a trunk beneath the window.

Molly shook her head miserably. "'Arry's holding on, but 'e's not thriving, James. I fear I'll lose 'im."

"Don't give up hope, Moll. Look, I've brought you something." James removed a bloody muslin-wrapped package from his leather satchel and held it up for Molly to see.

"What's that ye got there?" she asked, her eyes opening wide with surprise.

"Beef. Perhaps you can make some beef tea for Harry, and your own milk will be more nourishing if you eat better."

"Did ye take that from 'is kitchen?" Molly asked, her voice laced with disgust. "I want nothin' from the likes of 'im."

"No, Moll, I purchased it. You've made your feelings plain, and I wouldn't go against you."

"I thank ye, then," Molly replied as she sighed wearily. "I 'ear the old goat's gone and gotten married. A girl less than 'alf 'is age. So, what's she like?"

"I don't really know," James mumbled, his eyes sliding away from Molly, who gave him a suspicious look. "Were you not invited to the wedding?"

"No."

"But ye have seen 'er?" Molly persisted. "Ye must 'ave."

"Yes, I've seen her."

"What is it, James? Ye are not usually so tight-lipped. What's 'appened?"

James gave up his position by the wall and sat down on the trunk, suddenly tired. Molly was the only person in the world he could share his troubles with, but they were nothing compared with her own. She'd lost a baby boy only a year ago, and now Harry seemed to be showing the same symptoms. The girls were hale and hearty, but the boys were weak and lacking in appetite. James knew that Molly was a lot more frightened than she was letting on. Here, in Blackfriars, there wasn't a family that hadn't lost a child or two, but knowing that others had endured the same kind of suffering didn't make it any easier when it happened to you.

"Come, Jamie. Tell me." Molly only called him by that name when she wanted to remind him of her status as big sister, even though she was only two years older than him.

"I've lain with her," James finally choked out, too ashamed to look Molly in the face.

"Who?"

"Father's new wife."

"What?" Molly stared at him open-mouthed, unsure of whether to be amused or horrified by this bit of news. "Why would ye do a thing like that?"

"He asked me to. He wants a son."

"'E has a son," Molly replied bitterly. "You are 'is son."

"I'm a bastard, Moll. He'll never recognize me as his own."

"Ye know my opinion on the subject," Molly replied curtly. She'd voiced it often enough.

"Yes."

"So, he expects ye to lie with 'is wife, get 'er with child, then just step aside and pretend the babe 'as nothing to do with ye? How convenient. But then, that's what 'e'd done all those years ago, so it must seem natural to 'im."

"He took care of us, Moll."

"'E farmed us out the day after our mother died and never enquired as to 'ow we were. 'E never even bothered to name ye or have ye baptized. For nearly thirteen years, neither one of us knew we 'ad a father, until 'e decided 'e might have some use for ye after all."

Molly was still bitter after all these years, but James didn't blame her. She'd been only two when their mother died bringing him into the world. No one had spoken to Molly or comforted her besides the elderly cook, who took pity on the child, but there was no kin for the children to go to, so Molly and James might have been left to perish had it not been for Edward Asher. James knew the truth; their mother had pleaded with Edward as she lay dying that he would look after his children. James supposed that Edward was too afraid to go back on his promise to a dying woman for fear of offending God, but he never so much as said a word to his daughter or looked at his son.

The children had been sent off to Kent to Cook's childless cousin and her husband, who took them in and raised them, glad of the added income that Lord Asher provided for the children's upkeep. He sent money once a year but never made contact with his children, not until James turned thirteen, and even then, he'd only been interested in the boy. Molly had been turned out, being of an age to marry or find employment. She married Peter, the carpenter's son, and they moved to London in the hope of a better life. There wasn't much work for two carpenters in the small village where they lived. Peter was a talented man, and now, more than a decade later, he'd made a name for himself and even enjoyed commissions from the palace.

Molly hated their father with a vehemence born of rejection and indifference, and she chided James every time she saw him for allowing Edward to manipulate him. James nodded and agreed for the sake of keeping the peace between them, but Molly didn't quite understand his predicament as well as she thought. By the time their father had finished paying for their upkeep, Molly had Peter had already been courting. She was nearly sixteen and of marrying age. James strongly suspected that she'd already been carrying Elizabeth by the time the two said their vows in the village church. He had just turned thirteen and was facing an uncertain future. Master and Mistress Dawson had been kind to him and Molly and had provided them with security and stability when they needed it most, but they had no obligation to him beyond that which they'd been paid for.

Edward had never made provisions for apprenticing James, nor had he made any monetary arrangements for his future. On Master Dawson's instructions, James made his way to London and presented himself to Edward, who'd been expecting him. His father sized James up as he stood meekly in front of him, praying that the man wouldn't throw him out into the street to fend for himself. James had always been taller and bigger than most boys his age, and for once, his size worked in his favor.

"I have need of a man-at-arms, James," his father said thoughtfully. "These are uncertain times, and a man is never too cautious to seek protection, especially when he finds himself at odds with the politics of his country."

James didn't know much of Edward's politics, or politics in general, but assumed that his father was not a supporter of Oliver Cromwell and his ill-fated Commonwealth. Master Dawson was a staunch Royalist who fought in the Civil War and had been severely wounded in the leg. He would have died had he not been nursed back to health by a farmer's daughter who came across him in a field. Master Dawson rewarded his savior by marrying her, so the arrangement worked out nicely for them both. He spoke to James often, especially when in his cups, of the people's desire to restore the rightful king to the throne. Perhaps James's father felt the same.

"Do you know how to wield a sword, James?" Edward asked. James didn't, but he wasn't about to say so. He'd learn. He was a quick study.

"You will be instructed in the art of swordplay. I think you'll do quite well. What say you?"

"Thank you, your lordship. I'm happy to accept your offer," James replied, feeling a surge of hope. His father wanted him by his side, and if James proved himself, perhaps they might forge a relationship after all, and he and Molly would have someone to rely on besides themselves. Their father paid the Dawsons to have them looked after, so perhaps now that they were nearing adulthood, he would finally treat them as his kin.

Edward must have guessed something of James's thoughts, or maybe he'd anticipated the sense of hope that his offer would inspire in his bastard son. He took James by the chin and forced the boy to meet his gaze. "I am offering you a place in my household, but you must remember your place, James. No one is to know of your relationship to me, least of all my wife, and to ensure that, you must never speak of it. Servants gossip, and if you tell a single soul, and I discover your perfidy, you will be cast out. Make no mistake."

Edward let go of James and stood back, head tilted to the side as if he were gazing at a painting, hard-pressed to decide whether it pleased him or not. "You do have the look of your mother about you," he finally said. "She was a lovely girl. Taken too soon."

That was the most personal thing his father ever said to him and probably the longest speech he ever directed at James. He treated James the way he treated all the other men in his employ—with utter indifference. Whatever hope James had harbored that he would be singled out because of his relationship to his father was squashed within the first few days, but despite his bitter disappointment, James still tried to win the approval of the man who sired him. Perhaps it was a matter of pride or some stubborn need to prove that he was worthy of Edward's notice, but he worked hard in the hope that he would become indispensable.

James learned not only to fight but also to read, write, and speak like a gentleman. He had a desire to better himself, and this was his chance. Much had been expected of him in those years before the Restoration. Lord Asher schemed and plotted as the Commonwealth crumbled, and the people, who were tired of the tyranny of Oliver Cromwell, finally saw the wisdom of returning to a monarchy. James had been called on to protect his master more than once and had the scars to prove it. He took it all in stride, hoping that one day his father would realize his worth and see the value of his service.

Edward never asked about Molly, nor did he ever acknowledge James as his son, not even during the months after his riding accident when he'd relied solely on James. Edward had lost the use of his legs, and James had been called upon to carry him up to bed, lift him off the chamber pot, and help him into his carriage. James was always at his father's side during that time, and their relationship evolved somewhat. Bedbound, Edward had no one to talk to, and James, starved for affection and curious about his parents, took every opportunity to learn what he could.

In time, he'd even asked about his mother. He had a mental image of her since he was a little boy. She was gentle and kind, an angel with long golden curls and eyes of sky blue. He liked to think that his mother watched over him, especially when he was ill or upset, and it made him feel slightly less miserable to believe that he wasn't entirely alone. He never shared his fantasy with Molly, who was the most practical person he'd ever known. Molly would have ridiculed him and told him to stop being such a child. Speaking to someone who'd actually known Jane Coleman was a gift he never expected to receive, and he soaked up the details like bread soaked up broth.

"Oh, she was something, your mother," Edward said with a rueful smile, his gaze fixed on some distant spot beyond the window where the first buds of spring were just beginning to burst into leaf. "Jane came to us just about the time I married Ellen. There was a girl I was in love with, Caroline, but she rejected me despite the life I could offer her and married a man who had neither title nor wealth. My mother was pleased, that I can tell you. Caroline came from good stock, but her family was impoverished, and my mother, romantic soul that she is, never put much stock in marrying for love. So, I married a woman of her choosing. Ellen was pretty enough, wealthy, and docile—the perfect wife, except that I couldn't abide being in the same room with her. She was meek, distant, and completely lacking in wit. She was like a marble statue: pleasant to look at but just a hunk of stone on the inside."

Edward took a sip of wine and leaned back against the pillows. "Jane wasn't nearly as comely as my wife. She was plump, with unruly black curls and eyes the color of a winter sea— deep gray, just like yours—but I was happy when I was with her; she made me laugh, and she made me feel." Edward sighed. "And she wasn't afraid to love, despite the fact that she knew our relationship could never be more than it was. She gave herself to me without reservation, and never asked for anything in return. She understood the rules."

"Did your wife know?" James asked, shocked to learn that his father had actually felt something for Jane Coleman. He might not have loved her, but he felt affection toward her, and clearly still thought of her fondly. How could he be so indifferent to the children he'd had with her, especially Molly, who must be the spitting image of their mother? But Edward wouldn't know that; he hadn't laid eyes on Molly since she was two.

"I think she did, but she didn't care. The less time I spent in her bed, the happier she was. Once I got her with child, I never visited her bedchamber until it was time to try again. And try I did. I wanted a son. Ellen bore two stillborn boys—and Barbara," he added bitterly. "I have no son."

Edward didn't notice the hurt in James's face as he made that statement. He was completely indifferent to his feelings, viewing James as just someone to unburden himself to in his hour of need. He didn't regard James as his flesh and blood, not even after all this time. Lord Asher was a nobleman, a man who tailored his life to fit society's expectations. He might have enjoyed his relationship with Jane, but he had no use for her baseborn children; they were a burden and an inconvenience. Had Jane not begged him to take care of her babies, he likely would have forgotten all about them.

It was that conversation that finally forced James to acknowledge that Edward saw him as nothing more than a servant, someone who was dispensable and utterly unimportant. He meant to leave his father's employ, but a few days turned into a week, weeks turned into months, and he was still at Asher Hall. He supposed what made him stay was the fact that he had nowhere to go, and at Asher Hall he was close to Molly and her growing family.

It wasn't until his father's wedding night to Elise de Lesseps that Edward Asher finally called him "son" out loud, a fact that blinded James to what was being asked of him. He'd lain awake half the night, remembering the look of fear on the girl's face. She'd been frightened enough at the thought of performing her wifely duties, but being defiled by a servant while her husband watched was more than any sheltered young girl could be expected to bear. And now he had to do it again. He'd given his word. He supposed there was some poetic justice to the situation. Edward refused to acknowledge him, but he would acknowledge James's child as his own. It was payback of sorts, but was it worth the price to his soul?

Chapter 13

February 1665

London, England

Elise wrapped her cloak closer about her to keep out the cold as she stepped out into the garden. The sky above was just turning a lovely shade of pink, the lavender clouds lazily floating overhead, signaling that a new day had come. The air smelled fresh, as if some invisible hand had washed everything clean during the night. She loved this time of day, a time when everything was coming to life after hours of slumber and the day was still full of promise. There had been a dusting of snow the night before, but spring was definitely on its way. Several purple smudges dotted the pristine snow by the far wall—the crocuses refusing to be discouraged by a little snow. They raised their cup-shaped heads toward the sun, undaunted by the cold. Elise stopped and smiled at the little flowers. They were survivors, unlike the other flowers that couldn't survive a frost. She liked to believe that she was a survivor as well, but the past few weeks had done nothing to restore her spirit.

After six weeks of marriage, Elise's life had settled into a routine. Her husband was always solicitous and polite, but he rarely spoke to her or spent an evening at home. He was a great favorite of the king, having campaigned vigorously for his return from exile, and his presence was expected at all the countless entertainments that the palace hosted night after night. The Dowager joined Elise for supper every night but retired to her room immediately after, leaving Elise to spend the evenings alone. Elise tried to make inroads with Barbara, but the girl, although always happy to be acknowledged, had the mental faculties of a three-year-old. Elise felt desperately sorry for her, but there wasn't much she could do to help. Perhaps, had a tutor been engaged years ago to try and cajole Barbara into learning something, she might be further advanced. But since she'd been treated like a baby due to her mental disability, she still acted and thought like one.

Maybe she was better off, Elise mused. Realizing that she was deficient and often ridiculed by her own family would only hurt her. As it was, Barbara seemed content to spend hours on her crewelwork. She preferred to work in bright colors and only embroidered flowers that all looked exactly the same. She usually hummed a monotonous tune to herself while she sewed, a half smile on her face, completely lost in her own world. Barbara spoke in short sentences when she needed something and enjoyed being read to, but Elise wasn't sure if she grasped the gist of the story or only liked the soothing cadence of the reader's voice. Elise had been surprised to come upon James and Barbara several times, James reading to her quietly while Barbara stared out the window of the library, her gaze completely vacant. Elise never stayed but left them to it, loathe to spend even a moment in James's company.

The only person she actually spoke to was Lucy, but Elise had to be careful of what she shared with the maid for fear of revealing too much. Instead, Elise encouraged Lucy to talk and pass on household gossip and news of the outside while she brushed out her hair and helped her prepare for bed. But the conversations didn't last long. Lucy was only too eager to finish her duties for the day and retire to her chamber on the top floor, where she could have an hour of private time before going to sleep. She awoke before dawn, in time to wait on Edward's mother, who had trouble sleeping and refused to wait till the sun came up to get dressed and come downstairs.

James came to Elise several times a week, entering through her husband's bedchamber and leaving the same way, so no one would know of his clandestine visits. He rarely spoke, and their coupling was quick and impersonal. He seemed as reluctant as Elise, and she might have felt sympathy for him if she didn't despise him with such passion. At least he didn't mistreat her. He wasn't precisely tender, but he did nothing to hurt her or cause her discomfort. He simply went about his business as if she were asleep.

"Good night, my lady," James often mumbled after he pulled on his breeches and headed for the connecting door.

It is now, Elise thought once the door closed behind him. But was it? There were no more good nights, just restless ones. Elise was plagued by hopeless dreams, and wishes for a future that could never be.

If wishes were horses, beggars would ride.
If turnips were watches, I'd wear one by my side.
If "ifs" and "ands" were pots and pans,
There'd be no work for tinkers' hands.

Elise sighed. Her mother used to tell her that rhyme when she was little, and Elise laughed, picturing all her childish wishes turning into beautiful white horses that would spirit her away to a world of magic and wonder. There was no magic now, just endless despair. She was a prisoner in this house. Lord Asher didn't like his wife wandering outside on her own, so even if she left the hall from time to time, she had to be accompanied by Lucy, who was only too happy to get away from her endless chores and take a walk. But the outings were rare, especially since Elise received no invitations nor had any friends or family to visit on this side of the river. Even her father hadn't been to visit her. She missed Amy and Anne desperately, but it was as if she were no longer a part of their lives or her father's. Who would even care if she were gone?

Elise stopped dead. Who *would* care if she were gone? That was a good question. She'd obeyed her husband and had lived by the rules he'd set out for her for nearly two months, but who even noticed? Perhaps it was time to take matters into her own hands. Elise glanced back at the silent house behind her. The servants were already up, but Lady Matilda had caught a chill and had taken to her bed yesterday. Lucy brought her hot bricks for her feet every two hours, but the old woman was doubtless still asleep. And even if she weren't, she would remain abed today, given her illness.

Edward had come in only an hour ago. Elise heard him crashing about in his bedroom before he finally grew quiet. He would be asleep for hours and awaken in the late afternoon, just in time to eat, bathe, and head back to the palace, where he likely felt like an important man and not a useless, impotent cuckold on the cusp of old age.

She rarely saw James during the day. She had no idea what he actually did with his time, but it didn't matter. As long as he wasn't interested in what she did with hers, she was safe. Elise whipped about and headed back into the house. She climbed the stairs on silent feet and entered her room, breathless with excitement. She needed to put on her walking shoes since the slippers she was wearing would be covered in muck in no time and get soaked through. And she needed money.

Elise pressed her ear to Edward's door, but all she heard was rumbling snores coming from the other side. She eased the door open and entered the darkened chamber. She couldn't see Edward behind the drawn bed hangings, but she could hear him. He was in deep, alcohol-induced sleep. Elise crept toward the chair where Edward had discarded his clothes, careful not to trip over his boots. His purse was in the pocket of his breeches—she was sure of it.

Elise carefully extracted the leather pouch, making sure the coins didn't jingle, and pulled out a few coins. Edward would never notice, but the money would make all the difference to her. Elise replaced the purse and tiptoed out of the room, breathless with victory. She quickly changed her shoes, pulled on her gloves, and made her way down the stairs and back out into the garden. There was a door built into the wall, so no one would see her leave. The fluffy snow of the morning was already beginning to melt, turning into slush underfoot. Her footprints would vanish with the melting snow, which was an added bonus. Elise slipped through the door and closed it behind her, breathing the air of freedom for the first time since the wedding.

Elise pulled on her hood and walked briskly toward the river. Not many people were about just yet, but the city was coming to life: shops opening, farmers making deliveries now that the gates to the city were open, and wives and servants heading out to buy supplies for the day. Elise took a deep pull of fresh morning air. It felt wonderful to be out, especially on her own. She was as good as invisible, and the freedom of anonymity was intoxicating. She'd never given much thought to freedom before, but now that she was a virtual prisoner, it took on a whole new meaning, and she understood why men were willing to die for it. Having say over one's own life and future was worth everything—even one's life.

Elise stepped into a boat and took a seat in the stern. "Take me across, please," she said to the ferryman, who grinned at her, happy to have a fare so early in the morning. His lantern swung behind him as he pushed off and rowed them toward Southwark.

"Ye're out early," he commented as the boat sliced across the still waters. A hazy mist rose off the water, offering an extra layer of protection from prying eyes. Somewhere, a bell began to chime, and then several others joined in. It was eight o'clock.

"So are you," Elise countered.

"Well, I've got to earn me living," he replied. "A family don't feed itself, if ye know what I mean."

Elise nodded, not interested in pursuing the conversation. She felt exhilarated and reckless as the boat nosed its way toward Southwark. She only hoped it wasn't a wasted journey. Elise paid the ferryman and stepped onto shore. For a moment, she considered visiting the girls, but if her father found out that she had been wandering about on her own, he'd put a stop to her outing right quick. Instead, she headed in the opposite direction toward Borough High Street. The area where her family lived was still considered respectable, but this part of Southwark was anything but. There were many inns that catered to travelers, and the area was famous for its gaming stews, brothels, and various other base entertainments. Elise glanced toward the bulk of King's Bench Prison but hastily turned away and hurried along the street and past the Tabard Inn. She'd never actually seen the inn close up but had read of it in the *Canterbury Tales*, which she had "borrowed" from her father. The historic inn had served as a meeting point for pilgrims setting out for Canterbury.

Hugh de Lesseps would have had her whipped for reading such bawdy and irreverent balderdash instead of tracts more appropriate for women, but Elise had quite enjoyed the tales. A passage came to mind as she hurried past the sprawling inn and turned onto St. Thomas Street.

Bifel that in that season on a day,
In Southwerk at the Tabard as I lay
Redy to wenden on my pilgrymage
To Caunterbury with ful devout corage,
At nyght was come into that hostelrye
Wel nyne and twenty in a compaignye
Of sondry folk, by aventure yfalle

In felaweshipe, and pilgrimes were they alle,
That toward Caunterbury wolden ryde;
The chambres and the stables weren wyde,
And well we weren esed atte beste.

She felt as if she were making a pilgrimage but of an entirely different kind. Elise looked at the buildings, which leaned against each other like drunken men. There were countless narrow alleys that seemed to lead nowhere in particular, and only people who resided in them had a reason to enter. She finally found the house she'd been looking for and knocked loudly on the door, turning her head from side to side, as if she were going to be pounced on by her father or her husband at any moment. Elise's heart thumped in her chest.

"Oh, please be there," she whispered. "You have to be there."

She breathed a sigh of relief when she heard footsteps and the door swung open.

"Good Lord. Elise. Come in."

Elise slipped inside the house, glad to be away from the prying eyes of the city. She pushed back her hood and surveyed the humble dwelling. It was small but tidy, with one narrow window that didn't allow in nearly enough light. The room was dim, lit by a single candle whose flame flickered in the draft created by the opening and closing of the door.

Elise and Gavin stood facing each other for a moment before Elise walked into his arms and buried her head in his chest. She hadn't meant to cry or give in to self-pity, but seeing Gavin's smiling face was her undoing. He held her close as she cried, stroking her hair and murmuring words of comfort.

"You came," he whispered. "You really came. I'd nearly given up all hope of ever seeing you again. I started to believe that you were content in your marriage and had forgotten all about me."

"I thought of you every moment of the day," Elise confided. "I longed for you, and I wondered how you were."

"Come. Sit down. Let me get you some warm broth. You look frozen through."

"It was cold out on the river," Elise replied as she took a seat at the scarred wooden table. She gratefully accepted a cup of broth and wrapped her hands around the warm metal.

"Are you still planning to sail for the colonies?" Elise asked as she took a sip of broth. It wasn't very flavorful and lacked salt, but it was warm and dispelled some of the chill that had seeped into her bones.

"I am," Gavin replied. "I sail on April second."

Gavin studied her carefully, his eyes searching her face for answers. She'd come to him, so it was up to her to state her intentions.

"Gavin, does your offer still stand?"

"It does."

"Would you not mind living in sin with a woman who's married to another?"

"I don't put much stock in sin," Gavin replied with a smile. "Love between two people should never be a sin, even if it isn't sanctioned by the Church."

"So, how would we manage it?" Elise asked, hope swelling in her chest. Could she really pull this off, and was it still possible to salvage something of her life? She knew this was wrong, but something inside her refused to care. She would pay whatever price she had to to escape her joyless existence and snatch even the smallest bit of happiness for herself. She'd taken the first step; the second one would be easier.

"We would pose as man and wife. It would probably be wise to change your name, so no one would suspect anything. Elizabeth, or Elspeth, perhaps. Once in Virginia, no one would have any reason to question our union."

"But our children would be born out of wedlock," Elise said, suddenly realizing that she wouldn't be the only affected by this decision.

"So, they would. But as long as no one knows . . ."

"God would know."

"Yes, I suppose he would, but I don't think he much cares," Gavin replied. He'd always held some unorthodox views on religion, which Elise found scandalous, but at this moment, she was glad. He wouldn't reject her because she was already married and had lain with another man. Gavin knew it had never been by choice and wouldn't punish her for it. He was kind and understanding, and her life with him would be vastly different.

"Elise, I don't have much in the way of possessions. I have enough to pay for our passage and find us lodging once we get to Jamestown, but I cannot promise you a life of luxury. You must be prepared to work hard and make do, at least for the first few years."

"I don't need much, just a serviceable gown, a pair of shoes, and a cloak to keep me warm. Everything else will come in time."

"We'll build a life together, from the foundation up. We'll be happy, Elise. You'll see."

Gavin got to his feet and came around the table. He held out a hand to Elise and she took it gladly, tilting her face up to meet his. This kiss was sweeter than any kiss they'd stolen before; this kiss was a promise of things to come, of a life built on love and trust.

Elise gazed up at Gavin as they pulled apart, her mind made up. She took his hand and pulled him toward the bed located in an alcove and separated from the rest of the room by curtains.

"Elise," Gavin breathed as she reached for the laces of her bodice. "We can't. Not yet. I've a job at the Tabard Inn. I've undertaken to sort through their accounts. I need the money to pay for my lodgings until I leave so that I don't have to dip into my savings," Gavin explained apologetically. "I start at nine."

Elise nodded as disappointment tore through her. She wished to give herself to Gavin as a sign of her commitment. They would be as good as married then, even if that weren't so in the eyes of the law.

"You must go back. Pretend like nothing's changed," Gavin said as he reached for his coat. "If you come to me too soon, they'll find you. The ship is due to sail on the morning tide on April second. Come to me on April first. We'll be long gone before anyone suspects that you'd run away. Bring only what you most need."

"I will," Elise promised.

"I love you, Elise," Gavin said as he gave her hand a final squeeze. "Be careful getting back. You go first, and then I will follow in a few minutes. No one must see us together."

Elise couldn't imagine that someone would recognize her in this part of Southwark, but she didn't argue. Gavin was right: it was best not to take any chances.

"I will count the hours and the minutes until I see you again," Elise said as she smiled up at Gavin. "I hadn't realized how much I loved you until I lost you."

"You'll never lose me. I'm forever yours. Now go. I need to get to work."

Elise hurried out of the alley, her head bent low. A happy smile played about her lips and her heart sang a joyful melody. There was hope after all. She wasn't doomed to a life of loneliness and isolation with Edward Asher.

Chapter 14

James observed from a safe distance as Elise stepped out from the narrow house. She didn't look back but hurried out of the alley and down the street, her head lowered and her hood obscuring her face from passersby. James watched her turn the corner but made no move to follow. He knew where she was heading but didn't know whom she'd visited. He'd wait a few minutes and go knock on the door, pretending to be in search of someone. James was just about to carry out his plan when the door opened and a young man stepped into the alley. He appeared to be in his early twenties and had a pleasing countenance, his best feature being his eyes. Although his clothes were not as fine or fashionable as those of a gentleman, he clearly took pride in his appearance and tried to look the part of a well-to-do man. His step was unhurried, and once he reached the corner, James peeled himself away from the wall he'd been leaning against and followed the man. He didn't go far, only as far as the Tabard Inn, where he turned into the courtyard and eventually disappeared through a door.

James decided not to bother waiting and walked briskly toward the river. He spotted Elise in a boat that was still not too far from shore, her shoulders stiff, and her eyes fixed on the London side. Her hands were folded in her lap, but James could see the tension coursing through her body. He stepped into a boat and took a seat, his eyes never leaving Elise. The morning was clear, and Elise would easily recognize him if she glanced in his direction, so James pulled his hat lower over his eyes and huddled into his cloak. He could be any of a number of men crossing the Thames for business or pleasure.

Elise jumped out of the boat as soon as it docked, paid the ferryman, and hurried in the direction of Asher Hall. It made no sense to follow her, so James walked to a nearby tavern, found a table in the corner, and ordered a slice of pork pie and a tankard of ale. He hadn't had any breakfast, thanks to Elise, and since it was nearly time for the midday meal, he was ravenous. The pie wasn't half-bad, the crust flaky and hot and the filling flavorful and moist. James took a long pull of ale and leaned back in his chair, gazing out the grimy window at the river flowing past. The water sparkled in the morning sunshine, and the docks were a beehive of activity with men loading and unloading goods and going to and from the warehouses situated along the docks.

Edward had charged James with keeping an eye on Elise, but until today there had been no cause to follow her. Elise rarely left the house, and when she did, it was in the company of Lucy. They attended services at St. Martin-in-the-Fields and occasionally took a walk along the river bank on fine days. Elise met no one and had received no visitors since the day of the wedding, not even her father. James found that to be odd, but then he supposed that the notion of devoted and loving parents was something he dreamed about since childhood, not realizing that even those children who had living parents weren't always cherished or even cared for.

James signaled the barmaid for another slice of pie and returned to his troubled thoughts. He could tell Lord Asher that Elise had snuck out and gone to Southwark to meet a man, but did he wish to betray her? She had been inside the house no longer than a quarter of an hour and came out looking just as tidy and neat as when she'd gone in. Had anything of a lewd nature taken place between her and the man, she'd have emerged looking at least a little disheveled and looking guilty or elated. Instead, she looked anxious, no doubt wondering what awaited her once she returned. James hoped that Lady Matilda was still abed and would not give Elise a tongue-lashing. The old stick's only pleasure in life was to intimidate the servants, belittle Barbara, and chastise Elise. James hoped that on this occasion, she would be denied the pleasure since the servants would make no mention of Elise's absence, even if they had noticed that their mistress wasn't in the house, unless asked directly.

The truth was that no one particularly cared what Elise did. Edward wasn't outwardly cruel to her, but he made no pretense of treating her as one would treat a wife. He did not invite her to accompany him to court, nor did he entertain at home and present Elise to his friends and their ladies. She was there for one purpose and one purpose only, and James felt a stab of guilt as he considered his own part in her lonely life.

James gulped down the rest of his ale, threw several coins on the table, and stepped outside. Ordinarily, he would have gone back to Asher Hall, but the day was fine, and he felt too wound up to attend to his usual tasks. He strolled along until he came upon a small shop that sold candied fruits and marzipan and bought half a dozen of each before continuing on to Blackfriars.

Mercy opened the door, her elfin face lighting up when she saw him. "Hullo, Uncle James," she sang as she danced around him.

"Hullo, yourself."

"Mam went out to buy some fish. I'm 'ere alone with the baby. 'E's sleeping," she added.

"All right. I'll wait, then. Would you like a sweet?"

Mercy's eyes grew round with excitement. "Yes, please."

James took two pieces out of the paper cone given to him by the seller and handed them to Mercy. She couldn't be trusted with all the sweets, the little imp, and he had to save some for Molly and Elizabeth. Peter didn't like sweets and would likely give his portion to the girls anyhow.

"Wipe your face afore your mam gets back," James chided with a smile. Mercy's lips and chin were covered with sugar and her hands were sticky.

Mercy used the back of her hand to wipe her face. "There, all clean."

James was about to chide Mercy for being slovenly but bit back the criticism when he heard the thin mewling of the baby. Harry sounded more like a kitten than a child, and James's heart turned over for his sister. He'd heard the girls' lusty cries when they were hungry. They howled with rage and would not be denied, but this little mite just fussed. James turned to tell Mercy to get her brother, but she had disappeared outside. James left the bag of sweets on the table and went up to the sleeping quarters above. The baby was lying in his cot, eyes wide, mouth open in a soundless cry. He was pale and small and hardly weighed anything at all when James picked him up and held him close.

"How are you, little lad?" James asked softly as he rocked the baby. "Your mam will be back soon. Would you like to come downstairs with me?"

The baby just eyed him suspiciously, but James took that as a good sign. At least he wasn't crying. James carefully made his way down the stairs, mindful of the baby in his arms. Where was Mercy anyway? He'd never been alone with a child and was at a loss. The swaddling was wet and smelled of urine, and the baby was squirming in his arms, either from discomfort or hunger.

James breathed a sigh of relief when Mercy finally came back through the door. She looked at the bag of sweets with longing but made no move to touch it.

"Where've you been, girl?" James asked, irritated.

"Had to go to the privy, didn't I?" the girl replied with equal annoyance. "Give 'im 'ere. 'E needs 'is nappy changed."

James gratefully surrendered the baby and watched as Mercy skillfully changed him. She'd make a good mother one day, if she didn't dance herself into trouble. She was nothing like her sister Elizabeth, who was serious and diligent in everything she did. Mercy also wasn't as plain. Elizabeth favored her father in looks, but Mercy, with her bouncing dark curls and dark-blue eyes, reminded James of a young Molly. She'd been a beauty and had known it. All the young men in the village hoped she'd show them a sign of favor, but Molly had chosen Peter and never looked at anyone else.

James rose to his feet as the door opened, and his sister near fell over the threshold. She was carrying a heavy sack of flour, and the basket slung over her arm was full of fish.

"Here, let me help," James offered as he took the bag from Molly.

"Thank ye," Molly breathed as she set the basket on the table. She looked reproachfully at the sweets. "Ye spoil us, James."

"Can't I bring my sister and her children a small treat? I've got no one else to spoil," James replied, annoyed at being reproached.

"Well, maybe it's time ye did," Molly retorted, bringing up an old argument. She thought it was high time that James married and started a family of his own, but James, although not averse to the idea, had never met a girl he could see himself spending the rest of his days with.

"Mam, 'Arry is 'ungry," Mercy piped in. "I just changed 'is nappy."

"Right," Molly exhaled as she reached for the baby. Harry latched on to his mother's breast hungrily and James felt his heart turn over at the look of pure love in his sister's eyes. If anything nurtured the little boy, it would be the affection of his mother.

"Eat up, little mite," she told him as she settled herself by the hearth.

"Mercy, start the dough for the bread. Yer da will want 'is dinner soon, and I 'ave no bread to give 'im."

Mercy made a face of discontent but didn't argue and poured some flour right onto the table where she would knead the dough.

"What's new at the manor?" Molly asked.

James shrugged. There was so much he wanted to tell Molly, but suddenly the words deserted him. He wasn't ready to hear what she had to say about Elise.

"Ye daft fool," Molly breathed as she studied his face with a look of abject pity. "Ye care for 'er, don't ye?"

"Don't be ridiculous," James retorted but heard the note of panic in his voice. Molly always saw right through him; he didn't need to say a word.

"James, ye'll come to no good if you go on this way," Molly chided.

"I'm not a child, Moll," James replied, suddenly feeling defensive. "I'm a grown man who knows his own mind."

"Oh, really? Do ye? And what is in that mind of yers?" Molly demanded.

James was about to reply when Molly's attention shifted to the baby. He could tell by her look of dismay that Harry had stopped nursing. He couldn't have gotten much milk in the past few minutes, but his eyes were already closed and he looked tired and pale.

"Oh, 'ave mercy on us, Lord Jesus," Molly breathed as she gazed at her son.

James opened his mouth to speak but suddenly wasn't sure what to say. He didn't know much about babies, but even he could tell that Harry was barely holding on to this life. Molly turned her face away toward the hearth, but James knew that she was hiding her tears.

"I'd better go," James said awkwardly.

"Yes. Thank ye for the sweets. Elizabeth will be pleased."

James closed the door softly behind him and walked away, his heart heavier than it had been when he arrived.

Chapter 15

November 2013

Surrey, England

Quinn lifted her arm out of the deliciously warm water in the tub and reached for her vibrating mobile. She wasn't really in the mood to talk to anyone, having just spent time in the seventeenth century with Elise and James, but it was Gabe, and they hadn't spoken since he'd visited her nearly a week ago.

"Hi, Gabe," she said, hoping that Gabe called just to chat and not to discuss her investigation. She wasn't ready to share with him what she'd seen. Not yet. "How are you?"

"Splendid," Gabe replied sarcastically. "I've just had a call from Rhys Morgan. He wants a written proposal for the first episode on his desk by Monday morning."

Quinn sighed, annoyed. "Gabe, I've only just received the report from Dr. Scott. I've barely had any time to do any research. I'm simply not ready."

"I know, but Morgan wants an outline for the program, and he wants to discuss the dramatization."

Quinn growled into the phone, making Gabe laugh. She still wasn't sure how she felt about Rhys Morgan. He had impressed her, that was true, but he'd also put her on her guard, placing her at a disadvantage. He wanted her to headline his new series but somehow still managed to make her feel as if she should be the one impressing him and defending her reputation.

"Why don't you come up to London tomorrow? We'll have dinner, a couple of drinks, and discuss this when you're in a better mood," Gabe suggested. Quinn could hear the smile in his voice. Gabe knew her well enough to realize that she was growing weary of solitude and would love some company, especially if the company was as pleasant and undemanding as Gabe's.

"I have a better idea. Why don't you come here? I'll cook. To be honest, I'm a little travel worn right now."

"Even better. What can I bring?"

"Yourself and a bottle of sauvignon blanc," Quinn replied, smiling to herself. It'd been ages since she actually used her kitchen for anything more than making toast. It would be nice to have someone to cook for.

"Seven all right?"

"Perfect."

Quinn hung up the phone and slid deeper into the hot water.

**

Gabe showed up on time, bearing two bottles of wine and a happy grin. He opened one of the bottles while Quinn dressed the salad and sliced the loaf of Italian bread she'd picked up earlier. It was crusty and fresh, and it would go well with the seasoned olive oil she'd set out on the table next to a dish of olives.

"Something smells great," Gabe said as he handed her a glass of wine. Gabe appreciated good food but could barely boil water and ate most of his meals out. His refrigerator usually contained milk, chilled white wine, and not much else.

"Homemade gnocchi Bolognese," Quinn replied proudly. She'd spent hours making the meal, but the simple task of cooking made her feel relaxed and purposeful. She liked to listen to whatever music was appropriate to her menu, so she slipped in a disc of *Tosca* and allowed the soaring music to fill the previously silent space, making her feel less alone. She fancied herself an independent woman who didn't need a man to complete her, but the absence of companionship weighed heavily on her. It'd been a long time since she lived alone, and she was finding it a challenge.

Quinn heaped the gnocchi into a large bowl, decorated the dish with a few strategically placed leaves of basil, and set it on the table. "*Voilà*, dinner is served."

"Great. I've been saving myself all day," Gabe said with a smile. "I always enjoy your cooking."

"And I always forget how much I enjoy cooking. It's no fun cooking for one person," Quinn added as she took a piece of crust and dipped it into the oil before popping it into her mouth.

"Have you learned anything?" Gabe asked carefully as he helped himself to Caesar salad.

"I have," Quinn replied thoughtfully, "but it's not exactly something I can share with the tenacious Mr. Morgan. I can hardly tell him the truth."

"Have you met him?" Gabe asked, surprised by her response. It seemed that Rhys hadn't told Gabe of their meeting.

"Yes," Quinn replied without going into the details of their encounter.

"Just tell him what you know," Gabe suggested as he tucked into the food with relish.

"I know quite a bit, Gabe, but I can't support any of it with scientific fact, and Rhys Morgan doesn't strike me as someone who would just accept what I say without proof."

"Morgan leaves nothing to chance. That's why he's so good at what he does. Can you share with me what you've learned?" Gabe asked. Quinn knew he was curious, but for some reason, she was reluctant to tell him about Elise. Something about the girl's peculiar situation and her frustration and loneliness made Quinn feel as if she were betraying a confidence. She supposed it was ridiculous to feel this way about someone who was long dead, but she couldn't bring herself to tell Gabe of Elise's predicament.

"I'll tell you everything once I know more," she promised. "In the meantime, we have to figure out how to present my ideas to Morgan."

"Have you got anything at all that we can share with him?"

"Our lovers lived during the mid-seventeenth century. At that time, Mayfair was sparsely populated, not yet being the desirable location it became in the eighteenth century. There were several grand homes belonging to noble families in the area. There must be some record of who lived at the address where the skeletons were found during the period in question. Once I establish a tangible connection between the victims and the family, I'll have something to present to Morgan."

Gabe leaned back in his chair as he surveyed Quinn. "But how will you explain the rest?"

"I haven't figured that out yet, mostly because I still don't know what happened. Oh, I do wish you'd kept me out of this, Gabe. Rhys Morgan is not going to accept some theory without proof. He's too much the consummate professional to just wing it, no matter how intriguing it might sound."

"Let me help," Gabe offered. "If you give me the name of the family, I might be able to dig something up."

"The house belonged to Lord Edward Asher, but I really haven't looked into him yet. I haven't had the chance."

"Asher? Really?"

"Have you heard of him?" Quinn asked with interest. She'd studied seventeenth-century history, but it wasn't really her area of expertise.

"The name is familiar. I'm fairly certain that he served on the Privy Council and was a great favorite of Charles II, but I must double-check my facts."

"Yes, he was a favorite," Quinn answered dryly. It wasn't until that moment that she realized how much she despised the man. He'd been gone for hundreds of years, but the residue of his persona now lived in Quinn's mind.

"I take it he's not one of the good guys," Gabe remarked as he noticed the look of distaste on Quinn's face.

"No, he's not," Quinn replied with disgust. "The man is reprehensible."

"And long dead," Gabe pointed out, a smile playing about his mouth.

"Not to me. You see, Gabe, that's the problem with delving into the lives of these people." Quinn sighed. "I can't help getting involved. I know they died hundreds of years ago, and their problems died with them, but for as long as I'm investigating them, they are as real as you and I. They are living, breathing people who are trying to make the best of their lot in life. I don't only see their actions but hear their thoughts and feel their anguish, and I suffer alongside them whether I want to or not. See, it's not like reading a book or watching a film, where the immediate goal of the story is to entertain. I know that these people were real, and what they went through mattered."

"Did you feel that way with your Roman soldier?"

"Perhaps not as much. Atticus had enjoyed a fairly good life until he was cut down in battle. He made an educated choice when he joined the army. He wished to see something of the world and maybe cloak himself in glory while he was at it. He could have stayed at home and farmed the land alongside his father. Atticus would have lived to a ripe old age and raised a family of his own, unless some illness struck him down. Instead, he died when he was hardly more than a boy, but that was a risk he'd been prepared to take."

"So, how is this different?" Gabe persisted as he twirled the stem of the wine glass thoughtfully in his hand.

"Life has never been as straightforward for women. A young girl was at the mercy of her father until she became the chattel of her husband. Some women got luckier than others, or perhaps they were more cunning and understood how to manipulate the circumstances to their benefit, but some girls were thrust into unexpected situations where there was nothing they could do but find a way to survive."

"And this one clearly didn't."

"No."

Gabe poured her more wine and set the empty bottle aside. "Say you could get rid of this gift you possess once and for all. Would you do it, Quinn?"

"To be perfectly honest, I don't know. To have the ability to tell someone's untold story is a precious gift, but it's also a responsibility. I feel like I am no longer an impartial bystander; I become a part of the story."

Gabe looked at Quinn, his eyes soft with compassion. "Is it because you don't know your own?"

"In part. You have no idea what it's like not to know where you come from. There are all these people searching for their natural parents, despite the fact that their parents didn't want them. But, the need to know is stronger than any pain of rejection. They just want to know who they came from and why they were given away. I don't want another mother. I love the one I have, who's loved me all my life, but I want to know the woman who gave birth to me, and I want to know why she didn't want me."

"And you want to know if she had the same ability to see into the past," Gabe added.

"I do. I have so many questions, but there's no one to ask, and at this point in my life, I know that I will likely never know who my parents were. The trail had gone cold thirty years ago."

"Quinn, have you ever tried to learn anything from the blanket you came wrapped in?" Gabe asked.

Quinn nodded. "Yes, but I felt nothing at all. I can only connect with the dead, not the living, so I knew for certain that my mother was still alive. That might have changed since the last time I tried."

"Have you considered having a family of your own?" Gabe asked, his gaze soft on her face.

Quinn nodded, tears suddenly springing to her eyes. She thought she was going to have a family with Luke, but instead he broke up with her by text and left the country before she could come back and force a confrontation. She didn't want Luke back, but she did need closure.

"Quinn, you must move on. Luke was a fool to let you go," Gabe said. "Had you been mine—"

"No, don't," Quinn cut him off as she sprang to her feet and started clearing away the dishes. She hadn't meant to sound abrupt, but Gabe was her closest friend and also her boss. There was a part of her that longed to walk into his arms and let him kiss her, but neither one of them had an exemplary track record when it came to relationships. If their romance fizzled in a few months, she would lose not only a true friend but possibly her job, because working alongside him might prove to be too awkward or painful, depending on the circumstances of their breakup. She simply couldn't risk that.

"Quinn, it needn't end," Gabe said, as if reading her thoughts, but Quinn just shook her head.

"Gabe, please, don't."

Quinn never turned from the sink, but she sensed Gabe getting his coat and walking to the door.

"Goodnight, and thank you for dinner," he said softly, but still she didn't turn around.

"Goodnight, Gabe," she said to the empty room after the door closed behind him.

Chapter 16

Gabe scarcely noticed where he was going as he navigated the nearly pitch-black lane leading away from Quinn's house and toward the motorway. The windshield wipers were swishing madly, but still the visibility was no more than a few inches, the rain coming down in a torrent. He knew he should slow down, but his agitation clouded his judgment, and he stepped on the gas instead, racing blindly—not toward home, but away from Quinn. He hadn't meant to reveal his hand, not this soon anyway, but he never could think clearly around Quinn. Luke's departure had thrown Gabe into turmoil and upended his well-organized existence, forcing him to confront the truth. He supposed he was happy enough with Eva. He'd given up on the idea of ever finding the type of love that made him feel as if he'd come home at last and didn't wish to ever leave, but Quinn's altered status changed everything.

Gabe had come to terms with Quinn's choice a long time ago and braced himself for the moment when she'd tell him that Luke had finally proposed and she'd joyfully accepted, but Luke, damn fool that he was, had never made the ultimate commitment. Gabe tried to ignore the gossip in the archeological circles, had closed his heart to the black rage that made him want to kill Luke when Gabe heard that he was playing the field. There had been more than one indiscretion, mostly while Quinn was away on a dig and Luke was left to his own devices or was on an assignment of his own. The liaisons were brief and meaningless, by all accounts, but it still made Gabe burn with a helpless fury to know that the woman he'd adored for the past eight years was being deceived by that philanderer who took her for granted. She deserved so much better than Luke, but Quinn appeared to be blind to his faults—or perhaps, given her history, she was just desperate for a family of her own.

Gabe supposed that Luke could be charming and urbane. He had a certain polish that many academics lacked and had a knack for making women feel beautiful and special. Quinn had been no exception. Luke had managed to charm her and steal her away because Gabe had made the mistake of hesitating too long and putting his professional commitments before his romantic feelings. Luke got there first, and there wasn't a day since that Gabe hadn't regretted his decision to wait until the end of the dig to pursue Quinn Allenby.

For some while after that dig, Gabe lived in the hope that Luke would tire of Quinn and clear the way for him, but Luke seemed to love her, as much as he could love anyone, until Ashley Gallagher came along. Gabe had seen her several times: a bouncy American graduate student with golden tresses and wide blue eyes set in a china-doll face, atop a body that was all legs and large breasts. Luke seemed charmed by Ashley's American accent and her giggly forwardness. She played the ditzy Barbie doll to perfection, but Gabe could see the shrewdness behind the eyes.

Ashley was no fool, and she got her man in the end. A flirtation turned into something more, and Ashley had staked her claim while Quinn was in the Middle East. Luke had gone to the States to be with his new love and to put an ocean between himself and Quinn, whom he couldn't face. Quinn clearly knew nothing of Luke's betrayal, and it wasn't for Gabe to enlighten her. But he finally had a chance, and he'd be damned if he let it slip away. He'd ended things with Eva. It'd been easier than he anticipated, for both of them.

He was free, and now all he had to do was wait for the right moment. Quinn was skittish and on the rebound, and he had to give her the time and space to mourn her loss and get to a place where she was ready for a new relationship. Sound reasoning, except that all his plans went tits up the moment he saw her again. He'd blurted out the words before he could stop himself. She clearly wasn't ready to hear what he had to say, but there was no going back. He'd made the opening move and now he had to play the game to the end.

Gabe swerved as a stray dog ran into the road, its wet fur clinging to a skinny frame and lips stretched back in a snarl. Gabe forced himself to slow down and took the next turn with more care. He was still upset, but he was beginning to regain perspective. His carelessness this evening had been a minor setback. He'd lost the battle, but he hadn't yet lost the war.

Chapter 17

Quinn threw down the dish towel and retreated back to the sofa, suddenly too tired to tidy up. She'd seen a lot of Gabe over the years, but this was the first time he'd referred back to that night in Ireland—well, the second, actually, in as many weeks, and it rattled her. Gabe had seemingly made up his mind to drudge up the past, and Quinn supposed that as an archeologist, that was what he was trained to do to clear up any unanswered questions.

"Had you been mine," Gabe had said. Perhaps it just slipped out, or perhaps he'd been waiting to say the words all along, his feelings for her buried but never fully forgotten. Had he carried a torch for her all these years, or was this something new, something built on years of friendship and not the attraction they felt for each other before? Had she made a mistake when she'd chosen Luke? She hadn't thought so, but looking back, she knew that her choice had been motivated by all the wrong reasons. She had been young and impressionable and perhaps a little dazzled by Luke, who'd always been the soul of the party and the bloke all the girls tried to get close to. She had been flattered by his interest, seduced by his good looks and his aura of unshakeable confidence.

Quinn knew that Gabe had feelings for her. She'd been drawn to him as well, and the intensity of her attraction to him frightened her. She was somewhat relieved that Gabe was in a position of authority, being the dig supervisor, and couldn't act until the dig was officially over and his pursuit of Quinn wouldn't be seen as unprofessional and inappropriate. She could have waited, but she hadn't. She'd gone for Luke, who was easygoing and fun, the polar opposite of Gabriel Russell, who was intense and demanding. In retrospect, she realized that she ran because she wasn't emotionally ready for him.

That night, after confiding in him about her gift, she panicked, and she'd allowed Luke to take her home, walking out of the pub without so much as saying goodnight to Gabe, who'd been waiting to walk her back to her B&B. She'd allowed Luke to kiss her that night and had invited him back to her room. She'd been a bit drunk, but not drunk enough not to know what she was doing. She was burning bridges with Gabe, and her plan had worked. She just hadn't expected her relationship with Luke to evolve as it had. He'd fancied her since they first arrived at the dig, it turned out, and wasn't about to pass up his chance.

Their summer romance turned into eight years, but now, looking back, Quinn wasn't sure how much of their relationship had been love and how much was comfort and convenience. They both had busy schedules and were often away on digs and at conferences. They came together at her little chapel, spent a few weeks or months together, and then parted again. She'd been content, but had she really been happy? She'd always taken it for granted that Luke was faithful to her, but had he been? Had he always gone to bed alone when he was away from her? She supposed she'd been blind to his faults, but the veil had lifted, and now she was finally beginning to see clearly.

She still believed that Luke loved her in his own way and had been devoted to her at one time. But Luke had only one great love—himself—and he'd discarded her as soon as something better for him came along. He could have asked her to come with him, but he hadn't. He wanted a fresh start, and he wished to be unencumbered and free to pursue new relationships. Well, he had it, but so did she. Like it or not, this was a fresh start.

Chapter 18

February 1665

London, England

    Elise sat up in bed and hugged her knees. It was still dark outside, but dawn would come soon and with it, a new day. She'd barely slept all night, thoughts of Gavin crowding her mind. She'd been elated and hopeful after their conversation, but once she finally got back to the house and snuck up to her room without being seen by anyone but Lucy, the doubts had set in. A part of her had no regrets about seeing Gavin or making him a promise, but there were other factors to consider. There were still nearly six weeks till their departure, and with James visiting her several times a week, she could still get with child. There had to be a way to prevent that catastrophe from happening, but how? She supposed there were ways, but she was completely ignorant of them and had no one to ask. Decent women didn't try to prevent pregnancy. Conception was God's will and a part of God's plan.

    And then there was the matter of her marriage. She was Edward's wife in the eyes of God and man, despite the fact that Edward wasn't her husband in every sense of the word. Running out would brand her an adulteress and a whore. She would never be able to marry Gavin, and their children would be born out of wedlock, a predicament that weighed on her heavily. They could lie to their neighbors, but they couldn't lie to God. How could she walk into a church with Gavin by her side, knowing all the while that she was another man's wife?

Had she still been a maid, an annulment might have been possible, but no physician would believe her now. She had no proof; it had been destroyed by James on her wedding night. And then there was her father. Elise had to admit that she felt hurt and betrayed by the father she loved, but running away would bring out Edward's thirst for vengeance. He'd threatened to ruin her father, and he would. Could she put her own happiness ahead of everything she held dear, and would it be possible to be happy despite the factors working against her and Gavin?

Elise rested her chin on her knees and peered into the darkness. The thought of remaining in her present situation for years to come felt like a sentence worse than death. There wasn't a glimmer of hope if she stayed. Her only escape would be widowhood, and although she despised Edward for his duplicity, she'd never wish him dead. So, she was back where she began: lonely, desperately unhappy, and utterly trapped. She wished she had someone to talk to, someone she could trust, but there was no one. Except Lucy. Lucy was a chatty girl who'd lived in and around Blackfriars her whole life. *Perhaps she can be of assistance without realizing it,* Elise thought. She had to deal with one problem at a time, and for the moment, her biggest concern was possible pregnancy.

Elise got out of bed, poked up the fire, and threw open the curtains. A rosy light was spreading along the horizon, the tree line black against the lightening sky. It was a new day and a new beginning, and she'd be damned if she allowed her circumstances to break her spirit. She was stronger than that, and she would find a way out of her predicament.

Elise was already sitting at her dressing table when Lucy came in, bringing a pitcher of hot water for washing.

"Well, good morning, me lady," Lucy greeted her cheerfully. "Ye're up afore me again. Ye put me to shame." She pouted.

"I've always been an early riser. You get up early enough, and you need your rest."

Elise washed while Lucy put a few more logs on the fire and lit a brace of candles with a taper since the room was still in darkness.

"Shall ye wear your blue gown today?" Lucy asked as she opened the trunk. "It does go well with yer coloring." She sighed wistfully. "Yer hair is like liquid copper, it is."

"Yes, the blue gown. It looks like a beautiful day. Perhaps we can go out for a walk along the river today, Lucy."

"Aye, me lady. A walk would be most welcome."

"Lucy, I wonder if you might know of an apothecary nearby," Elise asked innocently as she sat down in front of the dressing table, ready for her hair to be dressed.

"Are ye ill, me lady?"

"No, but I thought perhaps I can ask about a remedy for Lady Matilda. She has such a terrible, wheezing cough."

"But Lord Asher had the physician in only yesterday. He gave her a tonic for her cough and advised a cupful of cow's blood mixed with milk twice a day to build up her strength."

"I see," Elise replied, thwarted. "I pray she feels better."

Lucy kept silent, which made Elise smile. Lady Matilda scolded and belittled the servants, and Lucy was always a ready target, being young and pretty. Her good nature particularly irritated the old woman, who tried to browbeat her into silent submission.

"I suppose there's an apothecary at St. Bartholomew's Hospital. The monks are very knowledgeable about herbs and such," Lucy said as she twisted Elise's hair into a knot at the nape of her neck. "Of course, his lordship had invited the court physician to attend on his mother. No monks for her ladyship," Lucy added bitterly.

Elise considered this information. St. Bartholomew's was out of the question. The monks were renowned for their healing and kindness to those less fortunate, but they couldn't help her with her problem. Perhaps what she needed was a midwife. But how could she go about finding one? A physician would be summoned if she were with child, but by that time, it would be too late.

Elise allowed Lucy to dress her and went down to break her fast. Perhaps a solution would present itself. She just had to be patient. Elise was surprised to find her husband seated at the table with a plate of food in front of him. He rarely rose before noon, and this morning he looked pale and out of sorts.

"Ah, here comes my lady," he intoned sarcastically. "You are looking radiant, my dear. Dare I hope?"

"I'm sorry to dash your hopes, sir," Elise mumbled.

"Are you indeed? You are proving to be a great disappointment to me, Elise. We've been married for nearly two months, and still you fail to get with child," he hissed, his eyes suddenly angry.

"I'm sorry, my lord," Elise replied. "It isn't for lack of trying. You apply yourself most diligently to begetting an heir."

She knew she shouldn't have said that, but a hot fury rose up within her. How could he blame her for not being pregnant, especially when his bastard rode her every other day as if she were a broodmare?

"Perhaps you're barren," Edward spat out, rising from the table with such anger that his chair clattered to the floor. "I shall summon the physician to have you examined. I assumed when I married you that you would prove as fertile as your mother, but perhaps my assumption was incorrect."

With that, he strode from the room, leaving his food untouched. Elise sank into a chair, but her appetite had deserted her. What would he do to her if the physician found her incapable of bearing children? Perhaps he'd seek an annulment himself, but was it possible to get one on the basis of infertility? If that were the case, half the royal marriages would get annulled. And what would that mean for her and her family? Of course, Edward's displeasure with her would be a moot point if she ran off with Gavin.

Elise sighed and reached for a jug of ale and took a sip of the cool, sour liquid. She couldn't go on like this. She needed to make a decision. She was going round in circles, but there were only two possible solutions. She could please her family and Edward by remaining exactly where she was and producing a male heir, or she could follow her own desires and leave with Gavin. Each choice came with its own set of consequences, but she had to decide if duty was more important than hope.

Elise sat there until she heard the wheels of Edward's carriage rattling past the window, then pushed her chair away from the table, having decided to forgo breakfast. Instead, she went back to her chamber, where Lucy was busy making the bed.

"Lucy, leave off," Elise said softly. "I feel unwell. I think I might lie down for a spell."

"Is there anything I can get ye, me lady?"

"No. I just need to sleep. Please, make sure I'm not disturbed. Perhaps you can use the time to wash some of my undergarments," Elise suggested slyly.

"Aye, of course, me lady."

Lucy quickly collected Elise's chemise, several pairs of stockings, and a shift, and left the room, closing the door softly behind her. Elise stretched out on the bed and waited. The garments didn't really require washing just yet, but Lucy was an inquisitive girl, and it was best to have her out of the way for a little while.

Once Elise was sure that Lucy wasn't coming back, she put on her drabbest gown, pulled on a linen coif to hide her elaborate hairstyle, and put on an old, worn pair of boots that she'd meant to throw out. She peeked into the corridor to make sure that all was quiet before skipping down the stairs and slipping from the house unseen.

The day was overcast, with a gauzy mist shrouding the buildings in a blanket of moisture. It wasn't very cold, but a raw damp seeped into her bones as Elise got closer to the river, and her face was wet to the touch as mist settled on her skin. She picked her way carefully, avoiding piles of refuse and pools of mud. She turned off on Black Friars Lane and then made another turn onto Carter Lane, where she made her way slowly down the street. It wasn't long until she spotted what she was searching for. A heavily pregnant woman was walking carefully down the street, an empty basket swinging over her arm as she set off to do her daily marketing.

"Do excuse me," Elise called out to the woman. "Me mistress sent me to fetch the midwife, but I seem to have lost me way. Would ye be able to direct me?" If anyone knew where the midwife was to be found, it was a woman near her time, Elise reasoned, and she wasn't disappointed.

"I surely can, pet. Old Nan lives just round yon corner in Creed Lane. Third house on the left. Ye can't miss it. There's a birch tree as grows right in front."

"Thank ye, mistress," Elise said with a smile.

"Glad to help," the woman replied and got on her way, waddling down the street at a glacial pace.

Elise followed the directions and was in front of the house in mere minutes. The birch was still bare, its slender trunk silvery in the morning mist. It was the only tree in the street, the old Tudor houses standing so close together that they practically leaned on each other for support. The upper floors overhung the lower ones, blocking out daylight and casting the street into a gloomy pall. The lack of sunlight prevented anything green from thriving, so the birch tree was a surprise. Elise took a deep breath before knocking softly on the door. She hoped Old Nan was in. A woman in her thirties opened the door, a smile of welcome on her face.

"I'm looking for the midwife," Elise said.

"You've found me, then. Have someone's pains started?" she asked as she reached for her cloak.

"No, I'm here for a somewhat different reason."

"You'd best come in, then."

The woman stepped aside and invited Elise into the house. A single candle burned on the table, casting a glow onto the walls. The room was sparsely furnished, but it was clean and warm. Old Nan herself looked clean and warm as well. There was a kindness in her eyes, and she was motherly in her manner, which put Elise at ease.

"Here, have a cup of broth," Nan said. "'Tis bone raw out there today."

Elise accepted the cup of broth gratefully and took the proffered seat. The broth was rich and hot, and she took a few warming sips before setting the cup down and raising her eyes to meet Nan's.

"What can I do for you?" the older woman carefully asked.

"You see," Elise began but faltered. She wasn't sure exactly how to ask what she wanted to know.

"You wish to know if you're with child."

"No. I wish to know if there's a way to prevent getting with one," Elise blurted out.

"Are you married?" Old Nan asked.

Elise felt a momentary panic. She didn't want to lie, but if she told the woman she was wed, the midwife might think it a sin against God to try to prevent conception.

"No, not yet," Elise fibbed.

"I see."

Elise cringed inwardly. She just proclaimed herself to be a fornicator, probably a worse sin than not wanting to get with child. "I'm not . . . w-well, that is," Elise stuttered.

"It don't matter to me, love. 'Tis not my place to judge. I've seen it all by now, and let me tell ye, it isn't always pretty or proper. There are some decoctions that women swear by, but I myself don't believe them to be effective. Sooner or later, they all fall pregnant anyhow."

"Is there nothing?"

"There is something ye can do. It works for some, but nothing is guaranteed, save keeping your legs crossed. Find some thick cloth and cut it into small bits, 'bout this size," she said, holding her thumb and pointer about two inches apart. "Dip a piece in vinegar before yer man comes to ye and insert it as deep as ye can into yer quim."

"How would that prevent me getting with child?" Elise asked, curious.

"The thick fabric blocks the seed from spilling into yer womb, and the vinegar kills its potency. It don't always work, mind, but 'tis better than nothing. Just make sure to remove the cloth after ye've used it or it'll begin to fester inside ye."

"Are there ways to get rid of a babe should the need arise?" she asked carefully.

"There are, but I'm not one who'll tell ye about them. 'Tis a sin against God to do away with a child. I'm a midwife; my calling is to bring new life into the world, not snuff it out." She didn't sound angry, but Elise could see that Nan felt strongly and didn't persist.

Elise took a coin out of the pocket of her cloak and laid it on the table. "I thank you for your advice."

Old Nan inclined her head and pocketed the coin. "God be with ye," she said as she let Elise out into the street.

"And you."

Chapter 19

November 2013

London, England

Quinn looked around as she was ushered into Rhys Morgan's office. She'd expected it to be more posh, for some reason, but the room, although well-proportioned and with an excellent view, was a bit Spartan and almost completely devoid of color. One wall was painted a muted shade of blue and displayed several photographs and award certificates, but the rest of the office was done up in dove gray and chrome. Rhys was wearing a charcoal-gray jumper, black jeans, and a pair of beat-up leather boots. He looked trendy and comfortable as he tapped away on his keyboard. He glanced up as Quinn walked in, closed the laptop, and smiled in greeting.

"Dr. Allenby, do come in. Deborah, an espresso for our guest, please, and one for me as well," Rhys called to the departing assistant. "Please, make yourself comfortable. First and foremost, I'd like to apologize for the way I behaved the last time we met. I tend to get a little dogged when it comes to a new project, but I am very happy that you've accepted our offer of headlining the program. Deborah will provide you with a copy of the contract and all the other necessary paperwork."

"No apology necessary," Quinn replied, although she felt a little wary of his good mood. "It was only natural that you should wish to know more about my methods before offering me the job."

"Truth be told, I never considered anyone else. You were my first choice, especially after Gabriel Russell's glowing recommendation. He will act as a consultant on the program. I trust you don't object."

"Of course not. Gabriel has been my mentor since I was a student. I welcome his input."

"Excellent. I won't rush you to complete your investigation, but I would like to hear all about your progress to date." He leaned back in his chair, his face suffused with ill-concealed expectation.

"So, no pressure, then?" Quinn chuckled as she pulled a file out of the briefcase.

"None."

Quinn accepted an espresso from Deborah, who looked less than pleased to be treated like a waitress, and went on to fill in Rhys on the findings of Dr. Scott before moving on to her own conclusions. "Based on the fibers and bits of leather found with the skeletons as well as the style of buckles and jewelry, I would say that our victims lived in mid-to late-seventeenth century. I can't say for certain what the man's position might have been, but the woman was definitely not a servant. She wore a gown made of fine fabric, which was ornamented by this lovely brooch." Quinn passed Rhys a picture of the brooch. She hadn't brought the original with her for fear of having an unwelcome flashback if she had to handle it in front of him. All the samples recovered from the chest were securely stored at her office at the institute, except for the brooch and belt buckle, which Gabe had entrusted to her.

"There was also an earring found. It was consistent with something a lady of means would wear." Quinn slid a picture of the earring across the desk.

Rhys studied the pictures with interest before turning back to Quinn. "Do we have any theories as to who she might have been?"

"During the late-seventeenth century, the area now known as Mayfair was sparsely populated. The houses belonged mostly to wealthy nobles who needed land to build great manor houses but still wished to remain close to Whitehall Palace. The population of Mayfair grew exponentially in the eighteenth century, but we believe that the skeletons date back to the original occupants. The first house built on that site belonged to one Lord Asher. He was one of the men instrumental in bringing Charles II back to England and served on the Privy Council until his death in 1699. Asher was a great favorite of Charles II and was mentioned in several documents from the period."

"Could the woman have been his wife?" Rhys asked, now clearly intrigued with the picture Quinn was painting.

"She could have been. Asher's first wife died when he was in his early forties, and he eventually remarried, but there's no mention of his wife's name, at least not in the documents I've studied so far."

"Where there any children?"

Quinn took a sip of espresso to give herself a moment to think. She knew about Barbara, but hadn't seen her mentioned anywhere. She couldn't very well bring her up before she had factual proof of her existence.

"I'm not sure. I'm still looking into that."

Rhys shrugged good-naturedly. He seemed more interested in the second skeleton.

"And you don't think that our *Romeo* was of noble birth?" he asked.

"He enjoyed good nutrition and fine health for the period, but his clothes were not of the same quality as those of the woman, and he seemed to have used his right hand extensively, which would lead me to believe that he might have had to work for a living."

Rhys looked thoughtful at this theory. "Or, he could have been a nobleman who enjoyed swordplay."

"That's a possibility," Quinn conceded.

"Excellent work, Dr. Allenby. We have a starting point, and now I can get the costume and set designers to start working on some ideas. In the meantime, we need to find out who the woman was and what happened to her. If she were a noblewoman, it might be easier to trace her rather than her companion. Have you any leads?"

"I plan to visit all the churches in the area and see if I can find a parish registry from the period. The entries are not likely to be online, but most churches still keep the old records, if they weren't burned—which is, of course, a possibility given the timeframe we're working with."

"Yes, of course, the Great Fire of London."

"Precisely."

Quinn replaced the documents in her folder and put them away in her briefcase, ready to leave.

"Dr. Allenby," Rhys said, his expression thoughtful, "would it be common for a house built during the period you suggest to have an oubliette?"

"No, it wouldn't," Quinn replied, startled by the appropriateness of the question. She'd been so focused on the players that she hadn't given any thought to the location of their remains. The chest had been found in some sort of shaft, which would have been well beneath the ground, even during original construction.

"Oubliettes are mostly found in old castles, ones that had subterranean dungeons. They might have been used by royals to dispose of those who'd been accused of treason or had fallen afoul of them in some way. Or by overlords whose word was law on their lands. I've never come across any mention of an oubliette in a private residence in London."

"Any theories?"

"Perhaps the space was never intended as an oubliette. It could have simply been part of a cellar or a separate chamber used for hiding objects of value. Lord Asher was a wealthy man."

"Could it have been a well?"

"Had it been a well, there would've been water damage to the chest. No, I believe the space was dry, even at the time of our victims' death."

"So, someone locked two young people in a chest—as a punishment, I presume—lowered said chest into the shaft, and left them to die? And no one noted their disappearance?" Rhys speculated.

"We have no way of knowing if anyone noted their disappearance, but clearly the young people weren't rescued."

He nodded in agreement, his eyes twinkling with interest. "So, for all intents and purposes, our couple was murdered?"

"Yes, they were. Whoever put them in that chest meant for them to die."

"I'll get onto my writers and see if they can come up with a couple of fitting scenarios for our dramatization. In the meantime, I look forward to hearing what you've discovered."

Quinn stood up to leave.

"Dr. Allenby."

"Please, call me Quinn," Quinn said. She hated the forced formality of her title.

"Then you must call me Rhys. I can't help noticing that it's almost lunchtime," he said with an innocent smile.

"So it is."

"I would love for you to join me. I took the liberty of booking a table. Do say you'll come."

Quinn tried to swallow down her irritation. She had no desire to have lunch with Rhys Morgan. In fact, she'd made plans to see her cousin Jill. Jill had turned her back on a high-powered position in an accounting firm just over a year ago and opened up a vintage clothing shop in SoHo. Quinn still hadn't seen the place, and she'd hoped she might take Jill out to lunch to celebrate her new venture. But to refuse his offer would be churlish, so Quinn nodded in acquiescence.

"Only if you promise not to force-feed me any more cake."

"Upon my honor," Rhys quipped as he held his hand over his heart.

Chapter 20

The restaurant Rhys took Quinn to was the type of place one would never take notice of just walking past. It was tiny and ultramodern, decorated entirely in white with abstract paintings adorning the walls. The servers all seemed awfully young—polished women and solicitous men, dressed in uniforms of pristine white. Quinn had to admit though that the food was sublime. Her swordfish served over pumpkin ravioli with feta cheese crumbles and caramelized onions was superb.

"Do you like it?" Rhys asked, eager to hear her opinion.

"Fantastic," Quinn replied. "You really are a foodie," she observed with a smile.

"I suppose I am. When I was a boy, my mother made the same dishes every week. She was a single, working mum, so she had no time or extra money to get too creative. I swore that when I grew up I would try something different every day."

"You must have been a handful," Quinn observed, trying to imagine Rhys as a precocious child.

"More than you can imagine. I had acute asthma when I was a child. Any type of strenuous activity or anxiety could set off an attack. My poor mother was always frantic with worry, imagining that I would have an attack whilst on my own and not have my inhaler nearby. She forbade me to participate in any afterschool activities or play with the other boys. I envied my older brother, Owain, who was always playing football and going swimming at the beach with his friends during the summer. I was only allowed to sit on the sand and breathe in the bracing sea air," he mimicked with a grimace of disgust, which made Quinn laugh.

"I suppose that's when my interest in television began. I used to read a lot, especially during the summer holidays, and I put on one-man productions of various plays for my mum. She worked as a hairdresser, but before she got pregnant with Owain and married my dad, she had aspirations of going to the university and studying medieval literature. She was a huge mythology fan, particularly anything to do with King Arthur."

"Where did you grow up?" Quinn asked as Rhys refilled her wine glass, clearly in no rush to get back to the office.

"Pembrokeshire, Wales."

"So, you speak Welsh?"

"Just a few words. I understand everything, but we always spoke English at home, being on the wrong side of the Landsker Line. Have you ever been to Wales?"

"Yes, many years ago while on holiday with my parents. We visited St. Govan's Chapel in Pembrokeshire. That must have been very close to where you grew up."

"Yes, but I've actually never been. My mum wouldn't let me go because of all the steps. She was afraid I'd have an attack. What did you think of it?

"I was just dumbstruck by it, even as a child. To me there was something utterly magical about building right into a cliff. You could hardly tell where the chapel ended and the cliff began, as if it simply grew out of the stone. My mum told me the story of St. Govan hiding from the pirates inside a crevice in the cliff face that shielded him from prying eyes. I had nightmares for days about being swallowed up by stone."

"You were an impressionable child, weren't you? Did you dig up your parents' garden looking for artifacts?" Rhys asked with a teasing smile.

"No, not really. I was more interested in genealogy when I was a child."

"Really, why is that?" Rhys looked at her with genuine interest, and suddenly something caught in Quinn's throat. She hadn't meant to have this conversation. He'd been so open about his own childhood that she suddenly felt as if she couldn't lie to him. She rarely told people the truth about her origins. It was a painful subject, and not one she cared to discuss with anyone. People meant well, but the look of pity on their faces was usually enough to undo her.

"Did I say something wrong?" he asked, his eyes widening with sudden anxiety.

"No, you didn't. It's just that I was abandoned as a baby. When I found out that I'd been adopted, genealogy became something of an obsession."

"Have you ever tried to find your parents?"

"I don't know who my parents were. I was left in a church pew and found by the priest. I was turned over to the state and eventually put up for adoption. I have no desire to track down my natural parents, but I would very much like to know who they were and why they gave me up. It would fill a void that has existed inside me since I was a child, and answer questions that have been gnawing at my mind."

"Like what?"

"Like why they couldn't just go through the proper channels and put me up for adoption legally. I tried to tell myself that being left in a church meant something, but there were times when I thought that I'd been disposed of like rubbish. Whoever my parents were, they couldn't be bothered with me, so they just left me."

Quinn was surprised to see that Rhys didn't look remotely pitying. Instead, he gazed at her with surprise, his eyebrows lifting in astonishment.

"Rubbish? I think not. Making films and documentaries is all about studying human nature, as I'm sure being a historian is, and deep down you know that no one leaves rubbish in a church. Whoever left you there wanted to make sure that you were found by someone who would do the right thing by you. They left you in what they perceived to be the safest possible place. It was a declaration of love, the final act of a caring mother. You might never know who she was or what prompted her to do what she did, but know that she loved you."

"My mum said the same thing, but I always thought that she was just trying to comfort me."

"She *was* trying to comfort you, but that doesn't mean that what she was suggesting wasn't true," Rhys replied. "And did it comfort you?"

"For a time. But I longed to know who my parents were, especially my mother."

"My situation is very different, but I can understand how you feel. My father died when I was two. I have no memory of him, except sometimes, I dream that I can hear his voice reading me a bedtime story. I suppose the memory is stored somewhere deep in my subconscious. Of course, I know who he was and have seen pictures of him and heard stories, but I would have liked to know him for myself. When I was a boy, I'd often wished that my mum would remarry, so that I'd have a dad. My brother is seven years older than me, so he had memories of our father and felt resentful of any man who might try to take his place, but I just longed for a man in my life."

"Did your mum remarry?"

"Yes, but only after I'd went off to the university. Dawydd had been in love with my mother for years. He'd been a friend of my father's when they were at school. I think he liked her even back then. She's happy," Rhys added with a warm smile.

"And your brother?"

"Oh, Owain never left Pembrokeshire. He owns a butcher shop and lives a few minutes away from Mum. He checks up on her regularly and drops off the children for a few hours in the process. Mum loves babysitting, so everyone wins."

"How many children does he have?"

"Owain has four boys and a girl, and Dawydd's daughter has three girls, so it's a full house when they are all there. I always go home for Christmas. It's a far cry from what it used to be when it was just the three of us. Of course, there are always the usual digs about my failure to produce more grandchildren for them," Rhys said with an irreverent shrug. "There's time."

"My parents moved to Marbella when Dad retired. They love it there. I've never told them this, but I actually dread Christmas since they left. I always have a place to go, but it's not quite the same as being with your family, is it?"

"No, it's not. Why not go spend Christmas with them this year?" Rhys suggested as he took a last sip of his coffee and rose to leave.

"I just might do that," Quinn replied. She gathered her coat and bag and followed Rhys out of the restaurant.

"Thank you for lunch, Rhys. It was lovely."

Rhys leaned forward and kissed her softly on the cheek before returning to his office. Quinn looked after him for a moment, then dashed toward the nearest tube station. Lunch lasted for over two hours, but she could still catch Jill before the shop closed for the night. She had some shopping to do.

Chapter 21

March 1665

London, England

Elise lifted the spoon carefully to Lady Matilda's lips, but the older woman refused to swallow any more broth. She'd taken a turn for the worse over the past few days and had barely eaten anything at all. Her already angular bones jutted out beneath papery skin that had acquired a gray pall over the past twenty-four hours. The old lady's breathing was labored, and her brow glistened with sweat but was cool to the touch.

"Cold," Lady Matilda breathed.

"I'll fetch a hot brick," Elise promised and picked up the bowl to return to the kitchen. Lady Matilda needed nourishment; perhaps she'd take some milk. Elise had asked Lucy to take out the chamber pot, but it proved to be empty, as Lady Matilda seemed unable to make water. That couldn't be a good sign.

"How is she?" Edward demanded when he met Elise in the corridor.

"She is very poorly," Elise replied truthfully.

"Thank you for everything you are doing for her," Edward said. He looked genuinely distressed. He'd even remained at home for the past few evenings and spent at least an hour each night sitting by his mother's bedside.

"Do you think she will improve?" he asked, barely able to keep hope from his voice.

"I pray that she will," Elise replied. "Dr. Fisk bled her again this morning."

"Dr. Fisk is a bloated old fool," Edward spat out. "She's gotten worse since he's been attending her, but he's the best physician in London. Even His Majesty seeks his advice on various matters of health."

"I've no doubt Dr. Fisk is doing everything he can to cure Lady Matilda," Elise answered diplomatically. She didn't think that bleeding an old woman who'd barely eaten for days would help, but what did she know? Dr. Fisk was a renowned physician who enjoyed the favor of the king, and surely he knew his business. Perhaps the bleeding would purge Lady Matilda of infection, as Dr. Fisk hoped, and restore her appetite. Once she was able to consume beef broth and meat, she'd make more blood.

"I'm sure you're right, Elise. I'm just too upset to think clearly."

"Is there anything I can do for you?" Elise inquired. "I was just on my way to the kitchen to get a hot brick for her ladyship."

"Thank you. I don't require anything. I'll just sit with my mother for a bit."

"As you wish," Elise replied and continued downstairs.

Since Lady Matilda had been ill, Edward had been kinder to Elise. No further mention of her infertility had been made, nor had James visited her chamber. Come to think of it, Elise hadn't seen James about the house at all. Normally, she caught sight of him throughout the day, mostly when gazing out the window, but she hadn't seen him for several days. She thought he might come to visit Lady Matilda, the dowager being his grandmother, but Lady Matilda never acknowledged James or spoke of him. Perhaps she had no wish to see him.

Elise kept a stack of heavy damask squares and a small stoppered vial of vinegar by her bed, but she hadn't had the opportunity to make use of them, for which she was grateful. She had to last one more month until the sailing, and then she would be free of James, as well as her husband, once and for all. Perhaps once Edward returned to court, she could risk visiting Gavin in Southwark again.

Elise handed the bowl to a servant and extracted a hot brick from the oven using iron tongs. She carefully wrapped it in a thick towel and hurried back upstairs. Lady Matilda's room was shrouded in darkness since the shutters were kept closed even during the day. The rosy glow of the fire cast shadows onto the great bed and the frail old lady in it. Edward sat next to the bed, his elbows resting on his thighs, his head in his hands. Gone was the fashionable courtier, replaced by a grieving son who suddenly looked years older than his age. Divested of his dark wig and elegant clothes, Edward looked like an old man.

Elise slipped the brick beneath the blankets and pushed it up against Lady Matilda's feet. They were ice-cold despite two pairs of wool stockings. Her mother had complained of being terribly cold just before she died. It's as if all the warmth of life had seeped from her body, leaving her a cold husk, ready for the grave. It was a morbid thought, but Lady Matilda looked like an effigy, her face still, like a wax death mask. Elise put her hand on Edward's shoulder in a gesture of sympathy and he took it and kissed, seeming grateful for the support. He understood only too well what was happening. No amount of leeching or bleeding would help his mother. She was in God's hands now.

"Go to bed. I'll stay with her," Edward said as he released her hand. "But ask James to send for Reverend Blackstock."

"Is James here?" Elise asked carefully.

Edward raised his face to hers in sudden confusion. "Ah, no, he isn't. Ask one of the servants, then."

Elise wanted to ask where James was but didn't dare. It was no business of hers. She wasn't even sure why she was curious. As long as he stayed away from her, she was safe. But thoughts of James plagued her that evening. *Where did he go, and when will he be back?* Elise wondered. *What does he do with his spare time? Whom does he see?* She knew nothing of his life.

Elise woke with a start when she felt an urgent hand on her shoulder.

"James?" she mumbled. But it wasn't James; it was Edward.

"Mother's gone," he said. "She passed an hour ago."

"Why didn't you wake me?"

"There was no need. Reverend Blackstock was with her. It was a peaceful passing."

Elise couldn't see Edward's face in the darkness, but his voice sounded teary. He really was distraught.

"May I lie down with you?" he asked.

"Of course."

Edward climbed into bed and rested his head on Elise's shoulder just as her sisters did when they needed to be comforted. Elise stroked his hair and held him close until he fell asleep. She tried to go back to sleep herself, but slumber wouldn't come. It felt odd to have a man in her bed, especially a man who was a virtual stranger to her. She was now used to the feel and scent of James, and she supposed sharing a bed with Edward wouldn't feel as strange, but he reeked of stale sweat and alcohol, and Elise's stomach clenched with revulsion.

Elise carefully pulled her arm from beneath Edward's neck and slid out of bed. The room was cold, and the floorboards were icy beneath her feet, but she couldn't bear to remain in the same room with Edward. She wrapped a warm shawl around her shoulders, stuck her feet into shoes, and crept from the room. She'd go to the kitchen and see if there was any broth left. She was thirsty and surprisingly hungry. She'd not had any supper at all, and the midday meal was more than twelve hours ago. Elise's stomach rumbled as she walked down the darkened stairs. She should have taken a candle, but she didn't want to wake Edward.

The house was silent around her, the boards creaking as she put her weight on them. The pale faces of Edward's ancestors materialized out of the gloom as she passed their portraits, their gazes seemingly full of malice. The house was forbidding during the daylight hours, but during the night it felt like a tomb. Elise thought of the fresh corpse lying in Lady Matilda's room. She hoped that the ground was thawed enough to dig a grave or the funeral would have to be postponed until warmer weather. It would be easier for Edward if he could bury his mother and return to his court duties before too long.

Elise was surprised to see a soft glow coming from the kitchen. Perhaps what she was seeing were the embers from the hearth, but that couldn't be. Cook banked the fire before she finished for the day for fear of burning the house down, and it was too early for anyone to be up. Elise stood still as the church clock began to chime at St. Martin. It was only three in the morning, hours yet till dawn. Perhaps one of the servants couldn't sleep and had come down in search of something to eat. Lady Matilda had run the house for years before Elise came, and she was tightfisted with household expenses. The servants ate poorly, only getting meat when there were leftovers from the master's table that couldn't be kept for the next day. They ate mostly pottage, bread, and cheese, and the occasional fish stew. Elise could hardly blame them for pilfering food in the middle of the night.

She walked into the kitchen quietly, so as not to startle whomever was already there. James sat at the wooden table, a jug of wine in front of him. He was awake, but his eyes were glazed with drink. A candle burned on the table in front of him and Elise noticed the moisture on his lean cheeks. He'd been crying. Had he loved his grandmother that much?

James turned slowly toward her, his gaze uncomprehending. "What are you doing here?" he asked, his words slurred.

"I came down for a cup of broth," Elise replied. "I'm sorry about your grandmother."

"What?" he asked, staring at her.

"I'm sorry about Lady Matilda's passing," she repeated.

James shrugged. "She was a nasty old woman," he replied. "I, for one, won't miss her."

"Oh. I thought you were upset," Elise said as she poured some broth into a pewter mug and held it over the flame to warm it up.

James shook his head, as if annoyed by a pesky fly. "I am upset, but not about her."

He looked like he wasn't going to say anymore, but a need to share proved to be stronger. "Harry died this evening."

"Was he a friend of yours?"

James shook his head again. "No, he was my nephew."

"You have siblings?" Elise asked, intrigued. Perhaps James's mother had married after Edward was finished with her and had other children. For some reason, Elise assumed that James had no family, but she must have been wrong.

"I have a sister—Molly. Asher's her father too. Molly is the only family I have."

"And your mother?" Elise asked.

"Died birthing me."

"How old was Harry?"

"Five months. He passed quietly. Just went to sleep and never woke up. Molly is devastated. She'd fought so hard to keep him alive."

"Was he ill?"

James shrugged. "He didn't eat enough to survive. Just didn't seem to have the strength to nurse. Molly had a physician look at him, but he could offer no advice. Just told Molly to eat more meat to fortify her milk for Harry. He was a sweet little mite. Looked just like Molly."

Elise laid her hand over James's, startling him. He looked like he was going to yank his hand away but thought better of it. "I'm sorry, James."

"Thank you."

"When will the funeral be?" Elise asked. She'd offer to come, if that was all right with James.

James shook his head in disgust. "There will not be a funeral. Harry hadn't been baptized. Molly kept putting it off till he was stronger, so as a consequence, he can't be buried in consecrated ground. If that cold bitch upstairs ever acknowledged him as her great-grandson, he might have been buried with her. As is, he'll have to be buried behind Molly's house. She's heartbroken. It's bad enough to lose a child, but to be denied a Christian burial is devastating for a mother. She needs to know that her boy is with the Lord, not moldering in a stinking hole behind the privy."

Elise pushed aside her cup and considered James for a moment. She thought she hated him, but at this moment, he was just a sad, bereft young man, and she wished to help.

"James, what if we could sneak baby Harry into Lady Matilda's coffin?" Elise asked.

"And how, pray tell, are we going to do that?" James appeared to be shocked by the suggestion, but he was listening, his eyes intent on hers as he waited for her to explain.

Elise smiled. "I have an idea."

"Tell me. I can't take Harry from Moll unless I can promise her that he will be buried properly."

"I will offer to prepare Lady Matilda's body for burial. I doubt Edward will object. I will dress her in one of her favorite gowns and place the baby's corpse beneath her skirts after she's been laid out in the coffin. The skirts are so voluminous that they will hide the child, and even if someone notices something, they will assume that it's just bunched up fabric."

James gave Elise a look of utter astonishment. "Why would you do that for me? You have every reason to despise me."

"I'm not doing it for you. I'm doing it for Harry. He was innocent of all wrongdoing, and I wish to help. I think it's beastly unfair that a child cannot be buried properly just because he hasn't been baptized."

"Are you a secret heretic?" James asked with a watery smile.

"No. I'm a person who thinks that there's much unfairness in the world."

"I won't argue with you there. I'll ask Molly tomorrow. You have until then to change your mind."

"I won't change my mind. I just hope that the gravediggers are up to the task."

"I'll help them myself if that grave will be Harry's final resting place."

Elise nodded. "We'll make it work, James."

"Thank you," he said and squeezed her hand.

Chapter 22

A brace of candles illuminated the darkened room, casting eerie shadows onto the walls and the open casket. It was before noon, but the shutters were closed out of respect for the deceased, and an unnatural hush permeated the room. Elise stood next to Edward as he gazed upon his mother for the last time. Edward's eyes drooped with fatigue and sadness. Elise hadn't noticed a marked closeness between mother and son while Lady Matilda was still living, but Edward seemed to take her passing very badly. Elise supposed it was a mark in his favor that he cared about his mother, if not about his children, one of whom was standing silently by Edward's side. Barbara was gazing off into the distance, as she often did, but the smile was gone from her face, replaced by an expression of complete incomprehension.

"Grandmother is gone?" Barbara whispered, bringing forth a stifled sob from her father.

Edward had readily agreed to allow Elise to prepare his mother for burial while he went out to order a casket. Normally, a servant would be sent, but Edward wished to choose the coffin in person to make sure it would be to Lady Matilda's standards. This was no simple pine box. The coffin was made of mahogany and decorated with fanciful carvings, the very kind of thing Lady Matilda would have thought frivolous and unnecessary had she been in a position to comment. Still, Elise had to admit that she looked dignified and peaceful, with her hands folded on her chest and her eyes closed as if in sleep.

Laying out her own mother had been a labor of love, but preparing Lady Matilda for her final journey felt utterly different.

Elise had to swallow down revulsion as she washed the old woman. Her skin was cold and wrinkled, and she smelled appalling after nearly two weeks of battling a fever. The stench of stale sweat and human waste assailed her, and Elise gagged with disgust. She gave up on her task and went to open the window, where she stood for several minutes, gulping in fresh air. The nausea finally passed and Elise returned to Lady Matilda, eager to be done.

Lady Matilda's limbs had stiffened during the night, and it took great effort to wrestle her first into undergarments and then into her favorite dark-blue velvet gown adorned with a dainty pattern picked in silver thread at the top of the bodice and hem. Had the dress come as one whole garment, Elise would never have been able to get Lady Matilda's wooden arms into it. Lucy panted with effort as she pushed the old woman onto her side so that Elise could tie the laces at the back. That done, Elise carefully rolled on silk stockings and pushed Lady Matilda's feet into matching shoes, then arranged her wispy hair into some semblance of order before dismissing Lucy and sinking into a nearby chair. She closed her eyes and let out a sigh of relief.

She was tired and glad to have the distasteful task over with. She hadn't liked Lady Matilda when the woman was alive, and she liked her even less in death. Elise felt a pang of guilt, but what was the point of lying to herself? Lady Matilda had watched her every move and delighted in making Elise feel worthless and ungrateful. Lady Matilda's death was a relief, truth be told, even if Elise didn't plan to remain at Asher Hall for much longer.

Elise sat up with a start as the door handle slowly turned. A pale face peered into the room, then the woman entered and shut the door behind her. She had a mass of dark curls spilling from beneath a linen cap and a generous mouth, so like her brother's. Molly looked hollow-eyed with grief as she approached Elise slowly. She was about to say something when she saw Lady

Matilda and stopped for a moment, looking at the old woman with a mixture of pity and disgust.

"She were my grandmother, ye know," she suddenly said. "If it'd been up to her, James and I would've been tossed out into the streets after our mother died, left to starve."

"She was not a kind woman," Elise agreed. It was considered uncharitable to speak ill of the dead, but she didn't care. She owed nothing to Lady Matilda.

"No, she weren't. My husband says that I should be grateful to have our little 'Arry resting with his great-grandmother, but 'e'd never known Matilda. I suppose I can derive some small sense of satisfaction knowing that she would have been livid if she knew."

Elise wasn't sure what to say to that, so she remained silent. Edward would be back soon, and she wondered how he'd react to finding his natural daughter in his mother's room.

"I came here to thank ye," Molly said, finally turning away from her grandmother. "I appreciate what ye're trying to do for my 'Arry more than ye'll ever know. If there's anything ye ever need, know that ye can turn to me."

"Thank you," Elise said.

"I will bring 'Arry tonight, once the old bag is in her coffin."

"Yes."

Molly turned to leave but thought better of it and approached Elise. She reached out and took Elise's hand in hers, squeezing it lightly as their eyes met. "Don't hate him," she suddenly said.

"Who, Edward?"

"No, James. He's a good man, Elise, but he feels a misguided sense of obligation to our father. James aspires to see the best in people, and his naïveté often leads to heartache."

"I don't hate him, Molly. Not anymore."

Molly nodded and slipped from the room, just as two men came up the stairs with the casket. They carefully moved the corpse to the coffin before taking it downstairs, where it would remain until the funeral. Lady Matilda was to be laid out in state on the dining room table, ready to receive final respects from the family and staff.

Elise tidied up the room, adjusted the counterpane, and closed the chest at the foot of the bed. It would be up to Edward to decide what to do with his mother's belongings and jewels. She was done here. Instead of going downstairs, Elise went to her own room. She felt tired and sad, not only for Molly—who was clearly mad with grief at losing her baby—but for James as well. Elise had never given much thought to what it must feel like to be a bastard, but now she began to understand. Molly was angry and bitter, but James seemed confused and unduly grateful to a father who treated him no better than a servant and used him for his own ends.

Elise would have gladly remained in her room, but an angry knock on the door roused her out of her reverie.

"Come downstairs," Edward demanded. "They're about to close the casket, and I would have you pay your respects to Mother."

"Of course."

Elise considered her duty to Lady Matilda discharged, but she obediently followed Edward to the dining room, not wishing to distress him further. She tensed as Edward reached out to touch his mother's hand in farewell before the carpenter nailed the coffin shut. He had no earthly reason to touch her skirts, but Elise was as nervous as a cat in an alley full of dogs. Baby Harry rested next to Lady Matilda's right thigh, the folds of the voluminous skirts hiding him from view. It felt wrong and disrespectful to stuff the child beneath his great-grandmother's skirts, but there was no other place where he could lie unnoticed.

Elise felt James's eyes on her as she stared at her folded hands, fearful of giving her nervousness away. He'd come in with the carpenter, there to help convey the casket to the cart that would deliver it to the church for the funeral. Elise looked up and met James's gaze. She saw a glimmer of gratitude in its depth and nearly smiled, catching herself just in time. James had come with Molly the night before to offer silent support as she delivered the remains of her baby. Elise hadn't seen Harry's face since he was wrapped in a shroud, but the corpse had been tiny, hardly bigger than that of a cat. Molly shook with sobs as she placed her son inside the coffin, then ran from the room, too distraught to speak. Elise adjusted the fabric to cover the child and walked away, leaving James to remain with the coffin overnight per Lord Asher's request. He didn't want his mother to be all alone on her final night above ground.

**

Edward nodded to the carpenter, who pulled several nails from his pocket before lifting the lid onto the casket with James's help. Edward rested his hand on Elise's shoulder as the man hammered the nails into the lid. The cart was already outside, ready to take Lady Matilda on her final journey.

Elise, Barbara, and James followed Edward from the room, ready to proceed to the church. All the servants were gathered outside and would follow the cart at a respectable distance. Edward hardly noticed when Molly and her husband joined the procession, bringing up the rear. Elise supposed that if he did, he might think that Molly felt some grief at losing the grandmother who never cared for her, but Molly needed to see her boy on his final journey, regardless of what her father thought.

    Molly and Peter came to the church but then stood well off to the side, where Edward wouldn't see them. Peter kept a protective arm around Molly's shoulder as she cried quietly into a handkerchief. They were gone by the time the service ended and the first clumps of dirt made contact with the coffin lid, thudding against the wood with sickening finality. Elise stood silently and watched as the gravediggers filled in the grave. Edward watched as well, his head bowed, his arms at his sides. He seemed defeated and indifferent to his surroundings, but in a few days, normal life would begin again. For all of them.

Chapter 23

James had no wish to return to the house after the funeral. Edward had invited some of the mourners back for refreshments, but neither James nor Molly would be welcome even if they wished to attend. Edward hadn't so much as glanced at his daughter during the funeral; perhaps he hadn't even recognized her, having not seen her in years. Molly was better off having no ties to this cold, manipulative man. Her life wasn't easy by any means, but it was hers to live as she saw fit, and she wasn't beholden to their father in any way. In an odd way, she was free.

As the mourners began to disperse, James left the graveyard and walked to Blackfriars. Molly could hardly tell any of her friends and neighbors that she'd just buried her infant son in someone else's coffin, so the wake for Harry was just for the family. Molly had prepared a mutton stew and baked rhubarb pie for dessert, which was a real treat. The sweet stuck in James's throat, but he did it justice anyway so as not to offend Molly. She'd likely been up all night preparing and cleaning the house. She was the type of woman who threw herself into domestic tasks to distract her mind from her suffering. Molly had always been practical and accepting of life's tragedies, but this was her little boy, and the second child she'd lost in as many years. James knew her well enough to note the rigid set of her shoulders and the barely contained storm of emotion that raged behind her dark-blue eyes.

"Molly, will you be all right?" James asked once Peter and the girls stepped out of the room. Peter suggested a walk by the river to give his wife a bit of privacy and quiet, should she wish to rest, but Molly threw herself into clearing up, as James knew she would.

"Of course, I will," Molly retorted forcefully. "The question is whether ye will be."

"I'll grieve for Harry, of course, but I'll manage," James replied, confused by his sister's vehement response.

"'Tis not 'Arry's passing I'm referring to."

"Then what?"

"Ye care for her. I can tell. I saw ye watching her during the burial. She didn't spare ye a glance, but ye were gazing at her the whole time, desperate for even a tiny spec of acknowledgement. Like a dog," Molly spat out.

"Don't be a fool, Molly," James retorted. Molly was feeling emotional, and he wouldn't do anything to upset her further, but she was talking nonsense and taking out her grief on him.

"It's ye who's the fool, brother," Molly countered, her eyes blazing with anger. She slammed a washed pewter jug onto the table as if it'd offended her somehow and began to dry the rest of the crockery, her movements jerky and unnaturally forceful.

"Molly, what's gotten into you? Elise just did something kind and selfless for a woman she'd never met and a child she'd never heard of. Why can't you show a little charity of spirit toward her?"

Molly shook her head as she glared at James, hands splayed on the table for support. "Ye just don't see it, do ye? It's not her I'm angry with. What she's done for 'Arry is nothing short of miraculous, and I will be grateful to her for as long as I live, but I've just lost someone I love, and I don't want to lose anyone else. She wouldn't have done what she's done unless she cared for ye. Why would she risk her husband's wrath otherwise? And now I know that ye care for her as well. Do ye not see where this might lead, James?"

"Molly, you know our father. He's no fool. He'll send me away as soon as Elise gets with child. I would have served my purpose, and he'll want me out of the way until my services are required once again."

"Well, I hope he does. Ye are right, James, he's no fool, nor is he a man who values the lives of others. Lord Asher is a ruthless, ambitious man, and he will not allow anyone to stand in the way of his plans. Go away, James. Find a life for yerself away from Asher Hall. I implore ye. I've no wish to see ye hurt."

James got to his feet and took his sister in his arms. Molly stiffened at first but then gave in to her need for comfort. She rested her head on James's shoulder as he held her close. "Molly, you are the only person in this world who loves me, and I value your loyalty and devotion above all, but I must do as I see fit."

"Ye should have never agreed to this scheme," Molly persisted. The fury had gone out of her, and now her voice sounded thin and frightened.

"You are right, I shouldn't have. But I did, and now I must deal with the consequences."

Molly pulled away from James and looked up at him, her eyes clouded with worry. "I know ye, James. Ye're too mule-headed to heed my advice, but mark my words: this won't end well for ye."

"Molly, I've made a deal with our father. Once Elise is delivered of a son, he will give me an agreed-upon sum of money and release me from his service. I have some education and skill with a sword. There's a place in this world for men like me. I will take my payment and go. At least I won't be walking away empty-handed after all these years of service."

"No, ye won't be, but ye'll be leaving behind a son and his mother," Molly persisted, refusing to let the subject drop. James reached for his cloak and hat. He'd heard enough, and he needed to leave before he lashed out at his sister and told her to mind her own affairs and leave him to deal with his. Molly meant well, he knew that, but she'd hit a nerve, which was exactly what she'd been hoping to do. She always knew just how to rile him up.

"They will not be my responsibility," James barked. He yanked open the door and strode out, slamming the door behind him for emphasis.

Molly shook her head in dismay, amazed by her brother's pigheadedness. "You just keep telling yourself that, Brother," she called after James, but he didn't hear her.

Chapter 24

Elise woke with a start, suddenly aware that someone was in the room. She'd taken to going upstairs after the midday meal to rest for a while. She wasn't sure why she was so tired these days, but the household ran smoothly, so there wasn't much for her to do during the afternoons anyway. She felt refreshed after an hour's nap and usually went downstairs to read or work on some mending, which never seemed to end. Edward always managed to snag his hose or tear a bit of lace on his collars. Elise diligently applied herself to fixing every garment, used to the economies of her upbringing.

Elise rubbed her eyes and sat up. She'd drawn the bed hangings to keep the bright light out and now pulled them aside to find her husband in her bedchamber. Elise sucked in her breath when she realized who was with him. Dr. Fisk treated Lady Matilda while she was ill, so Elise knew him well. He was considered to be one of the best physicians in London and was frequently consulted by members of the court for various complaints. Dr. Fisk had even attended on the king himself, but although he coveted the title of Court Physician, he had yet to achieve it. Edward said that His Majesty desired a younger doctor, one who was well versed in all the new advances in medicine and who didn't look as dour as Bernard Fisk tended to, even when smiling.

Dr. Fisk was a slight man with rheumy eyes and stooped posture, his physical shortcomings exacerbated by the unnatural blackness of his periwig and his elaborate attire, which nearly swallowed him up. Elise supposed that he was only in his fifties, but he appeared to be much older, perhaps because despite the rose water that he used in great quantities, he always smelled of illness and death.

"Is something wrong?" Elise asked, making an effort to sound calm. Her heart began to hammer in her chest as she stared from one man to the other. Edward had been preoccupied with his mother's illness, but now that she was gone, there was nothing to stop him from turning his attention to the business at hand.

"Dr. Fisk is here to examine you, Elise. Perhaps he can determine the cause of your infertility," Edward replied gruffly.

"My dear Lord Asher," Dr. Fisk began, "inability to conceive within the first few months of marriage hardly qualifies as infertility. Your wife is a healthy young woman. With regular visits from her devoted husband, she should become pregnant in no time at all."

Elise stole a peek at Edward. Dr. Fisk clearly didn't know of Edward's inability to perform his husbandly duties and assumed that Edward was applying himself diligently to begetting an heir. *What would he say if he knew that the mighty Lord Asher was using his baseborn son to impregnate his wife?* Elise wondered bitterly.

"You are right, of course, Dr. Fisk, but I would like to be sure that there's nothing physically wrong with my bride. She has been tired and wan lately. I only wish to make sure that she is hale and hearty and able to bear children. Please, proceed with the examination. Lie back, Elise."

Elise did as she was told. It was no use protesting since Edward would probably hold her down and force her to submit to the dreaded examination. She squeezed her eyes shut as the doctor began to touch her. He started with her throat and made his way down, squeezing her breasts, palpating her stomach, and then pushing her legs apart and forcing his cold fingers deep inside her until she gasped with pain. He seemed to be touching her very womb, and the sensation was most unsettling. The doctor finished his examination and patted Elise on the thigh before turning to her husband.

"Is something wrong?" Edward asked, his voice anxious.

"On the contrary, my lord. Your lady is with child. About a month gone, I'd say. I offer my most heartfelt congratulations to you both," Dr. Fisk said, his smile more of a grimace. It reminded Elise of a gargoyle, grinning from its perch atop some church for eternity, completely indifferent to the suffering of the people who passed beneath it.

Elise felt as if she were going to be ill. She'd been tired and out of sorts, but it never occurred to her that she might be with child. She wasn't familiar with the symptoms of pregnancy, so she attributed the fatigue to low spirits and lack of purpose. Elise closed her eyes, desperate to be alone. She couldn't allow her husband to see how devastated she was by the news, so she turned her face away as tears slid down her cheeks and into the down of the pillow. The two men paid her no heed and continued to talk about her as if she weren't even there, discussing her health like a mare's.

"She's got narrow hips," Dr. Fisk was saying with some concern. "It might prove to be a difficult delivery."

"She's shaped just like her mother, and she delivered six children in quick succession," Edward replied. He sounded gleeful and proud, just as an expectant father would.

"Did you know Mistress de Lesseps?" Dr. Fisk inquired as he washed his hands and dried them on Elise's towel. Neither man spared Elise another glance as they continued to converse, likely forgetting about her presence in the great bed altogether.

"Oh, yes," Edward answered bitterly. "I knew her before she married that buffoon, de Lesseps. Threw herself away on a man of no consequence. She was quite a beauty in her day and could have made an advantageous match had she allowed herself to be guided by the advice of her father, but the old man doted on her and gave in to her whim. Elise resembles her greatly, actually, but only in looks, not temperament," Edward remarked, leaving Dr. Fisk in doubt that Edward would not tolerate any rebellion from his bride.

"Sounds to me like you got the better end of the bargain, my lord," Dr. Griffin replied. "There's nothing like a young, beautiful bride to make a man feel virile again."

The two men turned to leave, and Elise heard Edward's voice just before the door closed: "Saving the child is a priority, Dr. Fisk. I can always get another wife."

Elise buried her face in the pillow as the tears began to flow in earnest. She was with child—Edward's child—James's child. It would be some time before her belly began to grow, and she knew that some women might take advantage of that and proceed with their plans, but how could she deceive Gavin? He was already willing to take on more than most men. He was prepared to take on another man's wife and have his children be born out of wedlock, but to accept another man's child was asking too much. Had Elise already had a child, as many widows did when remarrying, the situation would be different, but coming to Gavin newly pregnant with James's child would be a gross abuse of Gavin's love and trust.

Elise pressed her hands over her ears to block out the cheerful singing of the birds. She wished she could just die and put an end to this miserable existence. Maybe she'd die in childbirth, as Dr. Fisk feared, but then she would be leaving her child behind, and she couldn't do that. She'd been aware of her pregnancy for no more than ten minutes, but already the seed of motherlove had been planted. It was her baby. And James's.

**

James was just coming out of the stables when he saw his father striding purposefully toward him. Edward looked pleased, which was surprising so soon after the death of Lady Matilda. Edward had never shown his mother much affection in public, but James had been at Asher Hall long enough to know that Lady Matilda had been the driving force behind everything Edward did. She had been manipulative and harsh, but most of all, she had been cunning. Edward likely didn't even realize how his mother played him, and James was sure that she was manipulating him still from beyond the grave.

Edward stopped in front of James and looked around, as if checking if anyone was within earshot. "You are to leave today," he said without any preamble.

"Where am I going?" James asked. He'd been taken completely by surprise. His father had said nothing about sending him anywhere.

"Suffolk. My estate has been neglected for far too long, and that fool of an estate manager can use a swift kick in the rear; he's gotten too comfortable. I wish you to take up residence. You are to oversee the spring planting and examine every tenant's farm. Let me know if they can afford to pay higher rents. My coffers need replenishing."

"Has something happened?" James asked carefully. His father was not normally an impulsive man. He thought things through and formulated a plan. This mission seemed utterly contrived since there was a competent man in charge of the Suffolk estate. Master Grove would not welcome James's interference, or even his presence, since he was hardly more than a servant. But it seemed that Lord Asher wanted him out of the way—and quickly.

"Nothing you need to concern yourself with. Be off with you," Edward barked. He turned on his heel and strode back toward the house. James had no choice but to obey. He followed his father into the house to collect his belongings. If he left within the hour, he'd get to Asherton House before nightfall tomorrow, with a stopover for the night along the way. James was just walking up the stairs when he saw Lucy emerging from Lady Asher's room. She was flushed and nervous.

"All right, Lucy?" he asked, pausing on the landing. He liked Lucy, more so because she had such a transparent face and couldn't keep a secret if her very life depended on it. If James had learned anything from his father, it was that information always had value, and servants' gossip was not to be ignored since they always had their finger on the pulse of the household.

Lucy nodded, but refused to say anything and rushed off, leaving James standing outside Elise's door. He knocked softly and let himself in. Elise was lying in bed, her pale face nearly translucent in the harsh light of the spring afternoon. Her eyes looked puffy, and she stared listlessly toward the window, as if she were still alone.

"Elise, are you ill?" James asked as he approached the bed, belatedly realizing that he called her by her Christian name, which was inappropriate under the circumstances. He had no business being in her bedchamber, but since the death of Harry, he felt a bond with Elise and couldn't just ignore her despair. She hadn't ignored his.

Elise shook her head but failed to meet his gaze. She looked so forlorn that James thought someone might have died. He knew she had two younger sisters whom she loved dearly. Perhaps one of the girls or her father had taken ill.

"Did something happen?" he asked again, hoping she'd talk to him.

Elise finally turned to face him. "You mean he hasn't told you? He hasn't patted you on the head and thanked you for a job well done?" she demanded, her cheeks blooming with anger.

"Are you . . ." James stopped. Why was she so angry? Getting with child was the ultimate objective for any young bride. It was a wife's duty to produce an heir, and if she were indeed with child, she'd no longer have to endure his unwelcome visits. Elise nodded miserably and turned away again, her attention fixated on a gnarled branch just outside her window that was moving in the breeze like a waving hand.

"Congratulations," James said. "I hope you will resign yourself to the idea of motherhood and that all will go well for you and the babe."

Elise turned back toward him, her eyes narrowed. "Are you going somewhere?" she asked, studying him intently. She no longer looked angry, just defeated.

"Lord Asher is sending me to oversee his estate in Suffolk. I don't know how long I'm meant to stay."

Their eyes met for a long moment. Neither one said anything, but they both understood. There was no need for James to go to Suffolk. He'd done his bit, and now Edward wanted him out of the way where he could do no harm. Elise and James were both young, attractive, and had already crossed the forbidden line with his blessing. What was to stop them from continuing to fornicate, especially when Edward could not lie with his wife himself? He feared that Elise might have developed a fondness for the act and would invite James into her bed just for pleasure.

"Go with God, James," Elise said.

"Be well."

Chapter 25

November 2013

Surrey, England

Quinn collected her bags and locked the car before heading for her front door. Seeing Jill had been a real treat. They went to the pub after Jill locked up the shop and stayed longer than either of them expected, enjoying a few glasses of wine and chatting about everything from family to their less-than-satisfying love lives. It'd been a long while since Quinn spent time with a good friend. There was always a sense of camaraderie on a dig, but being around like-minded people didn't change the fact that they were more colleagues than friends who often dropped off the radar once they returned home. Quinn never lacked for company, but she rarely got too personal with anyone, especially about her love life. She'd spent several nights crying into her pillow after Luke broke things off with her but came to work in the morning exuding a false sense of cheer. She didn't care to be the object of pity or gossip, which was always rampant on a dig. Aside from Gabe, Jill was the first person Quinn had confided in, and she felt a cathartic sense of release. Jill had a way of putting things in perspective and following it up with much-needed retail therapy.

Quinn hadn't bought anything new in months and felt like a kid in a candy shop when she perused some of Jill's merchandise while Jill was busy helping customers. Quinn chose two pairs of jeans, a peasant blouse in a gorgeous shade of green, and a wraparound dress in a pattern of mauve and gray. It was very smart and could be worn to either a business meeting or a social occasion with high-heeled shoes or a pair of boots. A pale-pink mother-ofpearl vintage necklace completed the outfit. Quinn added it to the pile without even glancing at the price tag. She loved it, and since Jill's new business was still struggling, she wanted to give her cousin a helping hand.

Quinn inserted the key into the lock and froze in shock when the heavy oak door gave way and opened on its own, swinging back soundlessly on well-oiled hinges. Had she installed a security light above the door, as her mother always said she should, she would have noticed that the lock had been broken and there were scratches on the door jamb. The wise thing to do would have been to return to the car, drive away, and call the police, but Quinn wasn't thinking rationally, her veins pulsing with a heady mix of adrenaline and fury. Someone had dared violate her home, and she'd be damned if she ran away like a frightened child.

The front room was flooded by pale moonlight streaming through the stained-glass windows set high in the walls. The light was feeble but just enough to illuminate the destruction within. The place was a mess: books on the floor, files strewn across her desk, and every drawer pulled out and emptied. One wall had a circle of crumbling plaster, as if someone thought there might be something behind it and took a hammer to it. Quinn was turning toward the light switch when she was struck on the side of her head. Pain exploded in her skull as she crumpled to the floor, her mouth open in disbelief. She'd foolishly assumed that the intruder had gone, but she realized her mistake when she saw a dark shadow out of the corner of her eye, and then another.

Whoever hit her ran out the door and shut it behind them with a bang, leaving her in near-darkness. Quinn felt a wave of nausea brought on by the pounding in her head. She closed her eyes and focused on breathing deeply through her nose to get a handle on her rising sense of panic. What had she been thinking just barging in like that? She could have been killed or seriously hurt. Had the intruders been armed, they might have fired at her when taken by surprise. And what if they came back? Quinn had a splitting headache, but at least she hadn't been knocked unconscious, which was a blessing. She tried to sit up but was assaulted by such strong vertigo that she had to lie back down and close her eyes again until the world stopped spinning like a top. Once she thought herself able to try again, Quinn felt for her bag and fumbled inside, searching for her mobile. She called the police, then let the phone drop to the floor as a comforting blackness enveloped her.

Quinn's limbs felt heavy when she came round, and the pain in her head seemed to radiate in all directions. She lifted her hand and carefully touched her temple. Her fingers came away sticky with blood. *Bugger*, she thought angrily. She hoped she wouldn't need to go to the hospital, but perhaps she ought, just to be on the safe side. The pain became worse, making her head feel as if her skull was about to burst. Her head was throbbing, and her vision, which had become accustomed to the darkness, seemed to blur, the muted shades of the stained-glass windows turning into fuzzy smudges of color. The door opened and a dark presence filled the archway. Quinn squeaked in fear before realizing that she was looking at a police officer. The man knelt before her, his voice kind and soothing.

"Ms. Allenby, I am Detective Inspector Keane, and that's Detective Constable Hardy behind me. Now, you just remain where you are. The ambulance is on its way. Are you up to answering a few questions?" Quinn wanted to help the police but suddenly felt terribly sleepy. Her eyelids seemed to be weighted with lead, and the words no longer made sense, but the policeman kept talking to her.

"Stay with me. Don't go to sleep."

Quinn barely registered the other policeman who was already looking about the ransacked room. He didn't turn on the light but used his torch to assess the damage. He picked up an ebony statue Quinn had gotten as a Valentine's Day gift from Luke a few years back. It was a modern piece meant to represent mother and child. The figures flowed together and intertwined in a way that suggested that neither one could survive without the other. The statue was about two feet tall and made of solid wood.

"There's blood on this, sir," the constable said. "I think it was used to assault Ms. Allenby."

"Bag it and get it to Forensics. Maybe we can get some prints off it."

"Is there anyone I can call?" DI Keane asked as he bent over Quinn, his cool fingers on her wrist, checking her pulse. Somewhere in the distance Quinn could hear the wail of an ambulance, but it was muted, as if coming from underwater.

"Gabe," Quinn murmured. "In my phone." She hadn't spoken to Gabe since their ill-fated dinner, but at this moment, there was no one she'd rather have by her side. She had a few friends in the village, but she didn't want them fussing over her or blathering nonstop. Gabe was always good in a crisis—calm and in control.

"Right." DI Keane found Quinn's mobile and located Gabe's number. She heard him talking but barely registered the words. Her head felt as if someone had just taken an axe to it. A moment later, paramedics were hovering above her, taking her blood pressure and shining a light into her eyes. Quinn felt disoriented and confused. She hardly noticed when the two young men lifted her onto a gurney and wheeled her outside toward the waiting ambulance.

"You'll be all right, love," one of the paramedics said as he settled in next to her in the back of the ambulance. "It doesn't look too bad, but you'll still need a CAT scan to make sure there's no internal bleeding, and you can hardly stay in the house alone after what happened." He was an earnest young man with a thatch of ginger hair and clear blue eyes. He took her hand and held it as a gesture of comfort, which Quinn found oddly endearing. She hadn't realized it, but there were tears sliding down her cheeks, and the young man gently wiped them away with a crumpled tissue.

"My house," Quinn whispered, her voice watery with tears.

"Don't you worry. The police will secure your house. Everything will be all right. And your friend is on his way."

Quinn had tried valiantly to stay alert, but the swaying of the ambulance lulled her to sleep, and she finally gave up the fight. She closed her eyes and felt herself drifting away. It felt so liberating to just be and not worry about anything. There was still a nagging pain in her head, but it seemed to recede as she fell deeper asleep despite the paramedic's pleas to stay awake.

Quinn was startled by the bright lights of Casualty when she was wheeled in. She didn't want to go there; she only wanted to be left alone to sleep. She felt better, but now her head was pounding again, and her eyes teared up from the harsh fluorescent light. She shut them tight and remained that way until she was wheeled into a curtained-off alcove, where a nurse was ready to take charge.

Quinn endured what seemed like hours of poking, prodding, questions, and tests before being pronounced severely concussed. She'd grown agitated, and a mild sedative was administered, finally allowing her to sink into a deep sleep.

Chapter 26

It was hard to tell what time it was since the only light came from a bedside lamp. There were voices and sounds of activity, but they seemed muted, far away. Quinn's head ached and her limbs felt leaden, as if every ounce of energy had been sucked out of her. A bandage covered the wound inflicted by the statue, and an IV line snaked off the bed and toward the bag hanging off a metal stand. Quinn felt groggy and disoriented.

"Quinn? Are you awake?" A soft voice came from somewhere to her left. She turned her head a fraction and smiled despite the throbbing in her head. Gabe sat in a stiff plastic hospital chair, his disheveled appearance a testament to the fact that he took off as soon as he got the call. His shirt looked rumpled, and his jaw was shadowed by a day's growth of stubble. He looked tired and must have dozed off for a bit, but now he was leaning forward, watching her with a searching expression.

"How do you feel?"

"Like I've been hit over the head with an ebony statue," Quinn replied in a feeble attempt at humor. "I want to go home, Gabe."

"You can't go just yet, but I can get you a cup of tea if you like."

"Yes, please."

Gabe left and returned a few minutes later with a Styrofoam cup of sweet, milky tea. It wasn't strong enough, and the Styrofoam gave it a strange aftertaste, but Quinn drank it gratefully. Her mouth was dry, and her tongue felt unusually fuzzy.

A sudden unwelcome thought occurred to her as she handed the empty cup to Gabe.

"They haven't called my parents, have they?" she asked urgently. "I don't want them to worry."

"No, they haven't," Gabe replied, his tone soothing. "And they've secured your house."

"What?" Quinn asked as she gave Gabe the gimlet eye. "You are keeping something from me." He had that guilty look that she knew so well.

"It's nothing, really."

"If it was nothing you wouldn't try to avoid making eye contact with me, like you're doing this very minute."

Gabe held up his hands and smiled, caught out. "All right, but you won't be happy about this. There was a shooting in the village. Completely unrelated to your break-in, by all accounts, but there was a reporter here when you were brought in. He managed to snap a few photos and get the scoop. There might be something in the papers or online."

Quinn shrugged. This wasn't nearly as bad as what she expected. "Who in the world would care that my house was broken into? That's hardly newsworthy. I'm sure there are more important things to report. Who was shot?" she asked, concerned. She often went into the village and knew almost everyone, if only to say *hello* to.

"Some young punk. There was a dispute about a stolen car. He's in critical condition but is expected to make a full recovery. I don't think he's actually from the village. The lads were on their way from London to wherever they were going. The rest were arrested by DI Keane. He came to you straight after they were taken into custody. Busy night for the local constabulary."

Quinn nodded. Nothing ever happened in their little village. That's what she loved about it. This was practically a crime wave. Quinn sat up as DI Keane poked his head around the door.

"May I come in?" he asked and entered without waiting for an answer. He sank heavily into the other vacant chair. DI Keane looked exhausted, and no wonder: it had been a long night for him. Quinn felt comforted by his presence. He wasn't a particularly good-looking man. He was of average height but built like a prizefighter, his broad shoulders and well-muscled arms straining the fabric of his shirt. His hairline was receding, and he didn't look like the type of man who smiled easily, but there was something solid and warm about him, and Quinn knew that if push came to shove, she'd want DI Keane in her corner.

"How are you feeling, Dr. Allenby? I thought you looked familiar," he said, shaking his head in wonder. "Didn't make the connection until someone mentioned that you'd been on the telly. I quite enjoyed your documentary about that Roman soldier. Fascinating stuff. My son is obsessed with anything from that period, so we watched it together. He was very impressed with you, my Robbie."

"Thank you," Quinn said, smiling. "I'm glad you enjoyed it."

DI Keane nodded, his mind having already moved on to something else. "I'm told you will be discharged come morning. I just wanted to update you on the situation. We caught your intruders. Their mate was waiting for them down the lane in the getaway car, and they were speeding out of the village when they were stopped. All three are minors. We've recovered some jewelry and a few hundred quid. Your property will be returned to you after the hearing, but for the time being, it's state's evidence. One lad, Jimmy Barnes, sang like a canary when interviewed. He was more scared of facing his mother than of going to a juvenile detention facility."

"Was there any reason they targeted me?" Quinn asked. Her house was somewhat isolated, but she'd never had reason to be scared before.

"As it happens—yes," the policeman replied. "The lad's mother kept going on and on about that find down in Mayfair. Thought it was romantic. She mentioned that some items of jewelry were found with the skeletons. Seen it on the telly, I suppose. Seems our Jimmy is quite fond of history, particularly the Saxons, and got the idea in his head that the two skeletons were buried with grave goods which were now in your possession. He thought that if he and his mates got their hands on these items, they could sell them to a fence for a pretty penny. Jimmy didn't find what he came for, so he grabbed some of your jewelry instead, so as not to leave empty-handed." DI Keane shook his head in disgust. "He's the same age as my own boy. They were friends a few years back but grew apart. I know the family."

"You're only doing your job, Detective," Gabe said.

DI Keane nodded and rose to his feet. "Feel free to call me if you find that anything else is missing. I suspect you'll have to appear at the hearing, Dr. Allenby. Feel better," he added as he left.

"Grave goods—fancy that," Gabe remarked. "I'm almost surprised that a kid like that knows what grave goods are."

"Ah, the dangers of education," Quinn quipped.

"Do you still have the brooch and the buckle?" Gabe asked, suddenly worried.

"Yes. They're in my bag. I couldn't bear to be parted from them."

"You're getting too involved," Gabe observed.

Quinn smiled guiltily. "I can't help it. I've grown quite fond of Elise."

"I wish I could see what you see," Gabe said wistfully. "Will you tell me what happened to her?"

"Once I know the whole story."

Quinn was relieved when a few hours later, a young doctor came to tell her that she could go home. She checked Quinn's vital signs and took her blood pressure before signing the release.

"You're coming back to mine, and I will brook no argument," Gabe announced. "I will cook you a full English breakfast and make you watch TV until you're comatose with boredom."

"I'm comatose already, and you don't know how to cook."

"I can manage breakfast. Come." Gabe put his arm protectively about Quinn's shoulders, and she leaned against him. She was grateful that he hadn't mentioned their last meeting. What she needed right now was a friend, and Gabe was intuitive enough to understand that and let the other matter drop for the time being. Quinn was sure that the reprieve was temporary; Gabe wasn't the type of man to give up easily when he'd made up his mind to something.

"Gabe, I want to go home," Quinn said as they got into his car. "I thank you for coming, but I think I'd just like to be alone for a little while. The intruders have been caught, so I'm in no danger."

"All right," Gabe replied, his tone cool. He didn't appreciate being dismissed now that his services were no longer required. "I'll take you home. Are you sure you'll be all right?"

"Yes, I'm sure. I'll be fine. Really."

Gabe nodded as he pulled out of the car park. He remained silent on the ride back to Quinn's house and left as soon as he made sure that the house was in order and Quinn was able to lock the door behind him. Quinn leaned in to give him a kiss on the cheek, but Gabe took her by the shoulders and kissed her on the forehead in a fatherly fashion.

"Ring me if you need anything," he said before walking away. Quinn watched him through the open door, deeply aware of the rigid set of his shoulders and purposeful gait. He was hurt, and she was to blame. Quinn briefly considered calling out to him and asking him to come back, but she really did want to be alone. Or at least with someone who wasn't technically there. She wanted to be with Elise.

Chapter 27

March 1665

London, England

Elise took a shuddering breath as the boat glided toward the dock and came to a stop with a final splash of the oars. Her stomach heaved and she grabbed onto the sides of the boat and sucked in a breath of air in an effort to keep the bile from rising. This wasn't the sickness that had plagued her nearly every morning for the past two weeks—this was despair. The ferryman gave her an expectant look, and she handed over a coin and carefully stepped ashore.

"Mind how ye go," the man called after her, having noticed her pallor and unsteady gait. Elise gave him a wan smile, but he was already negotiating a new fare and forgot all about her.

It'd taken her nearly a fortnight to work up the courage to make this trip. Some part of her still hoped that things would miraculously work out, but she knew that was not possible. No matter how desperately she longed to get away and start a new life with Gavin, her conscience wouldn't allow it. Gavin deserved better than this, and so did her child. How could she deny it its legacy and condemn it to a life of financial struggle and obscurity? Gavin and the child were innocent of any wrongdoing—it was she who was tainted by deceit, and it was she who had to put an end to the dream.

Elise walked away from the river, determined not to lose her resolve. It was a beautiful March morning. Spring was in the air, and the tang of the river mingled with the smell of loamy earth, reminding her of the garden at her parents' house, where she used to sit on a bench on fine days and watch the Thames flow past. The sky was a pristine blue, and the sun, although still pale, now gave off some welcome warmth. The streets of Southwark bustled with activity, and no one paid any mind to a young woman walking alone. Elise decided that after her meeting with Gavin, she would go to her father's house. She longed to see Amy and Anne, and although her father would chastise her for coming alone, without so much as a maidservant to accompany her, she was willing to brave his anger if it earned her half an hour with the girls. But it would be even better if her father happened to be away from home. The thought of seeing him left Elise seething with a bitter anger that she wasn't accustomed to feeling toward her only living parent. She sighed with mounting misery. Today was going to be difficult, no matter what she encountered.

Elise approached Gavin's house and knocked on the door. Something about the place looked forlorn, not like before when it seemed quaint and welcoming. The shutters were open, but the windows were covered with a layer of grime, and there was rubbish strewn on the step. Elise waited a few moments, but there was no answer, so she knocked again. Then she suddenly remembered that Gavin would be at the Tabard Inn. She'd come a little later today, and Gavin would have already left for work. Elise retraced her steps and walked toward the inn. The place was surprisingly quiet. She supposed that those staying at the inn were still abed, sleeping off the aftereffects of strong drink consumed the night before. Southwark was known for base entertainments such as bear-baiting, gambling, and whoring. The Tabard Inn was more respectable than most, but men were men, no matter their station in life. They liked their pleasures.

Elise stopped in the courtyard and looked around. There were several doors, and she had no idea where Gavin might be. A young girl stepped outside carrying a bucket of slops from the kitchen. She stopped when she saw Elise and set the heavy bucket on the ground, taking the opportunity to tuck an escaped curl back into her cap.

"Ye lost?" she asked in a friendly tone, probably hoping for a quick chat before returning to her duties.

"I'm looking for someone. Gavin Talbot."

"Oh. Ye'd best speak to the landlord, then. He's just through yonder." The girl indicated a door to her left. "Doing 'is books, 'e is, so don't 'xpect 'im to be in good 'umor."

Elise thanked the girl and went in. She found herself in the taproom of the inn. It smelled of spilled ale and stale sweat. The polished bar gleamed in the dull sun streaming through the window, and rows upon rows of pewter tankards were lined on shelves behind the bar. The tables and chairs were all empty, save two. Two gentlemen sat in the corner drinking ale and partaking of a late breakfast of bread and cheese. They talked quietly but grew silent when they spotted Elise, their eyes drinking her in. One of the men gave her a welcoming smile, but she refused to meet his gaze and turned toward the other table.

A burly man sat alone, a ledger open in front of him and a quill suspended in his hand as he stared out the window thoughtfully. He wasn't wearing a wig, and his bald pate shone in the light, the skin as pink as that of a newborn babe. His belly protruded against his coat, and his calves looked like melons in a pair of mustard-colored hose.

"Are ye looking for employment?" he asked when he saw her standing there. "Can ye cook? I've enough serving wenches already." He opened his mouth to continue but seemed to realize that Elise was too finely dressed to be someone searching for a job in a tavern. The landlord leaned back in his chair, studying Elise with undisguised curiosity as he waited to hear the purpose of her visit.

"No, sir. I'm looking for Gavin Talbot. He works here," she replied timidly.

The man peered at her more closely. "Gavin, ye say? I hope ye're not in the family way, ducks," he added with a greasy smile. Elise balked. Why would he ask her that? Did Gavin have a reputation for getting girls with child?

The landlord pointed to a chair with his quill, inviting her to sit. Elise perched on the edge, her insides suddenly shaky. "Is Gavin here? I wish to speak to him."

"Gavin left a week ago. Sailed for Virginia," the man replied, watching her for a reaction.

"That can't be right," Elise protested. "He wasn't due to sail until the beginning of April. That's nearly two weeks away."

The landlord shook his large head. "Aye, that was his original intention, but he met a lady, our Gavin." The man looked at Elise with pity. "Had he promised ye something, ducky?"

"No, we are friends. I simply wanted to say good-bye and wish him a safe journey," Elise lied. She had no desire to tell this man the truth.

"Oh, well, that's all right, then. There was a wealthy tobacco plantation owner staying here with his daughter, awaiting passage to Virginia. Master Ambrose and his daughter wintered in England, visiting family in Kent. She is a comely thing but getting on in years, if ye take my meaning. Master Ambrose professed her to be twenty-two, but I think she were closer to twenty-five. That's quite an age for a woman," he added with an air of disapproval. "Another year or two and she'd be too old to bear children. The lass needed a husband, and the father needed an educated man to help him run his estate. Gavin fit the bill, so to speak. Once the old man dies, the girl's husband will inherit the lot."

"Did Gavin marry her?" Elise asked, shocked. This couldn't be right. What the landlord was suggesting was preposterous. Gavin made her a promise, had asked her to walk out on her marriage and sail to the Virginia with him. He wouldn't just leave her, having met a more attractive prospect. Not Gavin. He was an honorable man, a decent man.

"Master Ambrose was in a hurry to get back home and had no wish to wait three weeks for the banns to be called, so Gavin and Mistress Ambrose became betrothed with the intention of getting wed in Virginia. The proud papa even paid for Gavin's passage to the New World. And best of luck to them, I say. Seemed everyone got what they wanted."

"Did they?" Elise asked. Her voice shook with distress, but the landlord hardly noticed.

"Oh, aye. Gavin, he is a clever lad. Thought he'd marry the de Lesseps girl and be set for life, but wise Ol' Hugh sold the lass from under Gavin's nose. Married to some high-and-mighty lord, she is, and the other two are too young for marriage, so of no use to Gavin. No more than children, they are. I've no doubt Ol' Hugh will find them good matches in time. Why waste daughters on paupers when ye can marry them off to lords?"

The landlord guffawed with laughter at his own wit, doubly entertained by Elise's obvious shock. She felt as if she were going to be ill. "Thank you, s-sir," she stammered and fled the tavern. She needed fresh air. Elise ran for a few minutes until she was clear away from the Tabard and then stopped, gasping. She'd understood the words, but her mind still refused to accept their meaning. Gavin had become engaged to another and sailed off to Virginia without so much as a word of farewell. He told her he loved her, promised her a life and a future, and had cast her aside the moment something more lucrative came along. She had no right to judge him, she knew that, but he had no way of knowing that she was with child. She'd agreed to his proposal and had been eagerly awaiting their departure. Bitter tears spilled down Elise's cheeks as she imagined what finding out about Gavin's betrayal would have been like had she actually left home and come to him, expecting to start their life together. She'd agonized for weeks about her decision when there was no decision to be made—it had been made for her.

Elise felt hollow inside as she wiped the tears from her eyes and began to walk in the direction of her childhood home. The promise of seeing her sisters was the only thing that kept her from screaming like a wounded animal. Elise walked slowly, giving herself time to calm down. She couldn't show up at her father's house with puffy eyes and a red nose. She was Lady Asher, and she had to act the part, whether she liked it or not.

Elise slowly approached the house. Her heart leaped at the thought of seeing Amy and Anne, thoughts of Gavin pushed to the back of her mind for the moment to be retrieved and reexamined later. She missed the girls so much. They must have grown in the past few months, and they would have much to tell her. Elise was sure they'd be full of questions about her new life. The girls likely assumed, as anyone would, that she was a frequent visitor to the court of Charles II, being the wife of one of his favorites, but Elise's life was even more isolated now than it had been before she married. Elise approached the gate and gazed at the house. It looked just as it had before, solid and forbidding, but something seemed different. She couldn't quite figure out what.

Elise took a deep breath and knocked on the door, forcing herself to smile when it opened. An unfamiliar servant stared at her, waiting for her to speak. "I'm here to see Master de Lesseps. I'm Lady Asher."

The woman stepped aside and invited her in. "Ye'd best wait here, me lady," she said and disappeared down a passage, leaving Elise alone in the foyer. Elise stood still and listened. It was near noon. Her father always took his midday meal exactly at noon, and the girls were allowed to dine with him when there was no company expected. Elise would hear their voices and would smell roasting meat and baking bread. Her father liked meat at midday but often preferred to eat a lighter meal in the evening due to digestive problems. Sometimes he had nothing more than a bowl of broth and a slice of bread before going to bed.

Elise was surprised to see an older gentleman appear at the end of the passage. He was tall and stooped, with a dark, curly wig that fell way past his shoulders and yellow hose that drew attention to his long shanks and surprisingly large feet. He stopped in front of her and gave a stiff bow. "Lady Asher. A surprise indeed."

"Pardon me, but who are you, sir?" Elise asked. "Is my father all right?"

The man looked at Elise with an expression of utter astonishment. His feathery eyebrows seemed to disappear beneath the curls of his wig, making Elise suddenly weak in the knees. "Jonathan Collins, at your service," he announced, bowing stiffly over Elise's hand. "My dear lady, I can't imagine that your father hasn't told you. You must have forgotten. He sailed for the West Indies at the beginning of the month."

When Elise remained silent the man continued, "Surely you recall."

"I'm afraid I don't. When is he expected back? Did my sisters go with him?"

"He is not coming back, my lady," Master Collins replied. "He sold the house to me just after the New Year."

Elise felt as if she were going to faint. How could this be? How could her father just leave, and why? If he sold the house just after the New Year, he must have been planning his departure at the time of Elise's betrothal. He hadn't said a word. Could it be that his financial situation had been even more dire than he allowed her to believe?

"Would you like to sit down?" Master Collins asked. "Please, allow me to offer you some refreshment."

Elise nodded her thanks, and the man invited her into the parlor. "Do any of the old servants still work here?" she asked as she took a seat by the hearth, glad to feel the warmth of the fire on her ice-cold hands.

"Yes, I retained most of the old staff, with the exception of the lady's maid. I have no wife or daughters."

So, Rose is gone, Elise thought, hoping that Rose was given a glowing reference and some monetary compensation after years of service.

"Is Grace still here?"

Master Collins shook his head and spread his hands in ignorance, indicating that he couldn't be bothered with knowing the whereabouts of former servants.

"May I speak to Jasper then, Master Collins?"

"The groom? That's most irregular, madam."

"Please. I would be much obliged," Elise pleaded, bestowing her most radiant smile on the old man. Jasper would hardly have been in her father's confidence, but if anyone knew anything it would be him. Jasper was tall, fair, handsome, and the darling of all the servant girls. They told him everything that went on in the house, and he gleaned a thing or two on his own from frequenting the taverns. Jasper liked information and often made use of it in ways Elise didn't approve. She would never have known this for herself, but Gavin often told her not to say anything in front of Jasper since, if he had proof of their affection for each other, he might blackmail them to keep their secret.

Jasper entered the room a few minutes later, hat in hand, eyes glued to Elise. He looked subservient enough, but Elise could see a glint of amusement in his eyes as he looked at her. Master Collins excused himself, giving them a moment to talk in private.

"Hello, Jasper," Elise said with a smile. She didn't like the man, but she needed his help.

"Good day, Lady Asher. How may I be of service to ye?"

"Jasper, why did my father leave?" she asked without preamble. There was no point beating about bush. Jasper would either know, or he wouldn't.

"I wouldn't rightly know, yer ladyship," Jasper replied smoothly.

"Jasper, I have it on good authority that you know more than most."

"I can't imagine who'd say such a thing," Jasper replied, a small smile playing about his lips. Elise saw his gaze stray to the small silk reticule in her hands.

She took out a coin and held it up. The sum was more than Jasper would earn in a month. "Will you tell me now?"

"Certainly, yer ladyship." Jasper reached for the coin, but Elise pulled her hand back. She wanted the information first.

"If I don't believe you, I won't pay," Elise said sternly, although she knew that Jasper had the upper hand.

Jasper inclined his head in acknowledgement. "The master was in financial difficulty, as I am sure ye know," he said, giving her a shrewd look meant to remind her of her own hasty marriage.

"Property values in Southwark have gone up, so 'e decided to sell the lot and journey to the West Indies plantation, where 'e intended to invest the money in buying more slaves and then selling them on in the American colonies for a handsome profit."

"And my sisters?"

Jasper looked at Elise in some surprise. "They left with 'im, of course."

"Is that all?"

Jasper stepped from foot to foot, debating whether to tell her what she wanted to know. "Amy is to wed a plantation owner. The match was arranged by yer brother."

"But she is only fourteen," Elise gasped.

Jasper shrugged. He didn't care about Amy's fate any more than he cared about hers. Elise handed over the coin and rose to leave.

"Won't you have some spiced wine, Lady Asher?" Master Collins asked as he rejoined them.

"Thank you, but I really must be on my way. My husband will be worried," she added for good measure. She had no explanation for coming to call unaccompanied, and she assumed Master Collins surmised that her husband had no inkling of where she was. The sooner she returned to Asher Hall, the better.

"Jasper, see Lady Asher home," Jonathan Collins ordered.

"Really, there's no need," Elise protested. The last thing she wanted was to spend the next half hour in the company of the smarmy Jasper, but she could see in Master Collins's steely gaze that resistance was futile.

"There's every need. Please, I insist."

"Thank you, Master Collins."

The man bowed over her hand and wished her well, instructing Jasper to take the carriage to the river bank rather than going on foot. Elise was grateful of the offer. She was exhausted and emotionally overwrought. She'd braced herself for an unpleasant day, but she'd never expected this. Not only had she been left behind and betrayed by the people she cared about, but she was now completely on her own, with no one but her husband to care for her. The thought made her snort with the irony of it. Jasper threw her a look of disapproval, but she didn't care. His opinion was the least of her problems.

Chapter 28

November 2013

Surrey, England

Quinn awoke later than usual. Midmorning sun shone through the stained-glass windows of her bedroom and filled the room with a colorful glow. Birds chirped happily outside, and the wind moved through the trees, the leaves rustling as they fell from the branches and twirled silently to the ground, covering the grass with a blanket of autumnal color. The room was chilly, but Quinn was warm beneath her down quilt. Her head still ached, but she felt much better. She'd tidied up the house before going to bed—against doctor's orders, of course, but she couldn't bring herself to leave things as they were. It was too upsetting to see her private papers and possessions strewn all over the floor. A few things were broken, but thankfully, nothing truly important—like her laptop—had been damaged.

Quinn held the ebony statue in her hands for a long time, marveling at the fact that something so beautiful and innocent could have unwittingly become a murder weapon. She knew enough about human anatomy to realize that had the blow landed about an inch lower and struck her temple, she might have been killed outright. The interesting thing about the possibility of her untimely demise was that it made her feel giddy with the joy of living. Quinn got out of bed, took a hot shower, and dressed in a new outfit, putting it together from the items she bought from Jill's shop. She liked the way the vintage jeans fit her hips, and the peasant blouse brought out the green in her eyes. Quinn carefully lifted the corner of the bandage to see if she might be able to remove it. The wound didn't look too bad, so she pulled off the plaster and replaced it with a much smaller one from her medicine cabinet. She even applied a bit of makeup to make herself feel better and twisted her hair into an artful bun atop her head.

Quinn was just making some toast and tea when there was an insistent knock at the door. She frowned. She wasn't expecting anyone, and the only person who would show up at her door this morning would be Gabe. Quinn wiped her hands on a tea towel and went to answer the door.

"I'm sorry to come unannounced. Terribly rude of me, I know," Rhys said with a guilty smile. "But I heard about what happened and needed to see for myself that you were all right."

Quinn stepped aside to let him in. "Did Gabe tell you?" she asked, annoyed with Gabe for calling Rhys. She was quite all right; there was no reason whatsoever to alert anyone.

"No," Rhys replied sheepishly. "I saw it on the news."

"What?" Quinn gasped. "I'm on the news?"

"Yes. '*Historian attacked when she walked in on a robbery,*'" Rhys quoted.

Quinn nodded in disgust. "I might have known. There was a reporter at the hospital last night—for an entirely different case, mind you. I feel strangely violated," Quinn joked. "It seems odd that strangers know what happened to me."

"That's life in the public eye for you," Rhys replied as he shrugged off his jacket.

"I'm hardly in the public eye. I'm a historian, for God's sake."

"Get used to it. Once our program is aired, you'll get a lot more attention than you ever expected. Believe it or not, people lap this stuff up. '*History made real, the dead brought back to life,*'" he intoned, using an announcer voice that made Quinn laugh.

Rhys handed her a shopping bag. "Here, I brought you something to make you feel better. I know I promised not to force-feed you cake, but I think you'll like these. I made them this morning just for you."

Quinn pulled out a square plastic container out of the shopping bag and stared at the bell-shaped blobs of dough. "What are these?"

"Canelés. They're French. Caramelized crust on the outside, chewy on the inside, with just a small dollop of custard filling," he said, somehow making the description sound seductive. "I dare you to resist."

"You truly are evil," Quinn replied with a chuckle as she opened the container and inhaled the heavenly smell. "Are you trying to make me fat?"

"No, I'm trying to give you a moment of pleasure," he replied, all innocence. "And if you don't want to get fat, come for a walk with me. It's a lovely day outside. I've never been here before, so you can show me around the village. Was this a church?" he asked with some surprise as he gazed up at the vaulted ceiling and stained-glass windows.

"It was a private chapel a few centuries back. Now, it's my home, and I love it," Quinn said proudly. "There's such . . ."

"Peace," Rhys finished for her. "It just envelops you, doesn't it?"

"Yes."

"Will you show me the rest?" he asked.

Quinn was glad she'd made the bed before getting into the shower. She led Rhys into the bedroom, watching his expression of delight.

"It's breathtaking," he said as he took in the massive four-poster bed and the heavy carved armoire. "Simply stunning. It's like walking into another century. No television?" he asked as he looked around.

"No, I don't actually own a television. I do have electric lights and running water, but those are my only concessions to modernity. I like the ancient feel of this place, and I don't wish to spoil it. If I want to watch something, I watch it on my laptop."

"It really is beautiful. The candles are a nice touch," he added, referring to two massive candles in tall, medieval stands on either side of the bed.

The kettle began to whistle, and they returned to the main room, where Quinn poured them tea. She reached for a canelé and took an experimental bite. "Oh my God," she murmured with her mouth still full. "This is delicious."

"I know," Rhys replied with a satisfied grin. "My specialty. I make them only for the most deserving people."

"Flatterer."

"Guilty as charged. Now, pass me one of those."

Quinn laughed and passed him the container. She suddenly realized that she felt happy and light despite everything that happened the previous night. Gabe's presence had been comforting and reassuring, but there'd been a spark of tension between them. Gabe had made it clear that he no longer wished to be just friends, and Quinn felt cornered by his sudden intensity. She was flattered by Rhys's attention, but they didn't know each other well enough to have any expectations of each other, and it felt good just to spend time with him without feeling as if an answer were expected.

"Take a coat," Rhys said as they got ready to leave. "It's chilly outside."

"You sound like my mother," Quinn protested but reached for her leather jacket and wound a colorful scarf around her neck.

They walked at a leisurely pace down the lane and toward the village. The air was crisp and fresh. Leaves fluttered and twirled in the wind, slowly falling to the ground in front of their feet. A cool sun held court in the cloudless sky but didn't provide much warmth, and Quinn was glad that she'd listened to Rhys and taken a jacket.

"Did you grow up around here?" Rhys asked as he admired the pastoral views.

"No, my family lived near Lincoln, but I no longer consider it my home. Not since my parents left. I have a cousin who lives in London. She recently opened a vintage clothing shop," Quinn said. "She was in corporate accounting for years and then just up and left."

"There's always a fork in the road," Rhys replied. "You know when you reach it, but sometimes you're just not ready to choose. I guess your cousin took the right path."

"Yes. She's not turning much of a profit yet, but she is so happy. She even looks different." Jill had gone from wearing suits and a neat bob to wearing colorful kaftans and letting her hair grow. When Quinn visited her, she had it up in two buns on top of her head with several long tendrils framing her face. She looked like a teenager, but the style suited her.

"Have you reached a fork in the road?" Quinn asked.

"Not yet, but it is coming," he replied cryptically.

"I can't say that I know what you mean. I've always known what I wanted to do, and I'm doing it. I love it—every moment of it. I never want to do anything else."

"Then you are one of the luckiest people I know."

"I've never thought of myself as being particularly lucky, but I suppose you're right," Quinn replied.

"Most people spend their lives working at jobs that bring them no satisfaction, but they have too many responsibilities and too much fear to chuck it all in and pursue something they love."

"Not everything you love can be turned into a career," Quinn replied. "Don't you love what you do?"

Rhys shrugged. "I love stories and films, but once you see everything that goes on behind the camera, you can never recapture the romance of the dream of making movies. It's all about budgets, backers, temperamental actors, unions, and fickle audiences. A truly beautiful, emotional story can never hope to have the commercial success of a film based on a Marvel comic, and that saddens me. That's why I like working at BBC. We still produce quality television, or so I like to think."

"So, you are not courting any offers from Hollywood?" Quinn asked with a smile.

"God, no. I'm here to stay—at least for now."

"Come, I'll show you the St. Peter and Paul church," she said as they entered the village. "It's quite interesting. There's been a church on this site as far back as Saxon times, even before the Norman conquest. Of course, there's practically nothing left of the original church except for a few blocks of stone in the foundation. The current structure dates back to Tudor times."

Quinn took Rhys by the hand and pulled him along since he seemed to be hesitating. He'd been about to say something but changed his mind. They walked up the path toward the church, which sat squat and solid amid the ancient graves, its tower piercing the sky. Even on a sunny day like today, the church looked dour, its gray stone unchanged by sunshine nor enlivened by the foliage of the surrounding trees. There was something timeless and forbidding about the structure, almost as if it had made up its mind to withstand any turmoil or shifts in views and morality that had undermined the Church over the centuries.

Quinn only attended church on Christmas these days, more interested in festive ritual and feeling of belonging to a community than any type of communion with God, but she felt a proprietary pride in the ancient structure and was eager to show Rhys the interior. As a lover of history, there were a few points of interest he was sure to appreciate.

As they approached the church porch, Quinn noticed a woman standing beneath a yew tree. She was gazing up at the church, her expression so wistful that it nearly broke Quinn's heart. Maybe someone she loved was buried in the churchyard, or perhaps she was in sore need of divine intervention but didn't feel up to actually going inside and asking for it. She'd never seen the woman in the village before, but that didn't mean she didn't live there. The woman seemed startled when she saw Quinn and Rhys approaching, her eyes boring into Quinn in a manner bordering on rudeness. Quinn felt the woman's gaze follow her as she preceded Rhys into the church. She was grateful to step inside, hoping that the woman wouldn't follow. Her intensity was unsettling.

She was gone by the time Quinn and Rhys came back out a half hour later.

Chapter 29

Quinn was in much better spirits by the time Rhys left in the late afternoon. He'd walked her to the door but declined her invitation to stay for dinner, claiming that he already had plans in London, which was just as well. The time they spent together felt almost like a date, so Quinn was relieved when he said good-bye, kissed her on the cheek, and headed back to town. She liked him enormously and felt at ease in his company, but she had no wish to send any misleading signals.

The few hours she spent with him distracted her from thoughts of Elise, and more importantly, Gabe. If she didn't tread carefully, she'd lose Gabe for good, and her resolution not to get romantically involved with him in order not to risk their friendship now seemed pointless. She wasn't ready to face her feelings for him just yet, but deep down she knew that Gabe was the person her soul instinctively reached out to. Whenever she was worried, elated, or simply in need of a chat, it was Gabe she longed to talk to, to share with. She'd realized over the past two weeks that she hardly thought of Luke. She missed him from time to time, simply because they'd spent eight years together and he'd been intricately woven into the fabric of her life, but it was Gabe she most often turned to when she needed a friend. Luke could be dismissive and aloof when preoccupied with his own thoughts, but Gabe always found the time to listen and to help Quinn work things out without actually telling her what to do, the way Luke frequently did when his patience ran out.

Quinn shrugged off her coat, put the kettle on, and studied the contents of her fridge. She wasn't hungry enough to make a large meal, but she was feeling peckish and a little light-headed. Perhaps an omelet with fontina cheese and mushrooms. It was quick and easy. She was suddenly tired. Perhaps she'd overdone it a bit so soon after her injury. Quinn whipped up her omelet, made a piece of toast, and retreated to the sofa to enjoy her meal. She'd make a fire later, but for the moment, she felt too worn out.

As Quinn popped a forkful of fluffy egg into her mouth, she suddenly wondered about Rhys's private life. He didn't wear a wedding ring, and she was fairly certain that he wasn't married, but that didn't mean he was single. A man in Rhys's line of work probably met many interesting women. She'd felt a frisson of attraction on his part, but perhaps he was naturally flirtatious and attentive to all women. It'd been a long time since she was single, and the rules of the game had certainly changed since she was twenty-two. She'd found other men attractive, of course, but had never allowed her thoughts to stray any further, her loyalty only to Luke. Now she was single for the first time in nearly a decade, and she was no longer the starry-eyed girl who'd been easily seduced by good looks and a veneer of charm. She'd have to get out there whether she liked it or not.

Quinn was distracted from her thoughts by the ringing of the phone. She set aside her plate and went to retrieve her mobile. She'd left it on the nightstand and now noticed that she had seven missed calls.

"Quinn. Where've you been? I was about to come down there to see if you're all right," Gabe chastised her. "You should be taking things easy."

"I walked to the village with Rhys. Sorry, I forgot my phone," she replied in a conciliatory manner, but this was clearly the wrong thing to tell Gabe.

"Rhys was there?" Gabe demanded, his tone suddenly cool.

"Yes. He came by to see if I was all right and brought me canelés. He likes to bake," Quinn added lamely.

"Does he, now?"

"Gabe, what exactly are you upset about?" Quinn demanded, going on the offensive. She hadn't done anything wrong, and Gabe's ill-disguised jealousy was unnerving.

"Nothing. Never mind. Glad you're OK. I'll ring you tomorrow morning."

"I'm coming to London tomorrow. I plan to visit several churches in Mayfair. I'm going to look through their archives for any mention of Elise."

"Want some company? I have the morning off," Gabe suggested eagerly, his earlier pique forgotten. Gabe liked nothing more than doing research, especially if it culminated in a nice pub lunch.

Quinn actually cringed before answering. "Rhys is coming with me. He didn't think I should be wandering about on my own after being hit on the head."

"Right." Gabe growled. "I guess I'll see you when I see you." And with that, he hung up.

Quinn replaced the phone on the bedside table and returned to the living room. Her earlier good mood had dissipated, leaving her tense and upset. A part of her wished that Gabe was coming with her tomorrow so that they could recapture their easy camaraderie and delve into this project together as they had so often done in the past, but a part of her was annoyed with his attitude. He had no right to be angry, nor did he have any cause to feel threatened by Rhys Morgan.

Rhys's canelés still sat on the table, their aroma enticing Quinn to eat one. She was normally very strict about what she ate, but she felt she deserved a treat to lift her spirits. She reached for a canelé and took a bite, savoring it. She couldn't help smiling at the thought of Rhys baking these for her. He really was something of an enigma.

Chapter 30

May 1665

London, England

"Wakey, wakey," Lucy sang as she drew apart the bed hangings and flooded the previously dark space with bright spring sunshine. Lucy looked annoyingly chipper, which made Elise want to bury her head beneath the blankets and stay that way until the girl went away.

"I ain't leaving till ye get out of bed, wash, dress, and come down to break yer fast," Lucy said, her tone bossy.

Elise didn't bother to argue. It was pointless. Lucy wouldn't go away. She would just stand there, talking to her, until Elise was unable to go back to sleep, as she longed to do. The past few months had seen a change in her. A deep melancholy had taken hold, shackling Elise to her disappointment and grief. Lucy thought it was the pregnancy that was making Elise so tired and listless, but Elise didn't believe it was. What she felt was utter despair. She had no reason to get out of bed. What was the point of planning meals that no one would eat or dressing in gowns no one would see?

Elise spent her days in near solitude, her only company being the servants and Barbara, who hardly spoke and gazed off into the distance with a half-smile on her face, as if there was something beautiful just beyond the window that no one but she could see. Elise had tried to engage Barbara in conversation and cajoled her to take walks in the garden from time to time, but Barbara, although compliant, never left the confines of her own world, leaving Elise as miserably alone in hers as ever. Elise hardly saw Edward these days, but it didn't matter. They lived separate lives, and now that she was with child, he hardly noticed her, other than to ask after her health. She always told him that she was well, which effectively put an end to the conversation. And she was well, physically. It was her heart that needed healing.

Gavin was gone. Her family was gone. And even James was gone. Elise discovered that she missed him. James hadn't been much of a talker, but she missed his touch. He had been the only person to show her physical affection, but now even that was over. She supposed they'd developed a certain unspoken bond during the months before she conceived. He never spoke to her of his feelings or thoughts, but their lovemaking had changed over time. It had become tender, and more pleasurable for them both, although neither of them would ever admit to it. Elise found that she missed the feel of him inside her and the weight of his body as he lay on top of her and gazed into her eyes. He never uttered any words of love, but she could see in the depth of those gray eyes that he wasn't indifferent to her. They'd grown fond of each other without ever saying a word. And the secret of Harry's final resting place was something that they now shared, something that bound them in a conspiracy of silence.

Elise reluctantly sat at the dressing table and closed her eyes, refusing to meet her own scornful gaze in the mirror. She couldn't bear to see her reflection; she didn't recognize the person staring back. Her hair was tangled from tossing and turning during the night, but Lucy did her best not to hurt her as she pulled the brush through the thick mane and dressed it for the day, forgoing the elaborate hairstyles favored by the ladies of the court and just winding the hair into a bun at the back of Elise's head with a few playful curls left to frame her face. The simple style made Elise look more mature, like a married lady soon to be a mother rather than the girl she'd been only a few months prior. It was fitting. That girl was gone.

Elise placed her right palm against her belly, as she did every morning. She was hardly showing, but there was a tiny bump beneath her nightdress—just a slight swelling, almost as if she'd eaten too much. It was difficult to imagine that a human being was growing inside her. She didn't feel anything, not even the sickness that other women complained of in the early stages of pregnancy. Her mother had been terribly unwell when pregnant with Anne, retching into a bucket every morning, and, at times, well into the afternoon. But Elise felt like her usual self. Her breasts were a bit tender, and she got terribly hungry between meals, but otherwise, she felt no change. *What if it had all been a mistake, and I'm not pregnant after all?* she wondered. But she hadn't had her courses in three months now, so it had to be true.

Elise sighed. She tried not to dwell on her hurt, but every morning the misery assaulted her afresh. She'd put her trust in the men in her life, and they had all betrayed her. Her father sold her in marriage and left the country, Gavin had sworn his love then married another, and James had abandoned her to her fate. Did he not care about the child she carried? He might have done his father's bidding, but somewhere deep inside he had to have some feelings about the coming babe. It was his, after all. He'd been gone since the very day she discovered she was pregnant, and there had been complete silence since.

"How about the green gown today?" Lucy asked once she finished coifing Elise's hair. "Ye look ever so lovely in that shade. Shall I fetch it for ye?"

"It doesn't matter," Elise sighed. "I'll wear whatever gown you choose, Lucy."

"Come now. Ye must take care. A lady should always look her best."

"For whom?" Elise demanded. "There's no one here."

"Still, ye must do it for yerself. How about a walk in the garden after breakfast? That'll lift your spirits, I wager. 'Tis a beautiful morning, and mayhap Lady Barbara will join ye. She likes looking at the flowers."

"All right," Elise conceded. A walk did sound good. It was a beautiful, sunny day outside, and the prospect of getting out of this tomb of a house was suddenly very appealing.

"Ah, there ye go," Lucy cackled. "I see a ghost of a smile. I know I do. Just let me finish my chores, and I'll come with ye. His lordship said ye're not to go out alone."

"What, even to the garden?" Elise gasped. Did he know that she used the garden gate to slip out when she went to Southwark, or was he afraid that, given half a chance, she'd throw herself into the river? *He probably wouldn't care if I did, as long as I gave birth to a son first,* Elise thought bitterly.

"Now, now," Lucy chided as she watched Elise's expression in the looking glass. "No feeling sorry for yerself. Ye are young, beautiful, and wealthy. Life won't always be like this. Ye'll see. Things have a way of changing when ye least expect them, they do," she added wisely. "Me mam always said that the good Lord loves us the most when we are at our lowest."

Elise threw Lucy an amused look. "I must have a ways to go yet since the good Lord seems to take no interest in me."

"Don't blaspheme, me lady. The good Lord knows all, and he won't let ye down."

Elise chose not to point out that the good Lord let down countless people every single day. He wasn't there for the women who died in childbirth, the children who died before reaching adulthood. Nor was he there for the countless men who died on battlefields or the streets of the city from disease, hunger, or work accidents. And he certainly wasn't there for her.

Elise allowed Lucy to finish dressing her and made her way downstairs, where she ate a solitary breakfast of buttered bread and ale. She barely tasted what she ate. She had no desire for food this morning, but the babe was hungry, so she had to eat.

Chapter 31

By the time Elise returned to the house, she felt marginally better. They'd spent an hour in the garden, and despite her sour mood, the sight of colorful blooms and the heady fragrance of primroses lifted her spirits. Barbara drifted off to the parlor as soon as they came back in, intent on returning to her crewelwork, but Elise decided to stop by the kitchen for a cool drink. She was suddenly very thirsty. Elise walked along the passage, acutely aware of the silence enveloping the house. The only place bustling with activity was the kitchen, where Cook and several kitchen maids worked all day long to bake bread, roast meat, and prepare numerous side dishes that were hardly touched unless Edward came home. She supposed the servants ate well these days since all the leftovers went straight back to the kitchen for their own dinner.

Elise stopped just outside the kitchen when she heard Cook's cry of dismay. She sounded unusually upset, her voice trembling with unchecked panic. She was normally a level-headed woman who ran her kitchen as a captain would his ship, so her distress was alarming.

"We must double our order of flour. Or even triple it. We don't know 'ow long it'll last this time," Cook exclaimed. "And take stock of all our stores."

"Come now, Bess, don't ye despair. We've weathered it afore, and we will again," a calm male voice said. It was the gardener, Cook's husband, who'd come in for a cup of ale before returning to his work.

"Nay, John, I refuse to sit idly by," Cook screeched. "We ought to prepare. There've already been several deaths in St. Giles,

St. Clement Danes, and St. Andrew. A dwellin' 'ad been sealed up in St. Giles, but a riot broke out, and they freed the condemned, those soft-'earted fools. Don't they know what will 'appen?" Cook wailed.

"Bess, this 'appens every year," her husband tried to soothe her. "We are safe 'ere in 'is lordship's 'ouse. 'Tis the poor that 'ave to worry, living in such close quarters as they do. We're well removed from the city gates and slums."

"Not far enough," Cook retorted. "What'ya think, ye daft fool, that no people of quality die from the plague? Why, the king himself could be in danger. 'E'll be off to the country, ye mark my words, leaving the common folk to die."

Cook sounded quite hysterical, and Elise was suddenly no longer thirsty. She turned and fled, going back up to her bedroom. This was terrible news indeed. She'd been so wrapped up in her own feelings that she hadn't paid much heed to what was happening outside. There were deaths from the plague every year, but having lived in Southwark, Elise and the rest of the family felt relatively safe. The first plague deaths each year were reported in areas close to the docks, having been brought to London aboard ships from Europe. Measures, in the form of a quarantine, had been instituted by the Privy Council. Ships from infected areas were required to dock at Hole Haven at Canvey Island for a period of forty days before entering the Thames Estuary. Only ships with a certificate of health were allowed to proceed upriver, and they had to pass another checkpoint at Tilbury or Gravesend.

Elise could understand Cook's distress, but she thought the older woman was overreacting. Most deaths occurred in poor, overcrowded areas where people lived in squalor and filth. Those areas were found closest to the city gates and beyond city limits, in the Liberties. They were quite safe here; there was no need for panic. Besides, Edward was always at Whitehall Palace. He was privy to the latest news and would look after them should the need arise.

    Elise kicked off her shoes and crawled into bed. Sunlight flooded the room, but she didn't bother to draw the bed hangings. She was suddenly very tired and was asleep within minutes.

Chapter 32

November 2013

London, England

Quinn got off the tube at Charing Cross Station and walked briskly toward St. Martin-in-the-Fields, where Rhys was due to meet her at ten. She'd considered if it was worth visiting a few other churches in the area just to give Rhys the impression that she was searching for a needle in a haystack, but she dismissed the idea. If Elise lived at Asher Hall, as all evidence suggested, then it stood to reason that she would have attended St. Martin-in-the-Fields, as it was the only church in the area at the time. Several other parishes were created later on in the seventeenth century to relieve the overcrowding, but that would have happened after Elise's death. St. Martin's had been enlarged and beautified during the reign of James I, and it would have been the church Elise was married in and attended until her untimely death.

The grandiose building that towered over Trafalgar Square was not the original church of St. Martin. There had been a church on the site as far back as medieval times, but the neoclassical building that graced the square now had been built in the eighteenth century. The church Elise attended would have been the one built during the reign of Henry VIII with the intention of diverting plague victims away from Whitehall Palace. The Tudor building was constructed of brick and decorated with stone facings. It boasted a tall tower with buttresses that could be seen for miles. At the time of construction, the area was quite literally a field between the cities of London and Westminster, hence the name St. Martin-in-the-Fields.

Quinn ascended the steps and smiled at Rhys, who was leaning against a column, hands in his pockets as he watched her approach. He had a knack for looking casual and elegant at the same time, a trick that few men mastered. Gabe always looked a bit disreputable, no matter how much effort he put in. He joked that it was the dark stubble that shadowed his jaw by midmorning and made him look slightly piratical, a genetic "gift" from the Norman ancestors whose portraits graced the gallery of his family home.

"I'd nearly given up on you," Rhys said as she gave him a peck on the cheek.

"I'm only ten minutes late," Quinn protested, glancing at her watch.

"I know. Just teasing. Shall we go in?"

They walked into the building and instantly lowered their voices so as not to disturb the solemn hush of the church. There was no service in progress, but at least two dozen tourists milled about, taking pictures and craning their necks to admire the soaring ceiling illuminated by chandeliers suspended by cables at equal intervals. Unlike most churches, this building was filled with space and light, and it could have just as easily been used as a palace instead of a place of worship.

"So, you think this would have been the church Lord Asher attended?" Rhys asked as his eyes scanned the stunning interior.

"It would have to be, although, of course, it wouldn't have been this modern incarnation of the building. Everyone in his household would have attended it as well, unless they were Catholic, but given the jewelry we found and quality of the gown, the servants are of no interest to us. What we are looking for is anyone from the Asher family. The woman might have been his wife, or his daughter," Quinn added.

"How do you know he had a daughter?" Rhys asked, intrigued.

"I don't. I'm only suggesting that it's possible," Quinn improvised. She'd have to be more careful. She knew much about the Asher household from her visions, but ninety percent of what she had gleaned wasn't supported by any historical data. She'd done extensive research on Lord Asher but found only a few mentions of his name in relation to the Privy Council. What she needed was personal information, but Edward Asher had been a courtier—a man largely forgotten by history.

"I think this is a long shot, actually," Quinn said as they proceeded down the nave. "The records from the seventeenth century are likely no longer kept here, but I thought we'd ask."

Rhys stopped to admire the ceiling while Quinn approached a woman in her thirties wearing a clerical collar.

"Hello, I'm Dr. Allenby, and that's my colleague, Rhys Morgan. I was wondering if we might have a look at the archives. We are researching an individual who might have attended this parish in the mid-seventeenth century."

The woman smiled pleasantly. "We do keep some records here, but they date from the twentieth century until the present. All the parish records from the seventeenth century have been moved to the City of Westminster Archive at 10 St. Anne Street," the vicar replied. "We have so many people stopping by who are in search of their family history. I do wish we could be of more help."

"You have been. Thank you very much."

**

"Phew, I'm done in," Quinn said as she closed a dusty parish register several hours later. "But I'm glad we got something." She slammed her notebook shut with finality, stowed it in her bag and rose to her feet, easing her back.

"I'm starving," Rhys announced.

"Why am I not surprised?" Quinn laughed.

"Oh, come now, we've been at it for hours. Let's go get some lunch."

"All right," Quinn conceded. "I suppose I could eat."

They walked to Osteria Dell'Angolo a few blocks away—Rhys's suggestion. Rhys leaned back in his chair after they placed their order and studied Quinn across the table, his expression inquisitive. He looked as if he was about to say something, but he remained silent instead, waiting for her to speak. Quinn noticed that he did that from time to time, silently manipulating his companion into filling the void. It was a good way of getting people to talk, and Rhys liked information.

"Why are you looking at me that way?" Quinn asked. She felt disconcerted by his intense stare. It wasn't unfriendly, just full of expectation.

"There's something you are not telling me," Rhys informed her.

"Like what?"

"I don't know. You tell me."

"I'm not sure I follow," Quinn countered.

"Quinn, I watched you go through those registers. You weren't just searching, you were looking for something specific."

"Of course I was. I was looking for any mention of Lord Edward Asher."

"It wasn't him you were interested in. You were looking for a particular name. You came across a record of his first marriage and the baptism of his daughter, but you barely glanced at those. You kept searching, and you found the person you'd been looking for. Elise. How did you know her name?"

"Are you always this irritatingly observant?" Quinn asked in an effort to hide her discomfort. He'd noticed. She tried not to be too obvious, but her delight at finding Elise's name in the parish register had been difficult to hide. She'd given herself away.

"You know, I think I'd like a glass of wine after all," Quinn said, looking around for the waiter who seemed to have vanished when she needed him most.

"Don't change the subject."

"Was I?"

"Obvious tactic," Rhys joked. "Please, tell me."

"I'd rather not." Quinn looked away, unable to meet his steady gaze. She'd kept her secret for so long, but suddenly she longed to tell him the truth. He didn't seem like the type of person who'd make her feel foolish and ashamed of her gift.

"Quinn?" Rhys prompted.

"It's complicated," she mumbled, still hesitant to share with him. Rhys might find it fascinating, or he might immediately dismiss the possibility that her gift was real and relegate her to the category of a cheap charlatan who tried to capitalize on something she'd invented in her mind and was foolish enough to actually believe in. When faced with something otherworldly, most people were skeptical at best, filled with derision and disbelief at worst.

"What is it? What are you hiding?" Rhys persisted.

Quinn finally looked up to find Rhys's gray eyes watching her. He reached across the table and took her hand in his.

"Quinn, why won't you tell me how you know? It's not as if you're psychic. You found a reference to her somewhere."

Quinn laughed nervously. "You see, the thing is that I am."

"You are what?"

"Psychic. I've never really told anyone. Gabe knows, but I never even told Luke, my boyfriend. I thought he'd laugh at me. He was ever so much the scientist."

Rhys shrugged. "I won't laugh at you. I know there are a lot of scammers out there, but I do believe that a chosen few have the ability to see into the future—or the past. Are you one of those?"

Quinn nodded. "I can't see into the past at will. It's only when I hold an item that belonged to someone who's passed. I can see images of their life. And I can also feel some small measure of what they felt during certain events in their life."

"That must be amazing," Rhys breathed, "especially for a historian, or a filmmaker. What I wouldn't give to see things as they really were, not as we envision them."

"It is and it isn't. I get attached to them, you see. They become real, but I can't share what I've seen with anyone. People in the archeological community would ridicule me and question my scientific data. All I can do is find evidence to support what I have seen. It's sort of a backhanded way of doing research, but as long as I find what I'm looking for, I can use my knowledge to tell their story."

"You possess an incredible gift. You shouldn't be ashamed of it."

"I'm not ashamed, just wary of telling people about it, I suppose. I've often wondered if I inherited this ability from one of my parents, but I guess I'll never know."

"Do you think it's genetic?" Rhys asked, his eyes aglow with wonder.

"Isn't everything, to some degree? I can't imagine that I got this ability out of nowhere. Someone along the line must have had the same gift. Only I've got no one to ask."

"Yes, I can see how that would be frustrating for you. Still, I think it's incredible. So, you know who our lovers are, do you?"

"I know who the woman is. I'd decided to start with her. I can see glimpses into her life every time I hold her brooch in my bare hands. I usually use latex gloves when handling artifacts around other people, for fear of going off into a trance."

"Is that what happened when I came upon you that day by the institute? You looked as if you were a million miles away. Or a few hundred years in the past," he quipped.

"Yes."

"And I interrupted."

"You sure did," Quinn replied with a grateful smile. She'd been terrified of Rhys finding out, but he was totally fine about it. There was no derision or sneer of contempt. He looked fascinated.

"So, can you tell me about her? Elise," he said the name slowly, savoring it. Until that moment she'd been a nameless, faceless relic of another time, but now she had a name, and once Quinn described her, she'd have a face.

Quinn felt a pang of sadness as she began to speak, her voice low for fear of disturbing the dead. Hearing Elise's name spoken out loud had a strange effect. It was almost as if Elise was there, watching Quinn with those bright blue eyes, a small smile tugging at her lips. Quinn had known of her existence for only two weeks, but already Elise had taken over her heart, and Quinn felt a strange kinship with the young, friendless girl who was sure to meet with a tragic end.

"She's young and very pretty. What I found surprising about her is that despite her upbringing, she is quite spirited and doesn't just accept her fate. I expect that's what led to her untimely death. Elise understands the role of women in her time, but she can't come to terms with the fact that she is nothing more than some man's property."

"So, what we have here is the typical story of a young woman being married off to an older man and expected to produce an heir to title and fortune?"

"Not quite. You see, Elise's husband was impotent, but he needed an heir desperately and that weighed heavily on his mind. He was a wealthy man and needed a son to leave his estate to."

"What about his daughter? Could she not have inherited or produced a son for Asher to leave his estate to?"

"His daughter was what they called *feeble-minded* in those days. I suppose she might have been on the autistic spectrum or was severely learning disabled. She had some speech, but it was on a level of a five-year-old. Marrying her off would have been an act of unbelievable cruelty, not that any man in his right mind would want her for a wife, unless his only interest was in her wealth. To be honest, I'm not even sure if Barbara was physically able to bear a child. She was in her late teens when Elise met her, but she looked like a prepubescent girl."

"So, what happened?" Rhys asked. He leaned forward in his eagerness to hear the story, which Quinn found endearing. He was like a little boy, desperate to learn how the tale ended.

"Asher used his illegitimate son, James, to get Elise with child and then banished James as soon as Elise conceived for fear of them having formed an attachment to one another."

"And had they?" Rhys asked, a playful twinkle in his eye. He could sense a dramatic twist coming on, and the filmmaker in him was in heaven.

"Elise did warm to him after a time, but there was someone else in the picture. Elise had been in love with a young man called Gavin Talbot who worked for her father."

"But she married Lord Asher nonetheless."

"She did, and we have proof of that. But, what I found no trace of was any mention of a child, and we know from Dr. Scott's analysis that Elise had given birth to at least one child."

"She might have miscarried late in the pregnancy or given birth to a stillborn. It happened often enough."

"Yes, I suppose that's possible since there's no record of a baptism. I just can't help wondering if there are, in fact, any living descendants."

"Perhaps you will see something that will answer that question," Rhys suggested, watching her with interest. "I do envy you. I wish I could see it all for myself."

"I've made peace with my abilities, but when I was a child I wanted nothing more than to be normal. Seeing the past scared me."

"Who was the first person you saw?"

"My grandmother Ruth. I loved her, you see, and seeing her fear and suffering during the war scared me to death."

"Yes, I imagine it would. Can you control what you see?"

"To a degree. I seem to be privy to events that truly shaped the lives of the people I see. Sometimes the events are in sequence, and sometimes I find myself further down the timeline."

"How marvelous," Rhys said, shaking his head in wonder. "Will you tell me everything you see? We can create a completely realistic reenactment of Elise's life, all the way up to her death. The viewers won't know the story is real, but we will. What do you think?"

"I think that's a wonderful idea, but how will we explain this sudden knowledge?"

"We don't need to," Rhys replied. "What we are selling is a dramatization based on the few facts we do know. We try to connect the dots and fill in the blanks to the best of our ability. And our ability has just increased a hundredfold. What do you say to bringing Elise back to life?"

"I think she would have loved that."

Chapter 33

June 1665

London, England

Elise was surprised when Edward decided to join her for supper one night in June. She hadn't laid eyes on him in days, and even then it was only in passing. Any other woman might have thought that her husband kept a mistress at court, but Elise knew better. It wasn't the women that drew Edward to the palace—it was the men. He enjoyed the liveliness and intrigue of the court, and he seemed to feel most himself when distracted from his own troubling thoughts. Edward didn't share much with her, but from the little she knew of him, she deduced that Edward Asher was not a happy man.

Despite the ever-present loneliness, Elise preferred her own company to Edward's and felt more at ease when he stayed away. She didn't know what brought him home this evening, but she simply asked for another place to be set at the table and waited for him to join her. Edward was tired and ill-tempered, having just returned from the palace. He hadn't changed out of his finery, but he removed his wig and cleaned his face with a moist towel, wiping away any traces of the powder and rouge favored by some courtiers. It was almost as if Edward had removed a mask, allowing his wife a glimpse of what lay beneath.

"What news?" Elise asked as the first course was served. Elise had long since scaled down the evening meal to two courses, a broth and roasted poultry or baked fish. She didn't care for meat, and Edward was so rarely at home that it seemed wasteful to keep preparing dishes that no one ate. Once a week, Mistress Oliphant made Elise a sweet of some sort, claiming that if she stopped cooking puddings she might lose her knack for baking. Elise had never been one for sweets in the past, but now that she was pregnant, she found herself craving sugary treats. She also liked tea. Edward introduced it into the household a few months ago, saying it was the fashion at Whitehall Palace, brought from Portugal by Catherine of Braganza. Elise disliked the strange drink at first, but sometimes, especially in the mornings, she found it more palatable than ale, which left a sour taste in her mouth and made her belch. Tea had a bitterness to it, but when taken with a bit of sugar, it was quite refreshing.

Edward frowned as he stared at his bowl of broth. He was accustomed to eating rich, multicourse meals at the palace, and the broth displeased him.

"This is peasant food," he said scornfully and pushed the bowl aside. "Is there nothing else?"

"There's some roast fowl with root vegetables."

"Very well. I'll have that." He was surly, but beneath his gruff exterior Elise saw a man who felt frightened and helpless. "The news from the city isn't good," Edward said, finally responding to her question. "The death toll is rising. Some measures have been taken by the Lord Mayor, but they are too late. People are leaving London in droves. It took me nearly an hour to get home today. The streets are thronged with wagons and carriages. Many physicians and clergymen have chosen to leave at a time when they are needed most," he added hotly.

"They fear for their lives," Elise replied as a feeling of trepidation spread through her. No wonder Edward came home. Dread had replaced the gaiety of the court, and many had already fled the city, desperate to protect themselves and those they loved from a pestilence that struck indiscriminately. The plague didn't care for wealth or position. It simply killed.

"Should we not consider leaving?" she asked carefully.

"To flee London while His Majesty remains is cowardly and disloyal," Edward retorted. "I must remain, and so must you."

Elise couldn't imagine what difference it made to His Majesty if she were in London or not, but she chose not to argue. She was safe here, or so she wished to believe. The sickness was worst in heavily populated areas, where people came in contact with others and spread the disease. She came in contact with no one but the servants, and so far, everyone had remained healthy since they rarely went out. Elise prayed nightly that they would remain so.

"Has anyone at the palace been taken ill?" she asked as she picked at her food.

Edward didn't immediately reply, but she could see by the clenching of his jaw that her question unnerved him. She doubted that anyone of importance had been taken ill, but those from the lower orders were bound to have sickened. Servants, grooms, seamstresses, and cooks went into the city every day as part of their daily duties and came into contact with tradesmen and passersby. It was highly probable that more than a few had been infected.

Edward pushed away his plate with a snort of derision. "This is foul. I don't know how you eat this slop. Had my mother still been alive, she would have dismissed the cook for such a tasteless offering."

"Cook made this to my specifications. You rarely dine at home, and I like my food plain," Elise retorted. Rich sauces and overly spiced dishes gave her an upset, and she cared not what Edward liked since he was never there.

"Tell Lucy to bring me some hippocras. I'll be in the library."

"We haven't got any. You'll have to do with wine," Elise replied serenely, not caring overmuch if Edward was displeased. Edward stormed from the room, leaving Elise to finish her meal. Having endured Edward's bad temper, she reflected that perhaps eating alone wasn't so bad after all.

Edward spent the night at home, but Elise didn't see him again. She went to bed at her usual time and read a little before blowing out the candle, but she couldn't get to sleep. She heard Edward's snores through the connecting door, but it wasn't the rumbling that kept her awake. She was frightened. The servants tried to keep the truth from her, but she heard snippets of conversation as she floated through the empty house in search of something to do. Cook was glad that no elaborate meals were expected since she was hesitant to send the servants out to buy supplies. The less exposure everyone had to the outside world the better. The death toll was rising fast, and this promised to be the worst outbreak of plague yet. The warm weather didn't help matters, and Elise fancied she could smell the sickness in the air when she went out into the garden for her daily walk.

Elise lay on her back and stared up at the darkened canopy. She felt hot and irritable, and her mouth was dry with thirst. Elise kicked off the heavy coverlet and yanked open the bed hangings. She couldn't open the window for fear of letting in contagion, but laying there in just her nightdress helped. She folded her hands across her belly and tried to think of something pleasant, but nothing came to mind. She felt a strange little flutter deep in her abdomen. It felt like a trapped butterfly beating its wings against her skin. Elise moved her hands over her belly and tried to pinpoint where the flutter was, but it vanished as quickly as it came. A few minutes later, she felt it again. She hoped she wasn't getting ill.

She often felt queasy and bloated, but the feeling usually passed by midday. It rarely happened at night.

Elise rolled onto her belly, but had to turn right back again. She loved sleeping on her stomach, but she no longer felt comfortable. Her belly felt like a small hillock beneath her, and she felt a pressure she couldn't account for. Elise tossed and turned for what seemed like hours before giving up on sleep. She put on her dressing gown and went downstairs, still barefoot. The floorboards were smooth and cool beneath her feet and she liked the way they felt. The house was silent and dark; everyone was asleep. Elise went down to the parlor and threw open the window. She knew Edward would scold her terribly if he found out, but she just needed a breath of air. She felt so hot and restless.

The cool night air caressed her face as she stood there in the darkness, listening to the silence. Sunrise wasn't far off, and with it the heat would rise and the stench from the river would overpower the smell of flowers and grass. The river smelled foul at the best of times, but during the summer months the usual smell of rotten fish and sewage was almost unbearable, especially when combined with the stink of sun-warmed heaps of rotten produce and human and animal waste.

Elise was surprised to hear a noise coming from the direction of the kitchen. For one mad moment, she thought it might be James, but then she remembered that he was away in Suffolk, tending to Edward's estate. At least he was safe there. She shut the window and headed toward the kitchen. Perhaps Cook got up early and would make her some tea. Instead, Elise found Lucy, who was still in her night rail, her bare feet as pale as the linen of the garment. Lucy's dark hair spilled down her back, and her face was flushed with the heat of her attic bedroom.

"Lucy, what is it?" Elise asked, noting the pail of water in Lucy's shaking hands. Her eyes were huge with shock as she beheld her mistress, but she instantly looked away, a guilty expression on her face.

"I'm sorry. I didn't mean to startle you," Elise said, wondering why Lucy looked so spooked. She didn't seem to be doing anything wrong. Lucy set the pail down on the table and took a deep breath before finally meeting Elise's gaze.

"'Tis Janet, me lady. She's unwell."

Janet was the youngest maid in the household. She was only twelve, a thin mousy girl who'd come up from Kent to find employment. She was an orphan, and according to Lucy, she considered herself truly blessed to have found work in such a grand house with a kind mistress. Elise felt sorry for the girl but tried not to single her out for fear of setting the other servants against her. Elise did give Janet one of her old gowns since the girl had nothing but the clothes she stood up in. Janet treasured the gown and only wore it to church, seeing as she had no other special occasions in her dreary life.

"What's wrong with her?" Elise asked. "Is it her time of the month?"

"No, me lady. She's fevered. I came down to get some cool water to sponge her face and body. Her night rail is soaked with sweat."

Elise nodded. "Let me know how she is. And Lucy, I'll dress myself this morning. You just see to Janet."

"Yes, ma'am. Thank you."

Elise watched Lucy walk away, the pail carefully balanced in her hands. She hoped that Janet would improve by tomorrow. If she didn't, there'd be cause for concern.

Chapter 34

Elise didn't see Lucy for the rest of the day, but a feeling of dread settled over the house, as if all the inhabitants were holding their breath. Even Cook, who liked to hum a merry tune while she cooked, remained resolutely silent, torn between worry and guilt. Janet had gone out two days prior at her behest. She'd purchased produce and fish for supper and then helped Cook bake several loaves of bread. Everyone in the household had eaten the food that Janet had touched. If she did indeed have the plague, they were all at risk.

"How is she?" Elise asked urgently when she saw Lucy coming down the stairs. Lucy looked exhausted and pale, and her forehead was slick with perspiration.

"She's still fevered and has terrible chills despite this ungodly heat. Says her bones hurt," Lucy replied. She strove for calm, but the panic in her eyes was painful to behold. She understood the ramifications of sharing a room with Janet only too well, and she was the only person in the household who would be expected to look after her. "In for a penny, in for a pound," Cook was heard to say, referring to Lucy's amount of exposure to the sickness. It was too late to do anything for her now.

"Has Janet eaten anything?" Elise asked, keeping a safe distance from Lucy.

"Just a bit of broth and a cup of ale."

"Lucy, she needs to be examined," Elise said. She feared for Lucy, but the girl had already been exposed, so examining

Janet would not place her in any greater danger. "Do you know what to look for?"

Lucy nodded. "I'll just get some more water and a cup of ale for Janet."

"No. You mustn't go near the other servants. I will have Will bring up a basin of water and a jug of ale and leave it by the door. Lucy, I'm sorry, but you must be quarantined along with Janet." Lucy looked aghast but didn't argue.

"Check Janet over and let Will know when he comes up," Elise instructed. "And Lucy, don't worry. I will look after you. You have my word."

"Not much ye can do for me, is there?" Lucy asked. She sounded wary and defeated. They all knew the odds of surviving the plague.

Elise paced the parlor until Will finally came back down some time later, his face ashen. Elise didn't need to ask, she saw it all in his eyes, but she faced him across the room and smiled encouragingly.

"Janet has buboes, me lady. 'Tis the plague, as ye feared."

"Will, please ask everyone to assemble in the yard. I'd like to speak to them. And please wake his lordship. He'll need to be informed."

"Aye, me lady." Will left the room, his shoulders stooped and his gait slow. He was hardly older than Elise, but he seemed to have aged a decade in the past few minutes. Elise shared his fear.

Elise came out into the yard moments later. Nine frightened faces stared at her as she stood there for a moment, organizing her thoughts. "As you all know, Janet has been taken ill with the plague. We are now all at risk. I would ask you all to remain calm in the face of this threat. We must do what we can for Janet and pray that Lucy does not sicken. Janet and Lucy will be quarantined from this moment on. Will, you will bring food and water for washing, but leave them on the floor in front of the room. You are not to go in. No one is. If anyone feels fevered or achy, please let me know. You will be relieved of your duties and asked to stay in your room. Is that clear?"

Nine heads nodded. "Should we not inform the authorities that there's plague in the house?" Cook asked, her normally rosy face pale with fear.

"Not yet. They will have the house shut up with all of us in it. We will look to our own. You may return to your tasks."

Elise went back into the house and shut the door to the parlor. She didn't want the servants to see her fear, but she was terrified. One case was all it took to infect everyone in the house. Janet had touched their food, their bread, and likely their dishes. No one knew how the illness spread, but it stood to reason that anything Janet laid her hands on might have become infected. And Lucy had been in the kitchen getting food and drink for Janet. If she had been stricken, that increased their chances of illness.

Elise put her hands over her belly. The butterfly feeling had intensified over the past two days. Had her baby quickened without her even realizing it? She supposed it was possible. She was about halfway through the pregnancy, by her estimation. Elise pressed her hands to her growing stomach, searching for signs of life. "Are you in there, little one?" she whispered. "I'll keep you safe."

Elise sank down onto a wooden settle and closed her eyes. The only way to keep her baby safe was to keep herself safe, and she had no way to do that. They'd been granted a reprieve this past month, but now it was over. The plague was among them, and Edward wasn't about to do a damn thing to keep them from harm. She'd heard the thunder of hooves as he left the house, fleeing without even speaking to her.

Chapter 35

November 2013

Surrey, England

Quinn set aside the brooch and stared into the leaping flames in the grate. Her little chapel was frigid from October to April since it was built of stone and had no central heating, but the fireplace, which ingeniously faced both the living room and the bedroom, kept her cozy and warm. Quinn pulled a shawl closer about her shoulders and considered what she'd just seen. She'd learned about the Great Plague, of course, and had read the accounts of Samuel Pepys, who was the truest voice of his generation, in Quinn's opinion. Images of plague-ridden London were familiar to her, but it was different seeing it through the eyes of someone who actually lived through it. Quinn could feel Elise's fear and see the terror in the eyes of the servants. They'd believed themselves to be safe in Asher Hall, but no one was safe, not when an epidemic was raging just beyond the walls. Inhabitants of the house had to go out to buy supplies, and all it took for everyone to become infected was one person falling ill, as Janet had. Quinn felt a tearing pity at the thought of that frail, motherless girl who had little chance of survival. She was cared for by Lucy, but no amount of care would keep the disease from consuming her in the end. Few recovered.

Of course, in the seventeenth century no one knew how the pestilence actually spread, except that it traveled from person to person. People lived in close quarters with no running water or sanitation. Few washed their hands on a regular basis, and even fewer people bathed. Waste and muck covered the cobblestones, and open drains flowed down streets, the stinking contents splashing passersby as carriages and wagons drove by. Some of the greatest places of congestion were the city gates, where people and vehicles bottlenecked the archways and forced even closer interaction, allowing the disease to spread with greater efficiency. There were nearly seventy thousand deaths reported during the Great Plague, but historians believed that number was at least thirty thousand short of the real toll. Many of those who died hadn't even been infected but were victims of quarantine, shut up in houses with plague victims for forty days with a guard posted outside to keep them from escaping. *What a sad fate for someone who happened to be at the wrong place at the wrong time*, Quinn thought with an inward sigh. *And what a cruel world that forced people to resort to such extremes.*

  Perhaps the death toll might have been reduced had Londoners reported cases of plague to the authorities sooner, but fear of being quarantined forced many to keep an illness among them a secret. Quinn could understand Elise's reluctance to alert the authorities only too well. She was nearly five months pregnant, and being shut up in Asher Hall would be a death sentence for both her and her baby. Quinn wiped away a tear that slid unbidden down her cheek. Elise was long gone, but she seemed so real, so alive. Quinn was torn between the need to find out what happened to her and an equally strong desire not to know. She was so caught up in her thoughts that she nearly jumped out of her skin when there was a knock on the door. Quinn loved her antique door knocker, but at times the loud knocking frightened her, the echo reverberating through the house, bouncing ominously off the stone walls and forcing a shiver of apprehension to run along her spine.

  Quinn glanced out the window, hoping for a glimpse of her unexpected visitor. A powerful northern wind moved through the trees, and heavy rain came down in sheets, the thick clouds obscuring the moon and stars, and leaving the world in absolute darkness. Light from the window fell onto a sodden Gabe, and Quinn yanked open the door, a smile of welcome on her face.

"Let me in. It's a deluge out here," Gabe grumbled as he hurried inside, bringing a gust of wind and rain with him.

"You do own an umbrella, don't you?" Quinn asked with a grin as she stepped aside to let him in.

"Yes, but I can never find one when I need it. Any chance of a cup of tea? I'm soaked," he complained as he walked over to the fireplace, holding his hands out to the heat.

"Gabe, what are you doing here?" Quinn asked as she filled the kettle and took out mugs and some chocolate biscuits. They were a bit stale, but they'd have to do since there was nothing else she could offer him. She'd need to go into the village tomorrow to stock up on some provisions.

"I didn't like the way we left things the last time we spoke," he replied without looking at her, his eyes fixated on the fire. Quinn noted the rigid set of his shoulders and the way his feet were splayed, as if to achieve greater balance. Gabe wasn't sure of his welcome and was bracing himself for rejection.

"You could have called, you know," Quinn joked. Her heart leaped with joy at the sight of Gabe on her doorstep, but his unexpected arrival also put her on guard. Their relationship had morphed into something completely unexpected over the past few weeks, and she was no longer sure of the rules. The safety buffer of significant others had been removed, leaving them to face whatever it was that had hovered in the air between them for the past eight years.

"I could have, but I wanted to speak to you in person. Would you prefer that I leave?" he asked, watching her intently over his shoulder. He tried to keep his expression neutral, but

Quinn could see the tiny flame of fear in his eyes before he extinguished it, shrugging in pretend indifference.

"Of course not. Don't be ridiculous. Take off your jacket; you're dripping water on the floor."

"Sorry," Gabe muttered as he shrugged off his wet jacket, hung it on a coatrack by the door, then came back and sat down on the sofa, somewhat more at ease.

Quinn handed Gabe a mug of tea, and he took a sip, sighing gratefully. "Much better now."

Quinn perched on the armrest, keeping a safe distance from Gabe as she sipped her own tea. His intensity unnerved her, and she knew that this visit was going to be very different from the ones before. She wished she could forestall the conversation that was coming, but she supposed it would still take place sooner rather than later, and she wasn't at all sure how she wanted it to go.

Gabe sipped his tea silently for a few minutes, but his gaze never left Quinn's face. It's as if he were searching for clues. Quinn tried to look as nonchalant as possible as she waited for him to begin, but her stomach clenched with anxiety. She wasn't ready to have this confrontation.

"How was your day with Rhys?" Gabe finally asked. He tried to sound casual, but there was a bitterness in his voice that he was unable to hide.

"It was fine. We found what we were looking for." Quinn paused, debating whether to tell Gabe the truth. "He knows, Gabe."

"Knows what?"

"That I see Elise."

"You told him?" Gabe exclaimed, nearly spilling his tea.

"Yes, I did. I'm not sure why I did it, but it just seemed natural. He wasn't as surprised as I might have expected. He was fascinated, really."

"I bet he was," Gabe growled, his eyes flashing with anger.

"Gabe, what's your problem with Rhys? I thought you liked him."

Gabe's head shot up, his eyes boring into her as if she'd just slapped him. "Are you bloody serious?" he choked out, instinctively leaning forward toward Quinn in agitation. He seemed really rattled. She shouldn't have asked the question, but it just popped out and now she had to know.

"Quinn, I like Rhys, but it's your liking him that I'm concerned about."

"Why?" Quinn goaded him. "Why does my liking him bother you?"

"Because you are smitten with him, and the feeling seems to be mutual."

Gabe set down his cup and sprang to his feet, unable to remain immobile any longer. He paced in front of the fireplace for a moment before rounding on Quinn, who was watching him over the rim of her mug. "Quinn, I broke things off with Eve as soon as I heard that you and Luke had split up. I wanted my chance. I've loved you since the day you tripped over that boulder and fell into my arms at the dig. I wanted to ask you out right there and then, but I hesitated, afraid that my behavior would appear unprofessional. That moment of hesitation cost me dearly. By the end of the dig, you were with Luke, and the rest, as they say, is history. Quinn, I'm not going to let another chance slip away. I want us to be together, and I'll be damned if I let Rhys Morgan swoop in and take you away from me."

"He can't take me away from you because I'm not yours," Quinn spat out. "I don't belong to anyone. Not even to the man I thought I loved for eight years. Did you know, Gabe? Did you know that he left me for someone else?"

Seeing Gabe's expression told her everything she needed to know, and she felt fury well up inside her. She wanted to hurt Luke, but Luke was gone and Gabe was right there, ready to take the punishment.

"How could you?" she cried. "You call yourself my friend. You say that you care about me, but you stood by and allowed me to be lied to and humiliated, and you said nothing."

"I didn't want to be the one to hurt you," Gabe replied, desperate for understanding. "It wasn't my place, Quinn, and I thought he'd be man enough to tell you the truth himself."

"But he wasn't, and I spent the past few months agonizing over what I'd done wrong and why Luke just walked out on me without so much as a word of explanation. You could have spared me that hurt, but you kept silent and watched me suffer. I had to hear it from Monica Fielding, of all people."

"Monica told you?" Gabe asked, clearly surprised. He never quite understood the depth of Monica's animosity toward Quinn, having never been a target of her displeasure himself.

Quinn nodded. She couldn't recall the conversation with Monica without feeling physically ill. She'd stopped by the institute over the weekend to collect some papers from her office and thought she'd check out *The Diary of Samuel Pepys* from the institute library. She'd read it before, of course, but thought that it might be helpful in painting a more comprehensive picture of life during the plague for Rhys. Quinn was just coming out of her office when she saw Monica Fielding striding down the corridor, a stack of papers under her arm.

"Quinn," she exclaimed, her mouth stretching into her customary sneer. They had been friends once, a very long time ago, but professional jealousy got in the way of that, and Monica had never forgiven Quinn for outshining her in archeological circles. Unlike Quinn, Monica was a born gladiator—everything became a fight to the death rather than just friendly competition. Quinn's recent success was just another nail in the coffin for Monica, who'd failed to publish anything noteworthy in several years.

"Monica," Quinn countered. "What are you doing here on a Saturday?" Monica was the last person Quinn wanted to talk to at the moment, but it seemed rude to just push past her, so she resigned herself to chatting for a few minutes.

"I have a ton of papers to mark, and I simply can't concentrate at home. Mark can't go for five whole minutes without distracting me in some way, pleasant ways though they might be," she said with a smug smile, reminding Quinn that she was happily married. "Sorry to hear about you and Luke," Monica went on hurriedly, seeing that Quinn had no desire to continue the conversation. "I do hope you're all right, darling. Must have been quite a shock after all these years to find yourself single again."

"I'm fine. Really," Quinn replied. It seemed nothing stayed private for long.

"And so you should be. It'll never last between them, you mark my words. He'll come crawling back," Monica said, putting on a false show of support, her eyes searching Quinn's to see if she knew about the affair. "Although she's a fetching little thing, I'll give her that, even for an American. Father as rich as Croesus. Owns a string of car dealerships on the East Coast."

Quinn felt a wave of nausea as Monica's words sank in. Monica was the proverbial snake in the grass, but she was a historian and had great respect for facts. She wouldn't stoop to inventing an affair, not even for the momentary satisfaction of wounding Quinn. If she said that Luke left Quinn for another woman, then she knew so for certain, and that meant that everyone else at the institute knew as well.

"You did know, didn't you?" Monica inquired with a sad smile. "I do hope I haven't let the cat out of the bag, but Luke had been squiring that little hussy around town for months. He wasn't exactly what'd you call discreet. I figured someone must have told you by now." She meant Gabe, and Quinn felt as if she might be actually be sick. Had Gabe known? Quinn couldn't imagine that Monica wouldn't have mentioned it to Gabe in passing even if he hadn't. Monica was delighting in this. Quinn might be better known in academic circles, but her personal life was in shambles, and Monica was thrilled.

"If there's anything you need, don't hesitate. Nothing raises the sprits like a night out with friends. Us girls need to stick together," Monica purred.

"Yes, thank you, Monica. A night out with friends would be just the thing. I'll call a few and see if they're available," Quinn replied and walked away, leaving Monica smiling stupidly.

She'd confide in Monica when hell froze over, and maybe not even then. Quinn strode down the corridor and out the front door, forgetting her plan to stop by the library. She needed to get out of the building and away from Monica, whose eyes bored into Quinn's back as she walked away. Quinn had pushed the feelings of hurt and betrayal to the back of her mind, unable to cope with the knowledge that Luke had not only left her but had been carrying on behind her back for months. And now all that hurt came pouring out, having found its mark in Gabe.

"I was waiting for the right time," Gabe exclaimed, his gaze pleading with her as he ran a hand through his hair, making it stand on end.

"And you think this is it?" Quinn cried as unbidden tears spilled down her cheeks.

Quinn sank down on the sofa and picked up a cushion, holding it against her body as if protecting herself from an attack. She wanted to run and hide in a place where she felt safe and knew whom she could trust. She thought she'd trusted Gabe, but he lied to her just as Luke had and was now using her pain to serve his own ends. Quinn's hurt bubbled over, startling Gabe with the intensity of her anger.

"Get out, Gabe," she exclaimed. "Just leave. I can't deal with this right now. You might have loved me all this time, but that didn't stop you from being with other women. Did you tell them you loved them? Did you make promises to them just as Luke made promises to me? I gave him my love and my trust, and he threw them back in my face. How do I know that you won't do the same once you've tired of me? And then I will lose not only my closest friend but possibly the job I love, because working with you after that might prove impossible," Quinn cried.

"Is that what you really think of me?" Gabe asked, his voice dangerously low. "You think that once I've shagged you I'll get sick of you and move on? You think you'll just be another notch on my belt?"

"I don't know what I think. I thought I loved Luke. I thought he was going to propose to me when I returned from Jerusalem. More the fool me, because he clearly never planned his future around me. I also believed that you were my friend, but you clearly had an agenda of your own all along, and now that Luke's out of the picture, you expect me to fall into your arms and fulfill whatever fantasy you've created of us being together. Don't you dare put this kind of pressure on me," Quinn exclaimed as she threw aside the cushion and leaped off the sofa, staring down a stunned Gabe. "I don't owe you my love, and I'm a big girl. I can decide whom I want to be with, and if that happens to be Rhys, who incidentally has shown no interest in me, then it will be Rhys. Now, I'll say goodnight."

Gabe opened his mouth to reply, but nothing came out. He looked so stricken that Quinn wished the floor would open up and swallow her whole. She hadn't meant to hurt him, but she could see that she had wounded him deeply. He'd bared his soul to her, and she threw it on the floor and stomped on it.

"Gabe, I'm sorry," she muttered.

"It's fine. I'll see myself out. Thank you for your honesty, Quinn. I won't be troubling you again."

"Gabe!" she cried, but Gabe had already grabbed his jacket off the hook and strode out the door into the rain, slamming the door behind him with soul-crushing finality.

What had she done? She hadn't wanted to lose him, and now she lost him anyway. He would no longer be her friend, and that realization sliced through her like a knife. Not having Gabe in her life was one of the worst things she could imagine. Quinn grabbed her mobile and dialed Gabe, but he didn't pick up. She heard his calm, authoritative voice as he asked her to leave a message. She disconnected the call. What she had to say couldn't be said in a voicemail message. She wanted to speak to him in person, but Gabe needed time to cool down.

Quinn sank back down onto the sofa. She rarely cried, preferring to ignore her feelings of hurt, but hot tears poured down her face as the enormity of what she'd done finally sank in.

Chapter 36

Gabe revved the engine and tore out of the parking spot, eager to put as much distance between himself and Quinn as possible. The rain had let up a bit, for which he was grateful—he was in no mood to drive like an old lady. His Jag had the capability to chew up the miles, and at a time like this, he craved the release of speed. He'd been brutally rejected twice in as many weeks and felt as if he'd been drawn, quartered, and left to die of shock as he watched his entrails burn just before his heart was finally cut out. Gabe chuckled mirthlessly. Even when heartbroken, he thought like a historian, and only Quinn would see the irony in that. But Quinn didn't want him around.

Gabe merged onto the motorway, glad to see that it was practically deserted and he had the road to himself. He stepped on the gas pedal and felt the Jaguar pounce as it responded to his command. The car flew toward London, darkened countryside and empty petrol stations flashing past the windows. Gabe enjoyed the sensation for a few minutes before easing his foot off the gas. Where was he rushing to? There was nothing waiting for him at home, save an empty flat and an even emptier fridge. He didn't even have a few bottles of lager, and he was desperate for a pint. Gabe thought of calling his best mate, Pete McGann. Pete was always up for a few pints, especially on a Friday night, but Gabe didn't think he could handle Pete's rhapsodizing on marital bliss in his current emotional state.

Pete married his girlfriend the day after the university commencement ceremony, and although nearly the whole graduating class took bets on how long the marriage would last, given that Pete met a somewhat inebriated Jen in a pub only a month before and shagged her not five minutes later in the loo, Pete was still happily married nearly twenty years on. Pete and Jen had three strapping teenage boys who were always up for Sunday morning football or a trip to the arcade with their Uncle Gabe. They were fine boys, and Gabe secretly, or perhaps not-so-secretly, envied Pete his beautiful family.

Over the past few years, Gabe began to ache for a family of his own, the desire to have a child growing by the day, but despite always having women in his life, the only woman he could envision having a family with was Quinn. The thought of Quinn carrying his child filled him with such desperate longing that he nearly howled with the futility of his devotion to her. Luke was such an unbelievable wanker, a man who never put Quinn first and who discarded her like a piece of rubbish. Why couldn't she see that and give Gabe a chance?

Gabe swung the car off the nearest exit and turned around, getting back on the northbound motorway. He wasn't going to London, he was going to Berwick. He was too gutted to face spending the weekend on his own, and Pete and Jen's well-meaning platitudes were more than he could handle at the moment. He wanted what every man wanted when he was hurting too much for words. He wanted Mum. His dad liked to retire early, but his mum was something of a night owl and would still be up by the time he made it home. Gabe was close with his dad, but it was his mum who truly understood him, and she understood about Quinn. Phoebe Russell was the only person he'd ever confided in about his love for his friend.

Pete suspected, and Jen certainly knew, but Gabe had never said it out loud, never revealed himself to that extent. He was generally a private person, who liked to keep his feelings to himself. Besides, what kind of man admitted to carrying a torch for another man's woman for eight years? What kind of man was too honorable not to make a play for her at some point? Well, perhaps he'd refrained from making a play for Quinn not out of a misguided sense of honor but from some deeper knowledge that he'd be rejected, as he had been tonight. He'd allowed himself to believe that Quinn cared for him, maybe even loved him on some level, but that dream was over now. She'd made her feelings clear.

Gabe felt somewhat calmer by the time he pulled into the drive of the manor house he'd called home for the first eighteen years of his life. He'd notice signs of dilapidation come morning—his father had done little to maintain the family home since suffering a heart attack a few years back—but at the moment, the place looked like heaven. Warm light spilled from the library windows, where his mother was no doubt reading some juicy novel. His septuagenarian mum had discovered a liking for racy novels in her old age but diligently hid them from her husband for fear of giving him another coronary. Gabe didn't think his father would be particularly shocked. They hadn't been married for over forty years without learning something about each other, and Graeme Russell knew exactly what his sprightly seventy-two-year-old wife was into, just as his mum knew all about the online gambling his father liked to dabble in when no one was looking. Gabe suddenly realized how much he'd missed his parents. He didn't visit them nearly often enough, perhaps because he felt like a little boy the moment he walked through the door, but at times, that wasn't such a bad thing.

Gabe used his key to let himself in and walked toward the library, his footsteps echoing on the flagstone floor of the corridor. He should have rung, but he was in no mood to pull over, make the call, and explain to his well-meaning mum why he suddenly wanted to come home. Instead, he knocked on the library door gently, so as not to startle his poor elderly mother.

"Come in," she called eagerly. "I knew you'd come tonight," Phoebe Russell announced when Gabe stepped into the library. She was sitting in her favorite chair before the fire, an open book on her lap, and Buster the Lab asleep at her feet. Her heather-gray twin set was an almost identical match to her iron-gray hair, styled in a fashionable pixie cut, and her cheeks were rosy from the heat of the fire. Phoebe's blue eyes scanned Gabe from head to toe, checking, just as she did when he was a boy, that everything looked to be in the right place and that there was no cause for alarm.

"And how did you know that?" Gabe asked as he stooped to kiss her on the cheek and then sank into his father's chair, stretching his legs before the fire.

"A mother always knows," she replied cryptically. Phoebe gave Gabe another lengthy once-over, focusing on this face this time, and shook her head in disgust. "Foolish girl."

"Mum, have you suddenly become clairvoyant?" Gabe asked, smiling despite his misery. Truth be told, when it came to him, she always had been.

"Is it necessary to be clairvoyant to see that your boy is suffering? And why is he suffering, you might ask?" Phoebe asked dramatically, as if addressing a roomful of people. "It can only be because the woman he's worshipped for the past eight years is too much of a blind fool to recognize her good fortune when it's presented to her," Phoebe replied with a straight face, but her eyes twinkled with good humor.

"I'm not sure that Quinn agrees with you about the good fortune part," Gabe replied, staring miserably into the fire. Now that he was here, he wasn't sure he really wanted to talk about Quinn after all, but his mother was already off and running, going from relaxing in her chair to leaning forward in her eagerness to console him.

"Gabriel, you always were an impatient child," his mother scolded. "You could never wait for the right time. Why, I'd run out of places to hide Christmas gifts from you. Like a bloodhound you were, searching until you found every last one and ruining your own Christmas morning in the process."

"I'm no longer seven, Mum," Gabe sighed.

"No, you are thirty-seven, but you're still the same eager beaver you've always been. Quinn needs time, Gabe. She'll come around, you'll see, but you can't rush her. The man she loved just left her, for someone else, no less. She needs time to come to terms with that rejection before she can open her heart to someone new. Had she been the one to leave him, she might be ready to move on, but Luke's desertion came as a shock. You said so yourself. Stop hounding her."

"Is that what I'm doing?" Gabe asked, hurt that his mother would use such a harsh term.

"Isn't it? How many times since she returned from the Middle East have you made your feelings known?"

"Three," Gabe muttered, suddenly feeling like the biggest prat to walk the earth. His mother had that effect on him at times, but he didn't mind. He needed to hear the truth, even if it made him feel like a right fool.

"And that's two times too many. She knows how you feel, love. Give her a bit of time to come round. She has her reasons for not falling into your arms."

"And what might those be, Mum?" Gabe asked, smiling at his mother over the glass of brandy she just handed him, taking one for herself in the process. His mum loved a nightcap.

Phoebe Russell shook her head, as if astounded by her son's epic thickness. *One never finishes raising a son*, she mused as she resumed her seat. On some level, they remained little boys forever, always needing that little bit of guidance to come to the right conclusion, even when pushing forty.

"Gabe, you are not some random man Quinn met in a bar or at some dull archeological conference. You are her friend, her employer, and the man she's known the longest, other than her father and the pillock who ran for the hills with that teenage bimbo. You two don't have a clean slate; you have history already, and that history is holding her back. Crossing that line with you will jeopardize your friendship as well as her job, and she's worried and scared of losing you for good. You mean too much to her to be discarded like someone she had a casual drink with and didn't care to see again. I wager she's said something along those lines, hasn't she?" Phoebe inquired as she took a sip of her brandy, her eyes bright over the rim of her glass.

"Yes, she has," Gabe confessed, hanging his head in mock shame. "How'd you get to be so wise, Mum?"

"It comes with having a womb," his mother quipped. "You should know, my historian son, that women have always had to be wiser than men. Having no equal rights and being at the mercy of men their whole lives, they had to anticipate every eventuality and know how to deflect anger and injustice to protect themselves and their children. Women are not hotheads, my boy, they are thinkers and planners."

"You don't know modern women, Mum," Gabe countered, thinking of all the women who had thrown themselves at him over the years, interested only in a casual shag rather than a meaningful relationship. Women were liberated and as brazen as any man these days, if not more so.

"Don't I? Oh, they might be sexually liberated and free to speak their minds, but they still have to compete in the world of men in most areas, and they have to be twice as clever to achieve half as much because they are held back by misogyny and fear."

Gabe remained silent as he sipped his drink, considering what his mother had just said. She had a way of putting things in perspective and helped him see the situation from a completely different angle. Perhaps she was right, and he'd been impatient and overly aggressive. He thought that he was swooping in to save the day, when, in fact, he was making Quinn feel cornered and unsure of his motives. He needed to give her the time and space she needed to think and come to terms with Luke's betrayal. A slow smile spread across Gabe's face as he regarded his mother across the room.

"Thanks, Mum. I love you."

"And I love you," she replied, ruffling his hair as she rose to retire. "And do you know what does wonders for unrequited love?" she asked, a wicked grin tugging at the corners of her mouth.

"No, but I can't wait to find out."

"Hard work. The gutters need cleaning, the leaves on the lawn need to be raked, several lightbulbs need changing, and there's a drip in the master bath. And Buster could use a visit to the vet. He's been poorly lately, but your father keeps putting a trip to the doctor off. Afraid of losing his longtime pal," his mother added sadly. Buster had been with the family for the past fifteen years, son of the previous Buster who'd been Gabe's pup when he was a boy. At fifteen, there wasn't much a vet could do for him, but if the animal was in pain, perhaps he could offer some relief or a humane end.

Gabe got to his feet and saluted his mother. "Yes, ma'am. All will be done, and by teatime, no less. Make a list, Mum. I will fix it, change it, screw it in, rake it, and make it whole again."

"That's what I like to hear. At least you are not a procrastinator like your father. Now go to bed and dream pleasant dreams," his mother said as she reached up to kiss him goodnight. "I'll see to the fire."

Gabe trudged up the creaking steps, a silly grin on his face. It'd been the right decision to come home. His mother hadn't told him anything he didn't already know, but somehow, he felt remarkably better, and helping his aging parents around the house was something he looked forward to doing. It would help to assuage some of his guilt for not visiting them more often. Perhaps he could convince his father to take a ride to a nearby kennel and choose a new puppy. It would ease Buster's passing for his dad and give Gabe a chance to give his father an early Christmas present.

Chapter 37

June 1665

London, England

Elise cried bitterly as Janet's body was carried from the house wrapped in a linen shroud. Two grooms had donned leather gloves and tied kerchiefs over their noses and mouths, fearful of contracting the disease from coming into contact with the corpse. Janet had died peacefully, just slipping away in her sleep after days of fevered lucidity in which she kept crying out for her mother and begging God to help her. Lucy didn't appear to be infected but had to be kept in isolation for a period of forty days. And now they had no choice but to alert the authorities. A red cross would be painted on the door and an armed guard would be stationed outside to keep nobles and servants alike from leaving the premises.

Elise curled into a ball and rested her forehead against her knees. The position wasn't comfortable, and she was acutely aware of her small belly. The babe inside had begun moving during the past week. The movements were strange, almost like a fish on a hook thrashing in panic. They startled Elise and then stopped just when she got accustomed to them and longed to feel more. Elise put her hand on her belly, willing the child to move, but all was still. It's as if her baby felt her despair and tried to keep as still as possible to protect itself.

A knock sounded on her bedroom door, and Elise roused herself and wiped angrily at her eyes. The servants needed her to be strong, not come apart like a child. "Come," she called out.

Peg came into the room timidly. She was in her early twenties, with abundant fair hair and huge blue eyes that missed little. She was ethereally beautiful, but Elise suspected that she wasn't quite as innocent as she appeared. Peg was aware of her beauty and used it to her advantage, not that Elise could blame her. She'd learned a thing or two over the past few months, and perhaps being possessed of a little cunning wasn't such a bad thing for a woman.

"What is it, Peg?" Elise asked warily.

Peg lowered her eyes as she spoke, her voice reedy and frightened.

"I can't hear you," Elise said irritably.

"It's Judd, me lady. He's taken ill. The other grooms have taken him up to the loft above the stables."

"Oh, dear God," Elise whispered. "Not another one."

"I'm 'fraid so."

"Is it the plague?" Elise asked, already knowing the answer. What were the chances of a man simply getting ill when the Black Death was raging all about them?

"Aye, me lady."

Elise nodded. "Thank you for telling me. Make sure he has food and drink and that someone keeps an eye on him should he need anything."

"Aye, ma'am." Peg turned to leave, but not before Elise saw the terror in her eyes. "Are they coming to shut us in, me lady?"

"I'm afraid so, Peg." A desperate sob tore from Peg's chest as she fled the room, leaving Elise shaking with fear. She began to pace the room, taking deep breaths in an effort to calm down. She had just about mastered herself, when there was a loud banging on the front door, the thudding reverberating through the house. Had they come so quickly? Janet had died only that morning.

Elise took a shuddering breath and headed downstairs. She was the mistress of the house and needed to take responsibility for the people who relied on her. Peg was already at the door, her face contorted with fear as she pulled it open, half expecting to see soldiers. A man stood on the threshold. His hat was pulled down low and the bottom part of his face was covered with a kerchief. He looked dusty and travel-stained, and his leather-clad hand seemed to hover near the hilt of his sword. He wasn't there to shut them in, but perhaps he was bent on thievery.

"What do you want here, sir?" Elise spoke loudly. "There's plague in this house, so if you value your life, you'd better be on your way."

The man pulled off the kerchief impatiently, revealing himself to be James. "Aye, I know there's plague. Get your things together. We are leaving. Hurry, we don't have much time. They'll be here within the hour, and then it will be too late."

Elise nearly threw herself into his arms, but she had to preserve a sense of decorum. To the rest of the household, James was just another servant, a man who had no business telling the lady of the house what to do. Peg gaped at James for a moment, but she quickly got her bearings and whirled around to face Elise, her hands clasped in front of her.

"Oh, please, can I come with ye?" Peg pleaded. "I ain't sick. Not yet. And ye'll need a lady's maid to look after ye. Oh, please, me lady."

Elise would have preferred to take Lucy, but to break Lucy's quarantine was too risky. She showed no symptoms yet, but that didn't mean she wasn't on the verge of falling ill. "All right, Peg. Get your things and pack for Lady Barbara."

"James, how did you know?" Elise asked as she threw together a few items of clothing, a pair of sturdy shoes, stockings, and several small pieces of jewelry. She didn't have any money, but the jewelry could always be traded for goods, should the need arise. Elise took her mother's brooch from her jewelry box and pinned it to her bodice. She would never part with it, not even if she were starving. It was the only thing she had left—the only thing that meant anything.

"I didn't know. I heard of the terrible outbreak in London and waited for Lord Asher to bring you to Suffolk. I thought it was only a matter of time before he realized that he had to get you out of the city, but you never came, and I began to fear for your life. I saw them carrying out a body as I came up the street. Hurry, Elise. We need to go now," he added urgently. "They are coming."

"I know," Elise cried. She grabbed her cloak and thrust the valise into James's hands. "I must say good-bye to Lucy."

Elise ran up the stairs to the top floor and called out to Lucy, who opened the door just a crack.

"Lucy, I'm leaving with Master James. I thank you for what you've done for Janet, and I hope that you will be here when I return. I will pray for you every day."

"Thank ye, mistress," Lucy said, her voice trembling with misery. "It'll be a miracle if I'm still here, but I appreciate yer prayers on me behalf. Go with God!"

There was so much Elise wanted to say to the girl, but there were others within earshot, so she couldn't do more than nod and retrace her steps. Lucy had been her only friend during these lonely months, and she was leaving her to die while she ran toward freedom. Elise felt a stab of guilt, but there was nothing she could do. Even if she tried to take Lucy with her, James would not allow it. He balked at the notion of taking Peg, but Elise convinced him that she'd need a maid. Elise prayed that she hadn't made the wrong decision in bringing Peg. She could already be infected, but then again, so could she. They could all already be one foot in the grave, including James, who'd just traveled through London on horseback.

Elise snuck a peek at James. He looked tired, having just ridden through the night, but there was a vitality in him that gave her a small surge of hope. He was vibrating with determination and purpose, and she suddenly believed that not all was lost. He'd get her to safety, her and their child. The thought lit a warm glow in her belly, and the babe suddenly kicked, making her gasp with surprise as her hand flew to her stomach. James spun on his heel at the sound but was reassured by the smile on her face.

"So, it's quickened, then?" he asked, not expecting an answer. He held out a tentative hand toward her belly but instantly drew it back, aware of Peg's curious stare.

"Come now, my lady," James said instead. "There's no time to waste."

"Go with James?" Barbara asked as she took James by the hand and smiled up into his face. She didn't seem to fully understand what was happening but didn't appear to be put off by leaving with James. She seemed to trust him wholeheartedly.

"Yes, my lady. You are to come with us. You will be all right," he assured her with a patient smile.

"All right," Barbara repeated, still smiling.

Chapter 38

The day was oppressively hot but overcast. Thick clouds blanketed the sky, threatening rain, and the air stood still, as if holding its breath. Elise was surprised to see a carriage waiting outside when she finally emerged with Peg. Edward kept a fine carriage but rarely used it, preferring the sedan chair when he went to the palace. Still, he would be furious to find his carriage and horses gone. He did not ride since his accident, and the sedan chair could only be used for local outings. If and when he finally decided to leave, he'd have no means of transportation. Elise was about to mention this to James but changed her mind. He already knew, and he didn't care. James was in the process of tying his own horse behind the carriage, so as not to leave it behind. Two grooms watched from the stable, their expressions wistful.

The servants were sullen and silent as they gathered to watch their mistress leave, resentful of her timely escape. They understood only too well what awaited them within the next few weeks. Few would survive, if any. Elise was tormented with guilt, but there was nothing she could do for them. She noticed one of the servants pinch Peg as she walked by. Peg winced and paled visibly but didn't complain. She understood their anger and would have been just as envious if she weren't leaving with the mistress.

Cook pushed her way through the crowd of servants and walked down the steps. She approached Elise slowly, her mouth a grim slash across her face. She didn't smile, nor did she wish Elise well. She simply placed a bundle of food into her hands and walked away, her anger palpable. Elise accepted the offering with a nod of thanks. She made no apologies; there was no point.

James was impatient to leave, so Peg, Barbara, and Elise climbed into the carriage without further ado and shut the door. They felt the vehicle rock gently from side to side when James jumped onto the bench. He'd put on his kerchief again to block out the noxious fumes of the city and pulled his hat down to shield his face. Peg leaned back against the seat as the carriage began to move, breathing a sigh of relief. She had the look of a woman who'd just been spared the gallows while Barbara gazed about with interest. She never left the house, so to her this was probably an adventure.

Elise took one last look at the imposing facade of Asher Hall as the carriage turned into the street. Edward would be furious when he returned from Whitehall and found her gone, but she didn't much care. She had a chance at life, and she wouldn't forfeit it because of the deluded ideas of her misguided husband. If Edward wished to stay in London because His Majesty was still in residence, that was his prerogative, but he had no business sentencing Elise and her baby to death. Elise allowed herself a small smile. Had someone told her that she would become so defiant after only a few months of marriage, she wouldn't have believed them, but life with Edward Asher had changed her in ways she never expected—whether it was for the better remained to be seen.

Elise settled back against the padded seat and placed her hands on either side in an effort to retain her balance as the carriage jolted over the rutted street. She debated whether she should pull down the leather blinds. Covering the windows would offer anonymity, but it would also plunge the interior into tomblike darkness, not a prospect she relished. *A few more minutes*, Elise thought as she leaned forward to see how far they'd traveled. She saw several men striding toward the house with a determined gait. They carried a bucket of red paint and a brush, ready to mark Asher Hall as a plague house. One of the men noticed the carriage and raised his hand, demanding that James stop, but James whipped the horses and the carriage lurched forward, tossing Elise headlong into Peg and Barbara, who squealed with alarm. Elise grabbed on to Peg and the frightened girl, and they held on for dear life as James raced down the street, putting distance between the carriage and the angry men. Two men started after them, but the vehicle moved quickly and soon left them behind, their curses and threats still echoing in Elise's ears as she tried to calm her racing heart.

James avoided busy streets, which would force him to slow down, and sped down a narrow road for a few minutes before turning onto what Elise thought might be Holborn. She didn't know London that well, having grown up in Southwark, but Peg looked distinctly nervous as she pressed her nose to the uncovered window.

"What is it, Peg?" Elise asked the frightened maid.

"I think Master James is heading toward Newgate," Peg muttered, her expression worried.

"What of it?"

"He seems to be going toward the city rather than away from it."

"I suspect he knows what he's doing," Elise answered sternly. It gave her immense comfort to know that she trusted James. He had a plan, of that she was sure. Elise leaned back and tried to force herself to relax. They were away from Asher Hall, so at least they were safe for the moment. The carriage slowed down considerably as they approached Newgate. James had timed their escape well. The gates were the most congested in the mornings and before closing time when people were streaming in and out of the city. There was traffic at this hour, but at least it was moving. They were surrounded by carriages, sedan chairs, men on horseback, and those on foot. People's faces were grim and wary as they shuffled toward the gate. Some held handkerchiefs and bunches of nosegays to their noses, but most were too accustomed to the smells of the city to even notice and didn't think a sprig of flowers would protect them from the pestilence should it come for them.

Elise pulled down the shades, uncomfortably aware of the hostile stares she received from passersby. The interior of the carriage was airless and hot, but Elise was grateful not to be outside mingling with people who, if not ill, were filthy and disgruntled. The carriage offered a modicum of protection and sealed them in a tiny world of their own, offering a false sense of security. They finally passed through the gate and into the walled city of London, where Elise felt safe enough to open the blinds again and look out. The people who entered through the gate dispersed in various directions, and although the streets were congested with traffic, the city was quieter than ever.

Elise spotted many red crosses painted on doors, and the people who were out in the street hurried along, their eyes downcast. The cheerful bustle of the city had been replaced by a miserable pall, the fear almost palpable. Elise gasped with shock when she saw a cumbersome wagon make its way slowly down the street. An old man drove the wagon, his face covered with a black kerchief and his hat pulled down low. His eyes were fixed on the road ahead, glinting with grim determination. Two more men walked alongside, calling out, "Bring out yer dead." They banged on doors with red crosses, urging the inhabitants to dispose of corpses. Many doors remained firmly shut, but some opened, and frightened, filthy people came out and added their dead to the pile of corpses already stacked on the bed of the wagon. Elise couldn't see the faces of the dead, but she could see several pairs of dirty feet hanging off the back of the wagon.

"Will they get a proper burial?" Elise asked Peg, who was staring at the wagon fearfully. Her hands were folded in her lap, but they were shaking.

"They'll throw them into plague pits with a bit o' lye," Peg whispered.

"How do you know?"

"Me mam told me. Both her parents died in 1625. 'T'were a terrible time, then. She were only four. Her brother Jack was eight and took care of her until someone found 'em. An uncle took 'em in but only after the forty days. Me mam and Jack were shut in with their dead parents for near a month. They almost starved to death. Jack climbed out the window at night and foraged for food while me mam slept."

Elise shuddered at the thought. Would it get as bad this time? She hoped not, but judging by the number of marked doors, it was bad already. She stole a peek at Barbara, who was looking out the window and humming quietly to herself. She didn't seem affected by anything she saw, so that at least was a blessing. The carriage continued on, and Elise leaned back and closed her eyes, so as not to see any more. She was terribly frightened.

She must have dozed off for a bit but woke up when the carriage came to an abrupt halt. It was so hot inside, she could barely draw breath. Her chemise was soaked with perspiration, and her face was flushed and clammy. She gazed out the window. They appeared to have reached another gate.

"Where are we, do you think?" she asked Peg.

"I reckon we're by Bishopsgate now. I 'xpect Master James is making for the Old North Road."

It was now midafternoon, and the gate was bottlenecked with wagons leaving the city, the farmers having made their deliveries of produce, meat, and dairy and ready to return home to the outlying countryside. Elise could see several coaching inns from the window. One or two appeared closed, but the ones that were open seemed to have little business. The shutters were closed despite the hour, and the yards seemed deserted. Several doors had some type of proclamations nailed to the wood.

"They've closed them to keep the pestilence from spreading," Peg said knowledgeably.

"Does it help?"

Peg shrugged.

It took the better part of an hour to finally get through the gate. Elise noticed the bishop's miter built into the gate as they passed underneath. It grew momentarily dark, and then they were on the other side, but it wasn't a great improvement. Elise sucked in her breath as the stench assaulted her. Piles of refuse had been dumped outside the city gates, left to rot in the hot summer sun. Clouds of flies buzzed above the mound, and the stink was so evil that it made Elise's eyes water. She covered her nose and tried not to take deep breaths until they finally passed the dump.

The road was congested, but the farther they got from the city gates, the faster they were able to proceed. She suspected that James wouldn't want to travel through the night. It was dangerous on the roads after dark, and she was sure he was worn out after traveling from Suffolk the day before. She expected him to stop when they approached roadside inns, but the carriage kept moving, rocking from side to side as James whipped the horses.

As darkness settled around them, the air in the carriage grew cooler and fresher. Peg and Barbara were slumped against the side of the coach, asleep, but Elise stared outside, even though she couldn't make out anything in the darkness. She spotted candlelight occasionally, coming from a farmhouse window, but otherwise, everything was quiet and dark. Elise hadn't been able to eat before, but now she was starving. She reached into the bundle of food and tore a chunk of bread from the loaf. There was some cheese and a bit of sausage. She had some and washed it down with ale, gulping it directly from the leather flask. Despite the heat of the day, the ale was cool, and she felt marginally better. *James must be hungry,* she thought. He hadn't eaten anything at all.

Elise suddenly realized that she desperately needed to relieve herself. It had been hours since they left, and she had been holding it in without realizing, fearful of stopping. Elise wasn't sure how to alert James, so she knocked on the side of the carriage closest to the bench. She hoped he'd hear her. The carriage didn't stop, so she knocked again and again, waking Barbara, who stared at her in blind panic.

"It's all right," Elise assured her as the carriage finally slowed and came to a stop.

James opened the door and peered inside. "What's wrong?"

"I need a few moments of privacy," Elise said, amused by her own choice of words. This was no time to be delicate.

"Of course." James looked tired and irritable, but he'd pulled down his kerchief and taken off his hat, dragging his fingers through his damp hair, which had come loose from its binding.

"James, there's some food and ale. You must eat."

James shook his head stubbornly. "Not now. We still have a few miles to cover tonight. I'll take a drink though."

James gulped down the ale as Elise set off, holding Barbara by the hand. She was too frightened to go far, so she chose the first bush and squatted down behind it to do her business, urging Barbara to do the same. Peg joined them in a moment.

"I'm fit to burst," she said as she lifted her skirts. "Are we to keep going, then?"

"I think Master James has a destination in mind," Elise replied as she adjusted her clothing and walked back to the carriage with whatever dignity she could muster. James gave her the empty flask and helped her into the carriage before climbing back up onto the bench. Peg came back with Barbara and reached for the bundle of food, offering bread and cheese to Barbara first. Barbara didn't seem impressed by the offering but took it all the same, and she chewed the food with all the enjoyment of eating dirt, her expression never changing. They traveled for another hour or so before the carriage finally stopped. A small inn was situated on the side of the road, the ground floor windows alight. A young boy came out of the stables as soon as he heard the carriage draw up and smiled up at James, revealing several missing teeth.

"Shall I see to the 'orses, sir?"

"Yes. And take the carriage out back," James instructed as he threw the boy a coin. The boy caught it deftly and took the reins, ready to walk the horses toward a dark building behind the inn. He would unharness the horses for the night and feed and water the poor beasts. They'd earned their rest.

James escorted the women into the inn. "Good evening to you, Rupert," he said to the man who came out to greet them. "We need a room for the night and a hot meal."

"I've kept a room back just as ye requested, Master James. Shall I send the food up or would ye like to eat down 'ere?"

James glanced at Elise. She shrugged, indicating that she didn't care either way. And she didn't. She was so tired, she could have sat down right where she stood and gone to sleep, with or without eating.

"We'll eat down here, if it's all the same. I'd like some hot water sent up after the meal."

"Of course, sir."

Fatigue notwithstanding, Elise ate with relish. She was starving despite having a bit to eat in the carriage, and she was very thirsty. The stew wasn't half-bad, and the bread was fresh and slathered with butter. She drank three cups of ale and wiped her mouth with the back of her hand, making James chuckle. He ate like a man who hadn't eaten in a week. Elise wondered what he had been up to these past few months and what made him come for her now. James barely said anything as he ate, and she didn't press him. He was obviously exhausted, so questions would have to wait.

James waited downstairs while Elise, Barbara, and Peg used the warm water to wash. They undressed and climbed into the narrow bed in their chemises, their bodies pressed against each other for lack of space. When James finally came in, he bedded down on the floor with an extra blanket and went to sleep immediately, seemingly unaware of any discomfort.

Elise's back ached from hours of jolting, so she stretched out and tried to carefully massage her back without elbowing Peg, who was already sound asleep. Elise's mind was teeming with questions, so she began to hum a mellow tune in order to calm her mind. It worked, and she began to feel drowsy, her body sinking into the thin mattress as it began to relax. Elise closed her eyes and smiled. She was surprised to discover that despite everything, she was suddenly happy. Her melancholy had lifted, and she was eager to find out what tomorrow would bring. Elise rested her hand on her belly and waited for the baby to kick, pleased that it obliged.

"Good night to you too," she whispered and fell into a dreamless sleep.

Chapter 39

November 2013

Surrey, England

It took Quinn several hours to get to sleep after the confrontation with Gabe, and when she finally managed to doze off, her sleep was fitful and plagued by strange dreams. She was in seventeenth-century London, alone and terrified. Everywhere people were dying of the plague, and piles of dead bodies were carelessly left to rot, the stench so overpowering that it was nearly impossible to draw breath. She tried to run, but her huge belly slowed her down, and she felt exhausted and out of breath after only a few steps. Each street wound up being a dead end. Quinn felt overwhelming panic as she tried to find a way out of the labyrinth of tiny alleyways, but everywhere she went, there were red crosses on wooden doors and carts full of corpses.

Quinn breathed a sigh of relief when a carriage pulled up, driven by Rhys Morgan, who looked right at home in seventeenth-century attire. He smiled at her and invited her to get in. Quinn felt tremendous relief as she climbed in, but it was short-lived since the carriage wasn't empty. Gabe was slumped in the corner, his head resting against the side of the vehicle. He was gray and clammy, his eyes vacant as he stared at her. He was obviously ill. Quinn reached out to him, but he pushed her hand away, lifting his arm to reveal an egg-size bubo in his armpit. Quinn screamed and jumped out of the carriage, which drove away without her.

Quinn woke with a start, her heart pounding with fear and her forehead covered in cold sweat. It took her several minutes to calm down and remember that she was at home in her own bed. She put a hand to her stomach, breathing a sigh of relief to find it still flat. She'd never been pregnant, but the love she felt toward the baby in her dream had been all encompassing. She would have done anything to protect her unborn child, anything at all.

Quinn turned on a bedside lamp and angrily wiped the tears from her eyes. She supposed the feeling must have been there all along, but she was conscious of it for the first time. She didn't just *want* a child—she'd never feel complete without one. Luke didn't really want children, so she resigned herself to possibly never becoming a mother if she married him. It had been a sacrifice she was prepared to make, but now, suddenly, she realized that she'd never actually thought it through. They had both been busy with their careers, their lives too hectic to start a family, but now she was nearly thirty, and the desire for a baby filled her with the kind of longing that took her breath away. Was she channeling Elise somehow? Elise hadn't wanted a baby, but once she found out she was pregnant, her maternal instinct took over, her love for her baby as natural as day turning into night.

Quinn got out of bed and went to get a glass of water. She was still shaken by the dream. It left her confused and weepy. She sat down in front of the cold hearth and stared into the ashes of last night's fire. She'd been unusually emotional since "meeting" Elise, and some of Elise's feelings seemed to find their way into Quinn's own heart. She'd never experienced this before, not with any of the people whose lives she'd been privileged enough to see, not even Grandma Ruth's. She'd always been an impartial observer, not a participant.

"You're really losing the plot, Allenby," she said out loud as she finished her drink and padded back to bed. "Get a grip."

Chapter 40

June 1665

Road to Suffolk

The rain came down in nearly horizontal sheets of water. Elise ran toward the carriage, her impractical shoes getting soaked in mere moments and squelching loudly. The hem of her skirt was muddy, and rainwater ran into her bodice, but it felt good on her skin, and the air smelled fresh and summery. Elise turned her face up to the sky, put her arms out, and did a graceful pirouette, as if she were performing some pagan rain dance. She came to a stop and closed her eyes, savoring the moment. Elise couldn't recall the last time she felt such a sense of abandon. It was as if the chains binding her grew slacker with every mile that separated her from London and her husband.

Elise opened her eyes to find James watching her. Rain dripped from the brim of his hat and his coat was soaked, but he didn't seem to notice as he gave Elise a warm smile before handing her into the carriage. They'd barely spoken since he came to fetch her yesterday, but there seemed to be a kind of new understanding between them, an unspoken bond. Peg dashed from the door of the inn to the carriage and jumped in, collapsing onto the seat. She was remarkably dry.

"Ye'll get a chill," she said reproachfully. "Just look at the state of ye."

"Stop fussing, Peg. It feels good," Elise retorted, feeling chastened nonetheless. Her behavior wasn't ladylike, but she didn't feel much like a lady. She felt like her old self, a carefree girl who was full of hopes and dreams. The carriage lurched, and they got on their way. It would take longer to get to Suffolk than anticipated, what with the roads awash and the wheels getting stuck every few miles, but Elise didn't care. She was in no rush to get to their destination. While on the road, she was free. Once they arrived, she'd be Lady Asher again, and she would no longer be invisible. And sooner or later, she would have to return. The thought was soul crushing, so she put it out of her mind for the time being. She would enjoy this, no matter what.

**

The manor house was located two miles west of the town of Southwold on the shore of the North Sea and was built of forbidding gray stone. The crenelated tower was silhouetted against the leaden sky, its sections like giant teeth taking a bite out of the heavens. The estate was vast and well managed, by all accounts, the parkland full of game. Elise gazed up at the great house as the carriage drew closer. It stood atop a slight incline, like a fortress. She supposed that it might have been a fortress once, as the middle section appeared to have been part of a keep, and the dip in the ground that surrounded the house might have been a moat. Elise looked for any evidence of a curtain wall but found none. Perhaps her imagination was getting the better of her.

James did not drive the carriage up to the front door but stopped in front of the stables, where he unhitched the horses and led them away to be fed and watered after helping Elise, Barbara, and Peg alight from the carriage. They walked slowly toward the house, taking in their surroundings. All the windows were shuttered. The massive oak door remained firmly closed, and there seemed to be no activity in or around the building. There didn't even appear to be a groom to see to the horses.

"Where is everyone?" Peg asked as she looked around in dismay.

"The house is closed up," James said as he approached them, having dealt with the horses and carriage.

"Where have you been staying?" Elise asked, wondering what James had been up to these past few months.

"At the gamekeeper's cottage. The man died near a year ago, and it's been vacant since, so I took it over."

"Is that where we will stay?" Elise asked carefully.

"You are the lady of the house, so it's only proper that you stay in the house. I'll send word to Master Grove, the estate manager, that you have arrived, and he will see to provisions and servants. You can stay with me until the house is fit for habitation. Peg will act as chaperone," he added with a wry smile. "It's just through there."

James took hold of Elise's valise with one hand and offered his other hand to Barbara, who took it eagerly. He led them down a narrow, wooded path that seemed to stretch on for miles. Peg followed behind, muttering under her breath. Unlike Lucy, whose disposition had been sunny, Peg was a complainer, and her mouth was more often pouty than smiling. Having lived in London all her life, Peg wasn't used to walking long distances and was out of breath by the time they finally arrived at the clearing where the cottage was situated.

The cottage was small but clean and comfortable. The first room consisted of a large hearth, a table with two narrow benches, a wooden chest, and an alcove for a bed. The second room held a larger bed, another chest at the foot of the bed, and a nightstand with a pitcher, basin, and a pewter candlestick. There was also a loft accessible by a ladder.

"Have you been living here all on your own?" Elise asked, taking in the surprising orderliness of the place.

"Master Grove's daughter, Lizzie, comes by twice a week. She cleans and cooks for me." James seemed at bit uncomfortable at the mention of Lizzie, and Elise felt a pang of jealousy, which she quickly suppressed. What right did she have to be angry? James was a free man, and if he found some comfort in the arms of a comely maid, well that was his business.

"She's thirteen," James said pointedly, as if reading her thoughts.

"Ah. Is she a good cook, then?" Elise asked to hide her embarrassment. Was she so transparent?

"Passable." James glanced at Peg who instantly bristled.

"Well, don't ye look at me. I ain't no kitchen maid."

James shrugged and carried Elise's bag into the bedroom. "You can sleep in here, your ladyship. Lady Barbara, it's the alcove for you, and Peg can take the loft. There's a cot up there."

Peg didn't look pleased since she'd been clearly hoping that James would take the loft and leave her to sleep in the alcove, where it was bound to be warmer and dryer, but she wisely refrained from commenting. She was lucky to be away from London, and she knew it. Peg took her small bundle and climbed up the ladder, eager to investigate her sleeping quarters.

"And where will you sleep?" Elise asked.

"On the floor. I'll be fine, don't you worry," James added, seeing her expression. "It won't be the first time. I'll call on Master Grove and inform him of your arrival," James said as soon as Peg disappeared up the ladder.

James looked at Elise as if he wished to say something more, then turned on his heel and left. Barbara sat down by the window and took a piece of embroidery out of her basket, instantly content. There was nothing for Elise to do, so she stretched out on the bed and placed her hands on her belly. The baby gave a hearty kick, making Elise smile. She didn't wish to stay in the big, empty house. She liked it just fine here and would have gladly kept the knowledge of her arrival from the estate manager. How wonderful it would be to simply vanish for a while and live as she pleased with no one watching her or passing judgment. A place to sleep and simple, country food was all she needed to be happy, and James and Peg were company enough. But, she was Lady Asher, and James wouldn't hear of it. Besides, he wouldn't wish them infringing on his privacy.

Chapter 41

When James returned an hour later, he was accompanied by a young girl, who curtsied to Elise as if she were the queen, nearly dropping the basket she carried. Lizzie was thin and willowy, with abundant brown hair and large dark eyes. She unpacked the supplies she brought and went to work immediately, and within the hour the small house was filled with the smells of cooking. Once Lizzie got the stew going, she deftly kneaded some dough and made it into four loaves, which she placed in an opening on the side of the hearth to bake while the stew bubbled over the open flame.

Elise's mouth watered with hunger, but she'd have to be patient. Instead, she asked James to bring some water from the well and she washed hastily and put on a fresh gown. The one from that morning was still damp. Peg arranged it on the bench, which she pulled up to the hearth so that the gown could dry.

"That smells wonderful, Lizzie," Elise said as she inhaled the rich fragrance of cooking meat.

"Thank ye, me lady. Me da caught the rabbits just this mornin' and me ma skinned them quick-like once she found out ye'd arrived." Lizzie suddenly looked worried, realizing that she'd just unwittingly admitted that her father helped himself to the master's game. Some might see that as poaching, but Elise saw it as nothing more than good sense.

"Well, how clever of them," she said, smiling at the girl. "Do you have a big family?" Elise asked. She liked this sprite of a girl.

"I have three younger brothers, me lady. Two of them is twins, but they look nothin' alike. And me mam is breedin' again. I do hope 'tis a girl this time. I want a sister, I do. Brothers are useless," she added with a pout.

"You might change your mind once they're older," James said with a grin. "They'll look after you."

"Hmm," Lizzie said, her tone dubious. "More like I'll be lookin' after them."

Elise thought there was some truth to that but didn't comment. Perhaps Lizzie would be wed at a young age and have her own family to take care of, leaving her younger brothers to fend for themselves until they found brides.

"I'll have to take care of Joe for sure," she continued, warming up to her theme. "He's mute. Soft in the head too," she added, tapping herself on the temple.

"That must be hard on your parents," Elise said, wondering if Barbara heard what Lizzie just said, but her expression remained impassive as she continued to focus on her needlework.

"Neh. He don't do much, but he's strong, so Da puts him to work chopping wood and helping Ma round the house. He's harmless."

Lizzie pulled the pot out of the hearth and stirred the contents, releasing fragrant steam into the room. "This could use another hour or so, but I know ye're hungry, and the meat is cooked through. Shall I serve it now?" she asked.

"Please do. I'm famished. It's time to eat, Barbara," she said. Barbara obediently set aside her embroidery and took a seat at the table. Elise sat down next to her and accepted a bowl of stew. James sliced the bread, and Peg poured out some ale.

"Won't you join us, Lizzie?" Elise asked. "There's plenty for everyone."

"Thank ye, yer ladyship, but I must be away," Lizzie replied shyly. "If you'll leave the dishes, I'll do them first thing tomorrow mornin' for ye when I bring breakfast." She executed another curtsey and left, taking the empty basket with her.

The stew was delicious, and Elise ate her fill before declaring herself ready for bed. Peg helped her undress and brushed out her hair while James saw to the dirty dishes and covered the remaining bread so that it wouldn't grow stale overnight. There was no need for a fire since the night was warm, so Elise said goodnight and closed her door. Barbara was already in her bed, snoring lightly behind the curtains. Elise longed to talk to James, but nothing other than pleasantries had been exchanged between them thus far, and Peg was constantly about, making it difficult to find a moment of privacy. Elise wasn't concerned about Barbara overhearing them, but Peg was a different matter.

Elise drifted off to sleep only to be woken what seemed like a few moments later by the opening of her door. She peered into the darkness, trying to make out who it was. She thought it might be Barbara but discovered James standing by the foot of the bed. He looked uncertain for a moment, then came around and climbed in next to Elise. This was not what she expected, but she shifted her body to make room for him. James didn't say anything, just cupped her cheek, stroking her face with his thumb tenderly.

Elise opened her mouth to ask him what he thought he was doing when his lips came down on hers and he kissed her gently. This wasn't a passionate kiss, brought on by desire; this kiss was tender and full of feeling. She knew that she should push him away and ask him to leave, no good could come of this, but something at her core seemed to melt. It had been so long since anyone touched her, especially with love. James's hand slid downward and rested on the swell of her belly. He didn't say anything, but she knew the gesture for what it was. He was claiming ownership and making a connection with his child. He'd never touched her this way before, had never gazed into her eyes like this, fearing too great an intimacy. But now he was looking at her, and she was looking back.

Elise reached out and stroked his face. His jaw was covered with three-day stubble, and his cheeks seemed leaner than before, as if he hadn't been eating well of late. He sighed quietly when she ran her hand over his well-muscled chest. Elise felt James's heartbeat beneath her fingertips. His heart seemed to be pounding, or was that hers?

Elise expected James to say something, but he suddenly got out of bed, kissed her on the forehead, and vanished into the other room, leaving her completely bemused. Elise gazed after him for a long moment, unsure if he might be coming back, then closed her eyes and willed herself to go to sleep. It had been a long day, and they'd have plenty of time to talk later.

Chapter 42

November 2013

Surrey, England

When Quinn woke up on Saturday morning after her fragmented night of sleep, she felt grumpy and depressed. Her head ached, and random scenes from the awful dream kept popping into her mind. The row with Gabe weighed heavily on her mind, and she suddenly felt like a caged animal, desperate to get out. She made herself a cup of strong coffee, dressed hastily, and fled the house. She needed to talk to someone, and that someone was Jill.

Quinn glanced at the dashboard clock. It had just gone 9:00 a.m., so by the time she got to London, Jill would just be opening her shop. Quinn didn't think Jill would mind her popping by. She was in the shop alone all day, and Quinn was more than willing to help out with whatever needed doing. She had no wish to be underfoot, only to enjoy a bit of her cousin's company. She picked up two cappuccinos and several almond croissants on the way. She hadn't had anything to eat since lunchtime of the previous day, and Jill, despite her slender build, was always up for a cup of coffee and a pastry.

Jill was already working, rearranging some summer clothes on a rack closest to the door and marking them down for a clearance sale in order to make room for new winter inventory. She was wearing a long colorful blouse with a pair of black leggings and comfortable suede boots. Jill's blonde hair was piled high on her head, errant curls framing her lovely face as she smiled in welcome.

"Have you come to return your clothes?" she asked with a look of mock horror. "All sales are final," she added with a chuckle, although, of course they weren't.

"No, I've come to buy more. And to talk."

"And you've brought treats." Jill *oohed* as she took in the box of pastries and the steaming cups of cappuccino. "I've been here since seven, reorganizing all these racks. People just hang things up willy-nilly without any thought for size or order." Jilly pouted, the pedant in her clawing its way out.

"Not everyone thinks like an accountant, Jilly. Most people prefer chaos."

"Hmm, you're probably right," Jill replied as she scooped up several pairs of jeans and organized them according to size. She gave Quinn her full attention once the merchandise had been arranged to her satisfaction. Jill gratefully accepted the coffee, plucked a croissant out of the box, and perched on a high stool behind the counter, gesturing for Quinn to take the other chair. Quinn sat down as well and sipped her own cappuccino, unsure of how to begin.

"What happened, coz?" Jill asked, skipping small talk as usual. "You look like death warmed over."

"I had a terrible row with Gabe last night," Quinn confessed.

"Ah, let me guess," Jill said with an impish grin. "Gabe came by, told you that he's loved you for years, and demanded that you fall into his arms right there and then?"

Quinn bristled. "Now why would you assume that?"

"The man has been in love with you for nearly a decade. Everyone could see it except you. You were so blinded by Luke that a meteor could have struck central London and you wouldn't have noticed."

"I thought you liked Luke," Quinn protested, slightly wounded by Jill's assessment of her grasp on reality.

Jill gave Quinn a pitying look. "Quinn, you liked Luke. You liked him so much that no one could say a word against him, not even your parents. But now he's gone, and you have a chance to be with someone who might actually make you a priority in his life."

"And you think that person is Gabe?" Quinn asked, already sure of Jill's answer.

"I think that life gives us a couple of chances to be happy, and if we miss those chances, we regret them forever." Quinn knew that Jill was speaking from experience. She'd been single for several years now, and she bitterly regretted not making a commitment to someone who loved her when she had the chance, choosing her demanding career over her personal life. Jill's ex-boyfriend Paul, who'd proposed to Jill several times before finally taking the hint, was now happily married to someone else and a father of twin girls. He still sent Quinn Christmas cards every year, and last year's card had been the cutest yet. Jill had chucked in her career in the end, but it'd been too late to rekindle her romance with Paul. He'd moved on.

"I was happy with Luke," Quinn replied defensively, tossing the better part of her croissant in the rubbish bin. She was no longer hungry.

"Were you?" Jill asked, her expression all innocence.

"I thought I was. We wanted the same things in the beginning, but then my priorities changed," Quinn confessed. "I wanted to get married. And I wanted children," Quinn added miserably. She never told Jill that Luke never wanted children. She would have had something to say about that, and she would have been right.

"Quinn, I am all for the empowerment of women and equality in the workplace, but men and women are not the same and never will be. Our needs are different because our bodies are different. You might not have wanted a family in your early twenties, but you're thirty now, and like it or not, your body is reminding you of that. You wanted commitment and the promise of a family with Luke, but he still wanted the same things he desired when you first met, and he got them. He can play the field for another twenty years if he wishes and then change his mind and have a family after all. You, as a woman, are not on the same time schedule and cannot be expected to wait indefinitely until he's ready to settle down."

"He didn't want to marry me," Quinn confessed sadly. She couldn't bear to tell Jill that Luke had been cheating on her. It was too humiliating.

"He didn't want to marry anyone. Luke is ruthlessly ambitious and terrified of growing old and irrelevant," Jill said as she punctuated her statement with her half-eaten croissant.

"Are you suggesting that he's shagging his students to feel young?" Quinn chuckled, amazed by how close Jill had come to the truth.

"I wouldn't be surprised. There's a reason that's such a cliché. It happens more often than you think. Maybe it's time you shagged someone."

"Really, like who? And don't say *Gabe*."

Jill shook her head. "I would never suggest that. You can only shag Gabe if you're serious about him. Anything else would be unfair. What about this Rhys guy? Do you fancy him?"

Quinn shrugged. "He's nice."

Jill rolled her eyes dramatically, making Quinn laugh. "Nice? Is that the best you can say about him?"

"He intrigues me. I barely know him, but there's a connection between us that I can't explain. It's like he understands me."

Jill rolled her eyes dramatically. "I bet he'd like to understand you all the way to bed. Has he tried it on with you yet?"

"No. He's just been—what is the word I'm looking for—solicitous."

"Oh, what a knight in shining armor. I hate men like that. They kill you with kindness."

"And baked goods," Quinn giggled. "Oh, Jill, you are no help whatsoever," Quinn complained, but her dark mood had dissipated and she felt much lighter.

"Sure I am. You came in here looking like a thundercloud and now you're laughing. Now pass us another croissant."

Quinn slid the box across the counter and considered what Jill had said. Jill was right, as usual. She did feel happier. Both women looked up as two potential customers came into the shop.

"Time to work my magic," Jill whispered, giving Quinn a meaningful wink. "Be right back."

Jill went to help the customers while Quinn considered Jill's advice. She'd never been one for mincing words, and the things she said about Luke were hurtful but true. Luke was a self-centered, ambitious, selfish tosser. Quinn supposed that she always knew that on some level, but love is blind, and so is faith. She'd believed in him, believed that he loved her enough to include her in his plans. Well, now she knew different. And she also knew that once Gabe finally settled down with one woman and surrendered his heart, he would love her until the end of his days, which was exactly the reason she was so terrified to give him any encouragement. To give him hope and then yank it away would be unforgivable, so she had to be sure.

Jill rang up the purchases and wished the two women a good day before turning back to Quinn. "I actually have a new bloke," she suddenly announced, her mouth stretching into a ridiculously wide grin.

"Oh, do tell. I'm tired of talking about my toxic love life."

"He's one of the suppliers I work with. We've stepped out a few times," Jill confided.

"You really like him, don't you?"

Jill nodded as a rosy blush spread across her porcelain cheeks. "I do. We're going out again tonight. Would you like to come? I can ask Brian to bring a friend."

"I actually already have plans, but thank you all the same," Quinn lied. She'd just go home and catch up on some reading or watch a film. She simply wasn't ready to go on a blind date, but the thought of spending another Saturday night alone left her feeling more out of sorts than before.

Chapter 43

Quinn walked toward Hyde Park and plopped herself onto a bench by the Serpentine. The day was sunny and bright, if a bit chilly. The river sparkled as it lazily flowed by, its waters reflecting the fluffy clouds above. A canopy of russet and gold whispered overhead, leaves twirling and settling on the ground to form a thick carpet of vivid color. Another few weeks and these leaves would be nothing more than brown sludge decaying into the earth, but at the moment, they were beautiful.

The walk to the park restored her spirits, and Quinn felt more philosophical than upset, especially after speaking with Jill. On some level, she was grateful to Monica for telling her the truth about Luke, painful though it was. Knowing about the affair shed new light on his behavior and gave new meaning to Luke's abrupt exit. What struck Quinn the most was that Luke had apparently been flaunting his new girlfriend in front of their mutual friends. He wanted people to know, and he hoped Quinn would find out. He had no desire for an amicable split; he wished to hurt her— badly. That realization hurt worst of all. He hadn't just betrayed and humiliated her, but he'd also made her question her own judgment. She'd trusted him, relied on him, and thought that he genuinely cared for her. But now she had no idea what to believe. How long had he felt this way? Was this woman the first or the last in a string of many? Had there been signs that Quinn missed, trusting Luke wholeheartedly as she had?

Quinn was startled out of her reverie by the trilling of her mobile. She pulled it out of her purse and pressed the answer button, disappointed that the call wasn't from Gabe. He was the only person she would have liked to talk to at that moment. It was Rhys, who was not someone she expected to call on a Saturday. And so Quinn put on a cheerful voice, desperate to hide her pain.

"Quinn, I hope I didn't wake you," he said.

"Are you joking? I've been up for hours. I'm not one of those people who sleep till noon."

"Neither am I."

"As it happens, I'm in London. I came to spend a few hours with my cousin."

"Oh, sorry to interrupt."

"You are not. She had to work, so I took myself to Hyde Park with the intention of taking a brisk walk. Instead, I'm sitting on a bench and watching the ducks."

"If you'd like some company, I'd be more than happy to watch the ducks with you," Rhys suggested.

"If you have nothing better to do, I'll be glad to see you." And she would be. Rhys's company was undemanding and amusing. He was just the right antidote to brooding alone in the park.

"All right. Just give me a half hour. I'll meet you there. Say, by the Prince Albert Memorial?"

They agreed on a time, and Rhys rang off. The prospect of seeing him lifted Quinn's spirits. She wasn't sure what she felt for him, but she was being honest when she told Jill that there was some kind of a connection between them. Rhys made her feel peaceful, whereas Gabe brought turmoil and uncertainty every time they saw each other. It hadn't been that way while she was with Luke, but now Luke was gone, and Gabe wasn't prepared to wait any longer.

Quinn smiled happily when she saw Rhys walking toward her. He was casually dressed in jeans and his habitual leather jacket, with a tartan scarf in shades of blue and gray wrapped around his neck. He leaned in and gave her a kiss on the cheek.

"I woke up this morning thinking that my prospects for this weekend looked bleak, but now I couldn't be happier," he said sincerely. "I'm so glad you are in London."

"Me too. I love living in a village, but sometimes it does feel stifling. I miss the bustle of the city."

"So, what would you like to do?" Rhys asked. "We can take a walk, go for lunch, visit a museum, or go see a film."

Quinn pretended to give it some thought, then took him by the arm. "Let's take a walk, then have some lunch, and after that we can see a film. What do you say?"

"I say that sounds like an excellent plan."

They walked off together into the park, chatting animatedly. Rhys wanted to hear all about Elise, so Quinn filled him in, enjoying the shock on his face when she described plague-ridden London in great detail and told him of her strange dream. Eventually, they got tired of walking and sat down by the river. Quinn didn't really notice when Rhys's arm encircled her, but she rested her head on his shoulder as they sat together in companionable silence. They remained that way for some time before Quinn looked up at him. Rhys leaned down and kissed her, making her heart flutter in her chest. She hadn't kissed anyone since Luke, so it had been a long while since she'd been kissed by a new man. The kiss was lovely, but it lacked passion, and Quinn carefully pulled away, mindful of hurting his feelings.

Rhys looked at her. "You are so beautiful, Quinn."

"You must meet beautiful women every day in your line of work," Quinn replied modestly. She wasn't used to compliments.

Luke had been stingy with praise, but he showed his admiration in other ways.

"I do, but they are not like you. You're real and so very intelligent. Smart women are sexy," he said with a smile. He leaned down and kissed her again, but Quinn pulled away after a few moments. Something just didn't feel right. Perhaps she wasn't ready to get involved with anyone just yet.

"Rhys, I . . ."

"There's no need to explain. Come, shall we go? I'm famished, as usual."

Quinn smiled and allowed Rhys to pull her to her feet. He wasn't angry, but she felt a slight chill in his attitude. He didn't touch her for the rest of the day.

Chapter 44

June 1665

Suffolk, England

Elise moved into the manor house two days after arriving in Suffolk. The house was gloomy and silent, as if it resented human presence and wanted only to be left vacant to continue its slow descent into decay. It smelled of dust and disuse after months, if not years, of being shut up and seemed to squint in irritation as shutters were thrown open and light penetrated shadowy corners. Mouse droppings littered the flagstone floor in the kitchen, making Elise wrinkle her nose in disgust, and a layer of grime covered the pots and pans that hung from the ceiling.

Elise walked from room to room, noting those that appealed to her. There were few. The house was decorated in an old-fashioned, almost medieval style, with oppressive dark paneling and heavy, uncomfortable furniture that didn't boast so much as a cushion to soften the hard wooden seats. There were several faded tapestries, the colors muted by years of accumulated dust, and a few paintings of Edward's illustrious forbearers. She chose a back bedroom for herself. Decorated in shades of dark green and mauve, it wasn't overly pretty or feminine, but Elise was enchanted by views of the sea. She'd never seen the sea before, and the vast body of water that stretched all the way to the horizon and seemed to flow right into the sky intrigued and frightened her at the same time. When she opened the window, she could hear the sound of the surf crashing onto the beach, and a fresh, briny smell filled her nostrils. The fresh breeze blew away the stale smell of the room in seconds and fluttered the heavy curtains, releasing a cloud of dust.

"Ye'd best close that, me lady," a voice behind her said. "Ye'll catch a chill."

Elise reluctantly closed the window and turned to Mistress Benford. The older woman would act as cook and housekeeper, and there were two girls who would come in from town to help out with cleaning and laundry. Peg would see to Elise and Barbara, and two lads had been sent over by the estate agent to care for the horses and help with any heavy tasks that were too much for the women. There was no permanent staff because Edward had not lived in the house since his wife died and he met with his riding accident. They were to be a small household, but that suited Elise just fine. She didn't need an army of servants to spy on her every move.

"Mistress Benford, I will choose several rooms to be cleaned and aired out. The rest can remain closed for now since we won't be using them at this time. The kitchen and everything in it needs to be scrubbed from top to bottom and all the supplies laid in fresh before any food is prepared. I prefer simple meals of mostly fish, fowl, or broth, and I take my supper early," Elise informed her. She hated to eat just before going to bed with the food sitting in her stomach and making her feel ill.

"Surely ye need to eat well in yer condition, me lady," Mistress Benford protested. "Meat and blood pudding and such. 'Tis good for the baby."

"I don't much care for meat, but I suppose if you prepare a meat dish once a week, I'll partake of it. For the baby," she added. But really it was for James. He liked meat, and Elise hoped that he would dine with her at least several times a week. Of course, for the lady of the house to dine with her husband's manservant was unseemly and would reach Edward's ears sooner rather than later, but she didn't care. Here, in Suffolk, she would do as she liked. Elise smiled to herself, pleased with her decision. Exercising a modicum of control—no matter how small—over her life was intoxicating.

Chapter 45

December 2013

Surrey, England

Quinn tossed her purse and keys on the small table by the door and went to pour herself a drink. It had been a long day. Rhys had scheduled back-to-back auditions for twenty actresses, eager to choose his star for the reenactment, and he wanted Quinn to attend. She was the only person who knew what Elise had looked like, and he wanted to find someone who resembled her as closely as possible. Of course, no one would know that there even was a resemblance, but Rhys was a perfectionist, and it was important to him to get the details right. Once Elise was chosen, he would turn his attention to casting James, Lord Asher, and Gavin Talbot. Quinn pointed out to Rhys that there was no factual data to link Gavin Talbot to Lady Asher, but Rhys thought that introducing a forbidden love into the reenactment would add a bit of spice to the proceedings. After all, Gavin had existed and had been involved in a relationship with Elise, even if there was no physical proof of the romance.

Quinn dutifully sat through twenty auditions, but none of the actresses struck the right chord. There was one who had coppery long hair and blue eyes and bore the closest physical resemblance to Elise, but she hadn't captured her essence. How could she when she had so little to go on? Quinn supposed that with the right script and some coaching from the director, she would eventually come close, but somehow casting her as Elise seemed like a betrayal. Quinn felt a responsibility to Elise and didn't wish to see her portrayed inaccurately.

Quinn plopped down on the sofa with her glass of mineral water and let out a deep breath. It had been less than a week since she'd spent the day with Rhys, but their dynamic had changed already. Despite her lack of encouragement, Rhys exhibited a proprietary air toward her, as if they were in a relationship. He'd kissed her softly when she arrived at the studio and absentmindedly caressed her hand beneath the table as a string of actresses read their monologues. Quinn felt unsettled and confused. She liked Rhys and found him attractive; on paper, he was the perfect man. Maybe she was expecting too much. She was older now and not the girl she'd been when she first got together with Luke and was drunk on love, lust, and the heady feeling of being in a serious relationship for the first time. Perhaps feelings took time to develop and desire followed, but deep down she knew she was deluding herself. Her thoughts strayed to Gabe every few minutes, her gut twisting with guilt at the thought of how they left things last time they spoke. She missed him, missed talking to him and just hearing the reassuring sound of his voice. Quinn longed to call him, but she wasn't sure what to say. Gabe had made his position clear, and she was still marginally angry with him for backing her into a corner.

The December night was cold and damp, so Quinn laid a fire in the grate and rummaged through her cupboards in search of something to make for dinner. She didn't enjoy cooking for herself, but she was hungry, having had nothing since the sandwich she had a noon. Pasta would have to do. She had some mushrooms, tomatoes, and zucchini, so she'd make pasta primavera. She just set some water to boil when there was a knock at the door. Quinn's heart leaped, buoyed by the thought that it might be Gabe coming to make peace. Quinn wiped her hands on a tea towel and went to answer the door, a smile of welcome spreading across her face. She was surprised to see a woman standing on the threshold. She looked vaguely familiar, but Quinn couldn't place her.

"May I help you?" she asked, seeing the woman's hesitation. "Are you lost?"

"No," the woman mumbled. Quinn waited for her to state her business, all the while studying her features. She was sure she'd seen her before. And then she remembered: she'd seen her in the graveyard when she visited the church with Rhys a few weeks ago. The woman had stared at her then, making her uncomfortable. What on earth was she doing on her doorstep now?

"Dr. Allenby, may I have a few moments of your time?" the woman finally asked. "I need to speak to you regarding a private matter." The woman looked so nervous that Quinn felt momentarily sorry for her. She kept pleating the fabric of her coat, and her eyes were full of apprehension, as if she expected Quinn to slam the door in her face.

"And you are?" Quinn prompted.

"My name is Sylvia Wyatt."

Quinn had reservations about letting a complete stranger into her home, but the woman looked harmless enough, and she was clearly under the strain of some great emotion. Quinn had to hear her out.

"Come in, Sylvia."

The woman nodded her thanks and walked into the house, looking about in wonder when she realized that she'd walked into a converted chapel.

"What a lovely place," she said as she shrugged off her coat and accepted Quinn's offer of a seat by the fire. "I see you are drawn to places of worship," Sylvia observed. Quinn didn't respond. She had no desire to get sidetracked.

"How can I help you?" Quinn asked gently. She longed to be alone, and this woman seemed to have trouble coming to the point.

"May I call you Quinn?" Sylvia asked.

"It's my name."

Sylvia was scrutinizing Quinn again, gazing at her face as if she wanted to remember every feature, every expression. Her own expression was difficult to describe, and Quinn found herself wishing that she hadn't let the woman in after all.

"What did you want to speak to me about?" Quinn prompted, growing more uncomfortable by the minute.

Sylvia took a deep breath and locked eyes with Quinn, her gaze unflinching. "I saw your photograph on the news after you'd been assaulted," she began. Quinn noticed that her hands were shaking in her lap but didn't comment.

"Yes, it was rather an unpleasant experience," Quinn said, her hand subconsciously going to the bruise still somewhat visible at her temple. It had healed and faded but not completely.

Sylvia nodded. "I have never really been interested in history," she said suddenly, making Quinn wonder what she was getting at.

"Not everyone is."

"I mean that I might have heard of you sooner had I watched any of the documentaries you were in. I wish I had."

Quinn nodded, unsure of what to say. She was starting to seriously regret allowing this strange woman into her house. Perhaps she believed that Quinn was some minor celebrity and wanted to talk to someone who'd been on television.

"Go on," Quinn prompted Sylvia again.

"You look so much like my mother," Sylvia whispered as she reached a tentative hand toward Quinn's face and then yanked it away, realizing how inappropriate the gesture was.

Quinn suddenly felt cold despite the roaring fire. She had noticed the woman in the graveyard because she looked so forlorn, but there was something familiar about her. Her almond-shaped hazel eyes, the dark, curling hair. Sylvia was no older than fifty . . . old enough to be her mother.

"Are you . . ." Quinn asked, her voice shaking.

Sylvia nodded. "I know how angry you must be, and I was terrified of approaching you. I came here two weeks ago, but I lost my nerve and went away without speaking to you. I've been in hell ever since. Quinn, please give me a chance to explain."

Quinn forced herself to take a few deep breaths. Her heart was pounding in her chest, and gooseflesh covered her arms. She'd dreamed of finding her mother, of learning where she came from and why she'd been abandoned, but now that the moment was here, she wasn't sure that she wanted to know. Sylvia Wyatt was a stranger to her, yet there was a connection between them that needed to be explored and would be within the next few minutes. Quinn wished she'd had time to prepare for this meeting as Sylvia had. She'd obviously had time to consider how to best approach Quinn and what to say, whereas Quinn was completely at a loss. She wished that her other mother was there with her, or Gabe. Oh, how she wished Gabe was with her to offer moral support. She felt an almost physical need to have him by her side, but he wasn't. She was on her own.

"Why did you not want me?" she finally asked. Quinn held her breath as she waited for the answer. All this time, she chose to believe that her mother couldn't keep her, but now that she was looking at this well-dressed, attractive woman, she suddenly had doubts.

Sylvia shook her head. "I didn't think I could love you," she said. Quinn wanted the truth, but the words sliced like a knife through her heart, making her wish that she'd never laid eyes on Sylvia Wyatt. What kind of person said that, especially after going through the trouble of contacting her long-lost daughter after thirty years?

"Why?" Quinn cried. She wasn't ready for this, didn't want to hear any more, but she knew there was no turning back. Now she had to know.

"I need to tell you what happened before I can answer that," Sylvia said. She was infuriatingly calm now, almost as if, for her, the worst part was over.

"So, tell me," Quinn cried. "You are the one who approached me, so quit stalling and tell me the truth, or get out." She hadn't meant to have such an outburst, but her emotions were boiling over, and she felt as if she might cry. Nothing had really changed, but suddenly Quinn felt as if she'd been rejected twice. Having this woman tell her that she couldn't love her was more painful than she ever expected.

"Quinn, my parents divorced when I was fifteen. My mum had a string of affairs, and my father finally lost all hope of turning their marriage around and asked her to leave. I didn't really want to stay with my mother, but it wasn't as if I had a choice. She never offered me a home; she just left. So, Dad and I moved to a village outside Lincoln, where he opened up a gourmet shop. Dad used to be in the restaurant business and hoped to expand the shop into a café and maybe even a restaurant, but the divorce was costly and his savings were depleted."

Sylvia stared past Quinn's shoulder as she spoke, her voice strangely flat. "I helped out in the shop after school. We'd been there for more than a year, but I still felt like an outsider. I didn't have many friends and having to help my dad every day curtailed any social activities I might have joined in after school."

Quinn watched Sylvia as she spoke. She could see the emotion in her eyes, but Sylvia couldn't seem to bring herself to look at Quinn as she told her story. She stared into the fire instead, preferring its mesmerizing comfort to facing the daughter she'd abandoned.

"There was a grand old house just outside the village—Bixby Hall. It belonged to the Bixby family for hundreds of years, since Tudor times, but there was only one descendant left, and he had no wish to retain the family seat. The hall was sold to Jeffrey Chatham, owner of Chatham Electronics. *New money*, that's what people in the village called him, as if new money was tainted somehow. I'd met Mr. Chatham a few times. He was a charming man, very fond of good wine and French cuisine. He came in often, so my father ordered certain items just for him."

Quinn felt as if she might burst with impatience, but Sylvia had that faraway look in her eyes, and Quinn let her talk. She needed to tell the story her way, so she had to be patient despite wanting to scream.

"One day, just before Christmas, Robert Chatham, Mr. Chatham's son, came into the shop. I'd never met him before, but he had his father's charm and beautiful manners. He bought nearly a hundred pounds' worth of food and wine. Said he was having drinks and nibbles at the manor house that evening for a couple of friends of his who'd come down from the University of Edinburgh for the holidays. He invited me to come. Said he would pick me up at seven." Sylvia paused for a moment, clearly reliving the moment in her mind.

"I was flattered. He was so good-looking. He drove a red sports car that must have cost more than my father's whole shop. I agreed to come," Sylvia said and Quinn noticed the moistening in her eyes. Was Robert Chatham her father?

"Robert picked me up as promised and took me to the house. It was grander than I'd expected. It looked like something out of *Pride and Prejudice*. Like Pemberley," Sylvia said dreamily.

"What happened?" Quinn cut in, unable to hold back any longer. "I need to know."

"There were two other young men and two girls from my school. I knew them, but we weren't friends. They were from wealthy families and not interested in the shopkeeper's daughter. I was nervous at first, but I began to relax. Everyone was friendly, and Robert made me feel welcome. He flirted with me and told me I was pretty."

"So, you slept with him?" Quinn asked.

Sylvia shook her head. "The party lasted for several hours, and Christina and Tamzin eventually left. Tamzin was old enough to drive and had her father's car. I was left with Robert and his friends. I asked him to take me home, but he invited me to stay for one more drink. I wasn't much used to drinking, and I was tipsy already, but it seemed churlish to refuse. Robert poured me another glass of champagne and we all sat by the fire, just talking, laughing, and having one last drink."

A tear slid down Sylvia's face, and she defiantly wiped it away. "He'd spiked my drink. I began to feel woozy and confused. My head grew heavy, and I slid down on the sofa. I wasn't asleep, but I couldn't summon the strength to fight back. Robert pulled down my jeans and knickers, and I heard him laugh as he undid his own fly. I tried to call out, but I couldn't seem to find my voice. Everything looked distorted, like in a funhouse mirror. I put my hands up to stop him, but he bent down and kissed me, silencing my protests. He pulled me down onto the floor and got on top of me. I might have been crying, but no one was moved by my tears. Robert's friends just sat there watching. He went first, and his friends followed. All three of them had sex with me that night. Then Robert dressed me, put me in his car, and took me home. He told my father that I was drunk and needed to be put to bed. My father thanked him for bringing me home and walked me to my room."

Quinn looked at Sylvia, horrified. "Did you report them?"

"No. I got a terrible scolding from my father the next morning. He couldn't believe I got drunk and behaved like such a slag. I was *just like my mother*, he said. I couldn't tell him what happened after that. I didn't think he'd believe me, and even if he did, he'd think that I brought it on myself. Robert and his friends left on Boxing Day, and I didn't see them again. I tried to deal with what happened and just get on with my life," she said with a sad smile. "Of course, that was not to be."

"Why didn't you have a termination?" Quinn asked, surprised that Sylvia would want to keep the child after what happened.

"My periods were never regular, so it wasn't unusual for me not to have it for three or four months. By the time I discovered that I was pregnant, I was nearly five months along. I didn't feel any different, so I had no reason to suspect anything. I'd put the whole episode out of my mind, so desperate was I to forget what happened."

"Did you tell your father?" Quinn asked.

"I couldn't. It would break his heart. He'd think that he failed me somehow and that he should have been a better parent. He'd have blamed himself, or worse yet, would have thought that I was just like my mother and there was nothing he could have done to prevent what happened. I waited until the school year was over, then told him I was going to stay with Mum for the summer. He was upset, but he let me go. I knew that he wouldn't call my mother and check, so as long as I called him regularly, he would think that everything was all right. I went to Lincoln and found a waitressing job and a bedsit. I was hardly showing and wore baggy clothes in the hopes of keeping my pregnancy a secret. The summer went by, and I told my employer that I had to go back home in time for school. I'd found a midwife in the newspaper and called her when my labor began. I didn't want to go to a hospital since they would have insisted on calling my father because I was still a minor. The poor woman was surprised to hear from me since I hadn't consulted her before, but she had no choice but to assist me. The labor was quick, and before I knew it, you were born."

"What happened then?" Quinn asked. She already knew, but she wanted to hear it from Sylvia.

"I left the midwife's house and went back to my bedsit. I stayed there for several days, debating what to do, but I knew the answer all along. I simply couldn't keep you. You were a stranger to me, an alien being planted in my belly by one of three men who had sex with me without my consent. I was afraid that I would mistreat you or emotionally abuse you if I chose to be your mother. And then there would be the questions once you got older. So, I took you to the church. I'd been there a few times and thought you'd be safe there. I put you down when no one was looking and walked away."

"Why did you leave the note?" Quinn asked.

"I felt it was important for Child Services to know your birthday, and I thought of you as Quinn all throughout the latter part of my pregnancy. I thought you were a boy for some reason, and Quinn was a good strong name. I thought it might work for a girl as well. I assumed that your adoptive parents would change your name, but they hadn't, and seeing it on the screen gave me such a turn. I knew who you were as soon as I laid eyes on you, and it nearly broke me."

"Do you have children?" Quinn asked quietly.

"Yes. I have two sons. I returned home after you were born and, in time, married a local boy. I live in London now."

Quinn stared at Sylvia. She felt numb. It would take time to fully absorb what she'd just learned, but being an academic, she needed to learn as much as she could.

"Did you ever see Robert Chatham again?" she asked.

"Yes, I saw him several times in the village. He smiled and said *hello* to me as if nothing had happened. If I hadn't become pregnant, I probably would have begun to doubt that anything had."

"And the others?"

"I never saw them again. They only came down for the holidays that one time."

"Do you know their names?" Quinn asked.

"One was called Seth and the other Rhys. Rhys was from Wales."

"It's a common enough name," Quinn said, talking to herself. She was shaken to the core by Sylvia's story and couldn't handle one more shock.

"Yes, it is, but that man you were with at the church," Sylvia said. "I think that was him. He didn't recognize me. Why should he? I meant nothing to him," she said bitterly.

Quinn felt as if a bucket of cold water had suddenly been upended over her head. Was it really possible that the man she'd come to like and admire, the man who made romantic advances toward her, was a rapist? And what's worse, that rapist could be her biological father.

Chapter 46

Quinn remained immobile, staring into the dying fire long after Sylvia left. She scribbled down her mobile number and said that she would remain in the village until lunchtime tomorrow should Quinn wish to talk. Sylvia anticipated that Quinn would have more questions once she'd had ample time to think about what she'd learned. Quinn hugged her knees to her chest and rested her forehead on them, wishing to make herself as small as possible. The tears had dried, but she still felt as fragile as a glass bauble that could shatter into tiny fragments if not handled with the utmost care.

She'd spent over twenty years dreaming of her biological parents, imbuing them with all kinds of wonderful characteristics and inventing tragic love stories fraught with insurmountable obstacles in her desperation to believe that they would have kept her if they could. And now that she knew the truth, she wished that she could go back to her fantasies and never, ever learn the reality of what happened. Her father was a rapist, and her mother admitted freely that she simply didn't want her, couldn't love her despite the fact that Quinn had grown in her body for nine months and belonged to her more than to any of the men who'd forced themselves on her. And how was she supposed to work with Rhys Morgan after what she'd learned? The thought of facing him tomorrow was more than she could bear.

Quinn's first impulse had been to call her parents and tell them what happened, but after nearly dialing the number, she replaced the phone on the sofa next to her. She couldn't do that to them. They'd be devastated for her and suddenly unsure of their place in her world. Well, their place would never change. They were her mum and dad. They'd taken her in, loved her, cherished and protected her, and given her the encouragement and support she needed to be the person she was today. She'd rather die than hurt them. Perhaps they never needed to find out about Sylvia at all. Quinn had no intentions of ever seeing the woman again. What was the point? But she did need to talk to someone, and that someone was Gabe. It was just past ten, and she hoped that he'd be at home.

Gabe picked up on the third ring, his voice gruff. "Hello, Quinn," he said. Normally, he would have asked about her day and told her about his. Quinn would hear a smile in his voice when he told her of something funny that had happened or recounted some silly joke, but now his voice had a granite edge to it, and he was doing nothing to make things easier for her. It was up to her to do the talking.

"Gabe, something's happened," Quinn said quietly, desperate for him to care. There was a momentary silence as Gabe waged an internal battle between his wounded pride and his long-repressed feelings. He hadn't called her since the night she lashed out at him, and Quinn wondered if their relationship was over once and for all. Would he politely tell her that he no longer wanted her in his life?

"Gabe?" Quinn prompted when he didn't immediately respond. "Will you not speak to me?" It must have been a close thing, but love won in the end and Gabe replied, unable to reject her.

"Of course, I'll speak to you. What's happened?" he asked, his voice softening. "Are you all right, Quinn?"

"No, not really." Quinn hadn't even realized how not-all-right she was until she heard Gabe's voice. She opened her mouth to speak, but all that came out was a shuddering sob that turned into a full-blown breakdown.

"I . . . she . . . my mother," Quinn said, gasping as she tried to calm down. She hadn't meant to blub like this and had hoped to discuss the situation with Gabe calmly, but she couldn't seem to stop sobbing, a wave of devastation sweeping her along and smashing her against the rocks until she felt as if she were mangled beyond repair.

"Quinn, is your mother ill? Talk to me," Gabe pleaded with her.

"No. Not her." Quinn took a deep breath and tried again. It took several tries, but she finally got the words out. "Gabe, my birth mother came to see me tonight."

"What? You're kidding. Tell me everything." Thankfully, he'd forgotten all about his own hurt feelings for the moment. He knew what it meant to Quinn to find out about her past. "Wait. I'm coming over."

"It's late."

"I don't care. I need to see you."

Quinn rang off and hugged herself. Knowing that Gabe would be there in less than an hour made her feel infinitely stronger and calmer. She'd been such a fool. She'd been so thoughtless, so dismissive of his feelings when he had been the one to love her all this time. He'd always been there for her, even when she was in a relationship with a man he considered unworthy, a man who left her for another woman and didn't even have enough respect for her to break things off in person. Deep down she knew that Gabe would drop everything to come to her aid—he always had. He was the one man she trusted, the one man she loved. What had she been thinking when she rejected him so cruelly? She'd been mourning her relationship with Luke and coming to terms with the fact that the future she'd envisioned for herself was no longer hers when she should have been thanking her lucky stars that she'd been spared years of misery with a man who clearly didn't love her.

Quinn sprang to her feet and flung open the door when she heard a car pull up. Gabe slammed the car door and walked toward her. He didn't say anything, just took her in his arms as she melted into him, thankful that he hadn't forsaken her.

"Gabe, I'm sorry," she whispered into his shoulder.

"I know. No need to talk about that now. Come, tell me what happened."

Gabe threw his jacket over a chair and pulled Quinn down on the sofa next to him after pouring them both a large whiskey. Quinn took a sip and savored it for a moment before recounting the events of the evening without dissolving into tears again. The whiskey helped, and Gabe's presence made her feel as if she could handle this situation with some semblance of grace. She didn't have to deal with this alone. Gabe was there.

"I've spent all these years dreaming about meeting my mother, and now that I have, I feel empty and cheated somehow," Quinn said. "I know it sounds perverse, but I feel almost angry."

Gabe silently refilled Quinn's glass and studied her face. He wasn't the type of man who spoke without thinking, and although Quinn knew that he would try to comfort her, he'd also not bother with meaningless platitudes. He'd tell her what he really thought.

"Your feelings are natural," he said at last. "You have every right to be angry."

"How do you figure?"

"Quinn, like many children who've never known their parents, you've created a fantasy—a mother who was practically sainted. You imagined her as beautiful, loving, kind, and honorable. Tonight, you've been confronted by a real woman, a woman who made mistakes, lied, and exercised bad judgment. You also question her story."

"She was raped," Quinn protested hotly, shocked by her desire to defend Sylvia. She hadn't questioned what Sylvia told her, but now that Gabe brought it up, she paused to consider. She was a historian, and historians never took anything at face value. History was just someone's version of events until supported by facts, and all she had was Sylvia's version.

"Was she? Can you be sure that she didn't get drunk, have a bit of fun with three randy lads and then run off in shame when she found out she was up the duff? She didn't tell her father and never reported the incident to the police."

"Many women don't report rape," Quinn bristled, shocked by Gabe's lack of sensitivity. "The investigation can be more traumatic than the actual experience."

"True, but there are women who cry rape after consensually engaging in intercourse. This woman wants to gain your sympathy and forgiveness. Perhaps things happened just as she said, or perhaps she wants you to see her as a victim rather than someone who exercised bad judgment and paid for it."

"Gabe, I've never known you to be cruel," Quinn said, moving a few inches away from him and crossing her arms in front of her chest. She knew she had no reason to feel defensive, but Gabe was bringing up theories she didn't care to explore.

"I'm not being cruel, I'm being objective," Gabe replied, unfazed by Quinn's anger. "I'm simply exploring all the aspects of this story. What do you really know of this woman other than what she told you?" Gabe demanded. "Are you even sure that she is who she says she is? Perhaps she thinks she has something to gain by approaching you."

"She knew certain details," Quinn replied, wondering if anyone might have had access to that information. She supposed that anyone who was involved in her adoption would know about the circumstances in which she was found, not to mention anyone who watched the news or read the newspapers. The discovery of an infant in Lincoln Cathedral was well publicized.

"Details can be unearthed and manipulated if someone makes it their business to do so," Gabe replied, rational as ever.

"But not DNA," Quinn replied triumphantly as she reached into her pocket and pulled out a plastic bag containing a few strands of dark hair.

"Good girl," Gabe said with a grin. "Plucked it off her coat, did you?"

"It was easy enough. Most women have a stray hair or two clinging to the fabric of their scarves or coats."

"And what about Morgan?" Gabe asked carefully. "Will you confront him?"

"I don't know," Quinn replied truthfully. "What should I do?"

Gabe folded his arms and tilted his head, something he often did when he was thinking and didn't wish to be disturbed. Quinn let him have a moment. She had no idea how to approach the situation with Rhys Morgan. She had a contract with the BBC and was legally obligated to see it through to the end. Accusing Rhys of rape, especially when all she had to go on was the word of a woman she'd just met, would make working with him untenable.

Gabe finally turned to face her, decision made. "Say nothing to Morgan. Even if what Sylvia Wyatt told you is absolutely true, it's not your place to level such an accusation at him. She'd made her decision, and you must abide by it. Besides, the statute of limitations on rape must have expired by now."

"But how do I continue to work with him, knowing what he'd done and who he might be?" Quinn protested.

"First things first. You must find out if he's your father. Is there any way you can do that?" Gabe asked, practical as ever.

"He keeps a toiletry bag in his desk at work. I'm sure I can find something I can work with."

"Will you be able to keep your feelings to yourself until you know the truth?"

"I'll have to, won't I? I've waited this long to find out who my parents were. I can wait a bit longer. It will be hard to be in the same room with Rhys, knowing what I know, but I'll keep a lid on my emotions for the sake of the truth."

"Put on the old poker face?" Gabe joked. "I've never known you to be able to hide your feelings. Everything you think is always right there in your eyes."

"So, what am I thinking now?" Quinn asked softly, a telltale blush staining her cheeks.

"You're thinking what a fool you've been and how you can't possibly live without me," he replied with a smile.

"You know me better than I know myself, Gabriel Russell."

"Yes, I do," Gabe said. He was joking, but Quinn could sense the longing behind the humor. He wanted her still, despite the fact that she'd rejected him so brutally.

Quinn leaned forward and wrapped her arms about Gabe, drawing him toward her. She brushed her lips against his and pulled him closer as she deepened the kiss. This kiss was a long time coming for both of them, but Gabe's response wasn't nearly as enthusiastic as she might have expected. He took her by the shoulders and gently pushed her away. Quinn felt a wave of humiliation wash over her and lowered her eyes, wishing that she'd not been so forward. Gabe wasn't ready to forgive her, and perhaps he'd changed his mind. God knew, she'd given him enough reason to despise her. Gabe instantly picked up on her emotional turmoil and smiled ruefully, taking her face in his hands and forcing her to meet his gaze.

"Quinn, I want you more than words can say, but not like this. You are feeling raw and unsettled, and you want to make the hurt go away. What you need right now is support and understanding, and I would be the worst kind of prick if I took advantage of that."

Quinn nodded, still embarrassed but somewhat mollified by Gabe's observation. "You are right: I feel completely adrift."

"Well, what do you say to me anchoring you tonight? I'll stay, if you want me to, but as a friend." Gabe took her hand in his and smiled. "What say you?"

Quinn smiled back tearfully. "I say *thank you*."

Gabe drew her to him and they sat in companionable silence until Quinn fell asleep, her head against Gabe's shoulder. Gabe carefully lifted her into his arms and carried her to the bedroom, where he laid her on the bed, removed her shoes, and tucked her in beneath the covers. He climbed in next to her but knew that sleep wouldn't come for hours. He desired the woman next to him so much it hurt. Some small part of him wished that he'd taken her up on her offer, but he couldn't take advantage of her vulnerability. If and when he made love to her, it would be with her full consent and because she wanted him as much as he wanted her, not because she was looking for a bit of comfort. Gabe sighed and stared at the embroidered canopy, wishing it was morning.

Chapter 47

June 1665

Suffolk, England

Elise woke up with a start, clutching the counterpane to her bosom. A loud crash came from downstairs, as if a heavy wooden chair had been overturned. She sprang from bed, desperate to lock the door, but before she could reach it, it flew open, revealing her irate husband. Edward was panting with fury as he took in her disheveled state and frightened face.

"How dare you defy me?" he roared. "I ordered you to stay in London. We do not flee while our monarch sees fit to remain in the city." Edward looked exhausted, with shadows of fatigue staining the delicate skin beneath his eyes and a sickly pallor in place of his normally ruddy complexion. He hadn't shaved in days and wore his natural hair instead of the wig he favored, the hair carelessly tied back and nearly free of its leather thong.

Elise opened her mouth to reply, but no sound came out. She was terrified. She'd never seen Edward so angry. He was usually cold and indifferent, not spitting mad as he was now. The journey from London did nothing to cool his anger, giving him time to stew instead. He'd clearly traveled through the night and had had ample time to nurse his fury.

"I convinced her ladyship to come away." James appeared in the doorway. He'd obviously just gotten out of bed, and Elise said a silent prayer of thanks that it hadn't been her bed. Edward would have disemboweled them both.

"And what gave you the right to take my wife to the country without my permission, sir?" Edward roared, redirecting his fury to James.

"Common sense, your lordship," James answered, not bothering to hide his contempt. "People are dying by the thousands. Your wife is carrying the heir you so desperately wanted. Why would you put her life at risk? What does the king care where Lady Asher is? It's not as if he's even aware of her existence."

Edward flew at James and punched him in the face, his heavy ring striking James just below the eye and leaving a nasty cut. James winced with pain but didn't say anything to his father or retaliate. He stood his ground, feet apart, arms at his sides, hands balled into fists. He would not allow another blow to go unanswered, that was obvious, but he hoped that Edward would come to his senses and not strike him again. A thin trickle of blood ran down James's face, its slow progress resembling a bloody tear. James didn't bother to wipe it away, retaining his defiant position in case Edward should assault him again.

"Get out, you bastard," Edward growled. "You are no longer welcome in this house. And if I see you anywhere near my wife, I'll kill you with my bare hands."

James gave a curt nod and left but not before giving Elise a reassuring look. For all his bluster, Edward would be a fool to send Elise back to London. He was furious, but he was also sufficiently chastised. He knew that James was right, although he'd never actually admit it.

"I'm sorry, Edward," Elise said in a conciliatory manner. "James meant well. Surely you know that."

"If I want your opinion, I'll ask for it," Edward spat out. "Get dressed," he commanded.

Edward strode from the room, slamming the door behind him. Elise wondered if he planned to stay, but asking him when he was in such a state could be hazardous to her health. So, she dressed and sat patiently while Peg styled her hair. She had to do everything in her power to pacify Edward and get him not to banish James for good.

She came downstairs to find Edward eating alone in the dining room. He normally ate very little for breakfast, but the table was laden with everything Cook could find on such a short notice. Edward was devouring the food as if he hadn't eaten in days. He was pale and drawn, and cold sweat glistened on his forehead.

"Are you quite well?" Elise asked carefully. "Shall I summon the physician?"

"I'm tired and hungry. I traveled all night."

"Then I'm sure you'd like to rest after you've eaten. Shall I call for a bath?"

Edward made a dismissive gesture. "I'll sleep awhile, then have a bath after. Now, leave me in peace."

Elise was only too happy to be dismissed. She made her way outside and hurried to the stables in the hope of intercepting James before he left. James was saddling his horse, and Elise breathed a sigh of relief, noting his slow movements. He'd been waiting for her.

"Are you all right?" James asked when he saw her silhouetted in the doorway.

"Yes. He's angry as a bear, but he probably just needs time to cool off. Where will you go?"

"I'll stay at the gamekeeper's cottage for a few days. I can't imagine that my father will remain in Suffolk long enough to notice. I'm not leaving you, love." James reached out and cupped Elise's cheek. "I will be wherever you are, for all time."

"James, are you sure it's safe for you to remain here? I've never seen him so angry," Elise said as she walked into James's embrace. "I fear for you."

"What's the worst he can do, eh?" James shrugged, dismissing Edward from his thoughts. "Try to go for a walk by the beach each morning after breakfast. I will be looking out for you."

"All right. But stay out of sight until he leaves."

James lifted Elise's chin with his finger and planted a tender kiss on her lips. "Don't worry about me. I have a horse, my weapons, and a purse full of coin. I'm better off than most."

Elise waited until James galloped away before returning to the house. Edward's snores could be heard throughout the house, so Elise went to the kitchen instead. A strange man sat at the kitchen table, a mug of ale and a bowl of pottage in front of him.

"Good morrow, me lady," the man said, springing to his feet when Elise entered. He bowed to her and remained standing, waiting for permission to sit back down.

"Pray, continue with your meal, and then come see me in the parlor. I have a few questions to put to you," Elise said.

"As ye wish, me lady."

Elise didn't have long to wait. The man came shyly into the parlor, hat in hand. He was a simple peasant and not accustomed to being invited into the house proper.

"What is your name?" Elise asked. She considered offering him a seat, then changed her mind. This wouldn't take long.

"Aubrey Wilkins, yer ladyship."

"Did you bring my husband from London?"

"Aye, ma'am. I work for a livery, ye see. Yer husband wished to hire the finest coach available," the man went on, babbling with nervousness.

"And how are things in London?" Elise asked. She'd had no news of any kind since leaving with James, and the sights and sounds of plague-ridden London preyed on her mind day and night. James hadn't mentioned anything about his sister or her family, but Elise knew that he was terrified. Molly had nowhere to go, and her husband would not leave his business. It was their livelihood, so abandoning his outstanding orders was out of the question.

"Things are right bad, me lady. Thousands dead of the plague. The stench of rotting bodies fills the air," the man said and instantly regretted his choice of words. "Begging yer pardon, me lady. I didn't mean to be indelicate."

"That's quite all right, Master Wilkins. I prefer to know the truth. Are you returning to London today?"

"In truth, I wish I didn't have to, but the proprietor of the livery will be expecting 'is carriage back, so I must be on me way."

"Godspeed," Elise said. "Ask Mistress Benford for a parcel of food for your journey."

"Thank ye kindly, me lady."

Elise stared out the window. The stately coach that brought Edward from London rolled down the gravel drive, Master Wilkins on the bench. Elise wished that the coach was taking Edward away again, but he was still asleep, a small blessing in view of his current mood. A steady rain began to fall. The room grew dark, but Elise didn't bother to light the candles. The house felt cold and empty without James in it, and she wished that she could sneak out and join him in the cozy comfort of the cottage. Perhaps once Edward left, she would be able to see him again, but for now she had to play the dutiful wife and hope that Edward's ire had burned out, and he wouldn't seek a way to punish her for her disobedience.

Elise put a hand to her belly. Four more months till the babe was born. She had no illusions—the birth of the baby would not set her free, but maybe Edward would be happier once he had a son.

Chapter 48

Edward did not leave as Elise had hoped. He wanted to but seemed unable to get out of bed. He was ill-tempered and unwell, which concerned Elise. He might have been exposed to the plague before leaving London, but it was too soon to tell, and Elise had no choice but to look after him. She'd sent a groom to fetch the physician from town, but he'd been called out on some emergency and would not come until later, or possibly even the following day.

Elise brought Edward some beef tea and sat down at what she thought was a safe distance while Edward drank it. He'd been pale before, but now his face was flushed, and his eyes burned bright, as if he were possessed by an evil spirit. He smelled strongly of sweat, and his hair and beard were matted and greasy.

"Bring me some ale. I'm thirsty," Edward commanded after he finished the broth. Elise sent Peg to get the ale while she remained with Edward.

"You're fevered. I've sent for the doctor, but he might not get here until tomorrow. Edward, was anyone at Asher Hall ill when you left?" she asked carefully.

"How should I know? The house is quarantined," he replied, sullen as a child. "I spoke to one of the grooms through the gate. He told me you'd gone."

"What of Lucy? My maid. She'd been exposed to the plague. Had she taken ill?" Elise persisted.

"I told you, I don't know. I can't be bothered asking after a servant."

"No," Elise said quietly. Edward did not know most of the servants by name. To him, they were faceless, ageless puppets who saw to his every whim and had no right to expect any kindness or understanding in return. He gave them a home and a meager salary, and in his eyes, that was more than enough.

"Edward, have you heard anything of Molly and her family?" Elise asked.

"Molly who?" Edward growled, annoyed by her questioning. His eyelids were drooping again, but Elise saw a spark of recognition when she mentioned Molly. He knew exactly whom she was referring to.

"Molly your daughter."

"Get out and leave me in peace," Edward roared. "And send up that ale."

Elise left the room, her insides burning with rage. She knew that men often failed to look after their bastards, but what difference did it make whether a child was born in wedlock or not? They were still their flesh and blood, still their children. How did a man justify turning away from a child they had fathered, convincing themselves that they had no responsibility to either mother or child just because the union hadn't been sanctioned by the Church? How easy society made it for them. They sowed their seed wherever they pleased and then just walked away, free of any responsibility to live their life while some poor woman was left to raise a child in near poverty with no claim on the father.

She supposed that Edward's decision to look after Molly and James would be viewed by others of his class as an act of ultimate kindness and sacrifice, but Elise saw it nothing less than his duty. Edward had found a use for James, but Molly was of no interest to him, nor were her children, who were his grandchildren. Edward cared not a jot if they all died. He'd probably be more upset if one of King Charles's dogs died, mourning with his sovereign as if the creature had been a beloved child.

Elise sent Peg up with the ale and vowed not to see Edward again until the doctor came. Instead, she fetched her cloak and went out, making sure that no one saw her leave. The walk to the beach took her nearly a half hour, but she didn't mind. She liked walking by herself. It was a beautiful June morning, and the path was alive with birdsong and the rustling of small creatures as they went about the business of living. The ground was dappled with sunlight, the trees overhead forming a green tunnel above Elise's head. She'd never felt such peace or seen such unspoiled beauty in London.

The air became a trifle cooler as she neared the sea. James said that the water was always cold, no matter how warm the summer days might be. The currents carried water from up north, where it was cooler even during the summer months. Elise walked down the beach, carefully stepping on shingles and keeping far enough from the surf to keep her feet from getting wet. There was a desolate beauty, the relentless crashing of the surf disrupted only by the screaming of seagulls. She liked it and wished that she could keep walking until she was far away from this place and her unfeeling husband. She tried to tell herself that things would improve once the child was born, but she knew full well that she was deceiving herself. Edward felt no love for her and might not even care for the child since it wouldn't be truly his. He needed a son and heir, but there was no guarantee that he would be kind to the child. He might ignore the babe as much as he ignored Elise, using it only to fulfill his ambition. Would she spend the rest of her life hidden away and used only to serve her husband's purpose?

Elise had always pitied women who were widows, thinking them unfortunate and lonely, but now the idea of widowhood didn't seem so grievous. She didn't wish Edward to die—that would be unchristian of her. But she did long to be free of him.

What she wouldn't give to sail away from these shores and live a life with James and their baby. Would Edward care? Would he pursue them? She was his property, and so would be the child. He would not let them go, if only out of principle. Having a runaway wife would not look good in front of the king he so worshipped. Or did he? Elise often wondered why Edward spent so much time at the palace. Was it because he was truly devoted to His Majesty, or did he have some other agenda?

Elise put Edward from her mind when she saw James walking toward her. He looked handsome in the golden morning light, his dark hair ruffled by the wind, and his eyes fixed on her as if he was trying to memorize her every feature. He smiled in greeting, but Elise could sense the tension in his shoulders and the determination in his gait. He'd come to say good-bye, she was sure of it.

Chapter 49

December 2013

London, England

Quinn stopped in front of the building, suddenly unsure if she should go in. She'd spent the past few days agonizing about what she'd learned from Sylvia Wyatt, going from pitying the woman, to raging against Sylvia's gullibility and lack of courage, to wondering if she might have made the whole story up. Quinn came close to calling Sylvia several times, but Gabe talked her out of it, remaining steadfast in his opinion that she should wait until she knew more.

"Quinn, find out the facts before you make any decisions. This woman might be the genuine article, or she might be an opportunist who found information about you on the Internet and decided to take advantage. Perhaps she thinks you have money or you can do something for her."

"I do resemble her to some degree," Quinn countered, but Gabe wasn't persuaded by her argument.

"I've met people who've resembled me, but as far as I know we were not related, not even distantly. You are a scientist, and scientists deal with facts. I've called Dr. Scott, and he'll be expecting you. He'll run some discreet tests, and then you can know for certain what you're dealing with."

"Gabe, what if she really is my mother? Where do we go from here? Where do we start?" Quinn cried, suddenly alarmed by the possibility that Sylvia might be telling the truth. Wishing to find your birth mother was one thing; being confronted by one was a whole different thing entirely. "She has two sons," Quinn added. "They might be my brothers."

Gabe pulled Quinn close and kissed her on the temple, making her feel like a little girl. He'd been very protective of her since Sylvia's visit, and Quinn had to admit that his concern for her made her feel somewhat better about the whole situation. He was there, and no matter what happened with Sylvia, he'd catch her if she fell.

"If she is your mother, then you start slow. I know you want to believe that she will do anything to make up for lost time, but you don't know her at all, and she doesn't know you. You have to learn to walk before you can run, sweetheart."

Quinn nodded and squeezed his hand. "Thanks, Gabe. You are right, of course. I can't seem to think rationally these days."

"You've had a lot to take in. Go see Dr. Scott. He's the first step in determining what needs to be done."

Quinn yanked the door open and walked into the morgue. The smell of carbolic and decay assaulted her immediately, making her wish that she hadn't had to come here and could have met the doctor outside, but Dr. Scott was busy, and he was doing her a favor.

"Quinn, a pleasure to see you again," Dr. Scott beamed as he set aside a file he'd been working on. Thankfully, he wasn't in the middle of an autopsy, and his green scrubs were clean. "Hand it over," he said with a grin. "I hope you don't mind, but Gabe told me something of what this is about. I can only imagine how anxious you must be to get the results."

"Yes and no," Quinn confessed.

"Understandable. Your life will never be the same if these tests show that these two are your biological parents."

"Dr. Scott, may I ask you a question?"

"You just did," he quipped. "Of course, go on."

"Do you think psychic ability is genetic?"

Dr. Scott looked thoughtful for a moment before replying. "I tend to think that everything is genetic to some degree. I've never done any research on psychic ability, but I would think it runs in families just like artistic talent or an allergy to peanuts. Has this woman claimed to be psychic?" he asked, his curiosity piqued.

"No, nothing like that. It was just a hypothetical question."

"Well, I'll give you a hypothetical answer: It's possible, and it's probable, but nothing is certain."

"Thank you. When can I expect to get back the results?"

"Give me three days. You shall have them by Monday morning."

**

Quinn spent a restless night tossing and turning, finally dropping off to sleep after several hours only to be awoken by strange dreams. She couldn't quite recall what they were about, but they left her feeling unsettled and bad-tempered. There'd been a message from Sylvia on her answerphone when she got back from London on Thursday, but Quinn decided not to call her back until she had the results of the tests. The weekend would be hell, especially since she hadn't made any plans. Rhys tried to cajole her into seeing him, but the thought of spending time with the man set Quinn's teeth on edge. She'd have to see him sooner or later, but the way she felt now, it would have to be later—much later.

Quinn got out of bed on Friday morning feeling headachy and disgruntled. She had no idea how she'd fill the hours until Monday morning, and the prospect of three days of complete freedom filled her with dread. She'd hoped that Gabe would offer to come over, but he sounded uncharacteristically evasive when she spoke to him last night, making no mention of seeing her at the weekend. Quinn started when she heard the sound of an engine and then the slamming of a car door. She wasn't expecting any visitors so early on a Friday morning, and she hoped that Sylvia hadn't decided to take matters into her own hands and shown up at her door. Quinn pulled on a warm dressing gown and ran a hand through her wild hair. *I must look a fright*, she thought as she went to see who was at the door.

Gabe, looking fresh as a daisy so early in the morning, tried to keep the self-satisfied grin off his face as he stepped into the house and gave her a peck on the cheek. His face was cold and he smelled pleasantly of chilly winter air tinged with a hint of pine.

"It's bitter out there," he said as he unwound his scarf and shrugged off his coat. "Make us a cuppa?"

"You'd better have a good reason for being here before eight," Quinn chided Gabe as she went to fill the kettle. "I haven't even brushed my teeth yet." Secretly, she was thrilled to see him, her worries from last night put to rest by his unexpected appearance. They'd reconciled, but Quinn still had no clear idea where they stood. Gabe had been supportive and affectionate since Quinn's tearful phone call, but nothing had been resolved between them.

Gabe plopped down on the sofa and gave her a furtive look. Quinn suddenly felt her heart drop. Had Dr. Scott called Gabe with the results? That would be unethical, but they were friends, and this inquiry was completely unofficial. Perhaps Dr. Scott decided to tell Gabe first so that he could be there for Quinn when she got the results, thinking that she'd need the support when she learned the truth.

"Gabriel Russell, what do you know that I don't?" Quinn demanded as she stood over him, hands on hips. She was trembling behind the false bravado, praying that Gabe would just tell her, whatever it was.

"I know that you will spend the whole weekend pacing this room like a caged tiger, waiting for the results that, in your opinion, will change your life."

"Well, they will," Quinn replied, her tone defensive. She thought Gabe understood what this meant to her, but now he was making the outcome sound trivial and irrelevant and her anxiety unfounded.

"Quinn, you are who you are. It might be nice to know who your parents were, but it won't change anything in the grand scheme of things."

"Said the man who can trace his ancestry back to William the Conqueror," Quinn retorted, crossing her arms in front of her. She was pouting like a child, she knew that, but she was hurt by Gabe's lack of understanding.

"Said the man who's booked us into a lovely little hotel in the Cotswolds for the weekend. If we leave within the hour, we can be there before lunch. Shall I help you pack?" Gabe asked, all innocence.

Quinn stared at him in utter astonishment. She was torn between irritation with Gabe for making plans without even consulting her to overwhelming gratitude for his thoughtfulness. He understood what she was going through and did the one thing he knew would help, secretly planning a weekend away to distract her mind from obsessing about the outcome of the DNA test. She knew what this weekend would mean, and suddenly there was nothing in the world she wanted more. No matter what happened come Monday, she wanted Gabe in her life, and she was ready for their long friendship to evolve into something deeper. The thought of spending a weekend with Gabe in the picturesque Cotswolds made her grin with anticipation, and she dashed off to the bedroom to throw a few things together.

"Does this mean you're coming?" Gabe called out from the living room. Quinn could hear the smile in his voice as he went to pour them both mugs of tea.

Gabe came in with the tea but didn't advance into the room. He leaned on the doorjamb, as if he needed support, his expression saying it all. He was happy, excited, and nervous. He looked like a schoolboy who'd just come to collect his date for the school dance, unsure of whether it would be a night to remember or a disaster he'd recall to his dying day.

Quinn stopped packing and accepted the steaming mug from Gabe, rising on tippy-toes to kiss him on the lips. "Thank you," she said, smiling into his eyes.

"You can thank me by not bringing enough clothes to fill a trunk," he said, gazing at the growing pile on the bed. "It's only two nights. A pair of knickers and a toothbrush will do."

"Spoken like a man."

"I've perfected the art of packing light. All my possessions fit into a knapsack."

"Well, good for you," Quinn said as she added an aubergine-colored knit dress to the pile. "I certainly hope you'll be taking me out to dinner. Twice."

Gabe laughed and went to rinse out his mug. Quinn strongly suspected that he'd already had dinner reservations for both nights, in restaurants that he thought would be to her liking. It was nice to have him fussing over her like this. She would thank him again, properly, when she got the chance.

Chapter 50

Quinn smiled happily as she watched the countryside fly past. It had snowed during the night, and the normally green and brown fields were covered in a blanket of sparkling white. The sun peeked playfully from behind fluffy clouds that floated lazily past, and bare branches made intricate patterns against the pale-blue winter sky. Black crows looked like charcoal smudges on a sketch as they nestled in the branches, watching the car speed by with their beady eyes and crowing madly.

Gabe drove faster than was strictly necessary, but then he always had a love for speed, and Quinn felt perfectly safe with him behind the wheel. Not like there was much traffic. Gabe chose picturesque rural roads rather than taking the motorway, and they'd encountered virtually no other cars, making them feel as if they were alone in the world. They'd tacitly agreed not to talk about Sylvia, Rhys, or the pending results, and instead chatted about mutual acquaintances, the institute, and the latest news in archeological circles. The conversation was light, but there was a current of energy flowing between them that made Quinn catch her breath. Gabe felt it too, and when he pulled off his leather glove with his teeth, tossed it aside, and took Quinn's bare hand in his own, she nearly jumped out of her skin.

"All right?" Gabe asked, turning to look at her. Quinn nodded, unable to speak. She'd always felt a frisson of attraction for Gabe, but now that she was ready to acknowledge it, it seemed to have grown a hundredfold, ready to engulf her. He looked so relaxed, one hand on the wheel as he navigated the narrow roads. His hair fell into his face, and his dark-blue eyes crinkled at the corners as he turned to smile at her. He'd worn a short beard at one time but had shaved it off recently, shaving off about ten years as well. She liked him like this. He was a mature man, but there was still something boyish in him, something mischievous. Perhaps it was the happiness that radiated from him. She hadn't realized how controlled he'd been with her these past few years, not until she finally gave him some hope of a future.

They were both pulsating with nervous energy by the time they finally got to the hotel. It was a lovely house built of golden stone that the area was known for. The peaked rooftop, chimneys, and mullioned windows were dusted with snow, and the ornamental shrubs all wore caps of white. Gabe brought in their bags and quickly checked in while Quinn took in her surroundings. This was just the type of place she liked: beautiful, luxurious, and permeated with centuries of history. The hotel was decorated for Christmas, and the reception twinkled with fairy lights that were reflected in the colorful ornaments decorating the twelve-foot tree soaring to the ceiling in the foyer. Crimson poinsettias were artfully scattered about the place, adding to the festive atmosphere.

"Are you hungry?" Gabe asked. "Would you like to send our bags up and have some lunch first?"

"No," Quinn replied as she raised her eyes to his. Gabe correctly read the look in her eyes and reached for her hand.

"Right, then."

They were barely through the door before Gabe dropped the bags to the floor and swept Quinn into an embrace, kissing her until she was breathless. This was not a tender kiss of longing. It was hard and demanding, letting her know exactly what to expect. Gabe unzipped Quinn's coat and shrugged off his own, the rest of their clothes making a trail to the high canopy bed as he expertly maneuvered her toward it and lifted her onto the mattress. Neither one of them could wait a minute more, their desire for each other boiling over after the long drive. It was as if a dam had broken, sweeping away the past eight years, Luke, and all the unspoken hurts and misunderstandings of the past few months. Quinn yanked Gabe's jumper over his head and went to undo the zipper on his jeans as he pulled off her top. Quinn's hands shook with impatience as her mind emptied of all thought except that of Gabe and his hot skin beneath her fingertips. He sucked in his breath as she ran her hands over his well-muscled chest and allowed her hand to slide downward, wrapping her fingers around him. He gently pushed her hand aside and covered her body with his own, his knee pushing her legs apart.

Quinn arched her back and gasped with pleasure as Gabe's fingers slid into her. He lowered his head to catch her nipple between his teeth, and she cried out as the earth-shattering combination of pleasure and pain nearly brought her to the brink. There was no need for foreplay, she was more than ready for him, but he wasn't about to rush the moment he'd waited such a long time for.

"Gabe, please," she pleaded, but he wouldn't be rushed.

"Not yet," he murmured as he slid between her legs, pushing them apart with his eager hands. "Not yet."

Quinn grabbed fistfuls of the duvet in her hands and arched her back as Gabe's tongue followed where his fingers had just been. He took his time, tormenting her until her legs vibrated with tension, and she felt as if she might explode into a million pieces. She grabbed him by the hair and yanked him upward, unable to stand the exquisite torture a moment longer. "Now!" she demanded, not caring if he was ready or not.

Gabe plunged into her, bringing her to a shuddering orgasm with only a few rough thrusts and joining her in moments. He collapsed on top of her, his forehead resting against her shoulder, his breathing ragged. Quinn wrapped her arms around him and stroked his hair. Her bones felt like jelly, and a feeling of utter contentment flowed through her veins. There'd been no need to worry. They fit together like two pieces of a jigsaw, their bodies possessed of secret knowledge even if it took their hearts some time to sort things out. They remained that way for a few minutes, their heart rates slowing down as they descended back down to earth.

Gabe raised his face to Quinn's, his eyes filled with a combination of wonder and worry. He needed reassurance that it had been as magical for her as it had been for him, and she gave it gladly, wrapping her legs around him and guiding his stiffening shaft back into her body. The second time was slower, more deliberate, but no less exquisite. Gabe took his time, watching her face and enjoying her pleasure as he alternated between tender lovemaking and utter physical possession as he pinned down her wrists and drove into her, making her cry out in ecstasy.

He finally rolled off her and lay on his side, his head supported on one arm as his other hand cupped her breast, his thumb absent-mindedly stroking her nipple. The room was filled with the smell of arousal, and the sheets were tangled and damp beneath them. Gabe looked sated and happy as he gazed down on her.

Quinn reached out and stroked his cheek, and he leaned down and kissed her tenderly, the taste of her still on his lips. There was so much she wanted to say, but at the moment, she was speechless. Luke had been her first, so she had nothing to compare their lovemaking to except a few groping sessions when she was a teenager. It had been sweet and passionate at times, but never, not even at the start of their relationship, had it been like this.

"No, it wasn't," Gabe said as he smiled at her, his fingers now tracing a pattern on her stomach and moving lower.

"What wasn't?" Quinn asked, although she hoped that he'd read the unspoken question in her eyes.

"It wasn't like this with anyone else and never will be."

"Why?"

"Because with my body I thee worship," Gabe whispered in her ear, quoting the old-fashioned marriage vow and making her shiver. "And with my heart I thee adore," he added, staking his claim not only to her body but to her heart.

Chapter 51

The room was aglow with the crimson haze from the dying fire and the golden light of candles that had burned down to shapeless stubs. The hotel had grown quiet, the patrons having retired to their rooms and gone to bed. The clock at a nearby church struck the midnight hour, but Quinn and Gabe were still awake, savoring their last night away. They hadn't done much more than make love, eat, sleep, and take a couple of walks, but it had been exactly what they needed, and neither one was looking forward to returning to real life and the news that Monday morning would bring.

Quinn lay in the crook of Gabe's arm, her hair spilling over his chest and her legs intertwined with his. She felt wonderfully content, but she couldn't help but be aware of a restlessness in Gabe. He'd been wonderfully happy for the past two days, but now that the end of their getaway was drawing near, something was eating away at him, and Quinn meant to find out what it was, but she loathed the idea of tarnishing the idyll of this moment. Perhaps he'd tell her on the drive back, but Gabe couldn't wait. He carefully untangled himself from Quinn and sat up, looking down at her with an expression that instantly jolted her out of her somnolent state.

"Why?" he asked, his gaze intent on Quinn's face. "Why did you choose him? Surely you knew how I felt about you," he said. The anguish in his voice nearly broke Quinn's heart. She'd given herself to him body and soul, but he still couldn't forget the hurt that she'd caused him all those years ago. He needed closure before he could move forward.

Quinn sat up and covered her breasts with the duvet. She could make something up to pacify Gabe, but she intended to tell him the truth. He deserved that much, and truth be told, she'd asked herself the same question ever since finding out the truth of why Luke left her.

"I didn't know how you felt, but I suspected," she replied truthfully. "Gabe, I was twenty-two, and a young twenty-two at that. I'd never had a relationship that lasted longer than a couple of weeks. Luke was easygoing and fun. He made me feel light and carefree, whereas you . . ." Quinn shook her head in wonder at the way Gabe made her feel even back then. "You had an intensity simmering in you that would have burned me to cinders. Your love would have been all-consuming, all-demanding. You frightened me, Gabe, and I instinctively knew that I wasn't ready for you. I wasn't emotionally mature enough to be your equal, so it would have never worked between us, not then."

"And now? I can't lose you again," he said. "I won't recover."

Quinn reached out and took his hand, smiling up at him. No one who knew Gabriel Russell would believe that the strong, competent, urbane man they were acquainted with could be this vulnerable in the face of love.

"Gabe, I'm a grown woman now, and I knew what I agreed to when I came away with you. I would never toy with you, knowing how you feel about me. See, what attracted me to Luke is what ultimately drove us apart. I know you, Gabe. You are not a player, you're a man who sets his heart on a woman and loves her until the end. You want to possess and protect, worship and be adored in return. I'm ready for you now, if you'll have me."

Gabe's mouth stretched into a joyous smile, his eyes sparkling with relief. He leaned forward and kissed Quinn gently. This moment wasn't about sex, it was about something much deeper than that. The past was now behind them, and the future stretched ahead with infinite promise. Quinn took Gabe's face in her hands and kissed him back. "Yours," she whispered. "Forever yours."

Chapter 52

As the Jag gobbled up the miles and they drew closer to home, Quinn grew more fretful. She'd hardly thought of Sylvia or Rhys during the weekend, but now the anxiety returned full force, rendering her pensive and silent. Her feelings changed from moment to moment. A part of her wished that Dr. Scott would get a match and she could finally put the mystery of her birth to rest and start working on a relationship with her parents, or at least her mother; and part of her wished that things would just go back to the way they were. She hadn't mentioned anything to her parents. It seemed wiser to wait for the results before disrupting their peace of mind. Quinn knew that although her parents would be supportive no matter what she decided to do, they would still feel the sting of rejection, taking her desire to forge a relationship with her birth parents as some sort of criticism of the way they'd raised her. At the moment, they were the only parents she ever wanted or needed.

"You seem a million miles away," Gabe said as he stole a glance in her direction. "You haven't said anything in nearly an hour."

"I'm nervous about tomorrow," she admitted.

"I know."

"I don't know that I can ever grow to love them, knowing what I know of the way I was conceived," Quinn confessed.

"Darling, like most adopted children, you fantasized about your real parents and unwittingly put them on a pedestal. A child wants to believe that the reason they were given up was not because they weren't wanted, but because the situation was unmanageable. Everyone likes to imagine that they were conceived in love, but the reality is often very different."

"I suppose you're right, Gabe, but that still doesn't make this any easier. How do I look Rhys in the eye when I know what he did all those years ago? Do I confront him if he is my father?" *Thank God I never responded to his advances*, Quinn thought as she stared at the winding road stretching off into the distance. Sleeping with a possible rapist would be bad enough, but having sex with a man who might be her biological father would be something she couldn't ever come back from, at least not emotionally. Even the thought of the kiss they shared made her shudder with revulsion. Thank heaven Gabe didn't know that Rhys had tried to romance her.

"Quinn, why don't you wait until you get the results, and then we'll tackle those consequences together?"

Quinn nodded, her thoughts still in turmoil. It was going to be a long night, and she was glad that Gabe offered to stay. His presence was solid and comforting, his devotion unwavering. Quinn reached over and squeezed his hand. Gabe smiled back and blew her a kiss.

**

Monday morning came all too soon, and Quinn stared balefully at the phone as it refused to ring hour after hour. Gabe had waited with her until nine o'clock, but he had a meeting scheduled for ten and needed to get going. It was the last week before Christmas break, and there were finals to grade, paperwork to fill out, and a holiday do for the staff to organize. Gabe would have a busy few days.

"Call me as soon as you hear," Gabe said as he kissed her on the threshold. "I should be available by eleven."

"Will do."

Quinn went back into the house, made herself another cup of coffee, and settled in to wait. She tried reading, but the words just swam before her eyes, refusing to form actual words that made sense. There were three missed calls from Rhys, which she refused to return. She just couldn't bring herself to speak to him at the moment. He'd scheduled the shoot for the documentary for the beginning of January, so whatever the results, she'd have to work things out by then since she couldn't break her contract without incurring a lawsuit.

The wait became unbearable, so Quinn decided to take a walk instead. The day was brisk and overcast, and the heavens threatened to open up at any moment, but it was still better than staying indoors. Quinn tied a warm scarf around her neck, pulled on her wellies, and set off down the lane to the village. The snow had melted over the weekend, leaving behind a muddy slush that had frozen again overnight. It was easier to walk on the side of the road, where it wasn't so slippery.

Walking made her feel better. The physical activity relieved some of the tension, and Quinn increased her pace, almost trotting down the lane. A soupy fog swirled all around her, muffling sound and giving her limited visibility. Even the crows, who were usually out in full force in the mornings, were silent. Quinn finally decided that she'd gone far enough and turned in the direction of home. She was cold, and the moisture in the air made her face feel damp. She was almost back to the house when her mobile finally rang. Quinn fumbled for the phone and almost dropped it in her nervousness.

"Dr. Scott," she said. "Good morning."

"Morning, Quinn. I hope you had a pleasant weekend."

"I did," she answered truthfully, eager to get the pleasantries out of the way. "And you?"

"Very good, thank you. But I'm sure you don't want to hear all about my weekend with my partner's family," Dr. Scott joked. "I have the results."

"And?" Quinn felt as if the air was suddenly sucked out of her lungs, leaving her gasping like a landed fish. She couldn't breathe and had a stitch in her side that hadn't been there a moment ago.

"I can say with ninety-nine percent certainty that Sylvia Wyatt is your mother."

Quinn let out the breath she'd been holding. She thought she would feel either elation or despair at the news, but all she felt was a vast emptiness. She had no idea how to feel now that she knew the truth.

"Quinn? Are you there?"

"Yes, please go on."

"The man's DNA, however, is not a match. I hope you're not too disappointed." Quinn had not given Dr. Scott Rhys's name since she obtained his DNA by less-than-honest means.

"Yes. No. I mean, I'm not really sure how I feel about it yet. I suppose I need some time to think," Quinn replied.

"Of course you do. It's a lot to take in. Please, ring me if you need anything else. I'm always happy to help."

"Thank you. I appreciate your help, Colin."

"Anytime. Give my regards to Gabe."

"I will."

Quinn rang off, shoved the phone into her pocket, and walked on toward home. She tried to label her emotions but couldn't quite put a finger on what she was feeling. Relief, disappointment, despair, hope, and a tiny bit of closure.

Quinn kicked off her boots, put the kettle on, and called Gabe. He picked up after several rings sounding harassed. "Sorry, love, got pulled into another departmental meeting. What did Colin say?"

"Sylvia is a match, and Rhys isn't."

Gabe was silent for a moment while he absorbed her news. "How do you feel?"

"Honestly, I don't know yet. I think I'm actually relieved that Rhys isn't my father. If he were, it'd make working together very difficult—for both of us."

"Yes, I agree. Will you call Sylvia?" Gabe asked, his voice gentle. He wouldn't attempt to influence her, but he probably thought she should, if only to find some closure.

"I suppose I'd better. Of course, she already knows she's my mother," Quinn said with a nervous giggle.

"Quinn, you don't have to make any decisions today. Just take a little time to figure out what you want from your relationship with her."

"I don't know that I can ever think of her as my mother, but I would like to get to know her better. There are questions I still need to ask. And I've decided not to confront Rhys, at least not yet. I'm simply not ready to have that conversation with him."

"I understand. I'll call you later. Someone is waiting for me."

"OK."

Quinn made herself a cup of tea and sat down in front of the unlit hearth. The house felt cold and damp, but she had no energy to lay a fire. She suddenly felt drained, her heart heavy. Quinn slowly sipped her tea until some warmth returned to her limbs, and she reached for the phone once more. It was time to call Sylvia Wyatt.

Chapter 53

June 1665

Suffolk, England

Elise stood patiently by Edward's bedside while Dr. Samuels examined him. Edward had slept poorly during the night and was still flushed and agitated come morning. He had no appetite, and his chamber pot was full of vomit that permeated the room with its noxious odor. It was a testament to how ill Edward was that he hadn't demanded that Elise leave the room as soon as the doctor was admitted and had not objected to her opening the window just a crack to air out the chamber, although the doctor might have had he been able to draw breath without gagging.

"Take that out immediately," Elise hissed at Peg who poked her head into the room.

"Yes, me lady." Peg covered the bowl with a towel and took it away, allowing them all to breathe easier. The doctor looked visibly relieved and stuffed the pomander he'd been holding to his nose back in his pocket.

"It's not the plague, your ladyship," Dr. Samuels said as he walked out with Elise. "Your husband is suffering from a fever, but he will most certainly recover. He must stay abed for at least a week and have nothing but broth and thin gruel. Keep a fire burning in his bedchamber, and do not open the windows. You don't want him catching a chill, what with the sea air and all."

Edward's room was already stifling, and the smell of stale sweat, vomit, and illness was overwhelming, but Elise nodded in understanding. She would do as she was told.

"And how are you feeling?" the doctor asked as he took in her growing belly.

"I am well," Elise replied. And she was. She felt more energetic since leaving London, and her appetite had improved. She was actually hungry, especially after taking a brisk walk. The lethargy that plagued her in London seemed to have dissipated, and she felt a need to be active and spend time outdoors in the fresh air.

"You mustn't exert yourself," Dr. Samuels admonished, as if he could read her thoughts. "Women in your condition should remain indoors and rest as much as possible. You must attend church, of course, but walking should be avoided, as should all rich foods. Limit yourself to broth and porridge, and under no circumstances are you to consume any uncooked fruit or vegetables. Very unhealthy for digestion, I'm afraid. Have you consulted the local midwife?"

"No, not yet," Elise admitted. "I've been here only a week."

"I'll have Mistress Wynne call on you. She's a good pious woman," he added, wishing to assure Elise that no accusations of witchcraft had been made against the midwife. "She's devoted to Christ and the teachings of the Church, and she practices no pagan methods."

"Thank you, Doctor."

Elise didn't expect Dr. Samuels to attend her at birth if she were still in Suffolk. Male doctors were rarely called, seeing childbirth as the providence of women. If a male doctor was called in, either the mother, the child, or both were in grave danger. Elise hoped that Mistress Wynne was kind. She feared childbirth and, having no mother or other female relatives to offer her guidance, felt isolated and ignorant of what to expect when her time came. A midwife often brought the village gossips with her to ease the labor and offer support to the mother. The women told stories and comforted the laboring woman. Elise wasn't sure that anyone would come for her since no one in the area knew her, but she longed for the camaraderie of women, even if they happened to be strangers. Elise wished she could have formed more of a bond with Barbara, but the girl seemed even more withdrawn since leaving London. She found the new surroundings intimidating and refused to venture farther than the garden, terrified of seeing the sea. She kept doggedly at her sewing and embroidery and seemed to grow more animated only when she saw James. She obviously trusted him.

Elise went up to see Edward, who was now sitting up in bed propped up by pillows and wearing a clean nightshirt. He still looked deathly pale and was far from clean, his hair greasy and his beard smeared with dried vomit, but at least the air in the room was fresher. Edward waved her away as soon as she stepped into the room. "Leave me. You mustn't get ill. Send Peg back in. I need to use the chamber pot, and I'd like to wash and shave."

Elise was sure that Dr. Samuels would advise against such foolishness, but she saw no harm in allowing Edward to freshen up. He was a vain man, and getting clean would allow him to regain some dignity and control over the situation. And if he wanted Peg, well, so much the better. Elise was relieved not to have to look after her husband. His treatment of her rankled, and she'd resolved to spend as little time in his company as possible. She wished she could see James, but he'd gone to London. Elise could understand his need to see to his sister, but she worried so. James and the child were the only things that mattered in her life, but she had little control over their well-being. With James gone, every day felt like an eternity, and Elise had nothing to keep her occupied, save her sewing.

Chapter 54

James covered his face with a kerchief as he passed through Bishopsgate and into the city proper. He'd been in London just over a week ago, but things had changed dramatically during that time. A pall hung over the city, the people looking gray and frightened as they went about their business. The number of red crosses had multiplied drastically, and the streets were virtually deserted at a time of day when London normally buzzed like a giant beehive. No children played in the street, and few fine carriages passed by, the wealthy having either left the city or holed up in their houses, hiding from infection.

It was early July, and the heat of the summer combined with the raging pestilence made the air thick with evil smells. London reeked of death, open plague pits exhaling lye-scented fumes of putrefaction. James found himself holding his breath until he grew light-headed, but he could hardly stop breathing, so he tried to suck in air through the handkerchief, conscious that every gulp was laced with ill humors.

A gauzy mist curled between the houses, softening the sharp edges and obscuring the sky. It was thickest along the ground, almost masking the layer of muck and waste that coated the slimy cobbles. In some places, the refuse mixed with mud, forming ankle-deep rivers of sludge. James's horse picked its way through this swamp, its ears pressed back and its nostrils flaring as its hooves nearly lost purchase several times. The animal was nervous, and unusually skittish, especially after the fresh air and open spaces of the countryside.

James tried to avert his eyes as carts piled with corpses slowly rolled past him, the drivers staring ahead with dead eyes, correctly assuming that their own sorry carcasses would grace such a cart before the summer's end. James's horse reared as a cloaked man wearing a leather mask with a long beak materialized out of the mist. The man was a plague doctor, and he gave James a brief nod before vanishing down a dank alleyway. What hope did one man have against the tide of sickness sweeping the city?

The Tower of London looked even more forbidding than usual in the swirling mist, the ravens screeching loudly as they flapped their black wings and flew from one rampart to another. The stink of rotting fish wafted off the river, and James heard the plaintive cries of the ferrymen as they called out to one another to relieve their boredom. They got few fares these days since most people left their houses only when absolutely necessary and saw little reason to venture across the river. The sickness would claim many, but so would poverty. Almost everyone's livelihood had been threatened by the plague, and they were feeling the pinch.

An unnatural hush hovered over Molly's street, her normally nosy neighbors all hiding indoors, whether by choice or necessity. James tethered his horse and slowly approached the house, fearful of what he'd find. Several dwellings were marked with the telltale red cross, and James breathed a sigh of relief when he took in the unblemished wood of Molly's door. No plague, then, not yet. James knocked loudly, eager to see Molly and her family. Molly opened the door and yanked him inside, slamming the door shut behind him. She was hollow-eyed and tense.

"What are you doing here?" Molly hissed as she took in his travel-stained appearance.

"I came to see after the family," James replied, surprised by Molly's hostility.

"You must leave. Now."

"Why? What's happened?"

"What's happened? Are ye blind, man? There's plague all around."

James glared at Molly and took her by the shoulders. "What are you not telling me, Moll?"

"Beth's been taken ill. Two days ago. Oh, I can't bear to lose another child, James," she wailed. "If anyone finds out, we'll get shut in, and that will be the end of us all. You must leave. Save yourself, Brother. You still have a chance."

"Molly, let me take Mercy. I'll keep her safe."

Molly stared up at him, her mouth working as she bit her lip. "Where would you take her?"

"I'll take her back to Suffolk."

"Oh, you think our esteemed father will look after his granddaughter, do you?"

"No, he's banished me. But I can stay in the town, Moll. There are no cases of plague there yet. Life goes on much as before. The food is not tainted, and there's fresh air from the sea."

"All right. Take her, James. Keep 'er safe. I have to stay and care for Beth."

"And Peter?" James asked, realizing that he couldn't hear the sound of Peter working in his workshop.

"He's gone, James. He's been summoned to the palace. They need carpenters to make coffins. I haven't seen 'im in nearly a fortnight."

James nodded. Of course, there were thousands of people living in Whitehall Palace, and no carts would be collecting the dead in plain view. The nobility would have wooden coffins and proper burials, with a church service and mourners, not be tossed into lye-filled pits. The afflicted servants and other lowly members of the household would be discreetly disposed of, so as not to offend the sensibilities of the wealthy.

"And the king?" James asked. "Is he still in London?"

"Rumor has it that 'e's left for Salisbury with 'is court, but there are many who remain behind. Oh, James, it's terrifying, this is."

"Yes, it is. It's much worse than any previous year."

"There are shortages of food, and whole families die out once they're shut in. I'm scared, James."

Molly finally let go of her self-control and flung herself into James's arms, weeping. "I don't want to die."

"You're not going to die. Come with me, Moll."

"I can't leave Beth behind, and I can't bring 'er along. She'll infect the others and bring the pestilence to wherever we go. She doesn't 'ave long, James."

"May I see her?"

"No, ye fool. Ye may not. Just take Mercy, and be on yer way."

Molly grabbed an empty sack and began to throw in various items of clothing for her daughter. There wasn't much, and the sack was depressingly light. "Come," she called out to Mercy, who peered from behind the curtain of the alcove where she'd been sleeping. "James will take ye away from this accursed place."

"But what about ye and Father, Mam? And Beth?" Mercy pleaded. "I don't want to leave ye."

"We will come and fetch ye as soon as we can. Now mind yer uncle and don't be a burden to 'im."

Molly seized the child and held her close for a moment, kissing the top of her head. She squeezed her eyes shut to keep the tears from falling, then swiftly pushed Mercy away. "Go now."

Mercy looked frightened as she followed James out of the house. She glanced from left to right, shocked by the silence and stink of fear that permeated the narrow alley where she'd been born and lived her whole life. James lifted Mercy onto the horse and swung into the saddle behind her. She leaned against him, giving him her trust, but he could feel her slight shoulders shaking with silent sobs as they trotted away from Blackfriars. Mercy didn't say a word, but her body was rigid against James's chest, and she continued to cry, occasional sobs tearing from her as she took in the state of the city. James wished that he could comfort the child, but there wasn't much he could say. She knew the reality of what was happening and understood only too well the consequences of having a plague victim in the house.

James wrapped his arms about her and kissed the top of her head. "We'll be all right, Mercy. I'll take care of you no matter what. You hear?"

Mercy nodded miserably. "Thank ye, Uncle James. I know ye will."

Mercy remained silent for the rest of the ride through London, huddling against James as if she could meld into him for greater safety. She wasn't asleep, but she kept her eyes closed to block out the horror. James reached into his saddlebag and took out a piece of bread. "Here, have some bread, child."

"'T might be tainted," Mercy replied, stiffening.

"It's not. I brought it with me from Suffolk. I don't have much left, but we'll be able to buy some food in a few hours once we are far enough from the city."

Mercy accepted the bread and chewed it slowly, savoring every bite. James realized that the child probably hadn't eaten at all since yesterday, food being scarce. James took out a kerchief and gave it to the girl. "Tie this around your face once we get closer to the gate."

"Why?"

"It will keep you from breathing in evil humors."

"And how will that help?" Mercy asked, suddenly curious.

"I don't know, but the plague doctors wear those leather masks with the long beaks, and the masks seem to keep them safe. So, covering your nose and mouth must have some benefit."

Mercy nodded and tied the scarf around her face. She looked like England's tiniest highwayman.

"Will it get better outside the wall?"

"Not for a while. It's even worse past the city gates, but eventually we will get to open country. Just be patient till then."

"Not like I have much choice in the matter," replied Mercy wisely.

Chapter 55

"I'm glad to see you feeling better," Elise said as she entered Edward's room with the breakfast tray. Edward was sitting up in bed, a scowl of irritation on his face. The unnatural flush of a few days ago had been replaced by pallor, but at least the fever had gone, and Edward was no longer vomiting. He'd lost weight over the past few weeks, and his jowls sagged, loose skin wobbling beneath his chin in a most unbecoming manner. His hair appeared to be grayer than it had been even a few months ago, and there were fine wrinkles around his eyes even when he wasn't smiling, which at this moment, he most certainly wasn't.

"Will you try some breakfast?"

"Give it here," Edward replied and took the tray from Elise. She sat down and watched as he obediently ate a hot bun and drank a cup of broth. Edward handed back the crockery and made to rise.

"You are not fit to be out of bed, Edward," Elise protested. "You need a few more days, or you will undermine your recovery."

"If I don't die of sickness, I will perish of boredom," Edward growled.

"Better than dying of the plague," Elise replied. "They say in the village that the king and his court have left London for Salisbury. He will remain there until the pestilence begins to abate in the city."

"Then I will go to Salisbury," Edward said but made no move to rise. Surprisingly, he'd decided to heed her advice for once.

"Perhaps I can come with you. Salisbury is not so far, is it? I've never been." Elise already knew what Edward would say, but she thought she might try. Being in this house without James was unbearable. She floated from room to room, desperate for something to do and someone to talk to, but there was no one, save Peg, and it wasn't proper to chat with the servants as if they were friends. Elise had grown close to Lucy during her time in London, but Peg was a different type of woman, a woman who was best kept at arm's length if one didn't wish to have to pull a knife out of one's back. Elise was even lonelier than she had been in London, where at least she could take the occasional walk and see something of the hustle and bustle of the city.

"You will remain here," Edward replied, his gaze boring into her, daring her to defy him.

"Edward, what have I done to displease you so?" Elise cried, suddenly unable to contain her frustration any longer. "I have tried to be a good wife to you, but you are never at home, and when you are, you ignore me. Perhaps if you would explain things to me, I could learn to be a better companion to you," she begged.

Edward stared at her as if his horse had suddenly spoken. She'd never confronted him so openly before, and the experience was new to them both. He leaned back against the pillows and studied her for a moment, as if deciding just how much honesty she could handle. He let out a sigh of defeat, his shoulders slumping as he acknowledged the truth of her argument.

"Elise, my accident robbed me of my manhood, but it hadn't dulled my sight, nor has it done anything to dampen my lust. I might seem old to you, but inside, I'm still a young man who burns with desire and longs for pleasure. Having you belong to me, but not being able to use you as a husband should and seeing you grow big with a child that isn't mine enrages me. I long to punish

James and cause him the kind of suffering he's caused me, but I can hardly hold him accountable for doing what I asked of him."

Edward smiled ruefully at Elise's shocked expression. She hadn't considered that Edward might actually desire her or suffer torment because he couldn't consummate their marriage. He was right: he did seem old to her, and she just assumed that the passions of his youth had dissipated along with his ability to lie with a woman. Edward gave her a look of sheer disgust, guessing at her thoughts.

"You never spared me much thought, have you, dear wife? Well, let me tell you something: My youth was spent enduring the horrors of the Civil War and wondering every day if I might survive long enough to see the downfall of Cromwell and his accursed Republic. Those years were the bleakest of my life, but if I could turn back the clock, I would return to that time in a heartbeat rather than live this half-life that God has seen fit to *bless* me with. When I am at court, the glittering opulence and sheer extravagance of it all intoxicate me. I lose myself in the mad fantasy that is the reign of our king, and for a short while, I feel like my old self again, until I come home and see you—young, beautiful, and ripe for the picking by any man who's bold enough to try."

"Are you suggesting that I would have a love affair if you brought me to court?" Elise asked, astonished by the reason for her exile.

"I'm saying that you belong to me as much as any horse in my stable. I might not ride it, but that doesn't mean that I will tolerate anyone else riding it in my stead."

"I'm not a horse, Edward," Elise protested hotly. "You can't lock me away for the rest of my life just because you don't wish anyone else to look at me."

"It won't be for the rest of your life, Elise, but for the rest of mine. You might get lucky and end up being a wealthy widow. All you have to do is produce a healthy son who will ensure that all my worldly goods do not pass to my sniveling cousin, who is my closest male kin. Oh, how he would love to lay his hands on my fortune. Well, I've fought and plotted to have His Majesty restored to the throne, and he has rewarded me for my loyalty and valor. I will not have some spineless popinjay reap the rewards of years of deprivation and terror. Oh no. You will bear me a son, Elise, and then you will bear me another. I will keep you locked away and pregnant until you've fulfilled your purpose. And if you retain something of your looks, perhaps you will enjoy your well-deserved freedom then."

Elise gasped at Edward's words. He was nothing more than a bitter old man who wanted to punish her for his life's disappointments. And the tragic thing was that he not only could but would.

"I never took you for a cruel man, Edward," Elise said as she rose to her feet.

"And I never took you for anything more than an empty womb waiting to be filled," Edward spat out. A desperate sob tore from Elise as she fled the room.

Chapter 56

December 2013

Surrey, England

Quinn ordered a glass of white wine and found a table in a corner next to the window. She was early, but she needed a little time to compose herself before facing Sylvia again. She supposed she could have invited Sylvia to come over, but it seemed a better idea to meet on neutral ground, in a public place full of people where emotions would have to be kept in check. Quinn took a sip of wine and gazed out the window at the people walking by. The day was sunny but cold, and a bitter wind blew from the north, forcing the passersby to huddle deeper into their coats as they went about their business. The village was decorated for Christmas, wreaths of evergreens with red bows and fairy lights making the normally sober street look festive.

Quinn watched as Sylvia hurried down the street, her colorful scarf blowing behind her like a sail. The gusty wind blew her dark curls away from her face, and she bent her head into the wind to shield her face. Quinn gave a small wave as Sylvia entered the pub with a rush of cold air. She gave a brief nod, placed her order at the bar, and came to join Quinn at the table.

"Hello," she said simply. "I hope I haven't kept you waiting too long."

"No, I just got here. I normally walk, but today I drove in," Quinn admitted. "Too windy."

"I don't like this time of year," Sylvia said as she shrugged off her coat and unwound her scarf. "Some people love winter, especially the holiday season, but to me it's just a dark, cold stretch to get through."

The waiter placed a cappuccino in front of Sylvia and she inhaled its aroma, smiling in contentment. "I'm not much of a drinker, but I do love coffee."

"So do I."

Sylvia took a sip of her drink and raised her eyes to meet Quinn's. "I was really glad you called. I was beginning to abandon all hope of ever hearing from you."

"I had some things to work through," Quinn replied, being deliberately vague. There was no point in telling Sylvia that the test came back positive: she already knew she was Quinn's mother, and the news about Rhys was not something that Quinn was ready to share just yet. She still wasn't sure how she felt about seeing Sylvia again. When she'd imagined meeting her mother, there was always an immediate and natural bond, but she didn't feel anything except resentment for the woman sitting across from her. She'd tried to push it down and reason herself out of feeling so angry, but the feelings kept rising to the top and bubbling over, leaving Quinn with a deep sense of frustration. This is not how this was supposed to go.

"Have you ever regretted your decision to give me away?" Quinn asked. She knew what she wanted to hear, and she suspected that Sylvia would tell her just that to make her happy, but Sylvia shook her head, a stubborn expression that Quinn so frequently saw reflected in her own mirror hardening her features.

"No, Quinn. I know you want me to feel remorse, but I promised myself when I came to see you that I would be honest with you. I owe you that much. I thought of you often, and I wished that I had a way of keeping up with you, but I never regretted not being a mother to you."

Quinn sucked in her breath, feeling as if she'd just been slapped. "I was lucky to have been adopted by a wonderful couple who never treated me with anything less than love, but my fate could have been very different. I could have been shunted from foster home to foster home, becoming one of those children who fall through the cracks and eventually end up on the street, or dead of an overdose. Did you ever consider that?" Quinn demanded.

"Quinn, I know you're angry with me, and you have every right to be, but that decision was made by a frightened seventeen-year-old girl who thought she had no one to turn to. I did what I thought was best at the time, and despite all the ifs and could-have-beens, you've had a wonderful life. You are a beautiful, smart, successful woman, and I couldn't be more proud that you are mine, even if my claim on you is tenuous at best. I can't change the past, but I would very much like to be a part of your future."

"In what capacity? I already have a mother," Quinn replied spitefully.

"Perhaps we can just be friends, then."

Quinn took a sip of her wine. This wasn't going as she had planned. She meant to be cool and polite, but instead she was being hostile and accusing, pouting like a small child because she felt hurt and wanted someone to kiss her boo-boo, while Sylvia remained dignified and composed. Quinn looked away, suddenly ashamed of her behavior. She was a grown woman, and she would act like one.

"Are you married?" Quinn asked, turning back to face Sylvia. It was safer to change the subject and learn something about this woman whose DNA formed a large part of Quinn's being. Sylvia was right: the past couldn't be altered, but perhaps they could take a small step toward the future by learning something about each other.

"I was. My husband passed two years ago. Pancreatic cancer," Sylvia explained, her eyes filling with tears. "We were married for nearly twenty-five years, and most of them were happy ones."

"I'm sorry," Quinn said and meant it. "Tell me about your children."

"I have two sons: Logan and Jude. Logan just turned twenty-six, and Jude is twenty-two. I wanted more children, but it just never happened for us."

"Do they know about me?"

"They do now. They were angry at first and resentful. But they'd like to meet you, if that's something you might be open to."

"What about your husband? Did you ever tell him?" Quinn asked.

"No. I was too afraid to tell him in the beginning, imagining that he might think less of me, and once the opportunity had passed, it became harder to confess. I always knew I should have, but it was never the right moment. He would have understood, I think. He was a good man, my Grant. He was a primary school administrator. That's how we met. I was a teacher at the school he worked at."

"And Logan and Jude? What do they do?" Quinn asked, curious about these two lads who were her half-brothers.

"Jude is a musician. He plays guitar and sings. He's quite good, although I don't really enjoy his type of music. It's punk rock, or so he tells me. And Logan is a nurse. He works at the London, which is why I moved there. I wanted to be close to him after Grant died. I just couldn't bear to stay in the house all alone.

It went from being a place of comfort and love to a place of isolation and loneliness."

Quinn thought of her own little house. That's how it felt after Luke left, except that Luke was still very much alive. And he was no longer necessary to her happiness.

"Sylvia, may I ask you something?"

"Yes, of course. You must have loads of questions."

"Was there anyone in your family who had psychic ability?"

Sylvia looked at Quinn, clearly surprised by the inquiry. Judging by her reaction, it was obvious that even if there was someone, Sylvia wasn't aware of it.

"Not that I know of. Why do you ask?"

"No reason. It's just something I'm interested in," Quinn lied.

"I see. Well, sorry to disappoint, but no. I think the closest anyone came to being psychic was when my grandmother told my dad that my mother would come to no good. And she was right."

"Do you keep in touch with you mother?" Quinn asked, suddenly remembering that this woman's parents were her grandparents.

"I didn't for a long time, but we eventually made peace. As I got older, I didn't fully forgive her for leaving, but I tried to understand her reasons. I loved my dad, but I could see how he wasn't the right man for her. My mother was a very sensual woman who needed a man whose appetites matched her own, but my dad, God bless him, just didn't seem very interested in that side of things. He never remarried after Mum left. Never even had a girlfriend. Not everyone is cut out for it, I guess."

Quinn nodded. It was strange hearing about these people who were her close family. "Is he still alive, my grandfather?"

"No. He died a few years before my Grant. Just fell asleep in front of the telly one day and never woke up. I miss him," she added.

"Did he ever suspect anything, once you came back after having me?" Quinn asked.

"I think he might have, but he was too afraid to ask. He'd already lost my mum, and he was afraid to lose the only person he truly loved. He was happy to have me back and didn't ask too many questions."

Sylvia finished her cappuccino and reached for her bag. "I've brought some photos. I thought you might like to have a look."

"Oh, I would," Quinn exclaimed. She studied every photo, trying to find some small resemblance between herself and the people who were her family. She did bear a resemblance to Estelle, Sylvia's mother. She had been glamorous in her day, a woman who clearly enjoyed male attention. Her grandfather smiled benignly into the camera, and Quinn could see something of him in Sylvia, especially about the eyes.

Logan was a surprise. He was tall and lean, with shaggy black hair and sleeve tattoos. His lopsided grin was infectious, and his hazel eyes looked like they hid many secrets. He was the one who looked like a rocker, not his brother, who appeared almost prim by comparison. Jude must have taken after his father, his light brown hair thick and wavy, and his eyes a lovely shade of blue. He was almost classically handsome, unlike Logan, whose features were not as regular.

"That was before he started with his current band," Sylvia explained. "He looks a bit more wild now. Grew his hair out, and *got inked*, as he puts it."

"They must be popular with the girls," Quinn observed as she studied her half-brothers.

"Oh, aye, they are, except Logan doesn't go in for girls. He's quite the player, though—nothing like his dad, who never even had a girlfriend before he met me. He's been with the same bloke for a few years now. I hope it'll last. And Jude is artistic and sensitive. And single, as far as I know."

"I'd like to meet them," Quinn blurted out. She hadn't intended to, but seeing her brothers in the photographs loosened something in her heart. They were her flesh and blood, her siblings. Would they find common ground?

"Of course. You can meet Logan anytime, and with Jude, we'll arrange something."

Quinn returned the photographs to Sylvia. She felt a little more comfortable about spending time with her, and the anger of an hour before had faded but was still there at the back of her mind, gnawing at her. She'd found half of what she'd been searching for, but there were still questions she needed to ask.

"Sylvia, Rhys Morgan is not my father."

"How do you know? He has a one-in-three chance, just like the other two."

"I had a paternity test done. It came back negative."

Sylvia stared at her, shocked. "Does he know? Have you told him, then?"

"No. I just helped myself to some hair from his comb when he wasn't looking," Quinn explained, smiling guiltily.

Sylvia frowned, obviously coming to the wrong conclusion. "Are you involved with him?"

"Not in the way you think. There is someone special in my life, but it's not Rhys."

"Good. I'm glad. I want to see you happy."

"Sylvia, I'd like to know something of the other two men. I need to know who my father was."

Sylvia looked distressed but nodded. "I understand your desire to know, but I wish you'd leave it alone, Quinn. No good can come of it."

"Are you now being psychic?" Quinn joked, making Sylvia smile.

"I suppose I am. I'll tell you whatever I can, though."

Chapter 57

July 1665

Suffolk, England

Elise felt vastly relieved when Edward finally left for Salisbury. She tried to play the dutiful wife, but Edward's words had cut her to the quick and left her feeling despondent and frustrated. She wasn't foolish enough to believe that Edward married her for love—few people of his class did. But most couples, being put in a position where their lives depended on each other, at least attempted to have some sort of a relationship. Edward wanted nothing to do with her; he cared nothing for her or her feelings, but he held the key to her future, and legally she was his property. She was a bird in a gilded cage, a prize to lock away in a silver coffer and admire on occasion. Edward made it clear enough that to him she was something less than human: a vessel and a means to an end.

Elise wasn't precisely sure when she'd made the decision, but by the time James returned from London, she knew for sure. If her husband felt no obligation toward her, well, then she felt no obligation toward him. Perhaps this was a radical notion for a woman of her time, but she refused to allow a man to rob her of her chance of happiness. Edward might be her husband, and he owned her and her offspring, but he did not own her thoughts or her heart, nor did he own her loyalty.

Elise threw aside her sewing and rushed outside when she saw James canter into the front yard. James rode pillion behind a small, tired-looking girl whose head drooped like a flower as she slept. James said something to her, and the child stiffened, her eyes flying open once she realized that they'd reached their destination. James dismounted and helped the child off the horse, setting her gently on the ground. She took his hand and looked about fearfully.

"James, you're back," Elise cried as she approached him, but James made no move to go to her. Instead, he held up his hand to keep her from coming any closer, his expression closed. "It's all right, Lord Asher is gone," Elise said.

James shook his head. "Don't come any closer. We are both fine, but there is still a chance that we might take ill. I only came to tell you that I am back. I will stay at the gamekeeper's cottage with Mercy until it's certain that neither one of us has been infected."

"And your sister?" Elise asked carefully, stealing a peek at the child, who pressed herself to James's legs when her mother was mentioned, as if trying to make herself smaller.

"Molly and Peter are not ill, but Beth . . ."

"I understand," Elise replied and turned her attention to the little girl. "Welcome, Mercy. I hope you had a pleasant journey." Elise cringed at her inappropriate choice of words. There was nothing pleasant about fleeing a plague-ridden city, having left your family behind. Mercy was old enough to comprehend why her parents sent her away. Children grew up fast, especially when sudden death was all around them. Mercy might never see her parents or sister again, nor was it guaranteed that she wouldn't begin to display symptoms herself, having been exposed to the sickness.

"Thank ye, me lady," Mercy replied, her thin voice barely audible. "It was most pleasant. Uncle James took good care of me. He promised me mam." At this, Mercy nearly began to cry, but

James put a reassuring hand on her shoulder, and she got hold of herself.

"Well, I, for one, am very glad you are here, and I hope you will come to the house and visit me once Uncle James deems it safe."

"I would like that very much, me lady."

"Are you well, Elise?" James asked over Mercy's head. Elise nodded, unable to speak. What could she say? She was well enough physically, and there was no need to tell James of the conversation between her and Edward. He knew the truth of their arrangement and his own part in it, and he was just as bitter and angry as she was at being used so cruelly.

"I will send Peg to the cottage with a basket of food. She'll leave it on the doorstep. Get some rest."

"Thank you. I'll see you in a few days," James said as he handed Mercy her bundle and took his horse by the reins. He wouldn't be leaving it at the house stable, not when Edward could return at any moment. James's eyes softened when he took in Elise's rounded belly, and a smile tugged at the corners of his mouth as he raised his hand in farewell.

"And I will see you," Elise replied and hoped it was true.

Chapter 58

Elise spent the next few days in a state of acute anxiety. She kept waiting to hear that James had taken ill, and she asked Peg several times a day if she'd seen anything when she delivered the food basket to the cottage. Peg assured her that all was well. James promised that he would keep the curtains open as long as he and Mercy were well, and he would close the curtains as a signal if one of them displayed any symptoms. Peg often found Mercy looking out the window and waving vigorously when she spotted Peg walking toward the cottage.

Elise thanked God that Mercy didn't seem to be infected, but it was James to whom her thoughts strayed a thousand times a day. She'd never imagined what it would feel like to lose him, but now that the possibility was real, Elise realized that life without James in it held no interest for her. She'd hated him for so long that she hadn't realized how much she'd grown to care for him. James never spoke of his feelings, nor did he ask anything of her, but Elise knew with an unwavering certainty that James cared for her and their baby. Had the circumstances of their meeting been different, they might have enjoyed a courtship, but their entire relationship had progressed backward, starting with consummation and creeping slowly toward love and respect. And if James took ill, she would lose him as well, as she had lost everyone she loved.

Elise recruited Peg to walk with her to the church. She had no right to ask God to spare James; he didn't belong to her. But she prayed for him nonetheless. She hadn't asked Edward to bring James to her bed, nor did she give herself leave to care for him, but now that her feelings were crystal-clear to her, the fear of losing him was overwhelming. They belonged together; they were a family, and Edward was the outsider. Surely in the eyes of God she was wed to James, wasn't she?

The household breathed a collective sigh of relief when a week went by and no symptoms of the plague manifested. Elise and Peg walked to the cottage, eager to see James and Mercy. Mistress Benford tutted with disapproval as they prepared to set off, reminding Elise of Dr. Samuels's sage advice, but Elise waved her off. She was tired of sitting around and brooding. A walk would do her good.

"How are you feeling?" Elise asked Mercy who looked well rested and adequately fed after a week of doing little more than moping about the house.

"Bored," Mercy said with feeling.

"Then you must be well."

"Can I go to the 'ouse? I've never been to a grand 'ouse afore, and I . . ." Mercy grew silent, believing to have overstepped the bounds of propriety.

"Of course, you can go. You can walk back with Peg. I'd like a word with your uncle, if you don't mind."

"Oh, I don't mind," Mercy said. "He is surly and won't play with me."

"Well, maybe if you're nice to Rob he'll play with you after he's finished his work in the stables. He's only a few years older than you, and he knows all kinds of games."

Mercy's eyes lit up. "Oh, yes. But will 'e want to play with me? Boys don't like playing with girls, do they?"

"Depends what the game is," Peg replied with a wicked chuckle. "Come along, Mistress Mercy. We'll find some way of lifting yer sagging spirits."

Mercy skipped in front of Peg as they walked down the path leading toward the house. James remained in the doorway, looking at Elise as a slow smile spread across his face. He looked well, and Elise breathed out a sigh of relief, certain now that he wouldn't take ill.

"It'll take more than the plague to get rid of me," he said as he moved aside to let her through. Elise hesitated for a moment, then followed him inside the cottage. She'd expected to find squalor, but the cottage was clean and tidy, the clean dishes stacked on a shelf and a pot of something savory bubbling over the fire.

"Did you make that?" Elise asked.

"No, that was Mercy. Quite the little madam, that one. I have some ale. Would you like a cup?"

Elise shook her head. What she wanted was for James to take her in his arms, but the distance between them felt too great for some reason. Nothing had really changed but everything had. Elise looked up to find James watching her. His head was cocked to the side, and there was an odd expression on his face. Confusion mingled with longing as he took a step closer. This was her moment, and Elise seized it with all the impetuousness of the young. She walked into James's arms and laid her head on his shoulder. "James, I . . ."

James held her close and kissed the top of her head. He smelled clean, as if he'd recently bathed, and Elise could feel the warmth of his body through the thin linen of his shirt.

"It was inevitable, you and I, wasn't it?" he said quietly.

Elise nodded into his chest. Her heart thumped with a joyful rhythm as she turned her face up, smiling at him. "Will you not kiss me, Master Coleman?"

James lowered his head and brushed his lips against hers. They were soft and gentle, and her heart beat as if it might gallop straight out of her chest. She'd lain with James many times, but this was entirely different. This time she was a willing participant and not a pawn in a game she didn't know the rules to. This time she had a say.

James kicked the door shut with his foot and led her to the bedroom. The bed was narrow and hard, and the linens none too fine, but Elise didn't notice a thing as James helped her out of her gown. His hands shook with impatience as he undid the laces of the bodice and nearly ripped the ties of her skirt. At last she was standing in front of him in her chemise, and James sank to his knees and pressed his lips to the swell of her belly as he held it with his large hands. Elise felt a wave of tenderness for this man who'd never really known love. He would have it from her and their child; she'd make sure of that. Edward would have his heir, but Elise would have her love.

This time, their lovemaking was slow and tender. There was no rush, no ultimate goal. They had time, and they had each other. They explored each other's bodies in ways they'd never done before, taking pleasure in giving the other joy. Strange how something they'd done numerous times before had taken on a whole new meaning, and when they finally came together, it was as if they were two pieces of one whole, joining together seamlessly in a conclusion that had been inevitable from the very start. Instead of the tension that Elise usually felt, she experienced a pleasure the likes of which she'd never known. James wasn't just doing his duty, he was making love to her, and she soaked up his devotion as dry earth soaks up the first drops of long-awaited rain.

"How could something that was so wrong feel so right?" Elise asked as she nestled into James's arms. Her back was to him and he laid a proprietary hand on her belly, his fingers splayed over the child they created.

"We must be very careful, Elise. Don't think for a moment that my father didn't imagine this might happen."

"Well, he is not here, is he, and there's no one to tell him our secret."

"No, but that doesn't mean we shouldn't keep it to ourselves."

"May we walk by the sea?" Elise asked James shyly once they got dressed.

"As you wish, my lady," he replied with a smile. "Have you been to the beach since I left?"

"No, Peg wouldn't come with me. She's scared."

"I suppose it can be intimidating to someone who's never seen anything grander than the Thames."

James gave her a bow and offered her his arm. "Shall we?."

Elise accepted his arm and they walked in companionable silence, each one lost in their own thoughts.

"What will happen after our walk?" Elise asked as she followed James down the narrow track. They had to walk single file, but James held his hand behind his back, Elise's fingers in his.

James turned to face her. He looked momentarily puzzled, then lifted her hand to his lips and kissed it reverently.

"You will go back to the house, and I will return to the cottage. You're Lady Asher, and I am your servant."

"But what will happen with us?" Elise asked innocently.

"Nothing."

They had come to the sea and Elise stopped, staring at the sparkling water, James momentarily forgotten. A lovely breeze blew off the sea, and she turned her face into it and closed her eyes. The baby kicked, as if suddenly aware of her awe. The coast looked deserted and wild but also majestically beautiful. Elise turned her face toward the breeze. It was bracing and cold and smelled of brine and seaweed. Elise took off her shoes and stockings and allowed the surf to rush over her bare feet. She gasped as the cold water swirled around her ankles, but the feeling was exquisite.

"Be careful," James said as he took her by the elbow. "Wouldn't want to endanger the Asher heir."

Elise pulled her arm out of his grasp and turned to face him. "I am not your plaything," she exclaimed, wounded by his lack of initiative concerning their future.

"No. You are my love," he replied softly, his eyes caressing her flushed face.

"Did you know that people from this very town sailed to the Massachusetts Bay Colony nearly thirty years ago? They wished for freedom, James. And they found it."

"Many of them died," James replied, uncharacteristically pessimistic.

"And many of them didn't," Elise retorted.

James seized Elise by the elbow and pulled her away from the churning water. "Elise, I am a bastard. I am no one. I have no name and no fortune. I might snatch a few moments of happiness from this world, but I will never—you hear me?—*never* have a place in society or a comfortable life. Is that what you wish for our child? Yes, we can run away. We can even sail to America, but you will still be my father's wife in the eyes of God, and I will still be a penniless bastard. What kind of life will our child have? What hope for the future?"

"So, what do you suggest?" Elise exclaimed, "That we just go on as we are?"

"For now, yes. Once the child is born, my father will no longer be able to disown it. The humiliation would be more than he can bear, especially in front of the king he so worships. Our child will have a title and a handsome inheritance. And a future. And I'm prepared to put my own wishes on hold to see that happen."

"And what about me?" Elise demanded.

"What about you? You are a great lady. You have comfort, wealth, and an absentee husband. You also have a man who loves you and is devoted to you. Can you not make peace with the situation and just bide your time for now?"

Elise considered the wisdom of James's words. He was right, of course. She was too stubborn and too proud. She wasn't owed happiness, nor was she owed a livelihood. She didn't care about making sacrifices, but it wasn't fair to sacrifice their unborn child and condemn it to a life of penury and obscurity. If Edward openly disowned the child, it would have no name and be forever a bastard. James knew what that was like, and it had left an imprint on his soul that no amount of acceptance would ever erase. He wanted better for his son, and who was she to blame him?

"So, we sneak about?" Elise asked, but the fire had gone out of her, and she felt ashamed of her outburst.

"We bide our time," James replied. "And we wait for an opportunity."

"Do you really love me, James?" Elise asked, turning her face up to his.

"I do. And I swear to love you until my dying day." He bent down and kissed her. The kiss deepened and James drew her against him. They were so caught up in the moment that neither one of them realized that they were being watched.

Chapter 59

Elise suggested that Mercy stay with her at the house. James couldn't be expected to take care of a little girl, and Elise found pleasure in Mercy's uncomplicated company. She was articulate and surprisingly observant for a child of seven. Edward had never met Mercy, so if he returned unexpectedly Elise would just tell him that Mercy was Mistress Benford's granddaughter. He wouldn't care one way or the other, and Mistress Benford had taken a liking to the little girl and treated her as if she were indeed her granddaughter. Mercy had even managed to charm Barbara, who lit up every time the child walked into the room. Barbara liked to show Mercy her embroidery and listened intently when Mercy talked, mesmerized by the cadence of her childish voice.

Mercy's quick mind and desire to learn reminded Elise of her own sisters. She missed them so much, and she railed silently against her father for taking them away without so much as a goodbye. She'd loved and respected him, but he couldn't be happier to be shod of her, especially since the debt to Edward had been deferred. Elise strongly suspected that Hugh de Lesseps had no intention of ever returning to England. Edward would hardly follow him to the West Indies to collect what was owed to him. Her father had used her to pacify Edward and defaulted on the rest of his debt.

"Is there anything you'd like to do?" Elise asked Mercy as they sat in the parlor, a plate of sweetmeats in front of them. Mercy had helped herself to three already, and her fingers were sticky with sugar, but her eyes were filled with sadness.

"I'd like to bring some of these to my sister," she whispered. "She's never had anything like it, and now she'll go to 'er grave without ever knowing what she was missing. And me mam too. Will I ever see 'er again?" Mercy asked. She didn't allow herself to cry, but her hands were clasped in her lap, the knuckles white with tension.

"Mercy, I won't insult you by lying to you. You know as well as I do that I don't have the answer, but I will tell you this: Many people who are exposed to the illness never catch it. It just passes them by. No one knows why, but they live on. I will pray for your parents and sister every day, and you must too. It will give them a better chance."

Mercy scoffed at Elise's words. "Pray? God doesn't care."

Elise was shocked to hear such a sentiment coming from one so young. "Who told you that?"

"I heard me mam saying it to me da. She said that God took 'er mother to punish 'er for 'er sins and took 'Arry because 'e visits the sins of the parents onto their children. And now 'e will take Beth and me, and even Uncle James. Mam said that God is cruel."

Perhaps he is, Elise thought. She was overcome with sympathy for this little girl. God was a symbol of hope, love, and forgiveness, as long as one didn't question the word of the ministers too closely. There were people who saw God's mercy in everything, but there were those who railed against a deity they believed to be a despot. Of course, they did so in private because to question the Church could result in a trial for heresy. Was Molly one of those people who questioned the very existence of God? Was she a heretic? Or was she just a woman who was so crippled by her pain that she needed someone to blame? Many lost their mothers in childbirth, and many lost children. There were families whose graves took up whole rows in local cemeteries.

Elise placed a hand on her belly, suddenly aware that she wasn't immune to the whims of fate. Would she survive the birth? Would her baby? And if it did, would it live to see adulthood? So many didn't. Molly lost a child only a few months ago, and now she was about to lose another, if she hadn't already. Mercy might survive this round of the Black Death, but it would come back, as it did every year to claim more lives and decimate more families. Where was God when so many were dying? Were they all guilty of something and paying for a crime, physical or imagined? Or was death random, with nothing at all to do with the commandments of the Lord? Did it sweep through the streets of London, claiming anyone who crossed its path and laughing at the kind, loving God who could do nothing to stop it?

"What will happen to me if my parents die?" Mercy asked, interrupting Elise's thoughts. "Where will I go if Uncles James dies too?"

"I will look after you. You have my word."

"And do you have leave to make such a promise?" Mercy asked wisely. "Your lord might not agree."

My lord is your grandfather, Elise wanted to shout, but she kept silent and rearranged her features into an expression of calm and reassurance.

"My lord need never know," Elise replied. "I will keep my word, Mercy."

"You two are getting awfully maudlin," James said as he entered the parlor. He must have overheard the tail end of their discussion and was saddened by Mercy's questions. Mercy knew too much for a child—she could see right through Elise's hollow promise.

"It's a fine summer's day out. What do you say we ask Cook for a basket of food and take a walk to the beach? Would you like to see the sea up close, Mercy?"

Mercy's eyes grew round in her thin face. "Oh, yes, Uncle James, please. I would like to see the sea. Is it really vast? Can I wet my feet?"

"Yes, it's vast. Yes, you can wet your feet. And yes, you can run along the shore and look for treasure."

"What treasure?" Mercy gasped.

"Well, there are all kinds of things that wash up on the shore—mostly shells and small stones, but sometimes there are coins and bits of jewelry, carried on the waves from the treacherous depths of the sea, stolen by pirates who still rest in their watery graves as punishment for their Godless deeds."

Mercy squealed with delight as James scooped her up and twirled her around. "There are no pirates," Mercy said once he finally put her down.

"Are you sure? Will you not see what you can find?"

Mercy gave this some thought. "I s'pose I'd better. Just to be sure."

"Wise decision."

Elise smiled at James. He'd taken Mercy's mind off her fears and gave her something else to think about. Mercy had an inquisitive mind, so the story James had just planted there might keep her occupied for a while. Elise was sure that Mercy would take time to think about it and come back with a list of questions.

"James, does Mercy know how to read?" Elise asked as they walked toward the beach. James carried a basket over his arm and Mercy skipped ahead, singing some ditty to herself.

"I don't believe so."

"Does Molly?"

James shook his head. "Our father paid for our keep but never saw fit to educate us. The couple who looked after us were simple people, and illiterate like most. I learned to read and write once I was brought back to London. Once I mastered my letters, I helped myself to some books from the library. I never imagined that reading could bring such pleasure."

"What did you enjoy most?" Elise asked. She hadn't read many books but had been taught how to read, write, and do simple sums. Her father often required her help with the books. She didn't keep the accounts, but sometimes she took dictation and filled the numbers in the columns.

"There were some books on astronomy, and a few historical accounts. But what I really liked were the plays. My father had several folios of Shakespeare, Marlowe, Ben Johnson, and Thomas Middleton. My father is quite fond of the theater, or he used to be."

"I've never been to the theater," Elise said. "I've never been anywhere. Oh, how I would love to see a play or watch mummers perform. Have you ever been to the theater, James?"

"Yes, many times."

"Will you take me once we are back in London?" Elise asked.

"I would like to, but that's not a promise I can make."

Elise understood only too well. Edward would not welcome James home, even once the child was born. She might not see him again once they returned to town, at least not until Edward required his services again.

"I'm going to teach Mercy to read and write while she's here," Elise announced.

James stopped and looked at her. "Will you? That's very kind of you. It will serve Mercy well."

"I want to do something to help her, James. Whether her parents live or die, having certain abilities might give her more options as she gets older."

"There aren't many options for girls," James replied matter-of-factly. "Mercy will marry and look after her family at best or go into service and look after someone else's family at worst. Neither requires reading or writing. But perhaps she will find some pleasure in reading a story or having the ability to teach her sons their letters. Being literate can certainly help a man."

Elise nodded. She didn't wish to argue with James, but it rankled her the way men simply dismissed half the population. It wasn't just her own lot in life to be a wife and mother—it was every woman's. And if she had no family of her own, she spent her life doing menial work for pitiful wages. Even daughters of nobility had little say in their lives. They were paraded in front of eligible men, married off, and expected to produce as many children as they could before they either got too old or died in childbirth. There were no choices for them, and remaining unmarried was a fate worse than death. Unmarried women were treated like lepers—unless they were very wealthy, of course, in which case they were desirable prospects for fortune hunters.

Elise marveled at the fact that after having a woman—a strong and cunning woman—on the throne for nearly half a century, women were still dismissed as nothing more than a means to an end. *Someday that will change*, Elise thought hotly. *Someday women will be able to choose their own destiny.*

Chapter 60

The days settled into a pleasant routine. The house was far enough from the town to afford privacy, and there were no servants, save Mistress Benford, Peg, and Pete the stable boy, who had little to do since Edward had taken the carriage and horses. Mercy took to her lessons like fish to water, but what surprised Elise was how much time she spent in the kitchen. Mercy liked to cook, and she was eager to learn how to make new dishes.

"Me mam never 'ad much use for cooking," Mercy told Elise after one of their lessons. "She were always too busy taking care of us and the 'ouse to do much more than make a stew or a pot of pottage. Oh, we always 'ad enough to eat, mind ye, but there wasn't much in the way of variety."

"And what would you like to cook?" Elise asked, amused.

"I'd like to make pies and pastries, and roast a swan. Me da told me once that at court, they roast whole swans and then replace the feathers and insert rubies instead of eyes before presenting the birds to the king and 'is courtiers."

Mercy looked enthralled with the idea, her eyes sparkling with the wonder of it. "And they make other grand dishes too, using spun sugar and marzipan. 'Ave you ever seen such things?"

"Lord Asher had some fantastical dishes at our wedding feast. He'd hired one of the palace cooks to see to the preparations. There was a concoction of sugared fruit and nuts decorated to look like a blooming rose bush with a butterfly on each bloom. It was too lovely to eat."

"I wish I could 'ave seen that," Mercy said sadly. "I always dream of getting out of Blackfriars and living at the palace. If God sees fit to take me family, it's because I'd wished to leave them," Mercy whispered, her eyes huge with regret.

"Mercy, your desire to better your lot has nothing to do with what's happening in the city. It's no more your fault than yesterday's rain or tomorrow's drought. One little girl's dream cannot bring about the death of her family, and I won't stand for you blaming yourself. There's nothing wrong with dreaming."

Mercy nodded, somewhat appeased. "Thank you, me lady. Ye are very kind. I can see why Uncle James is so taken with ye. Me mam always said to put me silly notions out of me foolish head."

She would, Elise thought. She'd only met Molly once, but she got the impression that the woman didn't hold with sentiment or wild-goose chases. Molly seemed pragmatic to a fault, possibly a trait she'd inherited from her estranged father. Elise was sure that Molly loved her children fiercely, but she wanted them to find satisfaction in the here and now, not in indulging in daydreams of things that could never be. Well, perhaps Elise could do something for Mercy, something that would help her at least try to reach for her dreams.

Chapter 61

The next few months were the happiest Elise had ever known. For the first time in her life, she was her own mistress, having no father or husband to lord over her from day to day. She was free to do as she pleased, and although she didn't do anything out of the ordinary, it felt wonderful to do it without the watchful stare of a domineering male. Mercy was thriving, and so was the baby. Elise no longer fit into any of her gowns, so Peg sewed several new skirts to accommodate her expanding middle and laced her bodices loosely to allow extra room for her swollen breasts.

Elise completely ignored the advice of the doctor and went for long walks in the fragrant summer wood, enjoying the soothing tranquility of the country. James rarely came to the house for fear of betraying their relationship to the servants, but he joined her for daily walks, which inevitably led to a stolen hour at the gamekeeper's cottage. James's presence was like a balm to her soul. He gave her the love and affection she craved so desperately, but he made no move to control or patronize her. He simply loved her, which was such a novel feeling that Elise had to stop and remind herself that such a thing was really possible.

They spoke no more of the future, but Elise still harbored a hope that they might build a life together. Things had a way of changing when you least expected them to, and although she held no ill will toward Edward, she hoped that her marital status might change at some point in the future.

James often spoke of Molly, and Elise could feel the razor-sharp ache in his heart, the not knowing whether Molly and Peter were still alive worse than the actual news that they might have succumbed to the illness. Mercy resolutely did not ask about her parents, enjoying her time in the country as much as any child who'd never been farther than the next street would. Her reading and writing were coming along at a good pace, and she'd even taken it upon herself to share her newfound knowledge with Peg. Elise saw her sitting with Peg in the kitchen, teaching her the alphabet and writing out simple words that started with each consecutive letter, just as Elise had done to teach Mercy. Peg was not the most eager of students, believing that knowing her letters would do nothing to better her life, but Mercy was convincing, and Peg didn't mind staying off her feet for an hour.

There were days when Elise wished that they could just go on this way forever, but the summer was waning. Eventually, they would have to return to London, but not before the epidemic had abated. They had virtually no news other than what James heard at the tavern. Much of what was said was speculation, but even speculation was based on some measure of truth gleaned from travelers and through gossip. The king and his court were still in Salisbury, which meant that it wasn't yet safe to return. Elise and James remained in Suffolk, enjoying their idyll.

"What news of the city?" Elise asked as she lay in James's arms on a particularly lovely afternoon. The sun rode high in the sky, and it was so warm that James stripped off his clothes and went for a swim. He emerged a quarter of an hour later, covered with gooseflesh, but much refreshed. The North Sea often looked turbulent and gray, its waters icy even at the height of summer, but on this day, the sea was as smooth and shiny as a pane of glass, the blue expanse of sky reflecting in the tranquil water, sky and sea mirroring each other until it was hard to tell where one ended and the other began. The sun sparkled playfully on the surface, and the seagulls circled overhead, waiting for the right moment to dive for an unsuspecting fish.

Elise and James never saw anyone else on the beach. An occasional fishing boat sailed past, and once or twice they spotted a larger vessel, possibly bound for the shores of Scotland, but no townspeople came this far. There were still many who believed that bathing was hazardous to one's health, and it was only a brave few who dared to swim in the sea. Mothers scared their children with tales of sea monsters to prevent them from setting foot into the churning waves, fearful of their offspring being carried off by the current and drowned, their bodies never to be recovered.

James pulled Elise closer, enjoying the firm shape of her rounded belly against his side. The babe had been still before, no doubt lulled to sleep by the walk to the beach, but now it seemed to have awoken and was kicking vigorously, as if trying to get out before its time. James yelped with surprise as a particularly vicious kick startled him out of his reverie and brought him back to Elise's question.

"The situation in London is growing worse, according to some travelers who've passed through the town recently. No one is coming in or out, and merchants are leaving food outside the city. Payment is tossed to them from the walls. Some say that there are not enough death carts, and the corpses are piled on the streets and rotting where they lie. The streets are deserted, and diggers are working round the clock to provide enough pits for mass burial. Many deaths have been reported in villages around London, so the contagion is still spreading."

"But how?" Elise demanded. "If no one is going in or out of the city, how is this pestilence spreading?"

James shrugged. "All it takes is one infected person to pass through a village and come into contact with its inhabitants. A stop at a tavern, an exchange of coin, a handshake, and the illness takes hold. There's some talk of the king and his court leaving Salisbury. There've been a few cases reported there."

"Where are they decamping to?" Elise asked, fearful that Edward would return.

"Oxfordshire, I believe, but I don't know for certain. There's no possibility of returning to the city before the cold weather sets in. I won't let you go back, Elise," James warned, thinking she wished to return.

"I have no plans to go back, James. I will remain here until the child is born and then bide my time until the sickness abates. There's nothing waiting for me in London. Nothing at all."

Elise felt a stab of guilt as she uttered the careless words. There was nothing in London for her, but James was desperate for news of Molly and her family. There was no way to find out who lived and who'd died. Even those who kept records would most likely be dead by now, and all anyone knew were rough numbers of casualties which were nowhere near the real death toll.

"Have you heard anything about Master Pepys?" Elise asked. "Is he still in London, do you think?"

Edward often mentioned Samuel Pepys. He seemed to admire and despise him in equal measures. Edward never really explained his animosity toward the man, but Elise detected a note of jealousy in her husband. Samuel Pepys was loved and admired by His Majesty, and Edward carried on like a jealous mistress, fearful that he would be replaced in the king's affections.

"He was still in the city at some point during the summer, but most likely he's left by now, or he should have if he values his life and that of his wife."

"I would think that he'd leave once the king and his court departed," Elise mused.

"Not necessarily. Master Pepys is devoted to providing a chronicle of the times, and he can hardly do that from leagues away."

"I'd best get back before I'm missed," Elise said as she laboriously got to her feet and brushed sand off her skirt before slipping her feet into her shoes.

"Peg knows where you are. That girl knows everything. She's not as oblivious as you believe her to be," James said as he pulled on his boots and reached for his doublet.

"Peg is grateful to be here. Whatever she knows, she'll keep to herself," Elise replied.

"Don't be so sure, Elise. Everyone has a price, and a servant's price is laughably low. That girl has nothing to her name, save the clothes on her back. She'll spill all for a few shillings."

"You've a very suspicious mind, Master Coleman," Elise teased, amused by James's sudden gravity.

"Aye, I do, and it would serve you well to heed my advice."

"I do heed your advice, but the only way to remain safe is never to see you, and I refuse to do that. So let's not talk about it anymore. I must go back."

"I'll walk you," James said as he sprang to his feet and tied his damp hair into a loose ponytail.

"There's no need."

"There's every need. You're seven months gone with child. You shouldn't be wandering about on your own."

Elise smiled broadly, making James frown with disapproval. "I like it when you fuss," she said. "No one ever cared about my welfare this way except for my dear mother."

James just pulled her close and kissed the top of her head. "Of course I worry about your welfare. I couldn't bear to lose you."

"You will never lose me."

James nodded but didn't reply. Elise knew what he was thinking. She was something of a dreamer, but James was a realist to the core. He knew all too well that there were countless ways to lose someone, and that one had no control over when or where their loved one might stumble and fall. Elise supposed that James was worried about the birth, but she gave it virtually no thought. What was the point of fearing something she couldn't control? She would face her fate when the time came and pray that God was merciful enough to spare her and her baby.

Chapter 62

December 2013

London, England

Quinn set a cup of tea by the bed and bent down to plant a kiss on Gabe's cheek. "Wake up, you'll be late for work."

Gabe pulled a pillow over his head and growled. "Why must it be Monday already?"

"Because that's what generally happens between Sunday and Tuesday, but it's a short week, what with Christmas and all. If you get up now, you'll have time for breakfast."

"All right," Gabe grumbled as he sat up, took a gulp of tea, and reached for his dressing gown. "What's for breakfast?"

"Fried egg and toast. I'll even throw in some mushrooms if you behave."

"There's nothing in the fridge," Gabe replied, looking confused.

"I popped out to the shops while you were sleeping. I don't fancy going hungry," Quinn replied, arching her brow and making Gabe chuckle. Gabe hardly ever ate breakfast, but Quinn couldn't start her day properly without having something to eat, even if it was just toast and tea.

"Mm, I like having you around," Gabe mused as he gave her a sound kiss. "It's just like staying with my mum."

Quinn swatted him, but he jumped out of the way and disappeared into the bathroom. She had to admit that she liked spending the night at his flat and enjoying everything that London had to offer. They'd gone out to dinner and seen a foreign film last night instead of staying in, as they would have had they stayed at her place. There wasn't much of a nightlife in her Surrey village. Quinn smiled as she took out the eggs, mushrooms, butter, and bread. She'd been so lonely the past few months that doing something as mundane as making breakfast for Gabe made her giddy with joy. It was no fun cooking for one.

Gabe came out of the bathroom smelling of soap and aftershave and joined her at the table. His hair was still damp from the shower, and his dark-blue dressing gown matched his eyes. Coincidence? Quinn thought not. Probably a gift from a woman, hopefully his mum. Gabe buttered a piece of toast and tucked into his eggs.

"So, what's on the agenda for today?" he asked as he speared a mushroom and popped it into his mouth.

"I have a meeting with Rhys, actually. Gabe, what do I do?" Quinn asked, her tone plaintive. "How do I continue to work with him knowing what I know?"

"And what exactly do you know?" Gabe asked, eyebrow raised. "You know that thirty years ago, Sylvia Wyatt got pregnant and gave birth to you. Several days later, she left you in a church pew. Those are the only indisputable facts. Anything else is conjecture. Confronting Rhys with this—three decades after the fact—can result in nothing but ruffled feathers and harsh words. How do you think he'll feel if you accuse him of rape?"

"Guilty?"

Gabe shook his head. "Quinn, Sylvia made a choice not to go to the police or confront the men who did that to her. Whether it was because she thought no one would take her seriously or because she didn't really have a case is anyone's guess, but this is her fight, not yours. Rhys is not your father, so let sleeping dogs lie, at least with him."

"Meaning what?" Quinn asked, putting down her teacup.

"Meaning that there are two other men out there who might be your father. My advice to you is to focus on forging a relationship with Sylvia instead of hunting down your other parent, but I know that it will fall on deaf ears because I can already see that glint of refusal in your eyes."

Quinn couldn't help but laugh at Gabe's astute assessment. He was right: she couldn't simply let this go. Perhaps confronting Rhys was not a good idea, but she'd be damned if she gave up now. A few weeks ago, she had no idea who her biological parents were, but now she had one mother and two possible fathers, with a fifty–fifty chance that one of them was her biological dad. Whatever the consequences, she had to find out.

"All right, Gabe, I won't say anything to Rhys, for now, nor will I fly off to hunt down the other two men, but when the time is right, I will take this to its logical conclusion."

"Fair enough," Gabe said as he took a last bite of toast and got to his feet. "Now, I have to run. I have a meeting at nine. Did I ever tell you that being a department head is a colossal bore?"

"You did, but now I actually believe you."

"OK, I'll see you later."

"See you," Quinn replied. Gabe might be right about not confronting Rhys, but having to see the man and pretend that she didn't know about his past was going to be harder than he imagined.

Chapter 63

November 1665
Suffolk, England

A warm and pleasant September gave way to a rainy October, which seemed to drag on endlessly, one dreary day following another until Elise thought she might die of boredom, cooped up as she was in the big, empty house. Then November arrived at last, bright and frigid, the cold wind blowing away the last of the leaves and turning the waters of the sea a dark, forbidding gray. White caps danced on the grim surface, and great waves pounded the shore with relentless frequency. Mercy begged to go to the beach nearly every day, eager to see what treasures she could find. She rarely found anything other than shells and smooth stones, but on one occasion she found a coin and what appeared to be a man's silver shoe buckle. Her find only fed her appetite, and she believed that if she searched diligently enough, she'd find other valuables. Elise was too big and unwieldy to walk to the beach, but James was happy enough to take the girl, eager to get away from the gloom of the gamekeeper's cottage.

Elise spent her days in the parlor, gazing out the window with a book on her lap or sluggishly stabbing at her embroidery as she waited for James to come and see her. He came every day but stayed for a perfunctory half hour under the pretense of checking on her welfare and visiting his niece. To stay longer or show Elise any affection would get servants' tongues wagging, and now that they could no longer snatch an hour alone at the cottage, they had to be extremely mindful of appearances as they were mistress and servant, not expectant parents. At times, it seemed as if the babe would never come, comfortable and safe as it was in Elise's womb. Elise felt tired and irritable from lack of sleep due to the frequent demands of her bladder. Her back ached, especially when she sat for too long on the hard wooden settle, and her belly felt firm and tight, its weight and bulk disproportionate to the rest of her body.

By the time Elise's pains started, she was more than ready to face the terrors of the birthing chamber. The day was misty and gray, and a brace of candles was lit in the parlor despite the early hour, casting a pool of golden light that dispelled the gloom, but only just. Elise paced in front of the hearth, grateful for its warmth. The brisk wind from the sea seemed to penetrate every crack, and the room was frigid and drafty. The midwife had been sent for an hour since but had not arrived yet. Elise suddenly felt frightened and wished that she had female relatives or friends who might help her through the birth. Many women had a roomful of well-wishers around them while they labored. The women shared their own experiences, told stories, or offered silent support to the mother if they had no wish to share, having lost a child during or after the birth. There was Barbara, but she was better off kept in ignorance of what was going on, having no understanding of what Elise was about to experience. Barbara had caught a chill a few days since and was persuaded by Mistress Benford to keep to her bed. She didn't object; she just lay there quietly, staring at nothing in particular.

James mentioned once that Lord Asher meant to find Barbara a husband and make sure she produced a male heir if his scheme to use James to impregnate his wife failed, and Elise thanked the Lord that it hadn't come to that. Barbara was as innocent as a babe in arms, and the thought of some man forcing himself on her and Barbara going through the pains of childbirth without fully comprehending what was happening to her was inconceivable. What kind of monster would do that to a girl who was mentally deficient? Elise prayed that the child would be a boy.

Edward would be temporarily pacified, and poor Barbara would be safe from harm.

Elise asked Peg to look after Mercy and keep her occupied. She was too young to attend a birth, and Elise couldn't handle the endless questions the child asked. She'd been in the house when her brothers were born, but Molly wisely kept the child out of the bedchamber, most likely because she wished to hold on to her sanity. Elise could hear Mercy's piping voice as it echoed down the corridor.

"When will the baby come?" she asked Peg, her voice full of pleading. "Will it be a boy? Can I see him?"

"The baby will come when it's good and ready, Mistress Impatience, and ye will see it when her ladyship gives ye leave to. Now, why don't ye teach me how to write some more words? I've already memorized the ones ye taught me last week."

"Do you have a quill and ink, then?" Mercy demanded. "I don't recall them being kept in the kitchen."

"Bossy boots," Peg grumbled and retraced her steps to get the implements from the study.

Elise rested her hands on her lower back and leaned backward as far as she could. Stretching her back like that eased some of the tension, but her back ached almost as much as her womb when it contracted. Elise let out a low moan and resumed pacing. It helped to walk despite what Mistress Benford said, having birthed seven children herself in quick succession. She insisted that Elise ought to be lying down, but the idea of remaining completely immobile during the pain seemed like torture. Elise would walk about until the midwife arrived, at which point she would no doubt be bullied into bed.

"Where's Pete?" Elise asked Mistress Benford as the woman came into the room to bring her a cup of spiced wine and ask after her condition. Elise peered out the window as she spotted the midwife waddling toward the house, her head bent against the wind. She was an older woman, portly and short of stature, her cheeks ruddy with cold, and a look of fierce determination on her face. She knew her business, and she performed the service with dedication and kindness. Elise breathed out a sigh of relief, knowing that she was in good hands.

"In the stables, I expect."

"I wish him to fetch Master James."

Mistress Benford gaped at her in astonishment. Elise could almost hear her thinking that James had no business being there while the mistress labored, but it wasn't for her to question her lady's judgment.

"I'll send Pete to fetch him right away. Anyone else I should summon?" she asked, her tone acerbic. Elise didn't bother answering. A sharp pain tore through her, making her cry out. The pain didn't last very long, but it had been intense and frightening, and it occurred just as the midwife entered the parlor in search of her patient.

"Shall I help you to bed, me lady?" Mistress Wynne asked, having quickly assessed the situation.

"Perhaps you'd better," Elise conceded. She wished her mother was there to hold her hand and tell her that all would be well. The pain was intensifying, and she had to pause on the stairs to catch her breath and wait out a contraction.

Elise finally made it to her bedchamber and allowed Mistress Wynne to help her undress. She remained in her chemise and climbed onto the bed, suddenly grateful for a moment's respite from the pain and the support of the pillows behind her back. Her belly grew hard and taut as another contraction rolled over her, leaving her red in the face and panting. Elise glanced toward the window to see lashing rain soaking the countryside just before Mistress Wynne drew the curtains, shutting out all natural light. The birthing room had to be kept warm and dark, so she stoked up the fire and lit a few more candles.

Elise was surprised when there was a knock on the door and a young girl entered, followed by a strapping youth who set down the birthing chair, bowed deferentially to Elise, and departed. They must have set off in a wagon after Pete came to fetch the midwife and brought her back on his horse.

"This my daughter, Maisie, yer ladyship. I'm training her. I hope ye don't object to 'er presence."

Maisie was perhaps a year or two younger than Elise, and Elise felt instant kinship with the girl. "I've no objection. Maisie, will you sit with me for a bit?"

The girl instantly sat on the side of the bed and reached for Elise's hand. She had the same dark-brown hair as her mother, but unlike Mistress Wynne, whose eyes were dark, her eyes were a cornflower blue, fringed by dark lashes. They were full of compassion as she smiled at Elise. "All will be well, me lady. Me mam can bring a baby into this world whilst wearing a blindfold and with one hand tied behind 'er back. She'll 'ave yer precious babe out and swaddled before ye know it." Elise relaxed for a moment, soothed by Maisie's words. She was grateful not to be alone.

"If ye'll allow me, me lady," Mistress Wynne said as she pushed her hand between Elise's legs and into her womb. Elise cried out and arched her back, but the midwife was undeterred by Elise's discomfort, her face thoughtful as she took measure of Elise's progress.

"You're very close, me lady. It won't be long now. Ye'll have to push the baby out very soon."

"How will I know when?" Elise asked, panicked. She thought the baby would come out on its own when it was time, so the notion of pushing it from her womb took her by surprise.

"Oh, ye'll know. Yer body will direct ye. Now just try to save yer strength and roll through each pain as best ye can, and don't hold yer breath. Maisie, after the next contraction, let's help her ladyship onto the chair."

Elise's legs felt shaky and feeble as Maisie and Mistress Wynne helped her out of bed and settled her into the chair. She grabbed the handles, grateful for something to hold on to as the next pain rolled over her, leaving her breathless and exhausted.

"Now, lean back and spread yer legs like so," the midwife said as she pushed Elise's legs toward the sides of the chair, leaving the opening in the middle unobstructed. She bunched Elise's shift about her waist, leaving her lower body completely exposed. "There ye are, all ready now."

Elise felt an urgent need to bear down. She couldn't have fought it if she wanted to. It commandeered her body and tore its way through her, making her screech as she gripped the handles and pushed. The pain was unimaginable, but she couldn't stop now. She had to get it out, had to get his unbearable pressure to stop.

"Again," the midwife said as she crouched before Elise, staring between her legs, her hands at the ready should the baby come shooting out unexpectedly. Elise pushed again and again. It felt like an hour, but it was probably no more than mere minutes. The pressure was like a living force inside her body, forcing the baby out of her womb and pushing aside her bones. She felt as if her hips were being spread apart, yanked by giant hands, and there was a terrible burning in her quim as the baby's head passed through.

"It's ripping me apart," Elise cried as Mistress Wynne carefully maneuvered the shoulders. Tears were rolling down Elise's face and hot, sticky blood pooled in a basin beneath the chair's opening.

"That's what babies do," Mistress Wynne said matter-of-factly. "They put ye through unbearable pain and suffering, and once ye heal, ye can't wait to do it all again."

Elise doubted the wisdom of those words, but she had no time to wonder if they might be true. She let out an animal scream as the child slithered from her body into the waiting hands of the midwife. Elise's back seized and she went rigid from the pain as her legs bounced of their own accord to relieve the strain.

"Maisie, give 'er some brandy," the midwife said as she severed the cord and took the child away to be cleaned. Elise was still shaking as Maisie held a cup to her lips. "Here, take a sip. It will help relax ye."

Elise's teeth chattered and made a metallic noise against the pewter cup when she tried to drink, but she managed to get a few sips of the fiery liquid down her gullet. It burned its way down, but then a nice warmth began to spread as the brandy took effect. Elise suddenly forgot all about her discomfort. The baby wasn't crying. She tried to rise to peer around the midwife's wide back, which hid the baby from view.

"Is it dead?" Elise cried. "Please, I need to see it."

She cringed when she heard a resounding slap on the bottom and the child began to howl in outrage, no doubt wondering if it might be too late to return to the womb, where it had been safe and warm and no one was hitting it on the rump.

"A fine boy, me lady. A fine boy, indeed. And very large."

The midwife swaddled the baby, who was still screaming furiously, and showed him to Elise. She reached out and gingerly took the child. He felt heavy in her arms, but she held on tight, terrified of dropping him. He stopped crying and opened his eyes, studying her for a long moment before closing them again and opening his tiny mouth instead.

"Put him to yer breast."

"But I don't have any milk," Elise protested.

"Don't worry. There's enough there to sustain 'im until the wet nurse comes."

"I don't wish for a wet nurse. I'll nurse him myself."

Maisie and her mother exchanged shocked glances, but the midwife quickly rearranged her face. "Of course, me lady. As ye wish." Her tone was indulging, but her expression said that Elise would quickly change her mind.

Elise put the baby to her breast and he moved his little head about until he finally found what he was looking for. Elise yelped as the tiny gums clamped around the nipple and began to suck. It didn't feel as if anything was coming out, but the baby seemed content and dropped off to sleep a few moments later.

Elise glanced behind Mistress Wynne's shoulder, suddenly aware that the door had opened. James stood in the dim corridor. He was perfectly still, his face ghostlike in the gloom, but Elise could see the wonder in his eyes and the silly grin on his face. Their eyes met and she smiled just for him before he disappeared. They had a son, and Lord Asher had the heir he so desperately needed. Perhaps everything would work out after all.

Elise gazed down on her newborn son. Until this moment, the child in her womb did not seem real. She felt him move and knew that in time he would be born, but she had no clear idea of what to expect or how she might feel. She'd never witnessed a birth, although she had heard her mother's muffled screams when Amy and Anne were born, and she'd held her newborn sisters, feeling proud and overcome with tenderness for the little girls. This was different, however. As she looked at her son, she felt a kind of fierce protectiveness, the likes of which she'd never known before. She was seeing her boy for the very first time, but it felt as if she'd been his mother forever, and the love she felt for this tiny human being was beyond anything she might ever feel for anyone else. The fact that the baby was James's forged a new emotional connection between her and James, a connection which suddenly and irrevocably bound three separate beings into one whole—a family.

Elise wished that she could invite James to come into the room and allow him to hold his son, but that would be inappropriate and quite telling to the servants, so she focused instead on the beautiful child in her arms and took an extraordinarily long time to study his every feature and become familiar with his wonderful scent. The baby slept peacefully for a short while, but then his mouth began to open and close, and his head turned from side to side, reminding Elise of a blind newborn kitten seeking its mother's tit purely on instinct. She pulled down her shift and moved the baby closer to her breast. He began to suck fiercely, determined to get the nourishment he needed.

"Shall we send word to the master?" Mistress Benford inquired as she stood in the doorway, admiring mother and child. "He's a fine boy, no doubt about it, me lady. And looks so like this dear papa."

Elise almost blurted out that he did resemble James but bit her tongue just in time. Of course, people would look for a likeness between her son and Edward, and she was sure they would find it since people tended to see what they wanted to see.

"Yes, please send Pete with a message for Lord Asher. He'll be most pleased."

Elise smiled gently as Barbara materialized outside the room, ghostly in her white nightdress. "Take a look at your brother, Barbara," Elise called out as she turned the baby toward Barbara. Barbara remained outside the room, kept from entering by Mistress Benford, who warned about the baby catching cold and was insisting on Barbara returning to bed immediately.

"Never seen a live one before," Barbara said as she beheld her brother. "Always dead. Always sad."

Elise knew that Barbara was referring to her siblings, who had never even drawn breath, and the sadness of her parents, but Elise still felt as if someone just walked over her grave. She was glad when Barbara turned and left, unimpressed with the baby.

"May I take a look at the new arrival?" James asked, all innocence as he stepped into the room, having returned with Peg and Mercy, who was bouncing with excitement. "My most sincere congratulations, your ladyship," he said with a deep bow. "May your son know nothing but robust health, good fortune, and much love."

"Would you like to hold him, Master James?" Elise asked, matching his innocence with her own.

"If I may." James took the baby and studied his sated features. The child had drifted back to sleep and lay contentedly in James's arms. Elise couldn't help noticing the likeness between father and son. The baby had the same stubborn chin, the same full lips and dark hair as James. She was sure that no one else would notice these similarities, but she was so intimately familiar with the features of both her men that she couldn't help but see them.

"A fine boy, my lady," James said as he handed the baby back to Elise. "What will you call him?"

"I'll have to wait for Lord Asher to arrive. I'm sure he's got a name picked out for his heir."

"Doubtless, he has," James replied, a note of bitterness creeping into his words. James would never be able to acknowledge his child, not while his father was alive and maybe not even after, not if the child was to be the next Lord Asher.

"I'll go pen a note for Pete to take to his lordship, shall I?" James said as he excused himself and left. Mercy perched on the side of the bed and reached out for the baby's hand, tenderly holding it in her own.

"Oh, he's just lovely," she crooned. "Not like 'Arry at all. 'Arry was scrawny and red, but me mam said 'e were beautiful," Mercy confided in Elise. "Can I 'old 'im?"

"Not yet, Mercy. Maybe in a few days. He's still very fragile," Elise said, feeling a bit guilty at denying Mercy this small pleasure.

"I'm not a baby. I know 'ow to handle a newborn," Mercy protested, but Peg gave her an evil look and ushered her from the room.

"Come now, me lady, ye need to rest. Let me take the child. I'll look after 'im until ye wake," the midwife offered as she accepted the bundle from Elise and sat down by the hearth. Maisie quietly went about setting the room to rights. She wiped down the chair and put another log on the fire to keep the room warm before scooping up the dirty linens and leaving the room.

Elise was exhausted and overwhelmed by the intensity of her emotions. She sank into the pillows and closed her eyes, grateful for a bit of quiet. Her body felt battered, her breasts were swollen and tender, and she was sure that the baby had ripped her open during the birth, but the pain was nothing compared with what it had been only a half hour before, so she tried to relax. As long as she didn't move, the ache between her legs wasn't so bad. She thought she might not be able to sleep, but a heavy drowsiness pulled her deeper and deeper into its embrace, and she felt herself floating on a cloud of peace as she finally gave herself up to sleep.

Chapter 64

December 1665
Suffolk, England

Only the front few pews of St. Edmund's Church were full on the day of the baptism. Edward had been eager to baptize the child right away, but the baby had to be at least a month old, according to the midwife, to be safely taken into town, and Elise had to be churched in order to attend the baptism of her firstborn. Until then, she was considered unclean and couldn't receive the holy sacraments. Elise thought that she might chafe at being cooped up for a month after the birth, but her body needed to recover, and her fascination with her son kept her fully occupied. The servants thought she'd gone daft, besotted as she was with her baby, but Elise simply basked in the joy of being a new mother and relished being truly needed at last. She'd overheard Mistress Benford expressing the view that this was common enough in peasants, but not in women of higher station who handed off their babies as soon as they were born to be cared for by nursemaids and suckled by a wet-nurse. Elise had no such plans, but she feared that Edward might overrule her.

Edward arrived three days after the birth, by which time James was safely out of the way with Mercy. He appeared thinner and older somehow, as if the events of the summer had taken a personal toll on him, but he assured everyone that he was in fine health. Edward strode into the room and looked around until his eyes settled on the cradle in the corner. He approached carefully, as if the baby might unexpectedly pop out, and stood over the cradle, watching the child sleep.

"You are to be congratulated, madam," Edward said formally to Elise, who hovered behind him, awaiting his reaction to his newborn heir. "You have fulfilled your wifely duty." Elise was taken aback by Edward's stiff demeanor but decided to go along with it, hoping to tease him into a better mood.

"So are you, my lord. You have a fine son and heir and are the envy of all," she said with a smile.

"So I am. So I am," Edward replied, finally relaxing enough to smile. "What shall we call this little fellow?"

"I assumed you had a name picked out already," Elise said, hoping that Edward would permit her some input.

"Charles, I think, after His Majesty. The king adores flattery, and having children named after him makes him happy. Charles Edward. We should have him christened at the earliest opportunity."

"Middle of December, then," Elise replied. "I will be churched by then, and Charles will be strong enough to be taken out." She would happily accept the name Edward chose as long as she was allowed to be present at the baptism.

Edward looked irritated but conceded with good grace. "All right, middle of December it is. I shall remain here with you until then. His Majesty was most effusive in his congratulations and has given me leave to stay as long as I like."

"It's our pleasure to have you, then," Elise said with as much cheer as she could muster. She hoped that Edward would return to court and remain there until the christening, but it seemed he was determined to actually play the role of husband and father for a change. She couldn't imagine that Edward wouldn't grow bored after a few days, but she had to hold her tongue in check. He was master here, and she had to put on a show of obedience.

"What do you think of your brother, Barbara?" Edward boomed when he saw Barbara in the doorway. She never entered, just stood there, hovering and silent, her blank gaze fixed on the baby as if she couldn't quite figure out where he'd come from.

Barbara shrugged. "Brother," she said, but her attention was already on something else. She wandered off, leaving Edward even more annoyed than before.

"Dimwit," he said under his breath, and Elise prayed that Barbara hadn't heard that. She wasn't sure that Barbara would care, but it was still wrong of a father to speak so of his child.

"Have you engaged a wet nurse?" Edward demanded.

"No. I'm nursing him myself."

"That's most unseemly. I'll have Mistress Benford send to the village for a wet nurse. No lady in your position should suckle her own child. It's base and quite disgusting."

"Please, Edward. I enjoy it, and it's not as if anyone sees me. I know virtually no one here, so no one would care. It's such a pleasure to feed him. He is always hungry and has the most wonderful expression on his face when he's had enough. It's almost a smile."

Edward turned to Elise, his eyebrows comically raised with surprise. "You enjoy it?" he asked, his tone incredulous.

"It's a most gratifying feeling," Elise confessed, hoping that Edward wouldn't persist in hiring a nurse.

"The child seems to be thriving, so you may continue nursing him until we return to London. Then, a wet nurse will be engaged, whether you like it or not."

"Thank you, Edward," Elise said. They wouldn't be returning to London for a while yet, and by then Edward might have forgotten his decree. For the moment, Elise had to endure

Edward's presence and accept the separation from James. Not having him nearby made her feel vulnerable and lonely, especially since she couldn't share her joy of their son with the child's doting father. She missed Mercy too. Mercy infused the household with good humor and mischief, and without her, the others seemed gloomier and less inclined to laughter.

**

Elise tried to focus on the words of the reverend, but her mind wandered as she gazed around the beautiful church. Bright winter sunshine filtered through the stained-glass windows behind the altar, and rays of colored light streamed down, casting colorful shadows on the stone floor. The voice of the reverend seemed to carry all the way to the vaulted ceiling, traveling the length of the nearly empty church and disturbing the unnatural hush.

Lord and Lady Fillmore stood next to Edward and Elise, having been invited by Edward to act as godparents to little Charles Edward. Lady Fillmore was pleasant enough and expressed an interest in the baby and Elise's health post-delivery, but Phineas Fillmore barely glanced at her, his eyes searching the church instead, as if he expected an ambush at any moment. Elise met the couple briefly at the wedding feast, but she hadn't had an opportunity then to speak with them or observe them. She had been too absorbed by her own worries and expectations. Now that she had nothing to do but stand quietly, Elise studied the people who would be her son's godparents. She wasn't sure why, but she feared Lord Fillmore. His shifty eyes and prizefighter physique put her on guard. He held a noble title and dressed like a gentleman, but Elise knew a thug when she saw one. Beneath the elaborate wig and richly embroidered coat was not a man of refinement.

Elise turned her attention to Lady Fillmore. She was a few years older than Elise and very beautiful, with tresses of honey-blonde hair and wide blue eyes that constantly strayed to her husband, their expression watchful and at times even fearful. What bound Edward to this coarse man, and why did he choose him to be their son's godfather? Elise hoped that they wouldn't stay long and would return to Oxford—where the court had moved in September after cases of plague were reported in Salisbury—to the side of their king.

It was bitterly cold when they stepped out of the church. An icy wind picked up and blew with gale-like force off the North Sea. Shutters banged on houses, and brown, shriveled leaves cascaded from trees before being blown away like specs of dust. Elise held Charles close and covered his face with her cloak to keep the chill wind from freezing his little face. Her own face felt numb with cold and tears formed in her eyes from the force of the wind. Several carriages waited outside, ready to take everyone back to the house, where a christening luncheon would be served. Elise looked around as she was handed into the waiting carriage, hoping for a glimpse of James, but he wasn't there. Edward might fly into a rage if he spotted him, so James wisely stayed away. She wondered where he'd taken Mercy. What a shame it was that Edward was so rigid that he had no desire to even meet his granddaughter. Surely, he wouldn't even care if Molly and her family perished. They were of no interest to him.

As the carriage drew up to the manor, Elise squared her shoulders against the gale and followed Edward into the house, where she reluctantly surrendered Charles to Peg. Mistress Benford had been cooking and baking since the previous day, and a mouthwatering aroma permeated the first floor. Lord Fillmore rubbed his hands together in anticipation, ready to enjoy a hearty meal and Edward's fine claret. Elise wished that she could escape directly after luncheon, but it was her duty to play hostess and look after Lady Fillmore, who'd be left to her own devices as soon as the men's drinking turned serious. It would be a long afternoon, particularly since all Elise wished for was to be alone with her lovely boy. She pasted on a smile and invited their guests into the dining room.

Chapter 65

December 2013
London, England

Quinn sat across from Rhys in his office. He was going over some notes, so she forced her face into an expression of complacency as she looked at him. A part of her wished to confront him about Sylvia and everything Quinn had learned over the past weeks, but common sense told her to remain quiet. There was nothing to gain by confronting Rhys. Gabe was right: this wasn't her fight. Sylvia had made her choice, and Quinn had to respect that. But her anger was too close to the surface, and Quinn was afraid it would boil over if she remained in his presence.

"So, the child was born in Southwold, Suffolk, and was baptized in St. Edmund's Church on December fourteenth. This explains why we never found any reference to him in the London archives," Rhys said with an air of great satisfaction. That was one mystery solved, as far as he was concerned. Rhys pushed aside his papers and looked at her, his expression thoughtful. "But what happened to him? There is no trace of this boy anywhere. We know when he was born. We know his name. And we know who his parents were, but there's no record of this child anywhere after the baptism."

"I don't know," Quinn replied. The logical answer would be that the child died in infancy, and his death was never recorded, but Quinn hoped that wasn't so. She saw the baby in her visions, and he was as sweet and precious as only a newborn could be. To think that little Charles died shortly after the birth left Quinn feeling sad and weepy. Perhaps she would learn something of him once she got to the end of Elise's story. Quinn still had no idea when Elise actually died, or how, but the skeleton had been that of a young woman, and it stood to reason that Elise had only a few years left to live. Quinn almost wished that she could stop herself from finding out. She'd grown fond of Elise and hated to see her suffer. Elise was headstrong, and probably too naïve in some instances, but she was a young, vulnerable girl who'd been an innocent pawn in the game grown men played. Quinn sighed.

"You care what happened to her, don't you?" Rhys asked as he leaned back in his chair and put his hands behind his head. "She's long gone, Quinn. Her story ended many years ago. Don't take it to heart. The past is the past."

"Is it?" Quinn asked pointedly. "Sometimes the past has a way of catching up with you."

Rhys leaned back forward and gave her a hard look. "Are you referring to anything in particular?"

"I am, actually. Perhaps you haven't given it a thought since, but thirty-one years ago, you went to a Christmas party at the home of a friend. There was a girl . . ." Quinn let the sentence trail off, eager to see Rhys's reaction. She was gratified to see him go pale as his eyes widened in shock. She'd hit a nerve.

"How do you know about that?" he breathed, eyeing her with suspicion born of fear.

"That doesn't matter. Tell me, Rhys, was that the only time you raped someone?"

She hadn't meant to let that slip out, but now that the words were out, she was glad. She needed to know. She couldn't continue working with Rhys with this two-thousand-pound elephant casually lounging between them. He seemed like a good, kind man, but there was another side to him, and she needed to expose it, at least to herself.

Rhys got to his feet and turned his back to her, staring out the window at the gray London morning. Somewhere below, people went about their business, and cars moved at a glacial pace down the congested street. The London Eye stood still, not yet open to the public for the day. It was like any other weekday morning, except that it wasn't. Rhys finally turned around. His face was white, his eyes shadowed by either grief or guilt, Quinn couldn't quite tell. She thought he might lash out at her, accuse her of slander or deny it all, but Rhys simply nodded as if acknowledging her question.

"Quinn, I don't know what your connection is to what happened that night, but I have lived with what we did these past three decades. It was the worst thing I've ever done, and not a day has gone by that I haven't thought of that girl. Robert made me swear not to say anything to the police, especially if she pressed charges, but I promised myself that I would never hurt or disrespect a woman again as long as I lived."

Quinn exhaled a breath she hadn't realized she'd been holding. At least Sylvia's story checked out, and it meant the world to Quinn to know that her mother hadn't lied to her to cover up her own mistake. Quinn wished that young Sylvia could have been spared that awful night, but at least now they could move forward with a little more trust between them.

"Why, Rhys? Why did you do it?" Quinn asked, needing to understand why someone she found so likable would have stooped to something so base and violent.

"I was young, foolish, and easily intimidated. Robert and Seth pressured me into participating. I knew it was wrong, but I couldn't resist. I was a virgin, and the opportunity to finally lose my virginity to a girl who was half-conscious and wouldn't laugh at me was more than I could refuse. Robert and Seth were so drunk, they'd barely remember if I made a fool of myself, and they'd already taken their turn, so one more wouldn't really matter. We didn't hurt her, Quinn."

"Do you honestly believe that?" Even after all these years he couldn't own up to the truth.

"Well, not physically anyway. There was no brutality, just persuasion. She never said no. She never even tried to push any of us away. She went along with it."

"She was drunk," Quinn spat out, amazed by the man's propensity for self-delusion.

"I know. There's no excuse for what we did." Rhys suddenly grew silent, his eyes opening wide. "Is one of them dead? Is that it? Have you found something that belonged to them and saw what happened?"

"No, Rhys. I was approached by Sylvia. That was her name, in case you couldn't remember. Sylvia."

"Why did she approach you?" Rhys asked, suddenly nervous. He looked like a cornered fox, desperate to escape the hounds that were closing in.

"Because she's my birth mother, and you could have been my father, but you are off the hook. Your DNA didn't match mine."

Rhys let out a slow breath. "You're Sylvia's daughter?"

"Yes. I was conceived on the night you all took turns with her."

"Oh, Quinn, I'm so sorry." Rhys breathed. "I had no idea she'd had a child. Have you known all along?"

"No, I've only known for a few weeks, but I can barely look at you, much less work with you."

"I'd like to see her."

"Sylvia?" Quinn gaped at Rhys. Had he taken leave of his senses? What could he possibly have to gain to coming face-to-face with Sylvia now?

"Yes. Quinn, please. I want to apologize, make amends for my part in what happened."

"You want absolution, is that it?"

"Not absolution, but forgiveness maybe. I will never be absolved, but perhaps I can make amends," Rhys pleaded. He didn't look frightened anymore, just desperate.

"There's something else you can do."

"Name it."

"You can help me find my father," Quinn said, her eyes never leaving Rhys's. He seemed surprised by her request, but he shrugged in acquiescence.

"That should be easy enough. You know who the other two were."

"Yes, I know their names, but I want to get to know them without them knowing who I am. I want to take them by surprise and be sure of which one of them fathered me before I say anything."

"Robert Chatham is the head of Chatham Electronics. I haven't spoken to him in nearly thirty years, but I have seen articles about him from time to time."

"And Seth? Sylvia knows nothing about him at all. Just that his name was Seth and he was American."

"Yes, Seth Besson, that was his name. He was a friend of Robert's. I hardly knew him. He was from Louisiana, I believe. I'm afraid I don't know anything more."

"Will you help me find out what I need to know?" Quinn asked, challenging Rhys to say no, but he didn't. He really did seem to want her forgiveness, even if it was only motivated by his sense of self-preservation.

"I will help you with whatever you need. How does Sylvia feel about this quest you're about to embark on?"

"I haven't told her yet, but I can't imagine that she'd disapprove. I have a right to know who my father is, and I need to know where this psychic gift came from."

"I understand," Rhys replied. "Quinn, will you ever trust me again?"

"Maybe. In time."

Quinn felt almost sorry for the man. He looked so crestfallen. She didn't want to let him off the hook, but she knew that he wasn't unique in what he'd done. These types of situations happened more than people realized, with girls refusing to report the incident or press charges for fear of not being believed or being treated as if they'd brought it all on themselves. Date rape was common in the past and still was to this day. Perhaps the fact that Sylvia had been assaulted by three men rather than one made this situation worse, but it was certainly not exceptional. And many men who'd taken liberties with young women and crossed the line between being pushy and actually committing the act now had wives and children of their own, many of them fathers to daughters who might be in danger of experiencing the same thing on a college campus or while on a date. Rhys wasn't a monster; he was just a weak, spineless boy who gave in to peer pressure and did something he'd never planned on doing. At least he had the decency to feel guilty about it. Quinn wondered if the other two men ever gave Sylvia a thought.

Chapter 66

March 1666
Suffolk, England

Elise turned to take one last look at the house before climbing into the carriage that would take them back to London. Already the house looked abandoned and forbidding, just as it had when she first set eyes on it. It would be locked up until another outbreak of the plague or until Edward decided to spend some time in the country, something that Elise didn't expect to happen anytime soon. The court had returned from Oxford, so there was no longer any excuse to remain in Suffolk, but Elise wished that she could. She had been happy here, with James and her little Charlie.

This house never felt like the prison Asher Hall had become, but now she would be returning to London, and everything would change once again. Edward would hire a wet nurse for Charlie and force a wedge between mother and son. He said he would permit James to return, but on what terms? What would life be like once they were back in the city? Would Edward still neglect his family, or would he now spend more time at home? And would he expect Elise to give him another child? She hoped so since she feared she might be with child again, but it was too soon to know for certain. Her courses had not been regular since Charlie's birth, and after some light spotting in January, she'd not bled at all in February. If her courses failed to make an appearance later this month, she'd know for sure. The thought made Elise's stomach clench with fear. Edward would be furious if he found out that she'd lain with James without his express permission, and the realization that they'd gone behind his back would alert him to the truth of their relationship. They should have waited.

Elise had seen James only once since Charlie's birth, just after the christening in December. He'd sent her a note asking her to meet him at the cottage. Elise had bided her time, awaiting an opportune moment to slip out, but once she had, she ran all the way to the cottage, desperate to see James. James had fallen asleep by the time she got to him, so Elise quickly undressed and slipped into bed next to him, pressing her body to his and burying her face in his neck as she inhaled his familiar smell. She didn't think she'd ever feel aroused again after the agony of the birth, but natural instinct took over, and she reached for him, wrapping her fingers around his shaft and stroking him lightly.

James woke with a start, his lips lifting at the corners as he smiled at her. He didn't say a word, just rolled her onto her back and slid inside her, silencing her cry of pleasure with his kiss. Their lovemaking hadn't lasted long, but the intensity of it took them both by surprise. They weren't just lovers anymore, they were parents, their son making them a family and bonding them to each other forever. Elise still thought of that day often, reliving the memory of their last meeting when she felt lonely for James. It'd taken her time to get pregnant with Charlie, but it seemed that this time her womb knew exactly what it was for. Elise allowed her hand to stray to her abdomen. What would Edward do to them if he learned the truth? How severe a punishment would he devise? What could she do to avoid discovery?

Elise sat silently across from Edward, her questions locked away in her brain. Perhaps it was best to play the complacent wife and see what Edward had in store for her. It annoyed him when she questioned him, and he often did things just to spite her, like a child. Elise was glad that it was Peg in the carriage with them and not Barbara. Barbara made her uneasy lately. It was nothing specific, but the girl seemed more withdrawn than ever, except for times when she grew agitated and nearly hysterical. She was traveling in the second carriage with Pete and Mistress Benford, who'd been ordered to join the staff of Asher Hall in the role of cook. Edward worked under the assumption that half the staff were dead, and he was probably right. Getting new people would not be easy, taking into account the death toll. Everyone would be looking for new servants and stable boys—anyone who survived, that is.

Elise pulled aside the curtain and peered out once they passed through the city gate and were in London proper. She'd been away for nine months, but it felt more like a decade. The city looked gray and cold, the chimneys belching smoke into the air as subdued-looking people went about their business. There were no death carts rattling down streets, nor were there any corpses to be seen, but the streets were less crowded, the people wary. Many shops and taverns appeared to be closed, and there were still countless red crosses visible on doors, the paint not having been removed after the illness abated. Everyone seemed older and grayer, even the children who appeared hunched over and sickly, their eyes following the carriage fearfully.

There were still cases of plague, but the epidemic had passed with the cold weather, and the people were slowly returning to their homes and businesses. Easter was approaching, but there was no sense of impending holiday, no festive mood permeating the streets. Edward had sent a letter ahead, instructing the house to be prepared for their arrival, and Elise hoped there had been someone left to receive it. She was tired and travel sore, and she needed to use the chamber pot rather badly.

Charles slept peacefully, lulled by the rocking of the carriage. He was a happy baby, and he gave his mother no trouble as long as he was dry and well fed. Elise thanked her lucky stars for having been granted time with her baby. Once they settled into the London house, Edward would demand that she hand the child over to a nursemaid. Well-bred ladies did not rear their own children. Elise hated the thought but knew she would have to comply. Whatever time she spent with Charlie would be when Edward wasn't at home. There was no point provoking him into an argument she couldn't win; she'd simply go behind his back, as she did with everything else. She hoped that James would get to see his son. He'd be amazed at how much Charlie had changed in only four months, his expression now full of awareness and his toothless smile so beguiling. *Was there ever a more beautiful baby?* Elise wondered fondly.

She looked up at Edward and smiled sweetly. If she were indeed with child, every day counted, and she had to do something to prevent a catastrophe. At this stage, she could still say that the child came early, but if she waited much longer, there would be no way to hide the fact that she'd gotten with child long before they returned to London.

"Edward, would it not be prudent to give Charles a brother?" Elise asked as her heart pounded in her chest.

Edward tore his gaze away from the window and turned to face her, a look of astonishment on his face. "You've changed your tune," he said, giving Elise a piercing stare. Elise could see the suspicion in his eyes and cringed inwardly, wondering if she'd made a mistake.

"I only wish to be a good wife to you, my lord," Elise replied. "And children are so fragile," she added.

"Yes, I see your point," Edward said. "I thought to give you a reprieve, but perhaps it's time," he mused, giving her a smile at last. "I'm glad to see that you've come to understand and embrace your duty."

"My only desire is to please you, Edward," Elise said, lowering her eyes so that her husband wouldn't see the derision in them. She hated lying, and she detested Edward, but she would do anything to protect her unborn child and her love for James. Perhaps she was becoming well versed in duplicity at last.

Chapter 67

Elise alighted from the carriage, shook out her skirts, and took a moment to study the facade of Asher Hall. She wasn't sure what she'd been expecting, but the house looked the same as ever, solid and imposing, its numerous windows catching the afternoon sun and glowing, as if the house was afire. The red cross had been scrubbed off the door, and there was no indication that anything had changed since Elise left in such a hurry nine months before. A groom Elise hadn't seen before ran toward the carriage, eager to see to the horses and luggage.

The front door opened and Lucy stepped outside, ready to welcome her mistress home. She looked healthy and well nourished, and Elise breathed a sigh of relief at the sight of her. Elise would have hugged the girl, but Edward would disapprove, so they would have their own private reunion later. Lucy would fill Elise in on all the goings-on, but in the meantime, she had to play the part of the mistress of the house. To her surprise, everything was ready for their arrival, and most of the staff was there to attend to their needs. Only three people residing at Asher Hall had died, which was a blessing considering how much worse the situation could have been. Perhaps now Mistress Benford would be permitted to return home, since her services were no longer needed.

Elise ran her fingers over the damask bed hangings, remembering all the times James had come to her in this bed. She wondered incessantly where he'd gone and if he was thinking of her. If not for Charlie, her life would feel unbearably empty, and now it might be again. Edward had forbidden Elise to have a cradle in her room, saying that the child belonged in the nursery with his nurse. Elise would miss having access to him all day long, especially those precious moments when she took the baby into bed and they slumbered peacefully together, happy in their safe and warm haven. Elise wondered if Charlie would miss her. Perhaps he was too young to feel the absence of his mother and only needed someone to see to his needs, but she hoped that on some instinctive level, he would register that she wasn't the one taking care of him.

Edward was in the other room, settling back into his own bedroom after having instructed Lucy to take the baby away. She would be his nursemaid for the time-being until Edward found a candidate to his satisfaction. He wanted nothing but the best for his son, refusing to acknowledge that the *best* was to be cared for by his mother. Elise would find a way around Edward, but she needed time to see what his plans were and how often he intended to grace them with his presence. In the meantime, she would have a bath, dress, and join Edward for supper downstairs. He seemed more kindly disposed toward her these days, so no good would come from displeasing him.

Edward was already waiting for her when she came down. She smiled in greeting, and he bowed stiffly, watching her as if seeing her for the first time. The past nine months had altered them both—or maybe it was only she that was altered. Edward was the same stuffy, pompous man he'd always been. Elise looked around, wondering if Barbara would be joining them, but then remembered that Edward preferred that she eat in her own room when he was at home. The man couldn't bear the sight of her, so Elise decided not to bring up the subject. Perhaps in time, he would grow more tolerant of his daughter.

"There was a letter for you," Edward said as they sat down across from each other. "It's from your father. He says that all is well, and your sisters have adjusted to their new environment and are enjoying all that the West Indies has to offer."

"You read my letter?" Elise asked, incredulous.

"You are my wife, my property. You are not entitled to any private business of your own," he reminded her with a glint of warning in his eyes. "You may read the letter after we finish dining. It's in my study. I shall write to your father and inform him of Charlie's birth. I will also remind him of the debt he still owes me. He seems to think that all has been forgotten and forgiven, but there's still outstanding business between us."

"So, I wasn't payment enough?" Elise asked through clenched teeth.

"No, my dear, you were a deposit, so to speak. And Charlie is the interest on my investment."

Elise said nothing more as Cook served the soup.

"I shall leave it to you to hire another maid," Edward said. "It's unseemly for Cook to serve at table. I will see to getting more lads for the stable since the previous two died. There's just the one groom left, and Pete."

"As you wish," Elise replied woodenly. She longed to skip this awkward meal and go up to the nursery, where she could spend time with Charlie before Lucy put him down for the night. He no longer required night feedings, so she wouldn't see him again till morning.

"I have invited Lord Fillmore to join us for supper on Sunday. His wife has been poorly, so I thought the poor man might enjoy some company. James will be joining us as well," Edward added, his eyes never leaving Elise's face.

Elise's head shot up at the sound of James's name. "Is James in London?"

"Yes. I've summoned him home. I still have need of his services, as do you," Edward replied, giving Elise a meaningful look. "I must admit that although I was furious with him for circumventing my orders, his judgment had been correct. I owe him for your life and the life of my son."

"It's kind of you to invite him," Elise said, her tone flat. It took a lot of effort to keep the joy out of her voice, but Edward was watching her, so she had to feign indifference, even revulsion.

"It's the least I can do," Edward replied as he tucked into the fish course. He normally didn't care for fish, but he was hungry after their journey and ate with relish, even commenting on the delicacy of the baked cod.

Elise could barely eat, thrilled by the knowledge that she would see James in a few days. Having him back in the house would make things so much easier for them since no one would suspect anything if they saw two inhabitants conversing or taking a walk in the garden. And the rest would fall into place, whether she was with child or not. Elise couldn't wait for James to see Charlie. He looked nothing like the squalling infant James had seen the day he was born. He was such a sweet, handsome boy, and she would be so proud to show him off to his papa. *Perhaps everything will work out after all,* Elise mused as she picked at her fish.

Chapter 68

Elise dressed carefully for Sunday dinner. She wore her favorite gown of peacock-blue silk and pinned her mother's brooch to the bodice. Lucy coifed her coppery hair into an elaborate hairstyle with curls cascading over her ears and framing her face. Some women needed rouge to give the impression of dewy freshness, but Elise needed no artificial enhancement. She was rosy as an apple, her eyes bright at the thought of seeing James after their long separation. Perhaps Edward would even show off Charlie to him, so James could see the boy tonight.

Lord Fillmore and Edward were downstairs enjoying a cup of wine when Elise swept into the parlor. Her heart beat like a drum in her chest, but on the outside, she was a picture of calm and grace. Her eyes swept the room, searching for James, but he had not yet arrived, so she accepted a cup of wine and perched on a settle closest to the fire since the room was chilly, even with the fire blazing and the curtains drawn against the cold draught seeping in from outside. *What if James doesn't come?* Elise fretted. What if she never saw him again? But her anxiety was unfounded. James entered the room a few minutes later, looking splendid despite his modest attire. He greeted the men and bowed over her hand, his eyes meeting hers for the briefest of moments. Elise glanced at Lord Fillmore from beneath her lashes, curious to see his reaction to finding himself in the company of a servant, but Lord Fillmore didn't seem bothered. On the contrary, he was studying James with undisguised interest and smiling at him as if they were old friends.

"Come, let's eat," Edward invited. "Cook has made a wonderful meal for us, and I, for one, have missed the comforts of home."

Elise took her seat and waited while Peg, who was none too happy at being demoted to the position of downstairs maid once again, served the men first. There would be seven courses, and then they would walk over to St. Martin's for Evensong. Elise rarely attended Evensong, it being in the evening and inappropriate for a lady to attend on her own, so she was looking forward to it since the service was mostly sung, and she enjoyed music more than a verbal sermon. Elise hoped to snatch a private moment with James, but Edward seemed determined to keep them apart, making sure they sat across from each other, the distance preventing any intimate comments during the meal.

A light snow fell when they finally left the house, making the night somehow less dark despite the thick clouds that drifted across the sky, obscuring the moon for long moments and casting everything into near pitch-black darkness. They should have brought a lantern, but there was enough moonlight to guide them. Elise pulled up her hood to protect her hair from getting damp and accepted James's arm. Edward and Lord Fillmore walked on ahead, talking of some political matter that Elise didn't really care about. James made sure they fell slightly behind.

"How are you, my love, and how is our son?" he asked quietly.

"I'm well, now that you are here. Charlie is a wonder. I can't wait for you to see him. Oh, he looks so like you, James."

"Mercy was desperate to see him, so I brought her along. She stayed in the kitchen with Mistress Benford and Cook while we dined. I wager she got some lovely treats. You know how Mistress Benford dotes on her, and she was happy to see her once more before returning to Suffolk." Elise glanced up at James, reluctant to ask the question uppermost in her mind.

"Molly and Peter have weathered the storm, but Beth is gone," James said. "Molly lost two children in less than a year, but she's grateful for Mercy. She might not have survived had she remained in London."

"I'm so sorry, James. Now that I have Charlie, I can't even begin to imagine how painful the loss of a child must be. The thought of losing him is more than I can bear. I pray each night that he is never taken from me."

"As does every mother, but God has his own plan," James replied bitterly.

"How is Mercy?"

"She's well. She misses you and Peg, and especially Charlie. Molly was delighted with Mercy's newfound ability to read and write. She was so impressed, having never learned herself."

"I hope Mercy will make the most of it, even if only to read a book from time to time. I gave her two books to take home so that she can practice her reading."

"She's read them from cover to cover and asked me to bring her more books from the Asher Hall library," James replied with a smile. "She's taken to reading like a fish to water."

"Will you be moving back into the house?" Elise asked. Having him under the same roof would make everything that much more bearable, even if they would have to be extra careful to keep their secret. She opened her mouth to tell him of her possible pregnancy but then changed her mind. She'd wait a few weeks until she was absolutely sure. A part of her still hoped that it was a false alarm, but deep down she knew that not to be the case. Her body had changed, even in the last few days, her breasts growing more tender and an aversion to meat and wine making her feel bilious at meal times. Her milk wasn't as plentiful as before, making the need for a wet nurse for Charlie a necessity, and she felt tired and weepy, just like last time.

"I will take Mercy back tomorrow, then return. Nothing will keep us apart, Elise. Nothing. I will make sure of that."

**

Elise was relieved when the service finally ended and they could return to the house. The snow continued to fall during the service, and it now crunched underfoot, turning her feet to ice as the cold seeped through the thin soles of her shoes. She was tired and wished she could retire, but Edward insisted on having one more drink to warm them all up. It would have been churlish to refuse. Elise accepted a glass of claret and raised it in a toast with everyone else. "To our Lord and Savior," Edward said, surprising Elise. He wasn't a devout man by any means, so this newfound fervor was odd. Perhaps he was grateful that his family was spared and attributed his good fortune to God rather than to his baseborn son, whose good sense saved both Elise and their child.

"One more drink," Edward said, reaching for the bottle. "This is rather a fine wine, wouldn't you say, Fillmore? A gift from His Majesty."

"Excellent," Lord Fillmore agreed. "I'll gladly take a refill."

"None for me," Elise said. "I really must get to bed. I'm rather tired. Goodnight, gentlemen."

She took a step toward the door but grabbed on to the nearest chair for support. Her legs felt wobbly, and a thick mist seemed to descend on her head. She sank heavily into a chair.

"Are you quite all right, my dear?" Edward asked, solicitous as ever in front of others.

"I feel odd," Elise muttered. Her tongue felt unwieldy in her mouth, and it took a lot of effort to form the words. Elise forced herself to concentrate as she glanced at James. He seemed to be swaying where he stood, and his hand reached out toward the wall to steady himself. There was panic in his gaze as he turned to his father.

"Do sit down, James. You don't look at all well," Edward suggested and shoved a chair toward him.

"What have you done?" James croaked as he sank down on the chair.

Edward didn't reply but watched with interest as James fought to stay conscious. Elise tried to say something, but her thoughts scattered like beads from a broken necklace. She felt a darkness descending upon her and didn't have the strength to fight it off.

"You thought you could cuckold me, the pair of you?" Edward asked, his tone conversational. "You imagined that I was too dim-witted to see through your scheme. Well, I didn't get to where I am by being obtuse or overly forgiving. You of all people should know that, James. You've dispatched my enemies for me often enough to know that I don't forgive, and I most certainly don't forget. You owe me, and it's time to settle our account."

Edward's words came from a great distance, but Elise heard them just before she lost consciousness.

Chapter 69

Elise opened her eyes, but even after a few moments she couldn't make out anything. The darkness was complete. She tried to move, but a terrible pain ripped through her shoulder, making her cry out. She must have been lying on it this whole time. She tried to sit up and banged her head on something hard. Elise carefully felt around with her hand. There was something just above her head and behind her back. Her fingers found the contours of a face right in front of hers, and she ran her hand over a shoulder and arm.

James groaned as he came to. "My leg," he whispered. "I think it's broken."

"James, where are we?" Elise asked, her panic rising with every passing second.

James tried to raise his head, with the same result as Elise. He yelped as he hit his head against the hard wooden surface. Elise heard a sharp intake of breath as James felt around their prison. He tried to push against the top, but it didn't budge. They were squashed against each other, their limbs at unnatural angles. Elise tried to take the weight off her shoulder but only succeeded in causing herself more pain. James remained silent, which worried Elise even more than the discomfort. He usually had a plan, or at least an idea.

"James, what is this place?" Elise asked again. Her voice shook, and she grabbed his hand in the darkness. It felt warm and reassuring, and James clasped her hand and brought it to his lips, planting a kiss in her palm.

"He knows about us," James said. His voice was unsteady and Elise felt a jolt of fear pass through her cramped body when James failed to say anything more.

"Surely, he'll let us out once his anger cools," Elise whispered.

James didn't reply, and his silence sent a chill down Elise's spine.

"He'll let us out. He only means to punish us."

"Yes, I'm sure you're right," James replied, but there was no conviction in his voice.

"I need to feed Charlie," Elise cried, her voice shrill. "He needs me." But he didn't. Edward had already engaged a wet nurse, who was sleeping in the room with their son. She would feed him when he awoke; she would take care of him in Elise's stead.

"Are you hurt?" James asked.

"My shoulder and ankle hurt, but I don't believe anything is broken."

"A shame," Edward's muffled voice came from somewhere just above. "I was hoping you'd suffer before you die."

"Edward, please, let us out," Elise implored. "I beg you. I will never set a foot wrong again. Please, Edward. I need to be with my son."

"When Charles is old enough, I will tell him that his mother was a whore. Until then, he'll believe that his loving mother was carried off by the plague. Shame, that." Edward chuckled bitterly.

"Edward, surely you're not this cruel," Elise cried, terrified by the calm in Edward's voice. "Even if you won't think of us, think of yourself. You will be accused of murder. You'll hang."

"No, my darling, I won't. I've thought this through, you see. When morning comes, I will make a big fuss looking for you. I will turn the house upside down, and then I will discover that James's horse is gone and so are some of your possessions. I will be heartbroken, and everyone will feel sympathy for me, knowing that my young wife deserted me and our son and ran off with her lover. I will grieve for you, and then I will move on and forget you ever existed. No one will come for you. You will remain down here until you either die of hunger and thirst or suffocate. It will be a long and torturous death either way, and it will give you plenty of time to pray and repent for your sins. But even if the Lord forgives you, I won't. You will never receive a Christian burial or even have a few words said by a priest over your graves. You will simply vanish from this earth and from the hearts of anyone who ever cared for you. You've served your purpose, and I have no further use for you."

"Edward, please, I beg you," Elise cried. "Charlie needs his mother. James, say something," she implored James, who remained resolutely silent.

"He's got nothing to say. He betrayed his flesh and blood, and now he'll pay the price. I thank you both for my beautiful son."

"Edward, I'm with child," Elise called out and felt James stiffen next to her. His hand shook as he reached for her, clasping her hand in his in a gesture of love and support. "I will give you another son, another heir."

Elise felt cold with dread as Edward laughed merrily somewhere above her head. "Oh, I know you're with child, my sweet. Peg has been informing me of your activities and keeping track of your monthly flow. It would be nice to have another son, I admit, but I can't allow you to go unpunished. Charlie will have to do. I will send him back to Suffolk with his nurse, where he can remain safe from the pestilence of the city. That's my parting gift to you. You can die knowing that your son will be cared for."

Elise sobbed as she heard Edward's footsteps fade into nothingness. "James, why didn't you talk to him? Why didn't you beg him to spare us?" she cried.

"Because he wouldn't have. He's a cruel man, Elise. Even if we hadn't betrayed him, he might have done this anyway. He can't bear the thought that anyone might know that the child isn't his. Had the child been a girl, he would have us try until we produced a son, but he has his heir now, and he is content. He will keep Charlie safe, don't you worry about him."

"My son will grow up believing that I deserted him. He'll have nothing but bitterness in his heart."

James said nothing. He shifted his weight in an effort to ease the pain in his leg. As the minutes ticked by, the reality of what was happening finally sank in, and Elise began to shake, her teeth chattering loudly. They were buried alive. If Edward didn't come to his senses, they would die a slow and horrible death. Elise began to cry again, and James held her in his arms, pressing her head against his chest. Elise could hear the erratic beat of his heart. He wouldn't say it out loud, but he was terrified as well. He kissed her hair and murmured words of comfort, but nothing he said could soothe her. Her heart galloped in her chest as images of what would happen to them flashed in her mind. Was her life to end so abruptly and her baby's with her? Was God really this cruel?

The minutes stretched into hours, but no one came. No one would. Everyone believed her to have run away with James. There was no hope.

Chapter 70

The darkness was absolute. James lost track of time days ago. His throat was parched, and he was disoriented and weak. He could barely move. His leg hurt like the devil, but he hardly noticed anymore. He reached out and touched Elise's face. It was already cold. She was gone. He was grateful that she was finally out of her misery. The past few days had been harrowing, emotionally and physically. Edward had chosen their punishment well. No easy death for them. He'd inflicted as much suffering as he could manage to punish them for a few stolen hours of happiness. And now it was James's turn to go. He could feel life slipping from him, its grip on his heart loosening as the beating grew faint, and his mind seemed to produce phantom flashes of light. He inched his way closer to Elise and pressed his lips against hers in a final kiss.

"Sleep well, my love," he whispered as his eyes closed. They would lie together for eternity, locked in a kiss of love and devotion. James let out a final breath as his heart stilled.

Chapter 71
December 2013
Surrey, England

Quinn dropped James's belt buckle and collapsed into Gabe's arms, sobbing her heart out. "Oh, Gabe, he just left them there to die. It took days. They died of asphyxiation and dehydration, but most of all, they died of a broken heart. James blamed himself for Elise's fate, and Elise died believing that her son would despise her and never know how much she loved him. And she had been pregnant."

Gabe held Quinn close and kissed her tenderly. At this moment, he understood why she hated her gift. James and Elise would have died centuries ago anyway, but seeing their suffering in her mind was like having them die all over again and feeling a terrible helplessness at the inability to help them.

"It's all right, love. They are long gone, but you will bring their story to life. Their names will be heard again. And maybe there are descendants."

Quinn shook her head. "There are none. I looked and looked, but there's no record of Charles anywhere. Lord Asher died a decade later, and his estate went to a distant cousin, but there was never any mention of a son. Charles must have died in infancy."

"And Barbara?"

"Barbara died two years after her father. Of neglect, I imagine. Poor girl. No one would have cared enough to look after her after Edward was gone. He despised her, but he did see it as his duty to see her provided for."

Gabe held Quinn nestled in his arms until she finally calmed down. He was glad that this particular story was over, but Quinn was committed for two more hour-long episodes of the *Echoes from the Past* series. She was also determined to find the man who might be her father. Gabe tried to dissuade her from pursuing this quest, knowing that it could lead to nothing but heartache, but Quinn was adamant, driven by a desire to find out where her strange gift came from. He supposed he would feel the same if he were in Quinn's place. All he could do was offer his love and support, something he was prepared to do unconditionally.

"How about a nice hot bath?" Gabe asked, hoping Quinn would agree. A bath always put her in a favorable frame of mind.

"All right," Quinn sniffed.

"Be back in a moment."

**

Quinn lifted a soapy arm out of the tub and took a sip of her wine. It was cool and crisp, which made it even more delicious since she was warm and drowsy. A dozen candles flickered in the steamy bathroom, and soft music played in the background. Quinn leaned against Gabe, and his arms encircled her as she closed her eyes in contentment. She still grieved for Elise and James, but Gabe was right—they were long gone and there was nothing more she could do for them. Once the program was filmed and their remains buried, it'd be time to move on and put them to rest.

Quinn hardly noticed when Gabe lifted her left hand out of the tub. She felt an odd weight on her finger and forced her eyes open to see what Gabe was up to. An antique diamond ring sparkled on her finger. She'd seen that ring before. It had been in

Gabe's family for generations, and Quinn felt her stomach clench with apprehension. She couldn't possibly accept a ring that had belonged to countless women who'd come before her.

"Gabe, I . . ." Quinn protested as she made to remove the ring before images of owners past assaulted her.

"It's brand new. I had a copy made. The only memories associated with this ring will be your own, if you agree to marry me, that is." Quinn smiled as she felt Gabe's heartbeat accelerate and heard the intake of breath. He was nervous, poor man.

She flipped over, splashing water all over the floor in the process, and wrapped her arms around Gabe's neck as his arms came around her, holding her tight against his naked body.

"Yes," she said simply. "Yes. When do you want to get married?"

"Next week works," Gabe joked. He smiled hugely and kissed her, his worries of a few moments ago forgotten.

"How about in the spring? We do need a few months to plan a wedding."

"Spring, summer, whatever you want."

Quinn reached out of the tub and grabbed her phone, which was lying on a low bench. "I have to call my mum and dad," she said breathlessly.

"Can't it wait?"

"Absolutely not!" Quinn laughed. "I must tell them now. They'll be thrilled. Oh, there's message from Rhys. Let me see what he wants," Quinn said as she put the phone to her ear, trying in vain not to get it wet.

Quinn listened to the message and turned to Gabe. "The planning might have to wait a few weeks. Rhys says that a child's remains have been unearthed in Dunwich. The grave is several hundred years old, at least. The child was buried without a coffin, facedown, and appears to have a skull fracture. He wants me there tomorrow."

Gabe took a deep breath and sank beneath the water, pulling a giggling Quinn with him. Tomorrow she'd confront death once again, but today she'd be happy.

Epilogue

Mercy pressed herself against the wall when she heard the voices of the two men. Uncle James told her to stay out of the way since Lord Asher didn't want her in his house. She'd never met him, but she'd seen him at the funeral for his mother when they buried Harry on the sly. He did not look like a kind man, and the other man with him was downright frightening. She'd studied him when she peeked through the keyhole while they dined.

Mercy remained perfectly still as the two men dragged Elise and James down the stairs and toward the end of the dark passage that led to the cellar. She couldn't see them anymore, but she heard them. They were talking and laughing as they descended into the bowels of the house, pleased with the night's work.

"It will take them ages to die. I must admit, this is cruel even for you, Edward," Lord Fillmore said.

"They made their bed," came Lord Asher's reply. "A shame really, she could have borne me more children. But, I have a son, and that's what matters. Let's get them into the chest before they come to."

They both laughed as a body hit the floor with a thud. Mercy didn't wait to hear anymore. Lord Asher meant to kill Elise and James. There was nothing she could do to save them, but there was something she could do to save their baby. They thought she was young and naïve, but she knew about babies and knew about love. Elise was married to Lord Asher, but she loved James and he loved her, and they'd made Charlie together. She would not let their baby be raised by this frightful man.

Mercy climbed the stairs on silent feet and crept into Charlie's room, where the baby slept in his cradle. The nurse was fast asleep, her mouth slightly open and her arm over her face.

Mercy lifted Charlie carefully out of the cradle, wrapped his tiny body in a warm blanket, and slipped out of the room. She would take Charlie to her mam, who would raise him as her own. He was James's son, her mam's nephew. Her mam lost two children, so Mercy would give her one back. Charlie wouldn't be rich, but he would be loved, and he would grow up knowing that his parents died for loving each other.

Mercy froze when she saw the ghostly silhouette of Barbara in the corridor. Barbara gazed at Mercy and the baby, her face scrunched up in concentration as she tried to figure out what was happening. Mercy put a finger to her lips.

"*Shh*. Don't tell anyone, Barbara. It's a game, and it will be our secret."

Barbara smiled happily. "Secret. I like secrets."

"Go back to bed."

"All right," Barbara said and went back into her room.

Mercy slipped out of the house and ran through the empty streets, desperate to get home before daylight began to sweep away the darkness. She was cold and scared, but Blackfriars wasn't so far away, and her mam would tell her she'd done the right thing. Her father always wanted a son. Now he would have Charlie to follow in his footsteps and learn the trade. Charlie would be a carpenter. If it was good enough for the Lord, it would be good enough for the son of his servant James.

The End

Please look for *The Forgotten* (Echoes from the Past: Book 2)

Coming January 2018

Notes

I hope you've enjoyed the first installment of the Echoes from the Past series. There are more stories on the way, with new cases for Quinn and surprising revelations about her past. In the second installment, Quinn and Gabe are off to Dunwich, Suffolk, which is a place that is of great interest to me. Dunwich has quite a history, which I look forward to sharing with you.

I love hearing your thoughts, so please don't hesitate to reach out to me. You can find me at www.irinashapiro.com or on Facebook at www.facebook.com/IrinaShapiro2/. Please send me your information at irina.shapiro@yahoo.com if you'd like to be added to my mailing list.

And, as always, thank you for your support.

Printed in Great Britain
by Amazon